T0112667

DEMPOW TORISHIMA **SISYPHEAN**

SISYPHEAN

WRITTEN AND ILLUSTRATED BY
DEMPOW TORISHIMA

TRANSLATED BY DANIEL HUDDLESTON

HAIKA
SORU

SAN FRANCISCO

Sisyphean
Kaikin no To (Sisyphean and Other Stories)
Copyright © 2013 by Dempow Torishima
English translation rights arranged with TOKYO SOGENSHA CO., LTD.

Cover and interior design by Adam Grano

HAIKASORU
Published by VIZ Media, LLC
P.O. Box 77010
San Francisco, CA 94107

www.haikasoru.com

Library of Congress Cataloging-in-Publication Data

Names: Torishima, Denpō, 1970- author, illustrator. | Huddleston, Daniel,
    translator.
Title: Sisyphean / Dempow Torishima ; translated by Daniel Huddleston ;
    illustrations by Dempow Torishima.
Other titles: Sisyphean. English
Description: San Francisco : Haikasoru, [2018]
Identifiers: LCCN 2017037281 | ISBN 9781421580821 (paperback)
Subjects: LCSH: Genetic engineering--Fiction. | Science fiction. | BISAC:
    FICTION / Science Fiction / General.
Classification: LCC PL876.O75 S5713 2018 | DDC 895.63/6--dc23
LC record available at https://lccn.loc.gov/2017037281

Printed in the U.S.A.
First printing, March 2018

CONTENTS

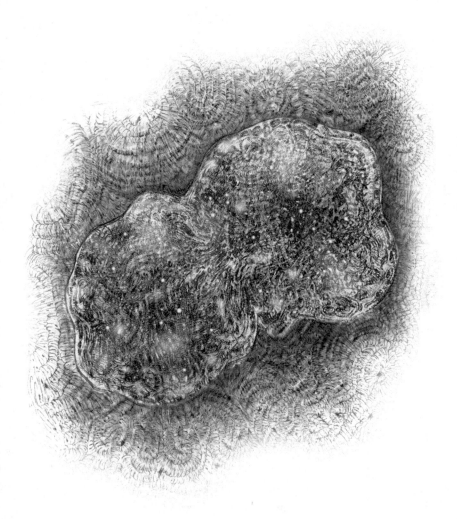

PROLOGUE

In stable orbit above a congealed accretion disc in the depths of galactic space, there swarmed untold millions of corporatians, who together formed the immense, nimbotranslucent corpuspheres of which an archipelagolopolis was composed. In the midst of their jostlings were two consolidated corporatians—<Gyo the Intercessor> and <Ja the Vigilant>—who together formed a stately, gourdlike shape over ten thousand shares in diameter. Seeking to engulf one another, these two had made mutual acquisition bids, and after the passage of a great length of time, in the midst of the unnatural equilibrium maintained within their incorporeated system, subordinapes dictated from life-forms sampled on countless worlds toiled each according to the standards of the corporatian to whom he belonged. They formed a vast, multifaceted ecosystem, wherein cycles of death and rebirth were repeated endlessly.

FRAGMENT:
PLUNDER

Many affiliated corporatians had created a transitory organizational confederation and into themselves enveloped an interstellar seedship of heretofore unknown make, which a Planetary Intellect had captured and sold to them. The corporatians ordered their subordinapes to disincorporate it, and with their tentacles they examined each and every piece. Although its chief part was missing, the coordinates of the world that had launched the vessel soon became clear, and based on the compatibility of its surrounding interstellar environment, that planet was identified as a candidate for Cradling.

The slide into instability began after the seedship had been divided among a great many corporatians via auction. A thorough investigation revealed that the hull of the seedship was in fact a dangerous mass of nanomachines, each no larger than a speck of dust, locked into their present form by a disc-shaped relic. As such, the ship was isolated from the incorporeate archipelagolopolis, and then in a follow-up investigation, it was learned that the seedship's world of origin was a bizarre collective life-form completely covered in the same sort of nanomachines—in a state of delerium, it was groping around blindly through every nearby star system. Planning for its wholesale affirmation was begun.

SISYPHEAN
(OR, PERFECT ATTENDANTS)

CHAPTER 1:
THE PRESIDENT WAITED ON

1

The date from which the tale is set forth matters little; to begin with the awakening of its protagonist is a mere convenience for the telling. Still, he had awakened just slightly later than usual this morning.

Clinging to the edge of a rusted metal deck one hundred meters above the surface of the sea was a row of tear-shaped sleepsacs, their gnarled and withered hind legs dangling from their undersides.

Nearly all of them were shriveled and dried, and only one, at the rightmost end of the row, yet retained its original form, swelling outward in the shape of a ripened fig. From the muscular tightgate that protruded from its upper tip there sprouted the rather dimwitted-looking face of a worker. Borne forward by the action of lickstrings connected to the sleepsac's inner membrane, the worker's slender, naked form was vomited out onto the deck, trailing behind it sticky threads of secretion.

The name of the worker was GyoVuReU'UNN. Although he had no memory himself of having ever been called by that name, there were no other freewalking subordinapes at his workplace, so this was not a problem for him.

The worker's shoulders quivered, and when he raised up his body, it was with movements similar to the curling of a burning piece of paper. His feet were dripping with amnesiotic fluid, and taking care not to let himself slip on it, he stood erect on a deck that lacked so much as a single guardrail. In his ears, he could still hear the indistinct voices of countless unknown colleagues whispering to one another.

"Stand up on the deck" / "I don't want to remember anymore" / "That was an awful sight" / "What's awful is it's just like everyone says" / "It's what they call collective unconsciousness" / "Like they had before" / "I don't remember that" / "I never seen it" / "Maybe you were just delirious" / "We've been horribly oppressed" / "By the way, I hear the next town over is closed off…"

The worker came fully awake as peeling, rusted iron bit into the soles of his feet. A sweetness and a grainy, figlike texture was spreading into every corner of his mouth. This was the flavor he always tasted whenever he came out of the sleepsac. Although the concentrated sweetness of dried figs was his favorite, the worker had never actually eaten one.

The last of the amnesiotic fluid dribbled out of his ears, a strong cold wind brushed against his eardrums, and the muffled sound of the waves came to him. The worker frowned at the creaking of iron that could occasionally be heard between their crashes.

Death awaited should he lose his footing. And yet it was always after the danger had passed that he felt most conscious of it. Seeking to ease the stiffness in his neck, he turned his head southward to look across the dark, steel-blue vastness of the sea and into the blur of mists in the distance.

It looked as though the deck were floating high up in the

sky. At one time, the worker had been quite sure that it was, but then one day he was made to assist in repairing the lift, and dangling from the edge of the platform, he had been lowered to a point about fifty meters beneath it. Or had that been the time he had tried to escape by way of the lift? In any case, he had learned that day that the platform was supported by many long, thick steel columns lashed to one another. And on the face of the sea right below his gaze, the waves had been crashing against a group of small islands. The steel support columns rose up from the centers of these islands—islands composed of rotting heaps of flesh: the piled corpses of stringbeasts such as coffin eels and bloodtide wayfarers that had tried and failed to climb up to the office building on the deck.

Pinching the left ear that was supposed to have been ripped off as punishment for having tried to run away, the worker looked up at the overhanging cliffs of landfill strata that towered above him on the eastern side. It was not merely a projection of his psychological state that made their striped patterns look different every time he saw them; even now, the willy-nilly counterfeiting of all manner of industrial products from the *eidos* of each one—and the collapse of those goods beneath their own weight—was ongoing.

Unable to entirely abandon his hopes of retirement, the worker made a visual estimate of the distance to the cliff. Although it looked rather close, he realized belatedly that there was no way he could leap across, and let out a long sigh.

He turned around and saw the company building, resembling the tongue of some giant that had been cut out and stood up on its end, right before his eyes. Skinboard-paneled walls that had been able to breathe when they were new now bore the scars of the canvassers' repeated sales calls. Now covered in scar tissue, the walls could no longer breathe at all.

The worker, having completed his commute to the office in only ten paces, set his center of gravity in his hips, slid open an iron door more than twice his height, and stepped into the stuffy, humid air of the corridor.

As he was closing the iron door, he felt an unpleasant, oppressive feeling, like being swallowed whole into the gullet of a coffin eel. He turned around and saw a pair of thighs right in front of him, with far too wide a space between them.

The worker's gaze crawled upward along the ridges of a special fabric knitted from muscle fiber, and sticking out from the wide opening of its collar was an eyeless, noseless, mouth-less, translucent head whose shape mimicked that of the office building itself. Tiny particles and a smooth, glossy sheen slid across its surface as it looked down at the worker.

"Mr. President!" the worker said shrilly—adding, "Good morning," once he had steadied his breathing.

Wrapped in its sleeve of knitted meat, the president's long arm twisted as it curled upward. Four fat fingers—their bones and nerves visible under translucent skin—pointed toward the inner room. Tiny bubbles of air fizzed from the spherical surfaces of his fingertips. When this was apparently insufficient to get his point across, he stretched his fingers still farther outward, and the pressure within his corpuscyte instantly ruptured the shells of the waybugs that lurked inside the digits. He showed the worker their still-beating hearts—about the size of sesame seeds—as they floated clear of the puffy clouds of red now spreading out in his fingers. The hearts continued to tick away with unnerving speed.

It dawned on the worker then that he had apparently come into the office later than usual. Was something wrong with his sleepsac these days? His regurgitation time was lagging.

The president's featureless face descended until it was right before his eyes. Within its interior, bone fragments, scales, and air bubbles floated, and a morel-shaped organ of unfathomable function bobbed back and forth with an irregular rhythm, managing to shift its position considerably though wrapped all around with winding, branching nerves and blood vessels. In the midst of a face that almost seemed more plastic than organic, an indentation suddenly began to sink inward. All around the deepening hollow, the face was starting to roil with waves, and then suddenly the hollow deepened and began to vibrate.

"GUEVOoOo—UENGuUuUNNuN—GUEPU, VV!"

The piercing cry reverberated all through the building. He was urging the worker to see to his disinfecting right away and get to his seat.

It was not, however, through the comprehension of words that the worker had arrived at that understanding—rather, it was the president's gestures and tone of voice that led him to that conclusion. The worker sometimes wrote down the president's words to try to learn to speak his language, but when he tried to say them aloud later, they would come out both resembling the original and sounding nothing like it. Given the structure of his larynx, the best the worker could do was make a noise like a clogged sewer pipe backing up. Or like someone doggedly clearing his throat to expel a mass of phlegm.

The worker threaded his way down a narrow path along which wound a synthorganic digestive tract, and went into the washroom. The space enclosed by its scaly walls was only barely wide enough for one person to stand. Still, being there allowed him to recover a slight trace of his composure.

Standing flush against the wall, he lifted up the grated floor, faced the hole, and let his immature excretory organs do their business into a pit through which whistled a distant, vacant-sounding wind. Replacing the grated floorpiece, he then stood on top of it and turned a brass, starfish-shaped handle on the scaly wall. Pure water, filtered through the purification tank, showered down on him from overhead. As beaded drops of lukewarm water drummed against every inch of his body, he grabbed a bar of winedregs hanging from the wall and began scrubbing away at himself, scouring off the filth that his eyes couldn't see. These dregs the worker had himself scraped from the bellies of winesprites.

A lock of hair got tangled in his fingers, knotted up, and came loose. Its gleam called to mind an image of glass fiber, and the worker stared at it, captivated. At what point had it become so faded and white? He was still too young to have his hair turning silver. He was only thirty-two, wasn't he? But in the instant that he thought that, he wondered again if he wasn't fifty-four. And after he had corrected himself yet again—*No, I was twenty-eight!*—he stopped thinking about it. He grabbed a meatpleat that was hanging on the wall and wiped off his dripping body. The intestines of sand leeches formed droppings hard enough to use as bullets, so it was hardly surprising that they dried his skin in no time.

He went back to the corridor and pulled a gray work uniform down off the wall. It was the sort of business suit that an accountant might have worn long, long ago; for some reason the clothes the company provided were all a little formal, though, so it wasn't like he had any choice.

When he arrived in the workshop, the president was slowly pacing in front of the faintly glowing dependency tanks, varied medicine bottles, and jumbled synthorgans lining the ten shelves built along the U-shaped wall.

Stepping forward at what he judged to be the proper moment, the worker slid—or was driven—into one corner of the workbench. When he lowered himself into a leather chair stained deeply by medicinal fluids, he found three slabs of slimecake spread out on the table, already sliced into shapes anticipating the organs they would be sculpted into. IV drips were keeping them in a state of quasi-life.

Hurriedly, he slid his hands into a pair of skingloves ridged with stillvein cords. Experiencing an odd sensation like joining hands with some total stranger, he opened his toolbox and laid out the needler, the tube-shaped reflex mirror, and the other implements he would need.

The worker jabbed his needler into a cross-section of slime-cake and injected the guidejuice. The president held out his thick fingers, and keeping them perfectly motionless, forced from their tips waybugs about the size of rice grains. At any given time, about five hundred waybugs were being nourished amid the currents of the president's body, receiving training according to their specialized functions. No sooner had the waybugs fallen onto the slimecake than they sought out the needle marks and burrowed in, expelling silver thread from their anuses as they tunneled along either vertically or horizontally, each in its turn raising a little ridge in the surface as it went. At last the waybugs emerged from the cut faces at fixed distances from one another, and the worker touched each with a pair of red-hot tongs. Their shells split open with brittle sounds, and their bodily fluids sizzled as they vaporized.

Every time the worker saw waybugs crawling around like ants, his breath started to seize up. The sight always took him back to the hills of Stillville, located thirty kilometers away on the mainland. With pointed jaws radiating outward from bodies about the size of a puppy dog's, the ants there had dug countless tunnels into the coaguland. Because of that, a large group of winesprites, their shells piled up one against the other on the surface, had all at once sunk into the ground. The worker vicariously experienced the torment of suffocating while caught up in the midst of that rescue operation, while the president stretched one arm all the way up to a shelf near the ceiling, grabbed hold of a few things, and tossed them down onto the bench.

These included three different kinds of neurofungi. Their threadlike, whitish bodies twisted and wrapped themselves around each other, painful even to look at.

The stupid things you come up with! If I'd died of suffocation back then, who is it that's handling these slime molds right now?

The worker drove the disquieting memory from his mind. He laid the molds down on a tray where a great deal of powdered dogshell had been sprinkled and turned them over. This step was to prevent them from taking root in the slimecake too quickly.

When he first started here, he had worked barehanded and had once let a neurofungus adhere to his fingertip. That had ended with him on the floor, writhing in white-hot agony. But now he was able to braid neurofungi into spiral cords with nimble, experienced hands.

It was a simple matter to tie the ends of these spiral-shaped cords to the waybug threads left inside the holes in the slime-cake slices, and—applying a steady rhythm from the holes on the opposite sides—tug them on through. The spirals would resist with all of their might, though, so it was necessary to pull and stretch that carpet of meat as he threaded the fungi into the tunnels. Whenever it looked like one was about to get tangled, he would loosen it using crochet needles inserted into adjacent tunnels.

TAPUVuu—the president expelled air from a vacuole, breaking the worker's concentration. When he returned his attention to the task at hand, he saw that the last remaining thread had snapped. He pushed his crochet needles into the web of tunnels to hunt for the broken end, and the president pointed out the correct position with a fat finger. That finger, however, blocked the worker's line of sight and brought with it an unpleasant sensation, like having his eye socket covered by it. The feeling gradually spread from his eye until at last he was assaulted by the feeling that his entire body was being sealed up inside that of the president.

The worker steadied his breathing and got back to work. In his thoughts, he retraced the correct route through which he should thread the neurofungus and set to the task anew, but even though he was still in the midst of this process, the president reached into the drawers and started taking out the first of the flesh-colored blood sedges, jibão-nets, and other tenants. He spread them out on a bracket that he pulled out from a column and started pointing at them with dogged insistence.

"If it's the tenants you're worried about, there's no need," the worker said.

Irritated, he had raised his voice, though the president quite literally had no ears with which to hear him. He did perceive sounds by way of a different sort of system, but it tended to interpret the worker's voice as static. A roar of criticism was still emanating from the vortex in his boss's face, but the worker wasn't listening, and it washed right past him as he finished prepping the slimecake.

The worker massaged his cramping fingers, and the president crossed his long legs and twisted his body all the way around from the waist down, causing undulations in his reversed right leg. From the area around his ankle, sticky, leaden-hued waste fluids came gushing out and oozed down toward a hole covered by grating.

At last, the worker took a limp jibão-net from the bracket.

Its webbed membrane, reacting to his body heat, began to slowly stretch and expand. Starving them a little made them clamp on better. A tenant that attached to a living creature would take the place of its original blood vessels, detouring the flow and skimming off what nutrients it needed to survive. The creature to which a tenant attached would not gain weight no matter how much it might overeat, and if there were some defect in its original blood vessels, its life might well be saved by it. For these reasons, there was even a tendency to see them as a welcome presence. However, once the parthenogenic tenant had finished budding and fallen into decay, the biological landlord would suffer harmful effects such as the bursting of atrophied veins under the pressure of a sudden return of blood flow, or obesity due to an appetite that had not gone back to normal after becoming thoroughly used to overeating.

As the worker was rolling out jibāo-nets on the slimecake, he started feeling hungry, even though it was still early in the day. This concerned him. For the past few days, his appetite had been increasing strangely. Though it was true that his tenants had been given subjection treatment, he was being given raw tenants as fodder every day, so they were in his stomach. He could hardly be blamed for suspecting he might be ill.

The president's leg bent as it passed through his line of sight.

A distracting thought welled up in his mind of the innocent roundfilers who had escaped the employment contracts into which they had been born. They had come to make frequent appearances in his dreams since he had heard the rumors.

Roundfilers did the work they chose on the land they selected, and although they were poor, they lived as they wished—the jibāo-net that had felt like ground meat in his hands was now like a cloth, thick with the water it had absorbed—and as the worker carried out his task, he began to imagine himself as a partaker in their lifestyle as well. As a washman, life was quiet and peaceful, his days occupied with cleaning all manner of grime and filth.

But then one day...

Here the worker's daydream began to take a turn.

A tenant masterhunter appears in the roundfilers' village, warning them that their bodies are being consumed from within by evil spirits. With a pair of shears, the masterhunter opens up the chest of a roundfiler, cuts out a jibāo-net, and holds it up high above his head. The shadow of the jibāo-net falls across his triumphant visage.

"See here! It's just like I told you. You see this disgusting thing? This is the evil spirit that possessed you. You have recovered your health."

Crowds of roundfilers, eager to have their own evil spirits exorcised, rush forward to stand before the masterhunter.

After the masterhunter departs with a great number of jibāonets, the roundfilers who recovered their health gain weight without ceasing. The image of them overlaps with that of the winesprites of Stillville, who continually secrete strong drink.

The worker shook his head, as if to drive away a swarm of leaf beetles. His head was enveloped in the odor of fluid waste, pungent as if from a rotting liver.

But that can't be. The winesprites couldn't have been roundfilers. Visible through their hemispherical, dimly transparent shells, those bloated, pitiful-looking subjugates resembled tumors. Once the worker had been concerned about one of the winesprites installed in Stillville. Its yield of spirits had been especially low. When he had called out to it, it had responded by spreading out hunting claws that resembled the pattern of veins inside a leaf, waving them about in midair, and drawing them up.

Ever since that day, the worker had carried the suspicion that the winesprites might not be mere jars for the brewing of spirits, but something more, something akin to workers such as himself. During one of the twice-monthly harvests, the worker had secretly brought over some tools from the office so as to pry loose a few of the hexagonal plates from its shell. In this manner, he had thought, it should be able to break through its shell from the inside and crawl out on its own. By blending into the thick fog that was peculiar to that area, it might be possible for it to escape from Stillville.

When the next harvest time came around, its shell was an empty hollow. Filled with joy at the thought that it had managed to escape, the worker had drawn near for a look, only to find a wrinkled, desiccated corpse lying inside.

At last realizing what had happened, the Board of Directors had gathered around the corpse of the winesprite, but then amid the fog there had risen up the shadow of a Crossing Guard, owing to which their investigation of the winesprite's untimely death had ended without conclusion.

2

The boards of the many shelves that surrounded the worker were rattling.

The worker looked up when he noticed, and on the other side of the worktable a chest wrapped around with muscle fiber had twisted perfectly sideways and turned around to the right, placing that rotating, mortar-shaped vortex close enough to touch his cheek.

"I'm sorry. My mind was wandering."

The worker took a skin threader in hand, gouged a hole into the slimecake, and once he had threaded it with a tube-shaped tenant known as a blood sedge, an oily spheroid was thrust right in front of his eyes. Its entire shape was expanding and contracting with a steady rhythm. It was a type of cicada, called a lubdub.

The instant the worker took hold of it, his arm shot upward. His own blood sedges resonated with it, throbbing to an accelerated beat and shattering the worker's composure. He pressed the lubdub down firmly against the workbench, jammed a guidepipe into its clover-shaped mouth, wrapped the wheezing spheroid up in slimecake, and attached a temporary fastener.

From a cage beneath the workbench he dragged out a coiled pinsnake and removed the cover from its nose. Checking to make sure a drop of poison was welling up on the tip of the pointed tongue darting in and out of its long snout, he pressed it against the throbbing slimecake and began sewing the edges together. While he was thus engaged, the pinsnake wrapped its long body around his arm and began squeezing so tightly that it hurt.

Using the wrapped lubdub as a base, the worker fashioned the rest of the slimecake into valves and atria, letting nothing go to waste as he sewed it all up into the shape of a heart. He stuck the tubular reflex mirror down into the blood sedge protruding from its upper portion to check the interior condition of the valves. There didn't seem to be any problems, so he peeled the pinsnake from his arm and returned it to the cage. Next, the president handed him the cardiopulmonary tube of the spherical creature itself, which he had violently dragged out after thrusting his hand back among the shelves. The worker connected it with a blood sedge, fastened a clamp onto the point of contact, and tightened the screws. He pressed down on the heap of flesh with overlapping hands, and blood flowed into the inner cavity. The cardiopulmonary tube began to pulsate, and at last it all stabilized enough to beat a steady rhythm even after he removed his hands.

His eye sockets throbbed with dull pain. The worker pulled off his skingloves, disinfected his hands, and pressed a finger against the middle of his brow. As his lower jaw receded into a yawn, he took a deep breath and felt disinfectant stinging at his eyes.

The president set a stainless steel tray on the edge of the workbench. It was his one feeding of the day. Stomach acid welled up in his throat, stinging like a rasp. Today's tray contained a maternity bug—its abdomen swollen to about the size of a fist—as well as some large and small scraps of slimecake, and a blood sedge that had died during its dependency and was just starting to go bad. As the president was lacking entirely the concept of meal preparation, each of these items was presented without garnishment.

The worker retrieved an antiregurgitant and a digestant from the bottles lined up on the shelf and popped one of each into his mouth. Both were tiny pillbugs, albeit medicinal in name only.

He pulled a hose out from the column beside the dependency tanks, sprayed one turn of the lever's worth of water into his mouth, and swallowed.

Taking the maternity bug in hand, he squeezed the giant blood-blister that was its abdomen, and popped its acidic, vitamin-rich juices onto the slimecake and blood sedge. He tossed the husk that remained onto the floor and picked up a scrap of slimecake that looked to be still somewhat edible.

With reluctance, he tossed it into his mouth; the acidic flavor vanished without a trace right away, leaving no flavor on the slimecake at all. He chewed and chewed, but it only grew soft and rubbery, until he swallowed it down without having ever bitten through. It was still stuck in his throat when he put the next scrap into his mouth. His diaphragm tightened as when filling his lungs with air. Even with medicine suppressing the revolt in his digestive tract, this was what he had to go through just to eat. For that reason, these had long been called "vomit meals," though vomiting was something to be avoided at all costs. Should he fail to hold it in, he would simply be force-fed his vomit once more. It made no difference to the president either way.

A memory surfaced: he was crying as he was eating his lunch alone in the center of the classroom, while all of his classmates were moving their desks and chairs in preparation for the after-lunch cleaning. No, wait—he had always been one to eat quickly, so perhaps he was the one sticking a mop out at his pitiful classmate's feet. Or was he the teacher who was forcing him to do that? Did that mean his present existence was his recompense for that?

That was when the president, moving as though to shelter a lover from a blast of wind, took a qizhong large enough to hold in his arms, and without so much as plucking a feather, shoved it into his collar and swallowed it whole with his highly elastic stomach.

The qizhong, perhaps sensing its impending death, awakened from its state of suspended animation and scattered feathers as it flapped its wings, though presently it was engulfed all the way to the tip of its tail. The president's solar plexus bulged outward as if with a tumor, its surface changing into a distorted shape, and then the bulge slid downward all at once to his side.

The worker picked up the blood sedge that he had put off till last, lifted his face up to the ceiling, and closed his eyes as he tried to imagine it as a grilled calcot like the ones he had eaten in a distant, foreign land that he could not have possibly ever visited. *I'm peeling back the black, burnt skins and inside there are steaming white onions*...He pulled the sticky strings from his fingertips and dropped it into the back of his throat...*and an orange sauce that smells of almonds dribbles from my mouth*...and ran down his cheek with a fishy stench.

Through stretches and contractions in his throat, the worker swallowed the blood sedge, but when he suddenly choked on it hard, it slid right back up into his oral cavity, slipping around and around his tongue. Helpless to do anything else, he started to push it back with his fingers when an embarrassing noise came bounding up from the back of his throat. The president, to whom this had perhaps sounded like spoken words, answered, "*ZoVoVo.*"

After repeatedly rinsing his mouth out with water, all that remained was a languid sense of relief such as one feels immediately after a completed dental procedure.

Perhaps because of his disgust at this feeding, his scalp was covered in gooseflesh that wouldn't go away. This eventually transformed into a sort of itchiness that felt like countless legs crawling about, causing the worker to run his fingers through his hair for fear that it was already crawling with lice. He didn't feel anything moving, but as he ran his fingers through his hair, tiny objects did stick to them. He caught some of them between his fingers and tried to comb them out, but they were stuck fast and wouldn't come loose. There was no mistaking it—these were egg cases.

They say that lice are attracted to certain types of brain waves, and although he had been tormented by their moist presence and the sensation of them threading their way between the hairs of his head, he had never actually managed to catch one, and even when he looked at his reflection in a dependency tank, all he was able to see was his own oily hair. Because of this, he had even wondered if the egg cases—which were the only things he could actually feel—might be something secreted by his scalp.

After spending the night in his sleepsac, the sensations of lice and eggs would be gone without a trace. Was this because the lickstrings inside fed on them, or because he recovered his peace of mind during sleep?

I just want to get back to my sleepsac soon, the worker thought.

The president bent over backward in apparent displeasure, and from this motion the worker surmised that a guest had arrived. Soon enough, the building began to vibrate, and even the worker could tell that the lift on the far side of the corridor was in motion.

Quite some time ago, a giant mutant coffin eel had tunneled its way into the lift and gotten stuck inside, its body bent in the shape of an S. Although the president had ordered the worker to dispose of it, the toxicity of the outer skin was strong enough to be listed in the Fishery Catalog of Hazardous Substances, so he had doused it in a putrefaction accelerant. Later, when scraping away the runny soup of liquefied rot that had dripped down onto the floor below, he had discovered an emerald-green magatama, such as should have only been possible to take from a canvasser.

The worker touched his shirt pocket. The magatama should have been hidden away inside, but his fingers couldn't find the dense little bead. Perhaps he had heard the story from a colleague.

There was a sound of folding doors sliding open and of faltering footsteps drawing near.

From out of the gloom there appeared a male boarhead, short of stature though sturdily built, carrying a packing case with both hands. Large drops of sweat clung to his wide face, and he was breathing with apparent difficulty. A worker from the fishery, he was in charge of on-site disassembly. Though he had always arrived by boat whenever he came here, to the worker's eyes he looked for all the world like he had crawled up from some Stygian pit.

The disassembler set the packing case on the floor and met his eyes for an instant, then immediately looked away in a most obsequious manner. This was in all likelihood because the worker had had some sharp words for him the first time they met, when the disassembler had referred to himself as "I."

"That's *my* name," the worker had said. "I won't have you referring to yourself as 'I.'"

In those days, the worker had believed that "I" was a proper noun and his own given name.

Even before that, he also had gotten indignant with the insect breeder for plagiarizing the way he looked.

The worker pulled on the skylight's control lever to close its slatted shutters, and when the workshop was completely dark, the president's body glowed with a faint light, and blurry shadows of his organs and skeleton became visible through his clothing. All of his waybugs could be seen crowding down into his feet.

The disassembler took a placoderm out of his case. Its shell looked as though it were made of complex crystals of stibnite, and its body reflected harsh flashes of light as it twisted and writhed. A high-pitched sound reverberated through the room as it abruptly snapped its jaws together.

The worker had heard that such fish could only be reeled in by a hook attached to a metal chain, and to that he could only nod agreement. The chained tendons that extended to its tailfin thrashed about vainly when held down against the lid of the packing case, but once the disassembler had pushed the long rod of his bonedriver in through the gaps in its armor plates to loosen a few of its screwbones, the tendons came loose with a grating sound and then quieted.

The wide blade of his butcher knife he applied near the fish's gills, and with a scattering of sparks and an eruption of steam and bodily fluids, he lopped off its head straightaway. As the fallen, armored head went clattering across the grated floor, the disassembler lifted the fish's tailfin and hung it from the shelf so that the cut surface faced a tubelike glass container positioned directly underneath it. The high-viscosity body fluid used as bait began dripping into it.

One after another, the disassembler butchered his placoderms and hung them from the shelf. When he was finished with them all, he turned a sweaty face toward the president and asked for his signature on the statement of delivery/completion-of-work report. As he did so, he shrank backward, however.

With a single stride, the president came forward, stood over the disassembler so as to entirely overshadow him, then pinned down his trembling shoulder and jammed a fat finger deep into one of his rapidly blinking eyes. The disassembler stopped moving, panted out short, steady gasps of air, and when he had endured the signature all the way to the end, he departed with languid footsteps and a hand pressed over one eye.

The president lifted up one section of the grated floor. The ominous, armored heads still had their jaws clenched tightly. One after another, he kicked them down into the darkness of the pit.

The worker took the mucus-clogged glass receptacle, fixed it to the bracket that stretched out from the pillar, covered his eyes with a pair of slitted protective goggles, and waited for the president to stretch out to his full height in the usual place. When the president was ready, the worker turned the control lever hanging down from the ceiling with his fingertips.

A single shaft of light fell onto the crown of the president's head. The beam was instantly refracted through his translucent body and shone out of the middle of his face, becoming a jittering point of light on the surface of the glass container. The worker gauged the turbidity level in the mucus, adjusted the lighting aperture, and when the formation was completed, pulled a number of solidified clumps out of the container.

Once he had wiped off the mucus that clung to them, the president's chest swelled out and let loose a *NVo* that sent several scales and a sulfurous odor dancing through the air. Shortly thereafter the top of his head began to foam. It was probably gas being released from the semi-digested qizhong inside him. The worker locked the next container into place. Although he endeavored to continue his work free of distractions, the beam of light veered wildly off course and touched his own shoulder, causing him to shut the aperture involuntarily.

The stinging pain lingered in his shoulder, and he was seized with an urge to fling the glass cylinder right at the president's face. Even if he did so, however, it wouldn't cause him any pain.

The president stuck a fingertip into his own face and began to slowly stir it about. His powers of concentration had reached their limit.

However, the job of solidifying the mucus still wasn't finished. In spite of that, the president reached up to the highest shelf and took down a skinbag shaped like a palm frond, pressed it against his ear, and squeezed it with both hands, injecting its contents into his corpuscyte. The fluid spread out through his entire body in a netlike pattern.

The worker couldn't hold in a sigh. It was still during working hours; moreover, they were in the middle of a job, yet here he was *drinking*! Actually, he wasn't certain it was liquor the president was drinking—it could have been some substance his kind needed to replenish in order to survive—but that eye-stingingly volatile aroma was clearly that which was peculiar to alcohol, and even if it wasn't, the president's careless actions became so awkwardly sluggish that it was embarrassing even to look at him.

The president straightened himself up, so the worker opened the aperture again. The beam of light refracted and spilled down onto the container, but its movements were slow and erratic. To make matters worse, the president interrupted him again midway through in order to gulp down liquor from a new skinbag. The worker felt like he was going to be drunk to the point of sickness from the aroma alone, but he somehow held together until the fourth batch of solidification work was completed.

Even after light returned to the workshop, afterimages of the beam remained in the worker's field of vision.

The president's upper torso turned toward the worker, tilted forward, and stopped just when it seemed he would tip over. Reversing direction, he turned back and slammed right into the shelves. Glass bottles filled with powerful chemicals rolled from the shelves and fell one by one. One of them broke and yellow bubbles spilled out. No sooner did they drip down below the grating than a cry arose like an alarm whistle, resolving itself into a voice saying, "Your mind is wandering." The worker's back broke out in gooseflesh.

It was a parrot. The creature was clinging pitifully to the underside of the grate, having crawled up from the bottom of the pit in hopes of partaking of some share of their leftovers. You could kill them off and then kill them off again, but eventually they would always show up once more, incoherently imitating the voice of the worker.

The arm that the president had reached out with to pick up the fallen bottle was knocking tools off the workbench one after another. The worker rushed over to pick them up, saying, "It's all right! I'll get them!"

His skingloves blistered on contact with the powerful chemicals. He felt a terrible itching deep within his eyes, his feet swelled up, and his joints stiffened.

He wished that the workday could just end here, but the job of finishing the project still remained. It wasn't that he was being forced to complete it by day's end, but the calendar on the middle shelf, which resembled a globe covered in synthorgans, indicated who would be coming in tomorrow. Should the product not be ready on time, he would be the one literally cutting his own stomach open to get them over the finish line. He shuddered, remembering the kinds of things that had happened to his colleagues as clearly as if they had been his own experiences—then he furrowed his brow, realizing that he had never even met those colleagues he was thinking about.

The worker lined up the misshapen, beam-hardened blocks on the workbench. The light around him was dim since the sun was beginning to set. He could see the president's body, thoroughly relaxed, sinking into blackness like the surface of a river at night. The worker took out a pair of torchburrs, each about the size of a fist and bound up tightly with pinnets. Giving each a good shake to make them glow, he hung them from the bracket. The synthorgans on the middle shelves convulsed abruptly.

Bathed in green light, the worker applied an iron file to one of the rough blocks and started shaving away the unneeded parts. Once a winged, batlike outline had appeared, he switched to a finer file and set about finishing the complex, hollow interior.

Suddenly, the worker's wrist leapt up, and he dropped his

file. This was because a wing that was supposed to have already been processed had started to vibrate in the space between the metal net and the torchburr.

Using tweezers, he plucked off the wing, and with it came vivid, sunset-pink muscle tissue that had been connected to the wing axis. It was still expanding and contracting. Frightened, he threw it to the floor. The wing with its attached flesh traced out a parabola through the stagnant air as it fell to the grated floor. There it stuck to the grate for only a moment before being snatched away by a tentaclelike appendage from beneath.

The worker set to the task of polishing the curved surfaces of the block using an emery cloth. To the steady sound of his polishing there was added another sound, as of some liquid coming to a boil. Despite a growing sense of puzzlement, he reached for the next piece and took it in his hand. The boiling sound grew louder, and he looked over at its source, which was the president. Beneath his clothes of knitted meat, great bulges were suddenly swelling out from his chest and side, then receding, only to bloom again.

Having surmised what was about to happen, the worker turned his face away. The grated floor resounded with a shrill noise, and he felt in his feet the vibration of something heavy crashing against it. The area filled with grayish white smoke, and though he switched to mouth breathing amid the nausea-inducing stench, his throat was still affected, and he started coughing very hard.

Turning back toward the workbench, he gave up all thought of cleaning the place up at quitting time and devoted himself instead to the work of polishing. The president's feet were behind the workbench, and it was his good fortune that he was unable to see them. He finished the second piece and tried to connect it to the first one he had shaped, but they would not fit together well, so he picked up the file again and pushed it inside once more. Next time, they fit together perfectly with a pleasant snap, so he then injected a buffering agent into the cracks using his needler.

The president wandered around the fogged work area. Having nothing in particular to do with himself, he stared meaningfully at the synthorgans on the shelves. The worker rubbed at his chest; a kind of white noise to which he felt an instinctive revulsion was making it hard for him to breathe.

"Everything left to do is my work..." the worker said, suppressing a cough and clearing his throat. "...so I, ah, don't mind if you want to go on ahead."

But for all his words accomplished, he might as well have been talking to himself.

At some point his legs had started to tremble. The cold air that came crawling in from below seeped into his pores and took root in his marrow, and even a slimecake—warm with advanced decay—wrapped snugly around his ankles could not have driven it out, let alone the tattered scrap of a blanket he actually had.

The worker had been complaining about the cold to the president in various ways for a long time. He had tried shivering exaggeratedly and he had feigned paralysis to the point of total immobility, but in the end his meaning had failed to get through, and an acquaintance of the president (a psychologist, apparently) had come in for a visit. That had been when the counseling sessions—or perhaps they were something entirely different—had commenced.

The translucent physician had sat down in front of the worker and encouraged him to speak using gentle gestures of fingers that swelled out heavily at their tips. The worker's puzzled face had cast a dim reflection onto the faceless, anthill-shaped head towering above him.

Relying on the nodlike gestures the physician would

occasionally send his way, the worker had made a desperate appeal, explaining just how horrible an environment it was he was made to work in.

"It's important not to interpret everything pessimistically. Let's stay on the same medication a while longer and see how things go. Try going in to work tomorrow as though it were your very first day."

The worker was remembering the time he had taken off work for a medical examination. Had that been at the company where he had worked previously?

"Ah, haven't people always told you your only saving grace is your perfect attendance?" "Oh yeah, it was because of that bunch who accepted leave that so many..." "I could see right through that, so I was the one who had to bear the guilt I might have otherwise..."

The physician had stared at the worker, though he lacked even eyes for doing so. The worker had blushed, realizing not only that he had been reminiscing, but that he had also been speaking aloud. Simultaneously, both of his arms dropped with a sudden weight and he returned to himself. Supported in both his hands was the unbroken chain of the thick, downward-arching spinal column he had just completed.

Before his eyes, the president was bending down to inspect it. The worker raised one hand while lowering the other, making the spine undulate, and even as he was demonstrating the smooth motion of its moving parts, he felt all the more puzzled, lacking as he was any memory of having completed so much of it. He pushed out a sigh from deep within his lungs.

The president's head moved like a tongue as it followed the curve of the spine.

Even after he had consulted with the physician, there had been no improvement in his workplace environment. Which was exactly why he was shivering even now.

"Bring me my samovar," said a sudden voice that the worker did not recognize.

"I've never heard of it," said somebody else.

"It must be some kind of anti-anxiety medicine," the worker muttered himself.

Making small talk, the worker moved the tips of his frozen toes. They were like the fake red noses of clowns; he could feel nothing with them. And he wondered: what kind of creature was a clown?

The feeling of a cold wet nose returned to his cheek.

I wonder if that was a clown? Wagging its bushy tail—that was definitely a dog—no, aren't dogs those hideous bugs with the exoshells that live underground? At any rate, I was raising a stem pet with a cold wet nose. Kyoro, John, Mukku, Rick... Several of them, even dozens of them. Even when they barked, all you had to do was rub their backs or their bellies and they would be as gentle as could be. Now, though, even the innocent interaction of calming a dog was something he remembered only as a symbolic sort of give-and-take to which neither thought nor emotion was attached.

Rather like the physician's counseling. At times when the subordinape displayed unusual behavior, he would be sat down across from him and made to start talking about whatever came to mind. At suitable moments, the physician would shake his head or make a show of dropping in an appropriate word or two. Mutual understanding did not occur. The worker was humiliated to know that in a corner of his mind a part of him was still longing for the next session, because in spite of everything, he knew his mind would feel a little clearer after it.

Walking backward, the president slid away from him and melted into the darkness of the corridor. Perhaps he was satisfied with the completion of the spine.

The moment the president was gone the workshop grew

very quiet, and sounds the worker had not noticed all day—of bubbles in dependency tanks, of the dull beating of the synth-organ he had completed this morning—became audible.

The worker lay down on his side, fitting the pointed projections of the vertebrae into their grooves in the shelf, and when he turned around, he saw a heap of excrement lying there like a rotting corpse, in a pile nearly as high as his waist. Broken bones peeked out here and there, and at the dungheap's base a number of trails and a scattering of holes remained, suggesting that it had been scavenged from beneath the grating in the floor.

The worker let loose in a groan what could not be expressed in words, and forgot to breathe in through his mouth. His sinuses were assaulted by a powerful, pungent stench, and tears welled in his eyes. Why did the president have to do it right here and not go to the bathroom? Or was that stuff not excrement? And even if it wasn't, why not lift up the grating first? Who was going to clean this up?

The back of his head was so tense that it hurt, but when he reached back to rub it, he found a solidified mass of piled eggs clinging there, with a number of short, needlelike things sticking out of them, writhing about. Lice legs?

With a sharp cry, the worker suddenly pulled his hand away. When he looked at his palm, he saw several red spots welling up, swelling into drops of blood.

Until that moment, he had doubted that lice really existed, so he had paid little mind to the story that went around about them—that late in the night their nymphs would hatch from the eggs all at once and consume their host's soft tissues entirely—but now that rumor suddenly took on a shade of plausibility that terrified the worker.

I've got to finish cleaning this fast so I can get back to my sleepsac, the worker thought. He lifted up one of the grated floor plates next to him, pulled out a floor brush from under the workbench, and started pushing the sticky, heavy excrement over the edge. Amid the excrement a tube that was apparently a tenant started to move, so he squelched it with the brush. Though it was cold enough to make him shiver, that was all forgotten as his forehead broke out in a sweat.

"Everything left to do is my work...so I, ah, don't mind if you want to go on ahead." Overcome with horror at his own words coming back to him out of nowhere, he held the brush upside down and jammed the point down between the bars of the grating. Out of breath, he tried to drive the unseen presence of the parrot into a corner, though perhaps in reality the worker was merely moving around by himself.

The legs of the lice bit into his skull. He wiped his sweat and turned back toward the last of the solid waste.

Sprinkling some pesticide on the nematodes that had erupted from the mass, he scrubbed it all through the grating with the brush as though it were a sieve, pulled out the hose, and sprayed down the floor, wishing fervently all the while that he could resign right now.

It always happened, however, that the end date of his contract would pass and then automatically renew before he realized. Try as he might to remember, the date always disappeared into an oblivion of forgetfulness. From the start, the sequence of events by which he had come to work at the synthorgan company and the manner in which he had contracted with it were all a blurred haze. For some reason, an image rose up in his mind of himself being carried by a preacher and submerged in a river.

What had ever become of that colleague of his who had set out for the office of the Labor Standards Administration to file a complaint? Ah, wait. He came back long ago. Someone had told him that. So where in the world...?

"Well, your story's hardly unusual, you know—" He had a

memory of being brushed off in that manner. "—Everybody exaggerates how harsh their conditions are, but the preposterous things you're saying are just a little...you know. You make your president sound like a total nutcase."

The worker put a hand to his forehead. A memory of his monologue in front of the physician came back to him. It occurred to him that the distinctive subordinape features reflected in that translucent anthill had both resembled his own and looked nothing like him. Could it be that that face had been the physician's true image, viewed through a phantom anthill?

His former workplace in his old hometown had come to appear frequently in his dreams, and the worker had grown to suspect that he might still be working there, undergoing some kind of treatment or other. *I'm having a hard time dealing with my reality,* he chided himself. *It's made me weak, and I'm swapping it out with fantasies of bizarre creatures...like directors called "human beings."* He squeezed the lever at the tip of the hose. That hypothesis was itself an escapist fantasy, the most impossible part of which was that the people living in that town were all dreaming of being allowed to work at the synthorgan company in his place.

His sweat having chilled so suddenly, the worker shuddered convulsively as he looked around at the dependency tanks, checking the temperature and density readouts of the dependency fluid and making sure there were no abnormalities in the color of the tenants slumbering away within.

He noticed that one of the blood sedges had turned dark, and used a pair of chopsticks to move it to a sealed container. That was when he heard a sound that was like thin chinaware breaking. Thinking it was just his imagination, he was about to move on to the next dependency tank when he was hit with the intense pain of flesh being rent asunder. Reflexively he reached back and ripped off the stuff clinging to his hair.

When he opened his palm, a swarm of nymphs burst forth like snowflakes from the broken egg capsule and started crawling up his arm. With his other hand, he tried to sweep them off, but the few that remained on his arm broke his skin with their pointed legs. The ones that had fallen to the floor also came crawling back at him, and it was as he was picking them off with a pair of tweezers and stomping them under his shoes that there came the sound of another egg case cracking open, and this time the nymphs started digging into his back as if plowing a field, sending the worker running out into the corridor.

His work clothes swarmed with larvae, so he tore them off and ran for the exit, trailing a low moan. Before the iron door had opened sufficiently, he had forcibly pushed himself through to the outside. Scattered nymphs danced into the darkness like snowflakes.

As he was stepping out onto the deck, the weight on his back grew heavier and began to squirm, as though he were carrying somebody there. As though heard from the bottom of a well of distant memories, there came a jingling metallic sound that drowned out all others, but he couldn't remember what kind of sound it was. His vision blurred with the piercing pain, and by the time that he in his panic had batted away the nymphs from his face, he was standing on the very edge of the platform.

Shoulders heaving as he breathed, he made his way to his own sleepsac, and forgetting his terror that a misstep would send him plunging down into the sea, leapt headfirst into the tightgate, into which under normal circumstances he would have carefully inserted himself starting with his toes.

Many fibers of spiral muscle undulated, and the body of the upside-down worker swayed forward and backward, rotating as it was enveloped by the inner cavity. By this process, most of the nymphs were pushed outside, and the ones that had attached to his skin were crushed one after another by the powerful pressure inside.

The worker, waving back and forth as he was moved by the lickstrings that grew so thickly amid the warm amnesiotic fluid, had already lost consciousness. And the thoughts of many others were beginning to show their faces.

3

Aah, the passenger planes are thriving, and every one of 'em's knocked up with a litter of Cessnas. **I thought that zone was supposed to be nanodust-resistant.** *Never dreamed that metamorphic nanodust could ever range so far without even having any ultimaterial.* **Track One's at an impasse too, thanks to abnormal pipe and train car breeding.**
I just came back from my baptism. **Transference registration? Why that, of all things?** *Don't call it that; this is different. Faith alone can make the cherubim open the doorway.* **What are you talking about? It's six of one and half a dozen of the other, right?** *The Great Dust Plague is going to spread, and every protective measure we have will fail; before that happens, I want to repent.* **But they're still building evacuation boats, aren't they?** *I just can't imagine exposing my bare self to the defilement at this point…not in a world where Kosmetics no longer function…*They were in the middle of an argument, but before he knew it the worker had begun to stare emotionlessly at the movements of this pair.

Their vigorous movements began to blur, trailing afterimages before at last transforming into flecks of rusted iron. Although he had awakened the moment his sleepsac spat him out, he had gone right back to sleep lying facedown on the deck.

He gazed at his painfully itching arms and found a swarm of small beetles clinging to them here and there. It was only when he tried to pull one off that he realized they were scabs. He looked at the inner side of his arms and found the legs of many nymphs sticking out like pins from the drum of a music box. He endured the pain as he plucked them out one by one.

He arrived at work and located his work clothes in the corridor, but of the nymphs there was no trace, and even the cloth that should have been torn into a million pieces bore not a single tear. Did the nymphs materialize only in front of him, then? That thought spun around and around in his head while he was putting on his suit, and then he heard the sound of the president groaning. The worker made a noise in his throat at the ominous presentiment this engendered. He wished that he could just go back to his sleepsac, but his legs would have none of that as they carried him into the workshop.

The president pointed at a dependency tank and opened up his face in the shape of a mortar bowl, revealing an organ within that resembled a rose. As he stood diffidently before the dependency tank, the worker was enveloped in a cry that by turns surfaced into the range of audible sound and submerged below its lowest frequency. He could not grasp the reason he was being reprimanded, though he did sense the seriousness of the situation. The surface of the fluid in the tank was covered in scum, and nearly fifty tenants whose color had darkened were jostling against one another.

At last he remembered that during the confusion last night, he had failed to check the last dependency tank. He felt something slick and wet on his right ear, and when he touched it expecting amnesiotic fluid, his fingertips came back red with sticky blood. One of his eardrums had burst, it seemed.

The president stretched forth both of his arms, brought

them under the worker's arms, and lifted him up off the ground.

Was his head about to roll? Would his retirement benefits be paid out even after the beheading?

The worker lowered his eyelids, and a flood of trivial and varied scenes whose ownership he neither knew nor could conceive of welled up in his mind's eye. *Aren't all of those my memories?* he thought as a sense of impatience ran through him. Even as he sought to dam them all up, his consciousness was drowning in memories, and just before his skull and his eyes were crushed by the overwhelming pressure, he slammed into the grated floor.

The worker, himself once again, looked up at the president, who was standing motionless over him as an organ resembling some kind of echinoderm retreated back inside his tongue-shaped head; a part of his congealed corpuscyte was rotating.

He was looking past the worker, beyond the wall, into the distant sky. The client should be arriving any moment now.

The president stuck a finger up in the air and caused it to rotate, and then calmly started walking. The fact that the president's indignation never lasted long was the one thing that the worker didn't hate about him.

Following behind the president, he went into a dock on the cliffside face of the company building, and there in a high-ceilinged space lined with exposed metal struts was berthed a groundship resembling a whiskey flask turned on its side. Its tin-colored exterior was covered in countless scratches and dents, from which it drew a faint whitish tint.

The president raised both arms up high toward the ceiling and first pulled down a pair of chains to which hooks were affixed at the ends. Once he had put them under both his arms, he stood up straight, and the worker started turning the stiff crank.

The body of the president elongated as it was lifted up,

and then slid—pulleys and all—along tracks in the ceiling, at last stopping directly above the groundship, at which point the worker climbed a ladder and began removing the president's pants as the president swayed back and forth as though executed by hanging.

Perhaps finding the sensation unpleasant, the president growled "*GyoVuVu*" and squirmed around, prompting the worker—who was having trouble with the fabric that had bit into the president's body—to coarsen his tone. "Please be still!" he said. Somehow, he managed to peel the pants down to the president's knees, after which they came off without resistance, exposing his bizarre naked form.

The worker looked away, but the following task of guiding him into the ship was also a part of his job. The president's corpuscyte began to collapse disgustingly, and as it did so, leg bones whose multiple joints had switched over to full articulation folded on top of one another and descended into the round entrance. His lower belly, however—through which his internal organs were visible—was sticking out of the ship in bountiful folds. Only his pale, wisteria-hued intestines unraveled as they slowly spiraled down into the ship.

The corpuscyte was like a festering tumor that the worker buried his hands in, fighting back a sense of embarrassment that felt like countless tiny fishes nibbling into the pores in his skin. At last, his hands found the hip bone that was caught on the hatch and shoved it down inside.

As the president's spine descended with graceful undulations worthy of an oarfish, his internal organs, tangled about with nerves and blood vessels, either clung to it or drifted away, only to be dragged down along with it. At last, when the remaining bones of his arms, pointing skyward, were completely inside the entrance, the worker closed the hatch. Up near the ceiling, there hung a shirt of muscle fiber that, like a discarded carapace, still retained the shape of the president's body.

Suppressing his fear, the worker climbed up onto a cargo platform in the back of the groundship. The platform was a carelessly made thing—nothing but a pedestal with railing, really.

The groundship started to vibrate. He gripped the rail with both hands, bent down, and braced himself. As he felt the vibrations running through it, images of oarfish and roses came back to him in sharp clarity for some reason. Could the nymphs that had hatched have stimulated his brain in some way? More and more of his memories—until now so vague and indistinct—were taking on such tactile clarity that it seemed as if he could reach out, take them in his hands, and confirm their existence himself.

The wall in front of the groundship, with its exposed truss structure, began to open up to the right and left. Just beyond that, a drawbridge had already been lowered, spanning the gap between the deck and the cliff face. A sticky rain was beating down against it. Following guidelines on the floor, the groundship slipped out through the door, and drops of rain slid down the worker's skin, trailing threads of wetness.

The steep cliff rose up before them. Unneeded industrial products, reproduced in perpetuity, collected there, forming many layers of unwanted things. The ship entered a tunnel in a layer formed of miscellaneous, tightly packed small items. The worker stared at the reproduced goods that had all melted together and taken on a tin-colored hue, and then the ship came to a stop at a dead end that was also the bottom of a vertical shaft. Once more, the worker was exposed to the rain. Presently, the ship began to rise, accompanied by a dull, oppressive sensation. Innumerable skeletons of elevators and countless crushed train cars and household appliances—replicated forever like reflections in a pair of facing mirrors—formed layers through which a vein of dust wound its way up and down and left and right, enfolding all like the arms of some tutelary deity. As they neared the top of the cliff, however, everything melted together, growing gradually more dim and indistinct.

The glossy surface of the ground passed beneath his line of sight and descended to his feet. The worker squinted. Beyond the threads of silver pouring down on him, a vast, bruise-colored expanse of coaguland extended for as far as the eye could see, covered all over in jellymire. It was so quiet here that he could hear the pulse of blood in his ears—as though the film that lay upon an out-of-focus land were absorbing all sound of the rainfall. With his hand he wiped away the sticky drops hanging from his chin.

The groundship was not yet moving, and the raindrops on its edges continued to swell like egg cases. When he was cooped up in the company building, he was always wishing he could go outside—any reason for doing so would be fine. But now that his wish had become his reality, he was oppressed by a nervous fear for the client and by the general unpleasantness of the rain. He simply stared off into the low-chroma sky, feeling nothing whatsoever.

Right before—or possibly right after—he had spotted a single ray of light shining beyond the indistinct clouds, he nearly fell off the landcar but grabbed onto the handrail. The groundship had started out across the jellymire. It gained speed as it advanced, and the wind that struck his face slid across his cheeks like a razor blade. Heavy waves rose up one after another with increasing power and slowly spread out into the distance, tracing smooth arcs. So far as the worker was aware, the groundship possessed no means of motive power; it seemed as though it were rather the coaguland that was moving.

Before his eyes, pillars of mud rose up without a sound. The ship shook violently as it was pounded by the crashing waves.

The worker adjusted his grip on the handrail as he endured the twisting in his stomach.

Far off in the distance, the landscape was broken by the pockmark of an impact crater. That was where the client would be waiting.

Many dark shadows were already beginning to rise up from that area, all of them towering to heights he had to crane his neck to see the top of. The mud sloughed off of them, revealing one gleaming black body after another, all covered in plates of shell that fit together like suits of armor. Segments of shell resembling mantis shrimp ran along arms so long they reached all the way to the ground, and in concert with their dispro-portionately short legs, each one swung its square shoulders back and forth, taking leaden, uncertain steps toward them. Pleopods lining the grooves in their shrimp-arms began to spin at high velocity, sending the packed-in mud flying everywhere.

This was a brand-new settlement. The worker had been told that this was a business run by canvassers aligned with hostile forces—that their way of life was entirely different from that of the presidents and directors of all the companies, who were not adapted as they were to life in an environment of coaguland. It was said that an ordinary canvasser used its pleopod-like cater-pillar treads to travel tens of thousands of kilometers through the landfill strata. However, it was also said that once assigned to office duty, they would remain motionless in fixed positions for many thousands of years.

For this reason, the footsteps of canvassers were as slow as those of penguins, though if the worker were to let his guard down and be captured by one, there would be no escaping it by his own strength. Every canvasser also carried the title of Head Collector, and as such could skillfully sever the head of a worker with its sharp radulae and wrap it up in its head of whisper-leaves.

Something grazed the worker's face, and a dull metallic sound resounded from the hull of the groundship.

Supported on appendages that branched out from their legs to grip the ground beneath them, the canvassers raised up their incongruously long arms and opened fire. Even so, their proffered business cards—Hades Thorns launched from barrels in the palms of their hands—possessed only firepower sufficient to dent the armor on the groundship. Hades Thorns had not been weapons originally; they were in fact nothing more than seeds for the dustveins, which gave life to the landfill strata. However, if a worker were to be hit by one he would not go unscathed, and should the seed remain in his body he might well end up being torn asunder from within.

Amid the flying thorns, the worker was exposed, unprotected, and practically a painted target. As he clung to the cargo platform's railing, his fury toward the president mounted.

Ahead of them, a great host of canvassers were standing in the way, but the president wasn't slowing down at all. Heedless of the worker's vain screaming, the ship was beginning to tilt so as to charge through a narrow opening bounded by a pair of them.

As they slipped through, pleopods bit into both sides of the ship, sending sparks flying through the air. Immediately afterward, the groundship, under a hail of Hades Thorns, executed a half-revolution and started sliding sideways. It barely managed to stop by the edge of the crater that had been formed by the fall, but the worker was thrown by the recoil from off of the cargo platform.

The jellymire heaved up around him ponderously, but there was no splash, and it stuck to every inch of the fallen worker's body as it flowed away from him in every direction. Fighting back against an icky feeling not unlike that caused by the touch of the president's body, the worker found his footing at the

mire's coagulation depth and pushed himself up to his feet. It was then that he looked beyond the geometric patterns formed of the intersecting trajectories of raindrops and thorns and noticed a soot-black rock that resembled an oyster's shell sunk low in the bottom of the crater. It was the meteor carriage carrying their client.

He shrank away each time a Hades Thorn flashed by, but they were missing him by enough that he suspected they were trying not to hit him. Steeling himself, he began to half swim his way back to the groundship, which was about as far from him as the office building was from the cliff. By the time he had pulled the towing cable on the tail end of the ship over to the rim of the crater, however, he was sunk to his waist in jellymire and unable to progress. As he was thrashing about, something suddenly blocked out the sun and his whole body went stiff.

A canvasser was standing right before his eyes, like the walls of some crumbling ruin.

It bent both its arms—each one by itself resembling some huge crustacean—and grabbed hold of the worker's midsection from both sides, easily lifting him up into the air. Its featureless, jet-black head unraveled as it pulled him near, its whisper-leaves slowly unfolding like the blossoming of a bowl-shaped flower. It was said that they used this organ to communicate with their proprietors and one another's departments.

At the center of the head of whisper-leaves was its saucer-shaped mouth, but what unexpectedly came out of it was not a radula but a swarm of insect larvae resembling snowflakes. In no time, a flood of them came crawling out, squirming in the midst of its bowl of whisper-leaves. The worker had no idea what was happening. Could the nymphs that had attacked him last night have been sent from this place? Or could it be that the canvassers too were tormented by eruptions of lice?

The worker let loose a scream from the pit of his stomach and kept twisting and turning as he tried to escape from the writhing things closing in before his eyes. By the time the canvasser had pulled him in close enough to see the differences in the nymphs' snowflake patterns, however, he had given up entirely and was sinking into memories of Christmas. He recognized that it was the flashing of the crystals and the bell-like ringing of their wings that had induced such memories, but he couldn't escape from their hypnotic glamour. And yet these dreams as well were short-lived, ending with the collapse of the whisper-leaves in the background and the scattering of the nymphs.

A rusted metal shaft had been thrust into the throat of the canvasser. It had come from beneath the worker's armpit and extended all the way to the groundship behind him. It was but one of many coaxers with which the ship was equipped. Some of the president's corpuscyte was squeezed inside it. The coaxer withdrew, and the upper part of the canvasser's body began to tilt backward, as slate-blue body fluids spurted from a joint between its armor plates, mixed with waybugs.

The worker slid down along the coaxer and landed hard on board the ship.

There was no time for relief, though, as the body of the ship began to tilt. He looked up and saw two more canvassers starting to lift the tail of the ship.

The groundship continued to resist, swinging about three coaxers now; a fourth it pointed toward the crater that lay behind the worker, urging the worker to hurry toward it. On the floor of the crater, three canvassers were already huddled around the client's meteor carriage, shaking it back and forth ferociously as they tried to break through its outer shell. With each shock, bits of its surface layer were flaking off.

The worker jumped down off of the ship and fought his

way through the jellymire as fast as he could. He reached the floor of the crater, and then, in the moment that the canvassers shifted their posture for a concentrated blow, reached out an arm and knocked away shards of broken shell. He slid the hook of the towing cable into a coupling ring that was revealed underneath and, dodging all the while the mantis shrimp-arms that came flying at him, climbed back up out of the crater. At least, that was what he had intended to do. His foot slipped and he fell back down, landing on top of the carriage, where he took a blow from one of their fists. Ribs shattered. The worker choked as he vomited blood.

For some reason, though, the assault stopped right away, and he felt the fists grow distant. Clenching his teeth, the worker opened his eyes. The multilayered heads of the three canvassers were all tilted in his direction.

There was nowhere to flee.

Looking out from between the canvassers and up toward the groundship, he could see the coaxers swinging about, feeling around among the insides of canvassers now lying flat on their backs.

The worker yanked on the towing cable with a strength born from all the rage he felt toward the president, but the cable was too long, and all he could do was haul in some slack. He could see the groundship's coaxer holding an emerald-hued magatama that it had extracted from the corpse of a canvasser. Almost adoringly, it raised it aloft toward the sunlight. But then the sight was hidden by the shadows of the ever-more-numerous canvassers. Each head of whisper-leaves suddenly inclined downward and blossomed.

Was workman's comp going to pay out for this? And if so, who was going to be the beneficiary?

The worker was steeling himself for the end when from out of nowhere a wave of jellymire came rolling in and swallowed him up in its swell. With no idea what was happening, he clung to the towing cable. The meteor carriage had suddenly tilted and gone under and then, as if rebounding, risen back to the surface.

The worker sensed panic from the president inside the ship. He took a look back, and the canvassers were scattering black splashes of mud across the landscape as they worked frantically to dive beneath the mire.

Clouded by rain, a colossal gray *something* rose up over them like a twisted, warped tower that was continually being built upon. As it slowly bent to the left and the right, it drew nearer, eliciting in the worker a sense of unearthly profundity.

Although its outline closely resembled that of the president, it was closer to the blood of the canvassers in color and, moreover, of a gargantuan size that would make either of them look like small children in comparison.

It was a Crossing Guard. Unaffiliated with any corporatian's corporation, it was a "nonprofit entity"—one that brought no profit to anyone—a bringer of death to canvassers, directors, and workers alike.

Against that receding backdrop, the worker could see the armored shells of canvassers tardy in escaping as they were pulled apart by fingers bristling from the ends of arms that swung down from overhead, as well as internal organs resembling sea hares being sucked up out of them.

Once the groundship was again parked in the company hangar, its hatch sprang open, and from its entryway the president's corpuscyte overflowed. The worker hurried to get the president's muscle fiber coat for him.

Each time a blob of the president's body tissue injected

itself into the clothing, a sharp pain ran through the sternum of the worker, who bore its weight.

The body and breast of the coat began to swell, a translucent head started rising up out of the collar, and twisted sleeves pulsated as they took shape once more. Face-first, the president laid himself down heavily on the floor, then dragged his naked lower half up out of the ship, crawling forward with arms that had not yet finished regrowing their fingers. Although the bones of both legs were visible, they were all still clumped together like the organs of a conch. Along with bubbles of gas, a large number of Hades Thorns were being ejected through his surface, and a reddish curtain was unfurling inside him.

When the worker brought him his pants, the president's lower body began to split, and through peristaltic undulations of his surface layer, he steadily drew the fabric onto himself.

Once he had finished dressing and restoring his body to a shape suited to bipedal ambulation, the president attached himself to the floor with suction cups formed from the soles of his feet, drew up his knees, lifted his waist, and slowly raised up his arched back until he stood fully erect. Then immediately, he stumbled as though drunk and slammed into a wall.

The worker cried out from behind, "Are you all right, Mr. President?" but the president only put a hand against the wall and set off down the corridor, dragging his feet as he went. Following along behind, the worker was still dragging his feet as well.

Lagging behind, the worker made his way toward the workshop, and when he arrived, the president's shirt was rolled up, and a long, cardiopulmonary tube meant for synthorgans was buried in his solar plexus. He was giving himself a blood transfusion.

The worker left the room and in anticipation of his next task went into the washroom. When he took off his work clothes, there was an unevenness in his chest resembling a fissure caused by geologic upheavals, and blue-black bruises covered every part of his body. He turned the brass handle on the scaly wall and closed his eyes. He could hear the sound of the water in only one of his ears. Carefully avoiding the bruise on his solar plexus—like an overripe fruit, it yielded too easily to his touch—he cleaned away the sticky gum left by the rain. The texture of the jellymire that had clung to his skin remained, though. Even now, it still felt like it was all over him.

The worker changed clothes and headed back to the dock, where he found the front end of the safely-recovered meteor carriage covered in a spiderweb pattern of hairline cracks and a clear substance similar in consistency to a mollusk's body oozing from the places where they intersected. As he looked on, the substance suddenly overflowed. After a glance down the hallway in hopes that the president might be coming, he resigned himself and put out both his arms. Then, remembering that the average client weighed four times as much as he did, the worker hurried frantically back to the wall and rolled a pallet driver up to the underside of the carriage.

The blob of corpuscyte oozing down onto the pallet now poured forth in earnest, and though the worker knew he was looking at a client, there was practically nothing contained inside it. It resembled nothing so much as a giant, glistening blob of fat. The blob timidly extended a slender antenna, twisted it to the right and the left, and then simply withdrew it. The entire mass began to sway as though it were being kneaded by invisible hands and then stopped. In its present condition, it was not even able to move about freely. The worker could not even imagine a time when the president had been this helpless.

The worker pushed the pallet driver with the client loaded aboard, and when they entered the workshop, the president pulled out the cardiopulmonary pipe and pulled himself away from the shelf he had been leaning against.

While the president was transferring the client's body to the workbench, the worker started prep for a series of delivery operations. From a medicine bottle, he pulled out a handful of stupa-toad eggs and swallowed them down to ease the pain in his ribs. He put skingloves on both hands and intertwined his fingers so that there were no gaps, then pulled a number of scrolls from the shelves, lined them up, and lifted up the spine that had been completed only yesterday. It was the first item for delivery.

The president took in hand the forward part of the spinal column, stuck it into the corpuscyte of the client on the workbench, and gradually pushed it in deep. The worker prepared the hips while the president worked in the spine all the way down to the tailbone, arranging it neatly for attachment to the body.

Next came the secondary tibia, and after that the primary tibia. As they repeated this process for each of the major joints, the client's body—hitherto nothing but a blob of fat—began to take on a shape resembling that of a director.

The worker placed a scroll of peripheral nerves on the client's head and worked his way down toward the toes applying more of them. When the network of nerves he had laid across the client's entire form had sunk into his corpuscyte and reached every corner of his body, the president divided out multiple fingertips and continued weaving nerve fibers together at the point of connection between the brain and spinal cord. Compared with the president's everyday behavior, this degree of manual dexterity was truly extraordinary, and the worker was amazed every time he saw it. However, this kind of work seemed to wear on the president rather heavily, and for some time after a delivery, he would often just sit out on the deck and drown himself in strong drink.

The implantation of the circulatory system was accomplished in a similar manner, by which point the client's "body"—his corpuscyte—resembled an ocean filled with bobbing and swaying sea anemones. They continued working, fitting each cnidarianlike organ into its place and hooking it up. The worker understood what a vastly different environment the presidents and directors had been living in; without undergoing a fundamental transformation, they could not hope to maintain their existence here.

An upper and lower jaw, each lined with splendid rows of teeth, were submerged into the client next, followed by a windpipe. As for organs of vocalization, those were provided only to middle managers who had charge of multiple subordinapes. Wondering to himself whether this client would be willing to listen to complaints about horrible working conditions, the worker pulled a bumpy length of intestine down from the shelf.

He handed it to the president, who began packing the intestine into the client, and that was when the president's usual roughness of hand started to return. As soon as he finished putting the beating heart in between the lungs, he grabbed a skinbag from the shelf and went out into the hallway.

The worker gasped. He wasn't just going to quit midway through, was he? And yet there was no sign of the president coming back. The client was still waiting for them to finish. The worker let out an exhausted sigh. With no other choice before him, he set to work alone.

One by one, he pushed the jointed ribs into place, shaped the chest cavity, and by hand drew the cardiopulmonary tube near to the heart and attached it, watching carefully until the veins began to throb and carry blood to the organs. As soon as the lungs began their cycle of expansion and contraction, blood came squirting out of a spot where two blood vessels were joined, spreading out disquietingly like a storm cloud. The metal fitting that the president had put in place to hold them temporarily had come loose. Immediately, the worker pushed his arms into the corpuscyte to try to deal with it, but that didn't go well: on top of the poor visibility caused by the bleeding, his hands were pushed back by body tissues designed to expel foreign objects. As he was moving his fingertips vainly about, there came a succession of hard noises, like the sound of a typewriter. He looked up and saw that it was the client's teeth chattering. Perhaps he was experiencing a phantom chill due to the sudden, steep drop in blood pressure.

"Every day, I have to be cold like this too," the worker muttered, but then he spotted a cloudy redness in the abdomen as well, and there was no time to indulge trite feelings of superiority. If an organ delivery turned out defective and had to be recalled, he might well be called upon to provide replacements from his own body.

The worker pulled off his coat and, naked from the waist up, breathed out a ragged breath to steady his nerves. Focusing all his attention on the clamps, he reset them. While he was doing so, new hemorrhages were breaking out one after another, and the client's entire body was stained a ruby hue. Suddenly, there came the resounding noise of something being torn asunder, but because it had apparently come from the hallway behind him, he paid it no mind and lost himself in the task at hand.

The worker stood motionless, his arms hanging limp at his sides. Both were dyed red to the elbows. His head was heavy with egg cases. He couldn't remember what measures he had applied where. The client lay still on the workbench. Too still. Amid the fear that all of his organs had ceased functioning, the client tilted his head lethargically and let his jaw fall slack like some bad actor hamming up a death scene.

"KaKaKa..Kaaaa..."

The client's thick tongue flicked haltingly in and out and, after making the same sound many times over, uttered in what was clearly its voice, "R'lizided. *Dreenkided.*"

The worker was relieved that the client was alive, although at the same time he despaired of drawing any meaning from the words. The worker could not tell whether they had been spoken to a subordinape in some linguistic sphere other than his own, or if his voice simply wasn't working right.

He was glancing toward the hallway, thinking of heading back to his sleepsac, when one of the wall planks blew off and went flying. The upper body of a male lipocorpus—it was unusual to have a chance to see one—stuck out from behind it, then lay down on the floor. The worker could tell that this male was a CP-type from the pair of cardiopulmonary arteries that protruded from its side and disappeared into the hole in the wall. As it regarded the worker, its eyes were like bullet wounds closed over with abraded skin.

Insensitively, the worker averted his gaze and turned toward the shelf. He suddenly felt very hungry, and without even wiping his bloody hands took a spoiled blood sedge from its sealed container and ate it raw. It didn't taste much different from when they were served at mealtime. He swallowed it with the intense nausea that accompanied it, and tears ran down from the corners of his eyes. As if in consolation, the client said, *"Telidagodabedd, herdares, eh, sodeforriseup."*

The tears didn't stop.

The client stayed with them for about a week, listening to lectures from the president on how to move like a human being.

The first time he stood up was three days after his organs had been delivered, on the same day that the CP-type—having ceased to function—was removed and a new CP-type was brought in. The client's joints bent backward when he stood erect, and the center of gravity in his waist was shifted too far to the left, but even so he set out in an awkward walk, stopped at the threshold, and watched as the CP-type was being carried in.

The next day, the client made a slow circuit of the company building, and by the time a few days more had passed, he had mastered the art of bipedal locomotion. His habit of raising his knees too high persisted, but it was still a more natural gait than that of the worker, who had not recovered yet from the blow he had taken at the crater.

On the last day, the metal fittings were removed from the junctions where blood sedges now adhered. Like a pair of conjoined twins, the client and the president buried their heads in one another, causing a rippling interference pattern to appear along their surfaces, after which the client departed, going down in the lift by himself.

The president came outside and leaned out over the edge of the deck. The worker did likewise.

A flatboat was pulling away from the base of the synthorgan company. On its deck, the client lay on his back, bathing his rippling body in sunlight, reflecting flashes of light just like the oceans once had. Was he saying something? His lower jaw was moving up and down. Matching its movements, the worker gave voice to it:

AI, WIL, TEL ZEM, TU DU, BETR.

4

After the president departed for the board of directors meeting, the worker should in theory have been able to spend some time alone—his first in a very long while. Even with jobs to do such as knitting nerve nets and taking care of dependency tanks, idle times were practically holidays for him, and more importantly, he knew that if he didn't give his body a chance to heal he would never make it through the post-Festival rush when casualties would be carried in in rapid-fire succession.

However, a seriously wounded auditor from the fishery was brought in while the president was away.

Although the surgical procedure needed was clear from the explanation of the disassembler who had accompanied him, the worker still could not quell the anxiety he felt. Visible inside the auditor's face and extending down to his chest was nothing other than the upper half of a subordinape's body, gripped in a full nelson hold by the auditor's articulated ribs. Skin remained only in places; the muscles and organs were exposed. Every time the worker moved around the room, those clouded eyes would follow him with a slight lag. The fishery worker was being used, apparently, as a stopgap life-support system for the auditor's organs. There could be no clearer example of what would have happened to the worker himself the other day if that client's delivery of goods had been unsuccessful.

As he was unaccustomed to the job of connecting nerve fibers, the surgery turned out to be one difficult problem after another. The work was completed in four days, the auditor sent away before he awakened, and then the president came back. Once again, cruel and hectic days commenced.

Even now, the injuries the worker had sustained from the canvassers were not healed, and his physical condition was hardly satisfactory. With his ribs broken, his chest was still terribly uneven, and the bruise on his solar plexus had swelled up horribly with pus that stained his clothing. His spine had bent into an arch from favoring the cracked bones in his knee and ankle. And maybe he had just taken too many stupa-toad eggs, but a strange pressure had started in his abdomen which was growing in strength day by day. He always felt like vomiting whenever he moved around, and as before he would be seized with coughing fits and vomit blood. In spite of this, there was no change in the amount of work he was called upon to perform, and perhaps because of his misery, outbreaks of lice and egg cases began to occur even during the daytime. When the president noticed, he would suck them off with his fingertips.

Had water started pooling in the worker's abdomen? It had expanded to an unbelievable size, until he was no longer able to even bend over. Abscesses emitting foul odors were breaking out everywhere, and he often grew forgetful to the point that it interfered with his work. The president never grew indignant, however, nor would he send for that quack physician anymore.

Those old memories he could never be sure were dream or reality became altogether impossible for the worker to recall, and locked into a cycle of depthless, two-dimensional days, his work came to be a merely reflexive activity, like the nervous twitching of a spine.

But then one day when a frightful amount of blood had appeared in his stool, there came a sign that he might soon be freed from that cycle—it was a part of his swollen stomach that had begun to protrude outward—and move.

He touched the surface with both hands, and as he caressed it, it dawned on him that he was with child, and without the slightest reservation, he accepted the fact that she was female. She could even feel a vague sense of her past as a female. She gave herself over to a joy that rained down from above and bubbled up from within, and no thought crossed her mind for the obvious question of whose child this was...or of those immature reproductive organs of which she had always been ashamed.

From the time that she realized she was pregnant, the worker would often sit in a chair in the workshop and, taking care not to put pressure on the fetus, doze off into slumber with her hands gently resting on her stomach. She was no longer in any kind of condition for working. She was not even in condition for walking.

With her jacket pulled up to her solar plexus and her pants pulled down away from her stomach, her exposed, whitish belly looked like an enormous peeled boiled egg.

Having perhaps awakened to a newfound respect for workplace safety regulations, the president turned down the next work order that came in. As if that were not enough, he even went so far as to display concern, making sure not to run out of the stupa-toad eggs that had become the worker's only source of nutrition. Cracks appeared on her stomach, making watermelon patterns as the belly swelled to three times the size of the pregnancies in her memory, covering and concealing her withered legs.

The eggs also had medicinal effects, and it was during a long day spent dozing in and out of drowsy slumbers that she suddenly vomited, and the birthing process began.

From the rounded surface of her stomach, amid scattered bits of undigested toad eggs that trailed threads of saliva and stomach acid, blood and body fluids erupted from around the abscess on her solar plexus, and something as black and as glossy as wet crow feathers rose up out of it and opened its eyes. After they had stared at one another for a time, her new self came suddenly sliding out. It was as though she'd beheld her own decapitation.

Then the worker's body twisted with an agony like she had never known, and in that moment her upper body was rotating around its own center of gravity. Her spinal column broke, bundles of muscle tore loose in rapid succession, and the ceiling and floor exchanged places. A grated pattern spread out across her field of vision. Its dark squares slammed into her face: her front teeth cracked open, her nose was crushed, and blood went flying.

With her damp nose pressed against the grated floor, clinging to a pain that pierced straight through to her parietal bone for proof that she was still alive, she turned her head to the side. She saw a newborn worker there, bending over backward as it was pushed from a stomach that now bore a shocking resemblance to a sleepsac. The president—when had he come in?—took it by the back and the nape of the neck, pulled the rest of its body free, and laid it down on the workbench.

The voice of the worker as she begged for help was not even a moan, but the president came over to her nonetheless. His face descended, made a noise that sounded like, *"GyoVuReU'UNN,"* and just as this was answered with a sound of creaking iron, the worker was flung down into the gloom beneath the floor.

She fell like a soul that had slipped out of its true, flesh-and-blood body, and going down the worker surely saw it: the truth behind the parrots that hung by both arms from the grated floor plates through which they wrapped their fingers.

That was me. That, and the sleepsac too, used to be me.

The dim light from the workshop fell farther and farther away. She was in an empty space with nothing she could struggle against. So empty that even when the end abruptly came, she wasn't aware of it.

CHAPTER 2:
THE DISASSEMBLER SEARCHED ON

1

When the on-site disassembler came to the synthorgan factory carrying his packing case, he stared for a moment at a worker who had assumed an awkward attitude toward him, apparently puzzled upon seeing another of his kind for the first time. He must have been born quite recently—his hair was jet-black and glossy, and his skin was fresh and young. *The cycles sure run fast here,* he thought with pity. He had just started to introduce himself as a worker from the fishery, when the young worker's face twisted into a severe expression.

"That's *my* name. I won't have you referring to yourself as 'I.'"

Just the same as before. The old memories didn't come back right away, so there were many cases where self-identification didn't go very well. They probably couldn't help latching on to a word that would provide a definition of who they were.

"I'm the on-site disassembler," he added simply, and then got down to work.

When the disassembler had finally finished disassembling the placoderms and was covered in oil, he requested the president's signature on the paperwork. The body tissues of presidents and directors were injected into his skull as recording media. By way of his eye socket, that swollen finger came feeling around inside his head, and he wet himself.

He had a headache as he got into the lift, the corpse of that coffin eel still wrapped around all four walls as though trying to climb up on the nearly four-meter-tall cage. The cage shuddered and slowly descended. From between gaps in the elaborate ribs surrounding him on every side, the skeleton of a subordinape who appeared to have been swallowed whole was peeking out.

The lift stopped. He stepped off onto an island of rotting flesh and was loading his packing case on the flatboat when his eyes paused upon a small, steeply ascending island located directly beneath a vertical drainage pipe. It seethed with the gases of decomposition.

"What's the matter?" asked the pilot.

The disassembler turned his short neck and indicated it with his jaw.

"You've tried how many times already? It's hopeless. It'll just be a parrot this time too."

"I know. You're probably right," the disassembler said as he started walking out into the shallows of the putrefying muck.

"That gas is dense. You watch yourself."

He waved a hand lightly behind him and pulled his scarf up over his nose. After crossing over to a tiny island covered in bas-reliefs of bones and organs, he sank to his knees in putrid filth that teemed with cockroaches and nematodes and headed toward a figure that was buried to its chest on the side of the highest hill.

It was looking up at the underside of the faraway deck. Its face was exactly the same as that of the worker he had met just moments ago. When, breathing heavily, he made his way to its side, its eyes moved. They turned toward the disassembler and stared.

The disassembler knew full well, though, that this was nothing more than a reactionary response. The magatama was always passed on to the newborn worker, so nothing of their former intellect could remain in those who had turned into parrots. The disassembler lifted up the parrot's half-body, and they regarded one another, face-to-scab-covered-face.

"Hey there, you remember me?"

Rows of sparse teeth began to quiver.

" 'Ey…member me?"

The disassembler's eyes grew moist. He recognized his tears as a form of self-pity.

Suddenly, he heard the sound of someone whistling with his fingers. It was the pilot urging him to head back.

"All right," he said. It was as he was setting the parrot back down, however, that the disassembler's fingers detected a small, hard bulge in the body's breast pocket. He undid its button and stuck his fingers inside. What came out was a magatama that gleamed with an emerald light.

2

At first, the worker thought himself—the pregnancy being little more than a biological and existential misunderstanding—submerged in water. This was because everything appeared distorted to him. He wondered if he had perhaps finally awakened from a nightmare in which he worked at a cruel synthorgan factory. After all, the room he was in looked a lot like the rooms in which the people of his hometown had lived. However, the familiar furniture and household appliances that were lined up against the wall were far too numerous, haphazardly pushed up against one another like animals snapping at each other's throats. The dim light was coming from a torchburr. Had there been a room like this at the base of the synthorgan company building? The terror of when he had been thrown from that structure came back to him, and he tried to get up, only to discover that he couldn't move in the slightest. It was as though he were buried to his neck on a sandy beach.

home> *<away>* *nothing>deep>depths>* *·<shell* *<seal* *<yoke<sin* *<*

Suddenly, lonely thoughts that beggared his imagination came welling up, and his eyes filled with tears. Without spilling over, they remained quivering on the surfaces of his eyes, only to be swallowed up in waves of concentric circles emanating from the midst of his field of vision. From somewhere, he could hear a sound like a backed-up sewer pipe.

sign> *flow>* *merge>* *destruction>* *·* *<desperation* *<void* *<execution* *<world*—his thoughts ached as though themselves possessed of a sense of pain.

Days spent in longing for a return from that place of exile beyond the bounds of society—days enough to turn boulders into sand. He could remember them as his own. *Is this somebody else's memory again?* He was thinking that it was, and the chain of thoughts that nested around the axis of that single point grew outward in every direction, forming a shell all around him, until they began both to complement and overturn one another.

Only in scattered fragments could he unlock their meaning, and when consciousness returned to him in that room, he could for some reason practically *taste* the presence of someone standing on the other side of the wall, and of corpses sealed within the disorderly layout of a multilayered, labyrinthine housing crystal lying farther in behind him.

Someone started walking toward him. It was not a worker

from his own company; he looked a lot like the disassembler from the fishery. Though hadn't he just been wondering where he worked himself? Coaguland...number four, it was the Fourth Coaguland Reaffirmation branch. He felt a pressure near his retinas, and the wall appeared again, and the disassembler appeared from a doorless entryway, confusing the worker.

"You were pretty slow to wake up. I'd just about given up on you." The voice that came to him sounded like it was passing through water. "We are presently located inside a vintage landfill stratum. The metabolism's slow here, though, so there's nothing to worry about."

Fwaa ii zii—

What is this? was what the worker had intended to say.

"It must still be hard for you to speak. Can you tell, by the way, that you're being preserved inside a director's body?"

Images rose up in the back of the worker's mind of a director caught in the grip of several canvassers...of organs and multiple yoked-in brains being smashed one after another. A shudder went through the corpuscyte that covered his entire field of vision, causing the disassembler's face to waver about.

"This director took fatal injuries in a canvasser attack. They brought him in to the synthorgan factory right away, but there was no way to restore him, so they threw him out. Yeah...no hope of helping them once they've had their brains destroyed."

No, that isn't right. Those yoked-in brains are internal prisons that greatly limit the functionality of cogitosome-bearing corpuscyte.

"You'd turned into a parrot and were buried in an island of rot. For some reason, you were carrying a magatama. During pregnancy, the magatama moves to the embryo, so what you were carrying most likely belonged to someone who was swallowed by a coffin eel. Magatamas govern the intellect and memory of subordinapes like us."

They were not merely memory organs for individuals. They

reminded workers in great detail of all kinds of things they had no way of learning by themselves, and in much the same way that landfill strata created counterfeit copies of things using eide from the past, they had also succeeded in making those things real.

Now he stood unmoving in a dark alleyway, staring silently as many of his kind began to come and go along a street where time had frozen over. One of the parishes that had once flourished in the inner world of the canvassers—which had long afterward remained compressed and frozen inside the magatama—was unpacking into his neural network like a tightly folded paper being opened to reveal a completed diagram.

"Since you're using some stranger's magatama as a foothold, it isn't clear whether you're the same worker as before."

The worker started walking. He was twice as tall as everyone else, but nobody seemed to notice. He tried touching a pedestrian on the back, but his fingers merely sank into him and got tangled up in the strings of letters there. It dawned on him that a subordinape was something chosen out of the collected data of the fifty thousand people that a canvasser's magatama contained. That data was then modified and forcibly incarnated. He realized also that while here in this parish, he was himself in a comatose state.

"If you're wondering who it was that merged you so splendidly with the director's body, why that would be your own newborn self. Not that he understood what it was he'd accomplished, mind you. I had originally hoped to play the role you're playing right now myself."

As he advanced forward, spatial distortions began to appear here and there, and the worker noticed that the space around him was dotted with gaps.

"Should've known I wouldn't be brave enough to be sealed

alive in corpuscyte, though."

The reason the warps and the gaps were appearing was that in regions where the medium differed from the rest—most likely near things like the cogitosomes that were scattered throughout the director's body—only space constructed through classical physics was being displayed.

"At the fishery, I couldn't even try to use a parrot unless I took it apart for disassembly practice."

The worker was headed toward a place of extreme distortion. It was a park where sunlight dappled through the trees. There a man in a white lab coat was sitting on a bench, nodding at no one in particular as he stared intently at a cliff face towering above the treetops. There was no mistaking that the cliff was made of landfill strata. Was there something special about the cogitosome handling its construction? It appeared that it was showing him space from before the end of the world.

A man in a suit appeared to his right. He held a can of coffee out to the man in the white coat and spoke: "With things having come to this point, I find it odd that you aren't getting registered to be Translated."

"Double-translation is an imaginary cyclical transaction. You should know that. Here even the magatama itself is nothing more than a concretion that the <World> brought into existence. Most likely, the replacement by ultimaterial that was done in order to effectively use our limited computational resources has caused some kind of—"

"What on earth are you talking about?"

"—harm from deprivation?" He stood up, gripping the can tightly. "All of this has already happened."

"Probably so. Like they say, history repeats itself."

"Not like this." The man in the white coat tossed an object, which at some point had transformed into a light bulb, into an ultimaterial bin, and stared firmly into the face of the worker.

"Can't you feel a presence there behind you?"

"I'm not the type to believe in ghosts."

"After you came out of your coma, you had your share of freakouts, though. 'It's the man I saw in my dreams,' you said."

"And that's been taken care of through cerebro-physiological means. Now I just have dreams about everybody floating in the darkness."

"Exactly. That's because Hanishibe is still drifting through interstellar space alone in that spaceship even as we speak. By continuing to speak, he's protecting us. The coordinates are—"

"I'm sorry, but it's time for me to go. Work is work, even in a world like this one. I'm off to the canvasser now, so I'll see you later."

The man in the suit crossed over the manifestation boundary as he departed, and disappeared. Dazedly, the worker moved away from that place. He knew that the scene he had just witnessed could not exist according to the law of causality. In other words, this was not the past.

"Hey, are you listening?"

Double-translation, interstellar spaceships—as he was strolling along unable to collect his thoughts, he bumped into an invisible wall. There were limits to the scale of the space that a magatama could contain. The other side of the wall was covered in fog through which another town could be dimly seen.

"Even you must've sought after answers any number of times. Why are we employed by directors? When did we sign such contracts? What are we getting in compensation? Oh, we remember these things dimly. That we signed a contract, that we received a baptism. But why aren't these things consistent even in our own memories? What were these directors and humans originally?"

Those who are forever damned…those who long to return… those who trick us into servitude.

"Why are there magatama even inside the canvassers? Does it mean that those disgusting things—I don't even know whether they're alive or machines—are our original forms? Why? Why? Look—you must be able to see it!"

The worker looked across the parish town, and simultaneously he was looking down at it with a bird's-eye view. Dimly, he could make out the ghost of the <World> constructed by the web of interconnectivity created by the canvassers'—no, the cherubim's—Whispering. But without whisper-leaves of his own, it was only possible to comprehend as a real image the parish with which he himself was affiliated.

"Whenever a fundamental question occurs to you, the lice appear and devour your thoughts."

The worker strained his eyes at the rows of houses and streets on the other side of the fog. Transforming his arms into Code, he pried open the invisible wall and stretched out his hand toward the mist-enshrouded town.

"So we forget the inconsistencies right away. The same questions occur to us, and we forget them again. This cycle has been repeating for generations. When the nymphs hatch from the lice egg cases—"

Those weren't louse nymphs. They were bits of Code as well, implanted by the directors in the roots of their hairs to prevent the lice egg cases from hatching—in other words, to prevent the activation of the snowpetal bugs, which were a self-defense mechanism of the magatama.

"—they cover your head like an umbrella and suck out every last bit of your soul. Even if you're disassembled afterward, there won't be a magatama inside."

That was because the snowpetal bugs would form temporary whisper-leaves and bequeath all of the magatama's data to the canvassers' <World> network. In the present, however, where such dramatic reaffirmation was taking place at the livable boundaries beyond which a certain sort of life support became indispensable, the cherubim—and thus their <World>—was on the brink of destruction.

"If that happens, you'll be left a CP-type, suffering from hyperfrequent hemo—φιλία·."

Regardless of business conditions, many things would be needed to preserve and reunify the inner world of the cherubim: magatama to serve as its seeds, its slate-blue development medium, cogitosomes to expand it, and corpuscyte to protect the cogitosomes. Even if this were to lead to a repeat of the world's end...

"W-what are you doin—?"

The worker was staring at the roads and the buildings of the two towns as they began to connect one to another, and at the same time, he was staring at the corners of the disassembler's mouth as the director's hands tore them apart; it opened wider and wider until the sides of the disassembler's face had split in half.

The worker grabbed hold of the magatama stored inside the disassembler's skull, then pulled his arm back out. The disassembler collapsed like a puppet whose strings had suddenly snapped.

On the second floor of a certain hospital in the midst of the expanded city, however, the disassembler, who had been lying comatose, opened his eyes, turned toward the worker—who was watching over him through the window from above —and nodded.

As he hallucinated the ghost of a planet. Of a <World>. As he was laid bare to the directors' hunger to return home.

CHAPTER 3:
THE RITE CAME OFF WITHOUT A HITCH

The workers who had been ordered to perform were standing in a line with nothing to do on a wharf near the outer edge of the ceremonial grounds.

The worker from the synthorgan company as well was standing on the cargo platform of the moored groundship, observing with a complicated expression the Festival that was also known as General Assembly. On the coagulating land whose reaffirmation had been completed, a great multitude of directors from all manner of businesses had gathered together and were crowded around a sacred palanquin. It was walnut-shaped, and about the size of an island. No canvassers came to attack. Already, many years had passed since the last sighting of them. With a presentiment that all things were coming to an end, the worker felt relieved and at the same time afraid, fearful of a future that he could not see.

Pushed along by the directors, the palanquin moved forward little by little, the ground beneath it crushed and turned up by its underside. Of those caught underneath and crushed there was no end; for workers, this was less a festival than an execution.

The shrine was ensconced in its appointed place, where it tilted just slightly before coming to a rest. Then the directors, bodies radiating visible light, began moving in ranks two or three deep around its circumference as the upper hemisphere of the shrine, rotating in the opposite direction, began to rise. At last it came to rest, floating in midair.

From the underside of this upper portion, long tubes known as fiddleheads extended downward, and the directors crowded around them. As the fibers of their clothing unraveled and dissolved, they were sucked into the tubes like snails going back into their shells. First one and then another; one by one, they disappeared from sight.

Suddenly, the bodies of those awaiting their turn began for some reason to undulate. All attention was drawn to a cluster of seven directors in their midst who were standing perfectly still.

They awakened in the worker an ineffable sense of otherness. The other directors surrounding them began to draw back.

It appeared as if those seven had leaned back to back against one another, when radiating outward from their feet there appeared cracks in the ground, exposing a greenish, translucent hill-like thing. For some reason, their fourteen legs were attached to its surface. Still crowned with the seven directors, the hill began to heave upward, rapidly expanding and growing in volume. It had apparently been buried at a considerable depth. In no time, the upheaval had become a giant figure with the seven directors stuck to its face, dragging itself up out of the ground with a terrible rumbling.

Its cyclopean body was ten times the size of a director, and a jumble of iron building materials could be seen inside its pale green form. It also contained a pattern of dark spots that in the right lighting would be revealed as the floating skulls of subordinapes.

The worker looked on in utter shock and surprise. He had never seen a Crossing Guard this close up before. It appeared vastly more massive than before. Mowing down the

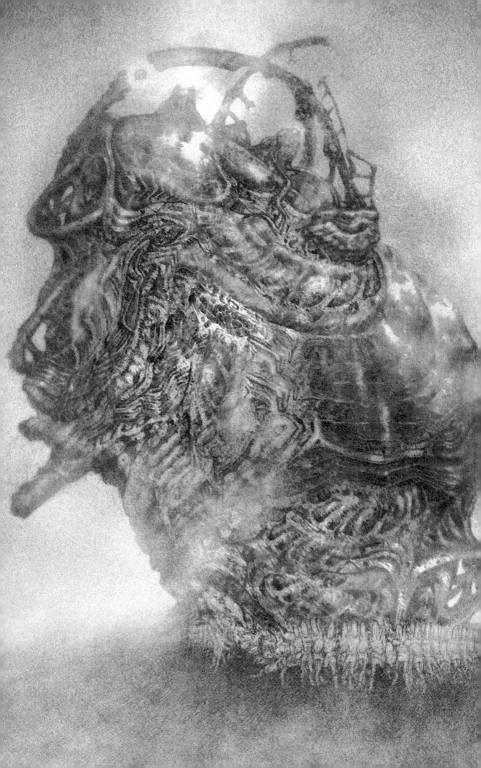

director-humans with its clusters of arms, the Crossing Guard swung from left to right a face where traces yet remained of the seven directors, and pressed that face up against the fiddleheads.

As the Crossing Guard invaded the shrine's interior by way of those tubes, steel towers, train cars, and the like came falling out of its body. They cracked the ground, and splashes of jellymire formed huge waves that began to engulf the entire area.

Many directors came running forward to try to pull the Crossing Guard's huge body out of the fiddleheads, but they were swallowed up instantly and their organs squelched. Numerous whirlpools appeared all over the Crossing Guard's body, and with a deafening roar it moved into the crowd of directors, who all cried out in baleful screams. There were also earnest protests from those who had voices to utter them.

INGuRoBaReMo, SoReBaDeSaGiMiDda, WaddaGoHome, DoToRe, WaddaGoHome—

As the worker looked on, the upper hemisphere of the shrine that the Crossing Guard had hijacked lost no time in withdrawing its fiddleheads and slowly began to rise higher. The directors lost themselves completely, and as they ran about in confusion looking for an escape, the space around the shrine grew distorted. In the space of an instant all fell dark as the light was sucked from the air in a radial pattern.

By the time a dim illumination had returned, the upper hemisphere of the shrine had vanished.

The many directors were lying on their backs, bobbing up and down with the waves of mud spreading out in concentric rings from the remaining lower hemisphere, and the survivors began to hurry as they tried to evacuate to the wharf where their attending workers awaited them.

This time, however, four long legs—wrapped about with thick, stringlike tissues through which not a gap was showing—emerged from the lower half of the shrine. They rose up vertically, started to twitch as they strained to their highest possible altitude, and that was when all of them bent at their center joints. Like sickles swinging downward, they stabbed into the face of the land.

Now these four legs had become support structures lifting up a gnarled, bony body from out of the shrine's lower half. All of the onlookers were staring up in fascination as its body bent farther backward. A thin steam was rising from its surface.

The scheduled one, the true settler: a Planetary Child—
said one of the terrified workers that had gathered together.
—come down to turn the screw of Earth's axis.

Beneath the four legs, the outer shell of the shrine rotated and began sinking into the ground. The Planetary Child crouched down to peer into the dark, ever-deepening shaft, and jabbed the tips of its four legs down into those inner walls. It raised and lowered its joints as though they were loaded with springs and then started to fall forward.

Amid intermittent rumblings in the earth, a few weak shadows that the directors could hardly be said to have cast came near the wharf. Among them was the president, his shriveled upper body bare and exposed. A cloudy pool of blood was visible inside his stomach. Utterly exhausted, he returned to the wharf. Then, as he was placing one leg on the groundship to steady himself, the body tissue of his face congealed into an oval shape that reflected an inverted image of the worker.

The worker nodded and said, "Shall we go back to the workshop, sir?"

A thought flitted through his mind of their remaining store of liquor. Would just that much be enough?

That was the end for him. Disassembled into more than a hundred different parts, that which had been the worker was suspended in midair. It was the president's judgment call. From among these parts, the lungs, the liver, the thigh bones and all

manner of defective parts were levied into the president's body.

Finally, the magatama was removed from his pineal gland, and the remaining fragments of the worker came pouring down like rain on the jellymire.

Even now, with the land handed over to the Planetary Child, the president was still waiting, and the next worker continued to do his work. Though the canvassers had been wiped from the plains of coaguland, a reconstituted <World> made up of many parishes continued to exist inside the departed interstellar spaceships. There the people were menaced by the Great Dust Plague and underwent Translation to become canvassers. They were beginning to wind the coils of an endless loop.

If a planet is a suitable cradle, exiles will surely be sent there to reaffirm it. Subordinapes will continue to be made from the magatama. And the date from which the tale is set forth will matter little.

FRAGMENT:
JEWEL

What <Gyo> had acquired at auction was nothing more than a large work animal held in perpetual stasis; the jewel concealed within, however, was a civilization frozen in time—a granary filled to overflowing with life's undiscovered phenovocabulary.

Dictating syntax from the jewel he extracted, <Gyo> created subordinapes of manifold purpose, his goal to improve work efficiency. Furthermore, he received syntax of investment from other corporatians and bred giant work-beasts as well. Their reception was exceedingly positive in terms of both words and nutrients. Orders came pouring in, and they were deployed one after another to the gelcase layers of incubation shells surrounding Planetary Embryos.

<Gyo> raised his liquidity, abounded in luxury, shamelessly expanded his physical volume, and at long last, succeeded in acquiring <Ja>.

CAVUMVILLE
(OR, THE CITY IN THE HOLLOW)

CHAPTER 1:
THE HEREANDNOW

1

Gentle ripples rolled across the classroom window, transforming the view into something like a reflection on a watery surface. Countless homes, clinging like shellbugs to petraderm walls outside, appeared to sway back and forth. Sound waves created the illusion as they beat against the translucent peritoneum stretched across the window frame. Nor was it only the classroom window; an inaudible roar echoing up from the depths was sending vibrations through every window worthy of the name in that funnel-shaped city.

"…the complex endoskeletal structure exists apart from the exoshelleton, and at first glance appears to be entirely without purpose. In fact, I can't see any use for it myself, and yet…"

Suspended in front of a sallow skinboard that accounted for the entire front wall of the classroom, Professor Shitadami lectured on without a pause, his head one-third the size of his entire body.

He pulled and manipulated the gutlines that hung down from the sliptrack overhead and began sliding from the left side of the skinboard to the right, moving along a spinal column that extended from one side of the ceiling to the other.

From either side of his overhanging chin there protruded a hard antenna that quickly and nimbly trailed scratches across the skinboard.

Long welts swelled up along the scratches, presently embossing the skinboard with a skeletal diagram of a momonji—a creature particularly simple in form and mysterious in its ways, even among the countless body plans and innumerable behavioral traits of its fellow petauristas. But for Hanishibe, sitting two rows from the back, everything in the tall, vertical space of the classroom was a blur, pushed from his mind by the vibrations of the silk-white city streets.

Why do I feel so uneasy? Hanishibe mouthed, not quite giving voice to the words. Descents from Heaven happened all the time. His sweaty fingers crawled along the spine of his rib-bound textbook, and he took comfort in the familiar peaks and valleys of its vertebrae.

"…if you know this part? Yes, Mr. Karikomo?"

"The roundbones are used as wheels or cogs. But even so, Professor, I have to think that from our standpoint, momonji are put together just a little *too* conveniently."

"That's an important point, but it's also a question that takes us into the realm of metaphysics. If you wish to pursue it, I'd suggest you transfer to the department of theology. Now, next is Mr.…."—Professor Shitadami turned toward the students and gazed across the classroom—"Hanishibe. What is this called, and what function do you think it serves?"

Hanishibe hadn't heard a thing the professor had said, but when twenty-three classmates turned around to look at him all at once, he realized that he had been called upon. A dazzling beam of sunlight was being reflected into his eyes off the hairless, hard, and finely cracked cranium of Yatsuo, who was sitting with perfect posture in a seat in front of him and off to the side.

There were four rows and six columns of seats, and about half of the faces occupying them were far removed from the human baseform. In the case of Monozane the Truncated Dodecahedron, who was bubbling away contentedly in an aquarium on a front-row desk, Hanishibe couldn't even tell what part corresponded to a face.

Grandpa's really amazing, Hanishibe thought, impressed anew by the outstanding work his grandfather did. Although humans came in all shapes and sizes, he could see right away that they were *people* and took measures to resurrect them.

Hanishibe was fearful that even if he did manage to become a taxonomist, he might misjudge someone and make a mistake he could never atone for. He had long had a feeling that it wouldn't be terribly unusual if people were found among the raw materials used in the mesenchyme-wrapped bones of the chair he was sitting in or among the ingredients of the broth that today's rhinoceros meat had been served in at lunchtime. His fear of making such errors was supposed to be why he was studying in this taxonomy department to begin with, but for some time now, Hanishibe had been afflicted by a sense of unease that he couldn't put clearly into words and had become unable to focus on his studies.

Professor Shitadami made a coughing sound.

"Hanishibe, didn't you hear?"

"*Zwee, Zu, Zwee*"

"He said, 'What's it called and what does it do?'"

"*UrryUpAnAnser*"

"Psst! The prof's calling you!"

Spurred on by his classmates' whispers, he looked up at the scowling face of Professor Shitadami, suspended in midair before the skinboard. The ridges that the blood sedges formed in his forehead were pulsating furiously, as was the swollen tumor in his left cheek.

The professor's right antenna was indicating the outline of an unassuming ossiform folded several times over, buried in the backshell ossiform beneath the momonji's skin. It wasn't yet listed in this year's textbook.

Hanishibe stood up from his seat.

"It's a wingtype ossiform," he said. "During their descent from heaven, they deploy from the backshell ossiform and push the skin outward, forcing it to spread out and tighten, and can exhibit movements similar to those of a bird flapping its wings. It can't fly, of course. Its original purpose, like that of the variable exoshelletons and the other unnecessary interior bones, are unknown, since the researchers are—"

Since he was just parroting what he'd heard from his grandfather, he could keep explaining for as long as anyone would listen, but the professor, with a wave of a shriveled hand that resembled some sort of dried snack, cut him off.

"Precisely. Strange though it may be, they exhibit behavior like that of a flapping wing. All we have to rely on is the *Book of the Heritage of the Hereafter*, but it's believed that the phylogenetic repetition that takes place up until a human fetus takes shape—changes in form such as the appearance of gills and tails—may contain the key to unraveling this mystery."

With perfect timing, then, a melancholy tone sounded out in the hallway. Hanishibe caught a glimpse of the "bell monitor" as he passed by the open door leading out into the hallway. With a forward-backward motion, he expanded and contracted his rust-colored, box-shaped thorax like an accordion, emitting the tone that marked the end of class.

"Well, that's all for today. To those of you on cleaning duty: don't forget to put ointment on the skinboard, and pay special attention to the spots that are festering. Next week, we'll be dissecting a real momonji, so wear something you won't mind getting dirty."

Someone smarted off at that, asking what those who don't wear clothes should do.

"Come prepared to molt," the professor replied. As his students wryly grinned, Professor Shitadami shook his head from side to side, retracting his antennae. He then slid his school rulebook into his backsac, pulled on a hanging line, and descended silently to the hardbone floor, facing downward. He crawled out of the classroom on all fours like a baby.

Hanishibe swept away the scales scattered across his desk, set his briefcase on his knees, and was just about to put away his stationery, when Yatsuo approached him. Hairline cracks ran across her glossy head in intricate geometric patterns, reflecting flashes of light. Her polyhedronal lips opened up like some cleverly designed mechanism, causing delicate distortions in the cracks of her face.

"There you were about to set him off with some snide remark, when the man himself pulled you out of the fire."

Her high, clear voice was easy on the ears, but Hanishibe couldn't figure out what she was talking about. He tried to return her gaze, to search her expression for the intent behind those words, but he couldn't tell which skin-shards concealed her eyes. Yatsuo sat down beside him in a vacant desk. There was a creak from the seat's pelvis.

"You were just about to wrap up that little speech of yours with something like, 'And as for the original function, that's still unclear due to researcher laziness.' Am I wrong?"

"Well, no, not really. What about it?"

"Exshuse me," said a hulking, dark green figure, interposing itself without the slightest hesitation between their two seats. It was Komorizu, who was on cleaning duty today. Large clusters of gourd-shaped appendages dangled from every inch of his fleshy upper body, covering him all the way down to the knees. For this reason he was exempt from having to wear clothing.

Komorizu was the son of Moitori, the highest-ranking official at the Department of Aquatic Resources. He had died at the age of sixty in his last Heretofore, and although six years had already passed since his revivification and metamorphosis from momonji, his attempts at recollection had gone nowhere, until at last he had been made to transfer into a second-year taxonomy program suited for sixteen-year-olds. Although no other case was as extreme as his, nearly all of the students treated him according to his provisional age.

The two desks were being gradually pushed apart into an arrowhead shape. While Hanishibe was staring at Komorizu's clusters of ponderously swaying, fleshy nodules, something finally occurred to him.

"Come to think of it," he said, "Professor Shitadami specializes in 'Determination of Function in Extraneous Organs.'"

"And don't you forget it," Komorizu said with a knowing look, passing between the two of them. At some point, the clusters of growths around his waist had sprouted innumerable pseudophalanges. A long, slender sort of rod was stuck among them and was gradually being carried up, up, and away. Hanishibe took a closer look and realized it was the marrowpen that was supposed to be resting on his desktop. Though Komorizu seemed unaware of it himself, his clustered gourdlets had sticky fingers.

Hanishibe leaned forward and quickly grabbed hold of the marrowpen, but the strength in those pseudophalanges was totally unexpected. Marrowink from inside came bleeding out and got all over his fingers, so he finally gave up and let it go. The marrowpen disappeared gradually into the shadows of his many appendages.

Yatsuo opened up Hanishibe's pencil box and handed him a piece of eraser-fat. As he was wiping off the marrowink, Hanishibe, speaking quickly, said, "You wouldn't have time to go out for hemomochi or something, would you?"

It was the first time he had ever asked Yatsuo out somewhere.

Yatsuo fingered the magatama hanging down from her neck. It most likely belonged to a family member awaiting revivification. "Don't make suggestions you don't have time for yourself. Tomorrow is fine; I can meet you at the hour of the monkey."

A bit thrown off by her own swift reply, Yatsuo changed the subject. "During class, you seemed absorbed in something outside the window. What were you looking at?"

"Oh…yeah. The peritoneum's vibrating. I was thinking it'll be pretty soon, you know."

"Oh yeah, Descent from Heaven. But was that really all that was on your mind?"

"Hanishibe?" a muffled voice called at that moment.

He turned around and saw Narikabura from the astronomy department standing in the doorway. He stood only as high as Hanishibe's waist. Positioned atop the three spindly, supple, knobby-kneed legs that accounted for eighty percent of that height was a formless blob that could only barely be identified from its outline as a human head. It was like a liposculpt abandoned midway by a craftsman.

"Today's your day for watchtower duty, isn't it?" said Yatsuo.

Hanishibe turned around at the sound of her voice. In the glossy flecks that covered her face, he saw several reflections of himself, his loose, scaly skin like a mask that hadn't quite been put on right—a relic of his having been born boneless.

Hanishibe could almost swear sometimes that his every thought was an open book to Yatsuo. At times, she even frightened him. Though his eyes would seek her out every time he came into the classroom, he felt a stifling presentiment that should their relationship advance, he would find himself trapped in a world where everything had been prearranged for him long ago. For that reason, he had always brushed off her invitations.

"Sorry about this, really. Tomorrow, then." So saying, Hanishibe pushed his writing instruments into his briefcase and got up to leave.

When he had walked as far as the front of the classroom, he found Komorizu resting several clusters of his gourdlets against the skinboard, rubbing in the ointment. Komorizu greeted him, waving the couple dozen pseudophalanges growing from the clusters on his back. Hanishibe waved back with his hand and walked past him on his way out the door.

When he emerged into the hallway, Narikabura stepped back on his three legs, drawing himself up against the bruise-colored cliff face that served as the wall. His movements were not unlike those of the terrified giraffe he had seen for the first time in anatomy lab half a year ago. Hanishibe could still remember the sweet taste of its meat, which everyone had shared after the dissection.

"You'll get landsoup on yourself," said Hanishibe.

"Oh, yeah," said Narikabura, moving away from the wall. Sticky, glue-colored landsoup was oozing from numerous cracks in the exposed cliff face. When it congealed, it would form a new layer of rock, though in time, pressure from within would cause that to crack as well, and the oozing would start once again. The moon's expansion was ongoing.

Threading their way between students absorbed in chatter, the two made their way down the hall.

"Where do you want to meet up?" Narikabura asked, inflating the lower half of his head, then releasing the air through many tiny holes as he spoke.

"How about in front of the watchtower?" Hanishibe said. "And don't forget to bring your own dinner."

"I know, I know. Watch duty or no, I've still gotta cook tonight—and make foods for weaning Dad too."

"How is he these days? Does he seem to be taking to you?"

"Not one bit. He's scared of me." Narikabura extended a vinelike glossophalanx out from between where his legs were attached. He held it up in front of his smooth, expressionless face and looked at it, sadly it seemed. "I tried to pet him, but Dad's head is, well…"

"Yeah, but he's only been revivified for six months."

"That's true. He's cuter than my last dad, so that's a plus, I guess. He's probably going to recollect the details of his Heretofore right away though and pass me by in terms of provisional age."

Last month, when he had visited Narikabura's house, his father's adorable, mutation-free baseform had been curled up in a rocking cradle. The father that had died two years ago had been the same age as Narikabura, however, and their relationship had been strained.

What was it like for people who raised themselves all by themselves? It was said that when people shared the same individual registration, their magatama would become attuned to one another, regardless of whether there were two of somebody or ten. Hanishibe was remembering being held by his grandfather once when he was sobbing as a child. He had become frightened imagining their home overflowing with himselves.

"There, there, you're not always necessarily you," his grandfather had said consolingly.

They passed by the classrooms of the theology department. Through the windows and the doors they could see students standing in rows, looking downward as if in meditation. Unlike the other departments, theology held classes until late at night.

Some of the students were twitching with nervous tics in their faces or arms. Perhaps their theological debates were intensifying. Their consciousnesses, it was said, traveled from the magatama in their brains, passed through the Divine Gate, and assembled in the Deilith—the place of advent for the eight million gods.

The Shrine Chieftain, who was also Minister of the three Imperial Treasures—the Mirror, Sword, and Magatama—was at the podium, teaching the class in person as he led his students in a ritual Shinto prayer. They were using words from the age of the gods, which Hanishibe and Narikabura could not even begin to comprehend.

Come to think of it, Komorizu—looking all smug—had been telling people lately that the Shrine Chieftain had invited him personally to transfer to the theology department. It made sense; after all, he had a good head for numbers.

"The Shrine Chieftain's wife is really pretty," murmured Narikabura. "Even a malformed freak like me she treats perfectly naturally. To me, she's everything a human should be."

Hanishibe didn't answer. This was because he held a secret admiration for her as well.

2

The sun was already starting to set when they passed through the school's fifth-level gate and emerged onto the cobbleshell road that traced out a loop above the neighborhoods of the lower levels. The whole funnel shape of Cavumville was dim with the coming of evening, but when Hanishibe looked upward, the slice of sky circumscribed by the city wall was still bright blue. An area a little toward the right where the watchtower stood was the only place still illuminated by golden sunlight.

"Well, I'll see you later," Narikabura said and started off down the steps outside the school's front gate on his three legs. Hanishibe, waving casually, slid his gaze beyond the fragile-looking form of his departing schoolmate as he gazed farther and farther downward.

Houses of irregular height were constructed along circular loops of gently rolling petraderm. The diameter of each level narrowed as one descended toward the filthbed that made up the floor of the funnel. The filthbed, at first glance, looked like nothing more than a dumping ground covered in remnants of bones and shells, but there in a bowl-shaped hollow formed by piled pleats of the moon's digestive membrane lay—the very depths of the world. In its center, the all-consuming Abyss sank downward like a navel. Near the edge of the filthbed, the object of worship known as the Deilith lay half sunk in its languidly undulating surface, so large that a thousand men would have been needed to move it. It was held in place by multiple cables affixed to the petroderm walls of the first and second levels. Legend had it that this huge stone lay on the very border between the Hereandnow and the Hereafter.

The Deilith was an oblong boulder that recalled a persimmon seed in both shape and texture. Constructed atop its smooth surface was the *shinmei-zukuri*–style main shrine, the shrine office, which was built to resemble a rocky mountain, and the Divine Gate, which rose up from its leading edge. The main approach was a train of floating barges that stretched from this gate to a pier on the bottommost city level.

Houseboats had been gathering around the Deilith. Ebisus appeared from huts on the boats and climbed one after another onto the Deilith, where they began wrapping their bizarrely long arms around the cables and hanging their weight on them. As they were doing this, the Deilith began to move just slightly, as if riding the undulations of the filthbed.

As Hanishibe walked along the road, the Deilith was gradually concealed by the row of houses on the first level. Absorbed in sight, Hanishibe walked right into a standing sideboard. "Watch where you're going!" shouted Old Man Tsunokiriroten. Seated in a chair next to the old-timer was a man whose skull grew straight upward like a tall eboshi hat; he was having the side of his face illuminated with a superb scene of Izanagi's descent to the underworld.

Chastened, Hanishibe passed by in front of them, and then the window of a tailor's shop appeared. Inside, seamstresses were deftly hand-sewing momonji skins, pinsnakes wrapped around their forearms.

Turning at the corner of the tailor's shop, Hanishibe began to climb up a wide, steep flight of stairs that extended both upward and downward along the slope of the funnel. Before he reached the next level, however, he came to a halt, rested his hands on his knees, and heaved his shoulders as he took a deep breath. He looked around and saw others here and there who were likewise exhausted and had sat down on the steps and the landing.

The moon's gravity had been increasing for several days now.

Even so, the stronger gravity didn't fully account for all the exhaustion. Everyone in Cavumville, for their own varying reasons, felt a sense of incongruity with their environment and were always complaining of some physical ailment or other.

Accordingly, life expectancies were short. Even when children were born, they almost never made it to adulthood.

Taking twice as long as he normally did, Hanishibe arrived on the seventh level, where his own home was located. The silk-white houses that stood in a row along the curved street were made of densely laid bonebrick painted with a mixture of ossipowder and landsoup. The outline of each was warped and distorted.

He walked along on cobbleshells worn down naturally by people's comings and goings. From up ahead, a man with a fibrous face and another with tentacles growing densely around his mouth approached, both swearing to one another about the "obliviates." Society looked coldly on the ebisus, who had abandoned their Heretofores.

A little farther on, there stood a single ebisu in the space between the incense-bun bakery and the hemomochi shop. His forearms, nearly as long as his legs' inseam, were raised up to the sky. Something about him reminded Hanishibe of a grass-hopper—his light-green work clothes probably had something to do with it—though with no mutations aside from his long forearms, he was the very image of baseform humanity. Suddenly, the ebisu raised his elbows, crossed his forearms, and flipped the palms of his hands over and back again several times. Using this kind of arm language, they could relay messages back and forth with their fellows, no matter where in Cavumville they might be.

When at last he arrived back home, a female ebisu with short black hair was standing in the gap between his house and his next-door neighbor's.

Hanishibe tried a polite greeting, but the woman remained motionless, and empty silence was her only reply. He gazed at her admiringly, as though she were some beautiful piece of sculpture, but then her forearms closed together like a pair of chopsticks, hiding her face. In the epidermis of those arms, he could see deeply gouged claw marks, scarring from bedfluid, and irregular bumps where bones had been broken and rejoined.

Hanishibe, ashamed of himself for staring, blurted out a hasty apology, then hurried into his house.

In the middle of the dim, narrow living room stood a stone statue, weathered by long years of wind and rain.

"What're you doing, Grandpa?"

The statue's hemispherical head turned left and right like a millstone grinding flour, and the facelid that covered the front of it began to slowly drag itself upward. It exposed an aged countenance that brought to mind a relief carved into a wall.

The left eyelid opened like a splitting fissure, revealing a socket tightly packed with tiny ocules resembling red grains, twitching this way and that. It was said that by using different eyes for different purposes, his grandfather could view the world from many perspectives.

"Hanishibe, is it?" said his grandfather, grimacing as he tried to force his other eye open. "Welcome back."

"Thanks," he said, then craned his neck in the direction of a recessed screen toward his right. "I'm home, Grandma."

"I was lost in thought just now," his grandfather said.

Of that Hanishibe was already aware. His grandfather shut his facelid anytime he had something on his mind. Lost in reflective contemplation, he would stand erect for hours on end, sometimes greeting the dawn without ever having budged.

"What were you thinking about? The structure of the universe again?"

"Well, that too."

"You should've been an astronomer, Grandpa."

"If I'd been an astronomer, you'd be saying I should've been a taxonomist."

Hanishibe's grandfather turned away and started walking toward the kitchen. A large knot was sticking out from his back. It had been growing steadily there for the past year, but according to a doctor with transparensight, it contained a thin, tubular substance that was coiled up in a ball. It wasn't a tenant of any kind, but one of his own organs apparently. He was undergoing some form of acquired mutation, though the cause was still unclear.

Squatting on a pedestal in one corner of the kitchen was a whirligig; it somewhat resembled a plantain lily but had a long, pipelike proboscis that was stuck in the side of a barrel beside the kitchen wall. Hanishibe's grandfather took an iron skewer in one hand and jabbed it into the insect's shrunken belly, which was wrinkled up like a dried-out fig. *KuKu! Kuuu!* the whirligig cried through its abdominal cavity. Afterward, the tip of its proboscis began spitting clean, clear water into the barrel at irregular intervals.

"The water isn't flowing very well," said Hanishibe. "Look at how shriveled it's gotten. I'll take it to the Department of Aquatic Resources tomorrow."

"Wouldn't it be better to wait until after the Descent?" Using the dipper, his grandfather drew some water from the barrel and drank it.

"It's always so crowded right afterward, Grandpa. You can hardly even walk up and down the street."

Hanishibe smiled as he said this and treated himself to a good look at the curio shelf on the wall in the foyer. Lined up on the shelf were a host of craftworks—vague replicas of implements used in that fuzzily defined otherworld known as the Hereafter.

Hanishibe's favorite was a headshell taken from some kind of petaurista, which had a stuffed cat foreleg resting on top. A roundbone, pierced with many holes, was attached to the forward face of the headshell. Hanishibe stuck the tip of one finger into a hole, then gave the roundbone a spin, picked up the cat's leg, and put its paw against his ear. When he did so, the insects inside it rubbed their bellyplates against one another, making a sound that was like someone whispering.

"You sure do like that one, don't you?" said his grandfather, facing the sink.

But Hanishibe's interest had shifted to another craftwork: a trilobite about the size of a cutting board. Its backplate had been inlaid with eighty-eight molars engraved with divine letters. "Whenever you press a combination of two molars," the craft shop owner had explained, "the common letters will blink in the back of the trilobite's mind."

There was no way of confirming whether or not this was true though. Even so, just by tapping the rows of molars with his fingers, he got the feeling that his thoughts at this moment were turning into words, and that those words were being transformed into reality.

His grandmother was also crazy about crafts of the Hereafter. Peeking behind the screen, he found his grandmother sitting cross-legged in front of a rectangular board. Her many legs were covered in innumerable thornlike projections, and her six eyes were pursed up like those of needles. All he could think was that she looked just like a petaurista. Shifting rainbow patterns were moving across multiple reflective membranes set in the face of a rectangular screen; his grandmother had been staring at them all day long like this without ever getting bored.

"Her memories of her Heretofore are too clear," his grandfather had once said, *"and what's worse, she believes the mutation she suffered during revivification is punishment for a crime she committed in her Heretofore. She tries to tell herself that she's just being superstitious, but..."*

"Here," his grandfather said.

Hanishibe turned around and saw him holding up a crustacean.

"You're on duty today, aren't you?"

"Oh, thanks." The shell of the lunchbox was warm when he took it, almost as if alive. "I saw some ebisus earlier, but tonight's still a little early for the Descent, isn't it?"

"You don't look very sure about that. But judging by the sky, it should still be all right. If anything does happen, just follow the procedures and ring the alarm bell. Still, we may yet have a good three months to go." With that, he gave a sigh. "But to think that I've still got to meet with that unclean *san'e* again..."

"You mean the Shrine Chieftain?" Hanishibe remembered the figure behind the podium in the theology department. He didn't understand why his grandfather hated him so. Hanishibe had often caught sight of the Shrine Chieftain making the rounds of the houseboats that dotted the filthbed, giving alms to the ebisus. The ebisus would take the smoked meat he gave them between their forearms and bow repeatedly as they fed. The clothes they were wearing had all been donated as well. The Shrine Chieftain had ascended to the high position of Minister of the Imperial Treasures, but he lived on the lowest level, amid the danger and grime of the filthbed, and was beloved of many for the good works he did.

Still, there were those like his grandfather who called him "san'e" behind his back. It was a slur meaning, "one born from a woman's body."

"You should take this too," his grandfather said, holding out a small package. Hanishibe opened it and found several cigar-shaped items lined up in a row. "They're smoked bitterbugs. Bite into one if you get sleepy. It'll wake you up."

Hanishibe thanked him, and once he had put the package of bitterbugs in his pocket, he put the lunchbox on his back, catching its two long legs on either shoulder. It hurt just a little as the claws on their tips bit into his skin.

3

The sun set early in Cavumville. When Hanishibe stepped outside, twilight was already falling. A good many stars were twinkling in the sky, and like a mirror image of the scene above, lights were glowing in windows throughout Cavumville as well.

The warm, humid air felt sticky on his skin. He struck a will-of-the-wisp and lit his lantern.

Hanishibe casually glanced down the narrow space between his house and his neighbor's (trying to look like he was doing nothing of the sort) but struck his lantern against the wall and dropped it. It made a terrible racket, bouncing on the ground three times, but then a white hand appeared in the dimness, grabbed hold of it, and picked it up. The indistinct form of that ebisu woman floated up from the dark recesses of the gap.

"Thank you. Um..." As he took the lantern from her, he noticed holes in the palms of her hands, as one might see in some pagan sculpture.

"I'm Hanishibe," he said.

"I am We. Please go quickly."

Her voice was just barely understandable. Hanishibe bowed once and started off again, walking along the smoothly winding cobbleshell street. He came to the large flight of stairs and hesitantly stepped onto it. His body was still heavy after all. Even so, he made his way doggedly upward, stopping to rest numerous times along the way.

After ascending three levels' worth of stairs, he immediately threw himself down on the roadside of the uppermost level, both arms spread wide. Sweat was pouring off of every inch of his body. A scattering of cottony clouds floated amid the starry sky.

Then an indistinct white thing blocked his field of vision, and Hanishibe gave a cry.

"It's me, Hanishibe. What're you doing here?"

Narikabura's non-face was staring down at him. Hanishibe got up with a laugh he didn't feel. Narikabura was carrying a lunchbox made of carapace on his head. Hanishibe started to ask him where his lantern was but then remembered: Narikabura could see in the dark.

The pair arrived at the base of the watchtower, which was touching the circular ringwall. The tower resembled a razor clam's shell jutting up overhead. As they came near, a door lined with tortoiseshell opened up as though it had been waiting for them, and two sleepy-looking men emerged.

Hanishibe took from them a bundle of keys—for the doors, for the alarm bell, and so on—and held the door open so Narikabura could go in first. Hanishibe followed him in, locked the door, and held up his lantern. Trailing behind Narikabura, he ascended a narrow spiral staircase that rose up along the wall, approaching as he did the giant, cylindrical alarm bell that hung down from the center of the ceiling. The myth of the Descent of the Sun Goddess's Grandson played itself out on its surface as he headed for the top: here was inscribed the figure of Ninigi-no-Mikoto, ancestor of emperors, receiving orders from his grandmother, Amaterasu Ōmikami. As the staircase turned, more images came into view, depicting his descent from the heavenly realm to the earthly one.

When Hanishibe emerged onto the mushroom-shaped lookout, a strong, warm wind came blowing up against him. The umbrella-shaped canopy was supported only by the central pillar where the control devices were clustered. In the open space that looked out in all directions, there were neither bars nor peritonea.

Holding on to a parapet that encircled the lookout, the two boys looked down on the lunar surface, which fell away like a cliff to form the outer edge of Cavumville. The many large and small craters covering the landscape beyond engendered a sense of extreme perspective as they receded into the distance, arcing around toward the far side's curved surface. Though it was impossible for the naked eye to take in the entire face of the moon, its shape could be likened to that of an olive whose seed had been removed. Hanishibe's knees trembled just slightly as his line of sight was pulled inexorably down toward the distant depths below. Through the thin atmosphere, he could see clearly a darkling plain covered in coaguland, extending outward until it blurred in the distance near the curved horizon. The sight brought with it a renewed realization that they were floating high up in the sky of the earth.

"I've heard our altitude is way too low for us to be recognized as a satellite."

"Did your dad tell you that? Me, I don't really know…"

Hanishibe sat down in a chair with an attached backrest, straddled the central pillar with both knees, and pressed his face up against a tubular viewport that stuck out from the pillar. Pulling a lever, he brought the device into focus, and a series of five lenses made of clear, compressed momonji eyeballs showed him a starfield in extreme magnification.

"They get bigger, don't they, the stars? My dad used to do research to try to find out why."

"I'll bet that's why you decided to major in astronomy," Hanashibe said in a distant, dreamy voice. "To carry on his work." Hanishibe turned one of the wheels on the pillar. The stars slid out of view and disappeared.

"It's not to take over his research. I want to make my baby

father recollect his Heretofore quickly, so I can help with his research."

Manipulating both of the wheels, turning them forward and then back again, Hanishibe aligned the telescope with a set of coordinates at which a great number of portents had been detected.

The two boys continued staring into a starry sky that showed no greater change than the occasional thin cloud scuttling across it. Now it was Narikabura who was sitting in the seat before the pillar; Hanishibe reclined on a low benchlike projection that jutted out of the parapet, the back of his head resting in a concave dip in the wall's edge as he watched the heavens with his eyes alone.

"Hanishibe—"Narikabura ventured, sounding like someone about to make a confession. "Why do you think it is that every single person looks so different from each other?"

"'Cause diversity's important. Having all kinds of looks makes the world more interesting. Don't you think?"

"That's fine for you, Hanishibe. You're close to baseform."

"Even I started out boneless. Took two years for the bone-seeds to grow."

"I don't think I'll ever find, you know, someone right for me."

"What are you talking about? You'll be fine."

"You don't know that," muttered Narikabura, as if to someone far away.

"There are married people with all kinds of variations, aren't there?"Hanishibe said, raising his head.

"You're not getting it. From the standpoint of pure physics—how can I put this?—strategies for carrying out sexual intercourse can vary from person to person." Face still pressed against the viewport, Narikabura continued: "I cannot love or be loved by anyone. The other person would—"

"I'm telling you, I'm sure you'll find somebody with the same mutations as you."

"The same kind won't work for me!"

An awkward feeling floated in the air between them.

Suddenly, Narikabura's upper body jerked upward.

"What's wrong?"

"I can see it. Something's falling this way."

Narikabura pulled on the lever that his glossophalanx was wrapped around, opening up the eight panels that enclosed the upper part of the watchtower. Then he shifted it over to a lever connected to the alarm bell's clapper.

Hanishibe placed his hands on a speaking pipe that jutted out of the floor over by the wall.

"It's odd how slowly they're falling—what're the…oh." Narikabura let go of the lever and leaned back in his seat, giving a dry laugh. "They're lees."

In which case, there was nothing out of the ordinary; those fragile, fist-sized lumps were falling all the time. Hanishibe let out a sigh. He could hear the wall panels creaking as they closed.

"I'm glad I died young last time. I think it would be even harder on me if I knew who I was married to." Narikabura had returned to his earlier topic, but now he sounded cheerful. "It's all right. After all, I've got my dad. I'll go on raising Dad. He's talented, my dad."

After that, the two of them continued to observe the night sky, switching back and forth between telescopic and naked eye observations. Trading items from their lunchboxes, shaking one another awake when they dozed off, biting into bitterbugs to dispel their sleepiness, they talked about nothing in particular until the changing of the watch early next morning. Simple lees in the sky could in no way diminish the gleam of the heavenly bodies.

Hanishibe left the watchtower at dawn and handed the keys over to the next pair on duty. His shoulders felt terribly stiff. Bathed in the strong morning light of the uppermost level, he raised up both arms to stretch his muscles. Narikabura as well bent his three legs like bows and then stood up straight with a pleasant look on his face. He cast a deep, sharp shadow across the ground, just like that of a sundial.

CHAPTER 2:
DESCENT FROM HEAVEN

1

Hanishibe slept past noon, then loaded the shriveled whirligig onto a cart, which he pushed toward the Department of Aquatic Resources. The windows of the houses that he passed on the way were being fitted with armored shutters by their residents, who were also using landsoup to caulk up gaps in bonebrick walls and daubing resinlike beastfat onto the bonetiles of their roofs, all in preparation for the Descent from Heaven.

The Department of Aquatic Resources was constructed in stairstep fashion, straddling the third and fourth city levels. The gentle line of its rounded rooftop suggested a loaf of bread. Hanishibe went inside through a doorway accessible from the fourth level loop-lane. There was only a thin smattering of other visitors. He pushed his cart to the department serving the zone in which his house was located and, without even having to wait in line, placed the whirligig on the reception counter.

The department employee was dangling down from beams overhead, with which four of his molluscean legs were intertwined. He handed a claim ticket to Hanishibe and in exchange picked up the wrinkly whirligig with a wriggling arm. Transferring his weight from beam to beam, he then disappeared into the back.

Hanishibe found a seat in the waiting area, and after about one torch had elapsed, the rafter-traversing employee returned, dragging along a delivery cart on which rested his whirligig, now so swollen it looked ready to burst. It had been attached to a live momonji, from which it had been allowed to replenish its blood supply to its heart's content. Its eyeholes were squeezed shut as if in satisfaction, creating radial patterns of wrinkles around them.

Hanishibe stopped his hand, which had been about to pet it on the head. From the tip of its proboscis, rolled up like a royal fern, he could hear the *su-su-su-su* of its peaceful breath in sleep. Hanishibe smiled, thinking, *I'll need to keep quiet on the way back.*

When he exited onto the loop-lane, white lees were dancing lightly in the air. The whirligig was very heavy now. He had not even made it halfway back to the great stairway when one of the cart's wheels broke. At a loss, Hanishibe looked up at the sky, wondering what he should do. It was blue overhead with not a cloud to be seen. Though it was still bright, the stars were out already. But it was as he was staring at that sight, thinking it rather odd, that each of those points of light began increasing rapidly in size.

The whole sky was full of them by the time the reverberating peal of the alarm bell began to sound from the watchtower on the uppermost level.

It was much too late in ringing. Hanishibe fretted as he looked around. Doom-proofed doors were going down in front of every entrance. The windows were already stopped with armored shutters. He pulled on the cart with the broken wheel, hoping to at least take shelter beneath the eaves of some roof, but it wouldn't budge an inch. The whirligig wheezed with the sound of a stopped-up proboscis.

Something bounced from the cobbleshell near his feet, and a little splash of blood radiated outward. Here and there, on the rooftops and the ground, bloody splashes were blossoming one after another like red handprints. At the moment, they were mostly insectoids known as carapaceans. Several of them were trying to get up, even with body segments half torn off.

One level down, something that looked like a coelenterate slammed into a roof, stuck there, and began extending tentacles out in every direction from its hemhorraging body.

Hanishibe turned about at the sound of a loud, wet noise, and flying chunks of meat stuck to his forehead and cheek. A petaurista shaped like a fava bean covered in black feathers had burst open, sending reddish brown organs flying. He wiped off the pieces of flesh and looked across the wide-open funnel-space of Cavumville.

Petauristas were falling in staggering numbers, like a waterfall plunging into the moon's hollow space.

There were brain-shaped lumps covered in tumorous growths; scaleless, sluglike fish shaped like bugles; spiral sponges that sprouted eyeballs…

—legless waterbears with elephant-skin that trailed multiple arms that ended in mouths; eel-like rays vibrating with innumerable sensory whiskers; hemichordates with comb-shaped antennae flowering out in every direction; discolored beetles under attack for some reason by the acorn worms they used as lures…

—priapulids joined together in radial patterns; pig pupas; fur seals bristling with gaudily colored, star-shaped projections…

—horned owls shaped like trilobites; tapeworms twisted into ghost-leg lattices; clouds of luxuriantly growing organs; streamlined water cicadas wriggling their parapodia…

Although "petaurista" was the catch-all term for all of them, it was hard to think any of these creatures belonged to the same planet's ecosystem.

The majority of them were falling toward the center of the funnel.

Though Hanishibe was frightened, he held up a hand to shield his eyes and looked up at the sky. The shadows of thinly scattered, lozenge-shaped momonji were beginning to appear. A sharp pain—it felt like a boulder had struck him in the back—assaulted Hanishibe, and he lost his balance. A crustacean resembling a rabbit rolled into view a few steps in front of him, coughing up green blood as it went into convulsions.

Hanishibe wanted to run away that very instant, but he couldn't abandon the whirligig.

While he was hesitating, though, he felt something tickling the back of his neck. At some point, a many-legged mouse had gotten onto his shoulder, and its vibrating, stamenlike feelers were rubbing against his neck. He was shooing it off with his hand—carefully, for fear that it might be poisonous—when he heard a fierce sound like an explosion. Hanishibe's entire body was enveloped in a huge spray of blood.

The thick, fishy odor clung to him. His body was starting to feel hot.

As the blood spray cleared, the corpse of the whirligig, burst open like the petals of a flower, came into view. The cart was split perfectly in half and drenched in frothing blood. The nearest wall was cracked in a spiderweb pattern, in the midst of which was buried an armored petaurista that resembled an infant child. Each time its body writhed it made a creaking sound, and finch-yellow fluid came pouring from its segmented body.

There was no further need to stay in this place. But even so, there were always short lulls during Descents from Heaven.

For the time being, Hanishibe sank back under the eaves. The petauristas that were pounding against the roof overhead broke apart into blood-smeared organs and meaty chunks and came falling down before his eyes in a steady rain. A piece of flesh with a shell attached had come to rest on his shoe. He kicked it away.

At the point where the loop-lane to his right began to trace out a visible arc, someone's house collapsed with a great rumble. A giant momonji had crashed right into it.

On the far side of level four—and level six and level five—clouds of dust were rising up from houses that had caved in, one right after the other.

No sooner did the fleshy chunks falling from the eaves seem to be letting up than the skeleton of the house made a noise and began to creak. It was getting harder for things to slide off the roof, and they were accumulating up there. Had that been a terrified voice from inside he'd just heard? He had the feeling that it was, though maybe it had been the dying cry of one of the petauristas piling up in the street. From smashed internal organs, from fur gone stiff with caked blood, and from cracked shells, innumerable tenants were now crawling out of the corpses. Was it Hanishibe's imagination, or was their crawling advance heading in his direction?

Presently, a ray of light began to shine through. The falling petauristas grew sparse, and for a moment the sky regained its former brightness. A midsized momonji was the last thing to fall, and then there were only the flurrying lees.

It was now or never. Shrugging away his fear, Hanishibe started walking, stepping over the accumulated piles of new-fallen corpses. He made his way along the street, accompanied by the merry crunch of exoshelletons breaking underfoot, nearly falling over when he slipped on bodily fluids, and stepping around the eruptions of tenants.

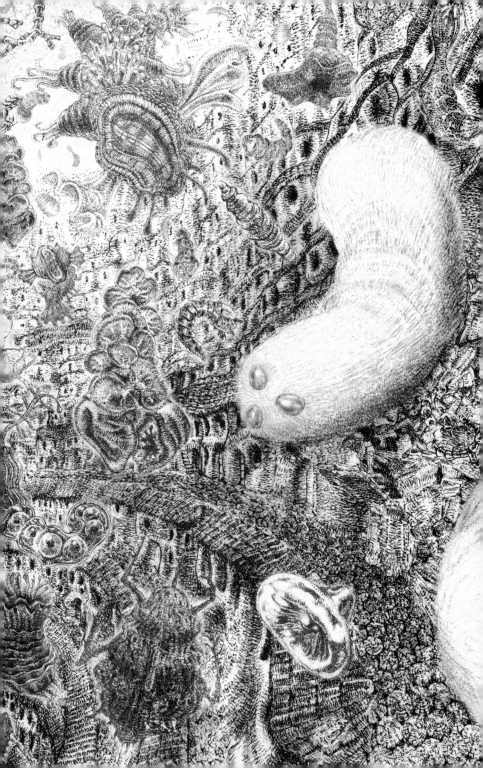

Suddenly, something latched onto his legs and clung to them tightly. Atop its hairless body there was no head, and the severed edge of its neck was swollen and quivering, just like a piece of hemomochi. As he tried in vain to peel off its luke-warm appendage, some passersby came and helped him.

"That just came out of nowhere…"

"Did you hear the first bell…?"

"Got yourself a good red dousing, there, didn't you…"

"You better run on home; you're like bait for all these tenants…"

"Be careful."

Hanishibe thanked them gladly and set off running. He had now gotten used to running on this unstable surface. The road ahead, however, was blocked by a single gigantic momonji. A quartet of ebisus were effectively using their long forearms to push it backward as it twisted its thick trunk in resistance.

Like a loaf of bonemeal bread, its body was of uniform thickness and covered in white down through which its rippling, pale-peach skin could just barely be seen. Whenever one half of its body reared upward, a double row of claw-legs could be glimpsed. Completely useless for locomotion, they were one more example of all the unnecessary body parts momonji had.

One of the ebisus held a palm out in front of the momonji's head, touching it right in the center of its three translucent eyeballs. Its eyeballs were uneven, as if they had been thrown at the creature haphazardly from somewhere far away and merely stuck where they had hit. For some reason, they invited pity. The ebisu's arm quivered for an instant, and then blood oozed out from the gap between hand and fur. The momonji went limp and had clearly given up its ghost. A reddish-black oval staining its white fur was growing larger.

The second floor of the house beside the creature had mostly collapsed. Hanishibe could see petauristas that had gotten inside crawling on its walls. The people who lived there were sobbing with both hands on their faces. He could also hear angry shouts directed at the ebisus, telling them to get lost this instant.

"Climb over," a solitary ebisu called from the other side of the momonji. "Here, give me your hand. Careful now."

The hand that was extended from across the momonji was hard and cold, as if carved from bone. With his left hand, Hanishibe clenched a clump of fur as if getting ready to rip it out. Then, pulled along by his right hand, he climbed up the side of the momonji. It had a fearsome overabundance of fur, making it very easy for his foot to start sliding on its exoshelleton. He somehow managed to get to the top and then slid all the way down the other side of its body.

"Go quickly! The next fall is coming in less than four and a half *doki*."

Hanishibe bowed and hurried on ahead, but when he reached the great staircase, his legs went weak.

All across the stairway, there were half-dead, half-living pet-auristas jostling against one another like scales from some gargantuan prehistoric fish. Step by step, he made his way upward between slimy piles of glistening, skinned wreckage, through overflows of bodily fluids and organs that came up to his knees, searching with the tips of his toes for steps he couldn't see. Though it might mean picking up a tenant or two, he made up his mind to press ahead and just endure it. His muscles gradually began growing stiffer though, and he soon realized it was getting harder to move. Midway up, he stopped walking.

It wasn't just the exhaustion. From his knees downward, tenants the size of phalluses had stuck to his legs and were expanding into conical shapes. There were even some that had attached to their fellow tenants. As he was knocking them off with his hands, he heard a wet noise like two pieces of raw meat colliding.

He looked up and saw a wrinkly meatrug come bouncing down toward him from about ten steps above. It hung for an instant in midair right before his eyes. In that instant, it blew outward, expanding with explosive speed into a meatnet that wrapped around Hanishibe's entire body, holding him fast.

Countless translucent needles awakened throughout the meatnet, making quivering movements like the blinking of eyes. The strength began to drain out of Hanishibe's body.

He resisted desperately, but it was in vain; his body was beginning to tilt. At last, he fell over onto the steps and slid down the stairs, sending petauristas flying as he went. When he slammed into cobbleshell, his back took the blow. The meatnet was crushed underneath and sent out a spray of strong, pungent ichor.

The blue of the sky grew pointillated and then became spotted. Several steps above, a piece of viscera that appeared to be a digestive organ rebounded up into the air. Right next to his ear, something popped. They were starting to fall again.

If this is my last day in the Hereandnow, he prayed, *please don't put me through this again in my Yet-to-come.*

That was when he spotted a figure on the landing of the great stairwell, and a sound reached him that was like people cheering. A memory of the Hereafter? There were fragmented voices blended with static—*lunar surface... Sea of Tranquillity... in human history... one small step*—the figure...the astronaut... came bearing a flag as proof that he was first to reach this lunar surface. As the Descent from Heaven grew fiercer, he walked step by careful step down the stairs, until he stood right next to Hanishibe. A voice emanated then from his closed facelid.

"Looks like you're paralyzed," he said. It was his grandfather's voice. The flagpole came near and peeled away the meat-net. Then, like a cold blade, the realization hit him that it wasn't a flagpole at all; it was an axe.

"You did well to make it this far during a Descent from Heaven." The older man lifted up his grandson's body as though it were as light as a feather and carried him in his arms, shielding him from the petauristas with his broad upper body. He stepped back onto the stairwell and started climbing up again.

"I'm sorry, Grandpa." Tears overflowed from the shame Hanishibe felt. "I let the whirligig die."

"It's all right. He's become one with the momonji and is falling toward us now. We'll raise him again."

"He was a good whirligig. I was horrible to him. I let him die."

"Yeah…he was a good whirligig."

Hanishibe couldn't peel his eyes away from the sights he glimpsed out in the open air from between his grandfather's arms. Petauristas in vast numbers—probably more than he'd ever seen in his current life—were plunging downward, practically climbing over one another in a mad scramble to hit the bottom first. It had long since become impossible to pick out individuals among them. Afterimages melted together with real images, and without his realizing it, time itself had seemed to come to a standstill. At last, the strangest feeling came over him that everything around him was falling up toward the heavens.

Hanishibe felt a flash of terror, as though he himself might be dragged into the plummeting horde as well, and lowered his gaze. The bottommost level, once a mortar-shaped basin, now rose up like a mound. Over and over, the central region would cave inward and then start swelling up again. This was because petauristas were still accumulating.

Suddenly Hanishibe's field of vision tilted, and the corpse-heaped cobbleshells came rushing up at him. Sure that he was going to hit them, his body went rigid, but with a painful gasp his grandfather managed to regain his posture.

"Are you all right, Grandpa?"

"Yeah." His grandfather swayed again perilously the moment after he answered. "It's really coming down now. We'd better hurry."

The door of their house was buried to half its height in petauristas. With his thick arms, Hanishibe's grandfather beat on the wall in what was apparently a signal. The first-floor armored door opened, and gray smoke billowed out. Then—as if materializing from its particles—a petaurista appeared. In shock, Hanishibe thought for a moment that one had even managed to get into his house. But when tenants came crawling up the wall, the petaurista began to precision-skewer them with her sharp legs.

"Grandma!" Hanishibe cried in a voice shrill with joy. "We're home."

Hanishibe was passed from his grandfather to his grandmother, who laid him down on the floor of a room where bitter smoke hung in the air. Due perhaps to the smoke's effect, the tenants began detaching from his body.

Hanishibe's grandfather slowly climbed into the house through the window, falling over in the process, and immediately his grandmother shut the armored door and window and extinguished the smoke pot. Leaving curling eddies in the drifting haze, his grandmother crawled along the floor, spearing one by one every last invading petaurista and tenant that she found crawling up the wall or across the ceiling.

2

Hanishibe awoke with an uneasy feeling, as though his stomach were turned inside out. There was a sticky sound as he got up, and the fat inside the sofa quivered.

"Grandpa! What time is it?" Surrounded by darkness, he had thought at first that it was already late at night. Relief spread through him when he realized it was just because the windows were covered with armored shutters. The noise of the Descent had let up.

"It's still the hour of the rooster," his grandfather replied. "What are you all in a tizzy about?"

"I'm supposed to meet somebody."

There was a scritching sound from the glowplates of a torchburr on the wall, and then the room brightened to a vague dimness. His grandfather was still standing. His grandmother, as always, was sitting on the floor in front of her rectangular board. He couldn't even tell if she were awake or asleep. A blood-splattered dishcloth was lying at her feet.

Hanishibe looked down at himself. The blood that had splashed all over him had been wiped away, and his clothes had been changed.

"No one'll blame you for breaking a date on the day of a Descent from Heaven. None of the levels are done cleaning up yet. It's dangerous to go walking around outside."

"Well, that's true, I guess."

"Where were you planning to meet up?"

"A hemomochi shop," Hanishibe said, stumbling over his words just slightly. "There's this girl named Yatsuo."

"Let's go together," said his grandfather, already headed toward the entryway before he even spoke.

The people who lived on the uppermost level were shoving the corpses of petauristas from their rooftops into the streets. By rule, this was done in a level-by-level order. As one went down to the lower levels, the danger of an avalanche increased.

Nearly all petauristas died instantly upon impact, and even the rare survivors never lasted the week. It was thought that they could not adapt to the lunar environment, though there were a few kinds, such as momonji, that were exceptions to this rule.

Hanishibe and his grandfather passed by children of all shapes and sizes who were sticking tenants on their arms to make bugmen of themselves.

He felt his chest tighten up when he saw his grandfather limping. He wondered if the pain was really bad and if that was why his silences were stretching out so terribly long.

At the place where the hemomochi shop was supposed to have been—a mountain of wreckage littered with bonebrick and hemomochi—a trio of ebisus wielding straw *shimenawa* from the shrine were trying to hold down a bizarre, man-shaped giant wearing clothing made of muscle fiber. Those were known as doomgods; once every few years, one would fall into Cavumville along with the petauristas.

The doomgod was pinned down on top of the wreckage by shimenawa wrapped around its arms and sides. It writhed powerfully as a whirlpool formed in its tongue-shaped, translucent head, unleashing an agonized growl of *VuVuRuRuVuVu*.

"Doesn't look like she's here," Hanishibe said a few minutes later. In spite of a growing sense of solitude, he felt relieved.

Across the surface of the ruins were scattered shards of porcelain tile—pale blue, like whenever she was happy. He bent down to pick one up. On the back side of the glossy rhomboid plate, there clung a piece of reddish flesh.

It's from a petaurista, Hanishibe thought as he crawled around on the pile of wreckage. He discovered a number of objects that were apparently fingers, and it was as he was averting his eyes from them that he spotted a geometric pattern peeking out through a gap in the bonebricks and hemomochi. In a sudden panic, he clawed away the wreckage.

Yatsuo's form—buried lying on its side—began to appear, her body severely twisted. Her crushed head was split into four large pieces, from between which peeked eyeballs and rows of amethyst teeth.

In eyes that had no pigment—in eyes he was seeing for the very first time—there yet dwelled some life. Even as they fluttered from left to right, they were staring at Hanishibe. The rows of teeth opened wider as she wrung out words in a faint voice. Hanishibe put his ear next to her mouth. From the rents in her face, hot breath was escaping.

"I...I knew."

"Knew what? No wait, don't talk."

"...knew you. 'Cause of...the kind of person...you are." Yatsuo swallowed down her pooled saliva with evident pain. "Now you...listen close...my dearest..."

He drew so close that his ear entered the gap in her sundered face.

"Don't offer...my magatama...to the shrine. Keep it yourself. It's in my head...And in your Heretofore..."

"In mine?"

"And then —"

"And then...what?"

"You...are the only one...who can stop *you*. You alone."

Hanishibe took hold of Yatsuo's digitless hand and remained bent over by her side.

At last he looked up, as if awakening from a light sleep, and reached in with his hand through the gouge in Yatsuo's head, sinking his fingers deep into her soft brain. When his fingertips felt a hard surface, he pulled it out without a sound.

"Come on, let's go home," said his grandfather. "The rest is the Level Association's job."

"Grandpa, what are you not telling me?" Hanishibe said. His back turned on him, he squeezed the blood-smeared magatama.

"I'm not hiding anything. It's just that...you can't recollect it."

"She had a very deep relationship with me, didn't she?"

"She did. The two of you were husband and wife."

"Why didn't you tell me?"

"Because it wasn't..." Hanishibe's grandfather fumbled for the words. "It wasn't a very happy marriage."

3

The petaurista disposal center stood along the petraderm of the lowest city level, whose ring enclosed the filthbed.

An abandoned building there had been refurbished for the job. Its ceiling was covered in a patchwork of peritoneum sheets, and its floor was covered with straw mats, where momonji of all shapes and sizes were laid out on their backs.

Amid a thick miasma that hung on the air, many taxonomists and ebisus were hard at work. Once the momonji were classified and disassembled, they were carried to the auction block next door, which was already buzzing with people involved in the processing industry.

The grandfather who was a taxonomist and his grandson who was studying to be one were staring at a relatively undamaged momonji from a vantage point near its head. Three ebisus had also taken position—one on its left, one on its right, and one on its stomach.

When Hanishibe's grandfather gave a nod, the ebisu on its stomach used his palm-spike to pierce the center of the momonji's brain and started cutting it open between its rows of claw-legs. At the same time, the other two ebisus started pulling off its fur from both sides. They scraped out its yellow fatty layer and divided it between them, stuffing it into huge, wide-mouthed jars. Then, removing several fragments of elastic shelleton, they exposed the birthingsac—swollen large and pale crimson with bloodshot capillaries. When they cut open its thick sacwall, a beast covered in black fur appeared—a monkey, apparently.

Hanishibe's grandfather stood in front of the monkey, but unlike the other taxonomists, he checked neither its pulse with his fingertips nor listened to its heart with his horn-shaped instrument. Instead, he simply stared at it with his many ocules and stuck a syringe into its thick-furred neck.

Spasming, the monkey sat up, coughing violently. Hanishibe's grandfather slapped it on the back. It vomited up gastric juice, and then it spoke.

"Where am I?"

The returnee was led away by a purifier from the shrine, and then they moved on to the next momonji, where the same operations were repeated. When the thick, sticky protoplasm came spilling out of the birthingsac this time, all that they found inside was a nerve plexus. Next was a pig without arms or legs, but after that they found a man who was quite close to the human baseform. Due to the shock of impact, however, he had terrible internal bleeding and they weren't able to save him.

When they had finished work on the seventh momonji, the ebisu in charge of signaling came into the disposal center from his post outside and informed Hanishibe's grandfather that the Shrine Chieftain was requesting his presence: a momonji too gigantic to move had fallen onto the mound of dead petauristas, he said, so he wanted the disassembly to be performed on-site.

Outside, petauristas were still being hauled in, and the acidic odor that was beginning to drift through the air no doubt meant that the filthbed was becoming active. The mound of petauristas was moving up and down as though it were breathing and slowly rotating as well. A Pillar would be rising within the next few toki.

Hanishibe, having been warned that it was dangerous, stayed behind at the disposal site as he was told. His grandfather, still limping, headed off toward the mound. His figure receded gradually into the distance, and then he started climbing.

Sometime later, Hanishibe was looking on intently as another taxonomist put his skills to work, when without warning the ebisus all rose to their feet as though they had forgotten what they were doing. Following their gaze, Hanishibe turned around and looked back. Through the peritoneum, he could see countless petauristas being thrown up and down on the top of the mound.

A mysterious lump of black flesh was sticking up from the top of it. It writhed about fiercely and then, as he watched, sank down, pushing petauristas out of its way like so much gravel. The mound itself began to collapse.

A huge wave of petauristas came rolling in. It smashed through the walls of the disposal center, closing in on Hanishibe and the others. Instinctively, Hanishibe dove into a momonji's hollowed-out abdominal cavity.

The world turned over again and again. Hanishibe was deafened by the violent crashing of meat and exoshelleton.

When the suffocating stillness became too much to bear, he tried to crawl out of the momonji, but a translucent membrane got stuck to his face. He ripped it apart at the seam with his hands and at last escaped, only to be greeted by an acrid miasma that stung his eyes.

It was said that disposal centers were constructed simply and designed from the start with the expectation of avalanches, which was why they collapsed so easily. Those ichor-splattered workers who had managed to hold body and soul together were already starting classification on the petauristas that had been swept over to them.

Out on the filthbed, geysers of bedfluid were now spouting here and there from what had become a lower, more gently sloping mound. Pungent steam clung to it like a thin gauze curtain and rose higher, taking on the form known as the Pillar, reminiscent of a white serpent. Mishaguchi, the red-mawed god of old who had descended with the innumerable petauristas, dwelt therein. From now until the time that the Pillar dissipated, divers oracles would be bestowed by way of the Divine Gate.

If only he had run. Those were the words spoken regretfully by the Shrine Chieftain.

Hanishibe's grandfather, he said, had been on top of the mound attending to the laparotomy of a momonji the size of a house. Jet-black skin had appeared from a rip in its gigantic birthingsac, and the moment that his grandfather touched it, he had immediately ordered everyone else to evacuate. An ebisu who had been rescued after being caught up in the avalanche had witnessed his grandfather's final moments. A dark, sinister-looking thing had burrowed from the topmost portion of the mound deep down toward the Abyss at the center of the filthbed, he said, and from there, a whirlpool suddenly began to expand outward. Hanishibe's grandfather, still only about midway down the slope, had just kept walking. There was no room for doubt: it was because of the injury to his leg he had received while rescuing Hanishibe.

When the whirlpool swallowed him, the ebisu said, the knot on his back had burst open, and a long, ropelike thing had shot up into the air. And then his grandfather had sunk into the whirlpool; it had not been a lifeline to save him.

His grandmother, having heard the news, had been rushing down toward the bottom city level when she was attacked on the way and beaten to death by citizens wielding giant shell hammers spiked at both ends.

They had mistaken her for a petaurista.

In the Descent from Heaven that day, thirty-six people lost their lives and twelve houses were destroyed. Two hundred sixty-seven momonji were disassembled, and from them were harvested forty-one returnees, seventy-eight large mammals, twelve lumps of clay bearing seeds of various plants, and many aquatic creatures and small animals in great variety.

CHAPTER 3:
THE BONDS OF FATE

1

The funerals for Hanishibe's grandparents were held at the main shrine, a *shinmei-zukuri*-style building that stood in the center of the Deilith.

Beneath the steep, straight lines of its gabled roof, Hanishibe was staring in a state of utmost lethargy at the sacred branches offered by the mourners.

Even after the funeral, he was unable to move from where he stood.

When he came to himself, he realized that someone was standing in front of him.

Without preamble, the man stated his business. "Why don't you come and live at the shrine?" he said.

Realizing that it was the Shrine Chieftain, Hanishibe looked up.

He required no explanation to understand that the Shrine Chieftain was feeling responsible for his grandfather's death. Hanishibe felt a resistance toward living in these filthbed-enclosed surroundings, but when he learned that he would be assisting the Reuniter-Pancarnate, he accepted the request.

The grounds of the Deilith felt even more cramped than

when viewed from the upper levels. In back of the solemn main shrine stood the shrine office, a four-story building with an area of only about two hundred *tsubo*. It looked like nothing more than a rocky mountain. A small, simple room on its third floor was Hanishibe's new quarters. Contrary to what the public might imagine, the rooms where the Shrine Chieftain's family lived were a far cry from luxurious as well.

His meals were usually taken together with the shrine purifiers in the second-story cafeteria, although he was also occasionally invited to dine with the Shrine Chieftain's family.

The Shrine Chieftain's wife, whom Narikabura and Hanishibe both held in high esteem, had retained her beautiful baseform without mutation, as had her two children—a six-year-old daughter who adored her father, and a three-year-old son who was always playing with a baby momonji. The simple petaurista cuisine, as befitted the priesthood, was mostly just carapaceans, yet the Shrine Chieftain's family would dig into it as though it were a sumptuous feast.

The Shrine Chieftain was kind to his family. And to Hanishibe, and to the ebisus. He treated everyone with kindness and affection. He was also a passionate educator. He took his divinity students into the Deilith's inner shrine—forbidden to the general public—and there he taught them about the eight million gods, training them in the use of Imperial Regalia such as the jeweled mirror that reflected the Sword of Gathering Clouds and the giant Magatama tied up with countless braided cords. He was also willing to seriously engage even the most preposterous discussions of Shinto ritual.

Komorizu, who had changed his major from taxonomy to theology, started dropping by Hanishibe's room frequently on his way back from theology department training sessions.

To hear him tell it, his head was ready to burst with matters theological. "The way you ushe your head is totally different," he would say. "I couldn't be more shatisfied, but shomehow... yeah, my forgetfulnesh is getting a lot worsh than before, and it's causing problems. Maybe thish is what they mean by 'academic tunnel vision.'"

It was always a sure bet that whenever Komorizu visited Hanishibe's room, something would turn up missing after he had gone.

Hanishibe began helping the elderly Reuniter-Pancarnate in the shrine office's first-floor Reintroduction office. One thing was a constant whether he was walking back and forth among the shelves lining the four walls of the individual registry, flipping through dermasheets, or reading line after line of flowing, reddish-black characters recorded in elegant marrowpen script: his ears had no reprieve from the voice of the Reuniter-Pancarnate, sitting in the center of the room declaring reunions.

The Reuniter-Pancarnate died within six months of Hanishibe's going to work there, but Hanishibe felt no unease about taking over the job.

Holed up in the Reintroduction office, Hanishibe attended to the stream of returnees freshly thrown into the Hereand-now. One after another, he dealt with each in turn, on and on with no end in sight. The returnees, having each attained their individual variations, were unable to remember even their names at first. Groping along blindly, Hanishibe would pile on question after question, unearthing their Heretofores little by little and comparing what he learned against what was recorded in the vast individual registry.

There were many who could not recollect anything right away. There were others who had to be investigated because their manner of conversation raised doubts about whether or not they were even people. Some of them, unable to accept their prior selves, spouted nothing but lies. There were even some imprisoned by ontological distresses, declaring, "I'm not me!" The declaration of a reunion required great fortitude and endurance. Tests of computational ability using divine letters and spirit numbers were administered, which thankfully made it possible to narrow down the possibilities somewhat. This was because most of those who showed superior ability turned out to have been theology students.

"There were buildings so tall they caressed the sky, rising up one after another like trees in a forest."

Mixed in among their memories of the Heretofore, fragments of the collective unconscious that was the Hereafter also came leaking out sometimes. Hanishibe had a feeling that he had memories of those sights as well. But what he himself had told the Reuniter-Pancarnate of long ago was a frightening world full of man-made things resembling furniture and household appliances all jostling against one another.

Memories of the Hereafter, whose landscapes could vary so vastly depending on the teller, continued to be compiled in the *Book of the Heritage of the Hereafter*. In recent years, however, the details of the content recollected had become terribly vague, and new additions were hardly ever made to that record anymore. The uncertain history of the Hereafter—that piled accretion of lives and deaths, of people recklessly multiplying through *san'e*—felt unstable and distorted, as though the slightest nudge could send it all crashing down.

When his work was finished and he returned to his room, Hanishibe would collapse into bed and be asleep in the space of a breath, oblivious to the stains on his hand from his marrowpen. He was worn down to the point of breaking, but when he thought of the possibility that his grandfather, his grandmother, or Yatsuo might be among the returnees, it became impossible to cut corners in the interviews. Yet even if they were revivified, the sense of remorse that Hanishibe carried would most likely be with him forever. In a small way, even Hanishibe could understand the feelings of those who threw away their Heretofores.

There were all kinds of reasons that led people to seek the obliviation of their Heretofores. Once they had signed their consent, a purifier would appear and jab the hooked ends of a sharp bonerod deep into their nostrils, cutting the nerve-lines connected to their magatama.

These obliviates, now no different from newborns, were then entrusted to the village of the ebisus, who lived on the rafts that floated on the filthbed. Immediately following their obliviation, they seemed innocent and happy, although others might feel flashes of envy toward them as their bodily variations gradually receded and they returned to the human base-form. Later, though, as their lives on the filthbed continued, their forearms would grow to an unearthly length, and individual characteristics would disappear from their faces until it became impossible to see any kind of expression there. As far as most people were concerned, this was merely nature's recompense for those who had fled their destinies.

For Hanishibe, stepping outside the shrine office at lunchtime made for a nice change of scenery.

Although the meat-colored expanse of the filthbed, strewn with bony debris, spread out before his eyes, and though the acidic smell of it was enough to burn his windpipe, the wife of the Shrine Chieftain, wrapped in an unbleached kimono and a beautiful pleated skirt, would often be out with her children for a stroll around the Deilith.

She would stare out across the houseboat-dotted filthbed as if lost in fascination, then spread out both arms as she took in a refreshing breath of air. From time to time, she would bow politely to no one in particular and sometimes delightedly let slip a few words spoken only to herself. Behind their mother, who was never quite in the same world as they, the children would chase around their baby momonji, smiling as though they hadn't a care in the world. Occasionally, Hanishibe even joined them.

On the houseboats floating near the Deilith, the ebisus were always dangling their long arms over the sides, digging out the small filthtail shrimp that burrowed between the pleated folds of the filthbed. Even when you peeled off a filthtail's vermilion lacquer shell, there was only a small part inside that was non-toxic and could be eaten. Moreover, their unpleasant odor was strong, and even flies wouldn't come near them. Yet they were the ebisus' main source of nutrition.

Hanishibe, when he was still unaccustomed to the stench of the filthbed and unable to get his food down, had once tried to do as the Shrine Chieftain did and give his lunch to an ebisu. Not one of them, however, would accept food from him. Unwilling to admit defeat, he had been about to place it in one of the boats when a voice had called to him from behind: "We can't eat anything except filthtail shrimp and shellfish." It was an ebisu who had been hired as a washerwoman. A number of wet garments hung from one of her forearms.

"I've seen you people wolfing down smoked meat."

"Our stomachs can't handle it."

"Don't tell me you throw it all up afterward?"

The washerwoman spread out the wrinkles in some dried clothes with her other hand. Hanishibe had a feeling he had seen the burn marks and fracture bumps on those arms before.

"Do you just force it down because you can't refuse?"

The woman tilted her head, not understanding.

"You're the one who picked up my lantern that time, aren't you?"

The woman held the laundry up high at a diagonal incline, then closed her eyes. She intended to stand that way until it dried.

Later, Hanishibe learned why the Shrine Chieftain bestowed gifts of food on the ebisus: it was in order to make them vomit up the store of fiber that was in their stomachs. "If I don't do that periodically," he said, "large masses of fiber will grow inside them and become impossible to remove without surgery."

As for the washerwoman, she was relaxing her guard little by little each time she ran into Hanishibe on the Deilith.

Ebisus had no names and didn't like to be named, so it was in secret that Hanishibe began calling her Matamade, meaning "hands like fine jewels." When through Matamade's good offices Hanishibe gained opportunities to speak with other ebisus, he began to realize that they were naturally low of intellect and unable to think about things at all unless the necessity arose. When sleeping, they experienced vivid dreams of the Hereafter, and it was said that even during the daytime, the fragrance of lawns would start to drift through the air if they grew drowsy, and the Hereafter would come breaking through.

Hanishibe, who harbored a strong interest in dreams of the Hereafter, volunteered for the duty of almsgiving and on that pretext made the rounds of the filthbed's houseboats one by one.

There were about twenty houseboats floating on the filthbed. All of these small boats were constructed by joining together momonji exoshelletons, so no fewer than ten would be living in the hut that took up most of each boat's deck space.

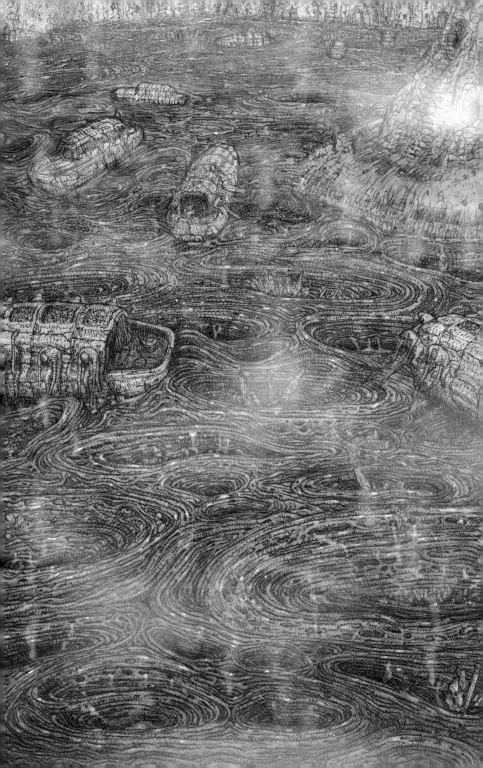

Several ebisus were sitting on either side of their houseboat's flat roof, fishing. Hanishibe came up and stood beside them, dodging the filthtails, nightclams, and grimeshells being tossed backhanded into the gutter in the center of the roof. With persistent questioning, he wheedled stories about their dreams from their reticent lips.

When there was no longer anything to catch, one ebisu thrust a spike from the palm of his hand into the meatpleats of the filthbed, causing powerful undulations that moved the houseboat. Unable to stand while the meat waves were rolling, Hanishibe evacuated to the hut. Beneath a ceiling hung with several birthingsacs, transparent through their webs of capillaries, sat a number of ebisus, arms and legs all tangled together as they peeled filthtails, ground them into paste, and crushed their shells into powder with a millstone. Hanishibe got them to tell him their stories as he helped them with these things. All the while, he was sweating profusely as he sipped at a boiled soup made from filthtail shells, brought out to show him hospitality.

When night fell, the ebisus curled up in birthingsacs like candies in their wrappers and slept. Or perhaps they were awakening into their dream.

What he was able to get from the ebisus' fragmented, halting words were detailed—one might say unnecessarily detailed—descriptions of everything under the sun, descriptions which differed vastly from what most people remembered of the Hereafter. Hanishibe, though dazzled by the torrent of information, was making many tweaks to the model he had hypothesized and focusing in on its essence. What was unfolding before him was a lakeside town with a pleasant climate, spreading out beneath a blue sky.

In that town, the four hundred households that he had been able to identify were living utterly ordinary, peaceful lives. The temporal axis of each was intermittent, but whatever correlation table one might draw, there was one family on which these segments converged, who lived lives free of interruption.

Facing the clear lake was a grassy garden enclosed by trees. Amid the chirping of birds and the refreshing aroma of the cut lawn, a little boy was running around trying to catch a dog with extremely short legs. The dog nimbly escaped from his little hands, and the young boy fell down into the grass. At the sight of this, a lovely young girl laughed and threw a ball. The dog leapt over the boy's back and lit out after it. Enjoying dark brown tea as they watched all this from their chairs on the terrace was their tolerant father and deeply affectionate mother—

No sooner did he put the story together in sequence than most of the things he'd been told would fade away.

Though it was true he felt envious of that peaceful lifestyle—so unlike that of Cavumville—Hanishibe had no words for such a world and could only describe it in pat, hackneyed phrases. As such, he couldn't escape the feeling that it was a boring place without any appeal for him. Before long, he had lost interest in that city by the lake.

2

When seventeen Descents from Heaven had occurred since Hanishibe came to live at the shrine, and when the number of returnees' reunions he had declared had risen as high as seven hundred, Hanishibe's promotion to court enforcer was announced, with words of appreciation from the Shrine Chieftain.

When told that it was work that only he—who knew the individual registry inside and out—could do, he did not feel uninterested and was grateful to be released from reunion declarations. Still, though, it bothered him that he had not yet been able to attend on the revivifications of his grandfather, his grandmother, and Yatsuo.

His first assignment as court enforcer was an unbearable one for him: to bring in for inquisition the astronomer Kubutsutsui, who had stirred up the people by promoting the Theory of Celestial Motion, a theory which rocked the very foundations of Shinto.

Hanishibe, having received his orders in the dead of night, greeted the dawn without having slept a wink and, leading a pair of purifiers, set out for the heretic's house. When he stood before the entrance, he inhaled deeply to steady his breathing, then knocked on the door.

When Narikabura appeared in the doorway, he thrust out his badge of divine office and ran quickly upstairs to the second floor. There Hanishibe sucked in his breath as he took in the sight of Narikabura's father. What had once been an adorable, baseform little baby had transformed into a mutated shape that was just like the body of a water flea. Through the whitish, translucent softshell of his head could be seen a series of multiple crystalline bodies. Apparently, it was no lie that he could perform observations of the heavenly bodies with his naked eyes alone.

Narikabura clung to his father, weeping and shouting. Hanishibe pulled him away and gave orders to the purifiers to take him in.

The inquisition was carried out as a holy rite in the midst of the main shrine.

"No annual parallax or aberration can be measured. Objective observations of this have led us to thith twuththat."Kubutsutsui's thick tongue writhed stickily in his thin softshell as he expounded upon his views. "The celestial sphere, on which the earth and the stars are projected, revolves around the moon where we are located, giving rise to the false Theory of Terrestrial Motion. This deep and profound universe is exceedingly small—far smaller than we had previously imagined. And now a distortion has begun to appear in the celestial sphere—and our destruction is at hand."

It was the kind of comment frequently heard from false prophets. The part that was most problematic theologically was the eschatological idea, which denied eternal recollection.

Surely Narikabura hadn't put such hard work into raising his father just so he could spread idiotic hypotheses like the Theory of Celestial Motion.

Hanishibe's chest was tight with sorrow and pity as the Shrine Chieftain handed him a fortune slip that turned his blood to ice. Hanishibe's voice went shrill as he obeyed the oracle written therein and pronounced on Kubutsutsui the sentence of death by sinking.

The pleated folds of flesh that ran throughout the filthbed converged in a depression called the Abyss, and it was there that Kubutsutsui was standing buried up to his waist. The thick, meaty tongue that had spread wide his heresies was tightly bound. The meatpleats, squirming like countless annelids, were swallowing up Kubutsutsui's entire body little by little.

As Kubutsutsui sank unresisting into the Abyss, packed crowds of residents lined the loop-lanes, staring on at him expressionlessly. From his vantage point in the execution boat, Hanishibe was unable to see Narikabura anywhere.

That night, sleep would not come to Hanishibe as he lay

in his bed. His eyes, wide open, were turned toward a translucent universe globe that glowed dimly on the shelf. It had been fashioned from one of the countless minute air bubbles scattered throughout a momonji's eyeball. Although he had confiscated it from Kubutsutsui on confirming that it expressed a heretical view of the universe, he knew that it was really nothing more than a teaching aid commonly used in the astronomy department and modeled after a Divine Implement.

During the week following Kubutsutsui's execution by sinking, two eschatologists were arrested on charges of holding illegal assemblies, and again, executions by sinking had to be carried out.

It came to be that when Hanishibe walked the streets of Cavumville, rotten organs and human feces would be flung at him. Classmates whom he passed in the way also stopped meeting his gaze. These were signs that eschatological thinking and the Theory of Celestial Motion had made much greater headway in the world at large than he had imagined.

Someone on duty in the watchtower discovered a series of long, large bumps rising from the upper part of the moon's outer crust and extending toward its backside in the direction of Ox and Tiger. This resulted in a huge uproar. In swift succession, ridges of bumps were also confirmed in the directions of Ram and Monkey, Dragon and Serpent, and Dog and Boar, spurring on greater devotion for heresy.

To the geologists, however, these bumps were nothing more than projections whose growth had been under observation since long ago. But although they argued that this was probably something no different than the expansion of petraderm caused by landsoup, the furor did not settle down. A connection was drawn between those projections on the lunar surface and earthquakes that had long occurred at irregular intervals. People were reading signs of the Eschaton into all manner of things.

At last, three young men employed a giant kite in an attempt to descend from the watchtower down to the earth. They never returned.

Inside the watchtower, a satirical sketch was found showing Hanishibe pushing the backs of that trio.

Only Komorizu continued to drop by his room at the shrine office as before. One day, as he was squeezing his way in through the door, several of his gourdlet clusters got stuck behind him. As soon as the now-doorframe-shaped Komorizu pushed himself over the threshold, however, they all snapped forward and knocked something off the shelf. Komorizu was fatter every time Hanashibe met him, so there was no helping the room being cramped.

Komorizu rotated his slimy head and frowned, flaring all three of his nostrils.

"What's that shmell? Don't tell me you're eating filthtail shoup in here? If you take the ebishus side too much, you end up having more trouble than you need. Out in the world, they think you're carrying out the shuppression on your own authority."

Hanishibe couldn't blame them. After all, he was the one carting people off, handing down their sentences, and standing witness as those sentences were carried out.

"The reputation of the great court enforsher has sunk deep down into the filthbed's Abyss…" Komorizu sang with silly inflections, "…and without shaking anybody's respect for the Shrine Chieftain."

Hanishibe was made cognizant of his own moral responsibility every day.

Komorizu, returning the universe globe to the shelf, suddenly groaned and put his head down on the floor. The bulbous clusters covering his body bounced, many of them scattering trash.

"What's wrong, Komorizu?"

"I…I'm fine." Many pseudophalanges had stretched out from his bunched gourdlets and adhered to the walls. His pseudophalanges crawled up the walls, hauling his body back up again.

"Oh, man…lately my head's jusht full. I'm reading the tracks of the gods in the cracks of burnt bones. How many times have I assembled the shpirit numbers and done the shilent chants? I've ushed my head too much, and it looks like I've caught a bad cold with a high fever. I shleep and I shleep, but no matter what I do, I can't seem to shake the exhaustion. Everybody in the department is like this. We've had three martyrs already. I gotta get through this shomehow."

"Martyrs, you say…? Why something like that all of a sudden?"

"A divine edict's come down, apparently. Probably shays that the folks upshtairs can't wait any longer."

After Komorizu had left, Hanishibe noticed a variety of items lying scattered around the floor and laughed out loud. There was the marrowpen Komorizu had taken off his desk in the classroom all those years ago.

Beside it was a bundle of dermasheets. They were covered in diffuse pointillistic designs, over which marks forming complicated curves had been traced. The diagrams thus created were spread out over three pages; you could only see the whole progression by laying the three sheets over one another. As he flipped through the dermasheets, marks that began from the same starting point transformed into many different shapes. These probably represented cracks in the burnt bones that Komorizu had spoken of, which showed the paths by which the gods had traversed it.

He picked up the celestial globe and stared at it for a moment. It looked like a part of it matched the density distribution of those points, but the starting point was not the moon. Far from it, it began in an area far removed from the solar system, where not a single star existed.

3

The next Descent from Heaven came, with the eschatological furor as yet unabated.

Hanashibe was standing by a third-story window at the shrine office, looking out at the mound formed by the accumulation of petauristas. Half the ground floor was completely buried, and the surface of the Deilith could not be seen at all. Out on the mound he could see many ebisus, each standing well apart from their fellows, signaling to one another in arm language.

An ebisu near the base of the mound took off running toward the shrine office, but Hanishibe was racing down the stairs already. Thanks to his time spent among the ebisus, he was now able to read their arm language.

When he climbed outside through a first-floor window, the ebisu was pointing toward a spot midway up the mound.

With uncertain footsteps, Hanishibe climbed up the wobbling mound of piled corpses, and when he reached the site, sure enough, an eschatological thinker who was supposed to have been disposed of by sinking was there, wedged in between the petaurista corpses. Had he been thrown free when the momonji he was in struck the ground?

The man had vomited a great quantity of blood and was already dead. His body was covered in marks resembling a striped pattern of burns.

Hanishibe stood rooted to that spot for a time, unable to arrange his thoughts, and then realized that an ebisu standing near the top of the mound was waving at him vigorously.

Hanishibe set off running. When he reached the top of the mound, the ebisu was pointing at a hole from which a gigantic petaurista had been removed. "I saw him fall from the sky," he was saying. Hanishibe got down on his stomach and peered down into the hole.

What he saw he couldn't believe at first. Peeking out from between the shells, the chunks of flesh, and the entrails under which he was buried was his very own grandfather, looking just as he had in the past.

With the help of one of the ebisus, he dragged him up out of the hole. Drawing near, he called out to him. His grandfather's facelid was closed though and did not open. He caressed the hard, rough skin, drenched though it was in a gravy of putrescence. His skin was much harder than it had been in the past. A long, ropelike flesh-tube was hanging out from the knot on his back, extending down into the hole, where it disappeared among the petauristas forming its walls. They hauled the flesh-tube in as they collapsed the wall and at its end discovered an object about the size of a human head that resembled a blob of glue. It was giving off a blue light.

Hanishibe stared at the torchburr-illuminated form of his grandfather lying in the bed. Sometime earlier, the blob's blue light had gone out. Hanishibe took a bite of filthtail soup from his bonebowl and took in a breath of air. The obvious question rose up in his mind: why had his grandfather and that eschatologist fallen with the Descent from Heaven?

A certain hypothesis occurred to him, based on the words of Kubutsutsui, but it was too absurd to take seriously, and he shook it out of his mind. Had a couple of momonji come apart in midair during the Descent after all? *Both of these men are returnees.* All he could do was keep telling himself that.

He tripped on the flesh-tube that lay in a writhing mass on the floor. He stripped off the sticky glueball and set it next to his universe globe, then coiled up the flesh-tube and put it away beneath his bed.

"If any of Grandpa's colleagues come by, I'll bring them up here," he said. Taking his lamp in hand, he put the shrine office behind him. Before the bedfluid erupted from the petaurista mound to form the Pillar, the ebisus would have to spend the whole night hauling the freshest-looking, most promising petauristas over to the disposal area. No one had asked him, but Hanishibe had made up his mind to assist them in the task as much as he was able.

A whitish haze hung over the whole of the filthbed now, rising up dimly from the blackness in the illumination of torchlight that shone from the perimeter. Gas was being given off by petauristas as bedfluid melted away their bodies.

As Hanishibe began climbing up the slope, his body could sense that the entire mound was slowly, almost imperceptibly rotating. The slope to his right collapsed, burying alive several ebisus who had been carrying a momonji. He started to turn to go and help them, but right away one of the buried ebisus stuck his torso up out of the jumble and signaled in arm language that they were all right.

Relieved, Hanishibe signaled back, and that was when he sensed the presence of someone standing behind him. He turned around. Through the whitish mist, he could make out a dim figure. The face still resembled a liposculpt, but now it had taken on a solid shape, with features more defined than they had been before.

"Narikabura!" Hanishibe cried. He started running toward him, but his foot slipped on a blood-smeared shell and he fell down on his back. "You...you must really bear a grudge for what I've done."

"Yeah. I've never forgiven you. Up until just now even, I was thinking about...about killing you."

The moment Hanishibe tried to sit up, the corpse he was sitting on began to slide, and he grabbed hold of an intestine that was near at hand. His fingers were sinking into a wall of flesh.

"I've been in hiding," said Narikabura, his face beginning to blur. "Together with the eschatologists. Because I'm sure even now that my dad was right."

"How can you blindly believe in things like eschatology and the Theory of Celestial Motion? What about the will of the gods?"

"Since moving into the shrine, you seem to have learned how to hide your true feelings in front of them. Even you must realize what's going on. Even you must suspect it. Food and drink offerings are being brought into the Deilith constantly. Divinity students are being forced to work their brains until they martyr."

Hanishibe felt his throat going dry as he waited for the next words.

"They only intend to escape themselves."

"Who's going to escape? And where in the world *from*?"

Shadows wavered in the growing swells of fog.

"I'm out of time already. But I'll tell you one thing before I go. Those ebisus you're on such friendly terms with? Why do you think it is their intelligence is so low? Because the same thing is happening to them that's happening to the divinity students right now: their intellects are suppressed because almost all of their brains' functionality is being used from outside."

"What in the world for?" A faint scent of grass brushed past his nose. "And how could you know something like that?"

Narikabura drew nearer through the fog. He was walking on two legs. What was then revealed before Hanishibe was the baseform of a woman wrapped in an unbleached kimono and a pleated skirt. The fabric covering her chest and shoulders bore dark stains.

"Right now, I am simultaneously here and in the village by the lake." The features of his liposculpt face began to run, as if melting in the heat. Bubbles appeared in depressions that formed, resembling eye sockets, as his lips and the ridge of his nose came protruding forward. There was no mistaking it: what was forming was the face of the Shrine Chieftain's wife.

At that moment, someone called out Hanishibe's name from below. Narikabura silently backed away. When Hanishibe twisted around to look behind and below, he saw the Shrine Chieftain standing there, holding up his lantern.

"What are you doing here?"

"Helping the ebisus like always. My foot just slipped." There was no lie in merely leaving out the details. "What brings you out here?"

The Shrine Chieftain looked around, and in a gloomy voice he told him, "I can't find my wife."

Just before dawn, the search for the Shrine Chieftain's wife was called off for the time being. Hanishibe headed for the disposal area, thoughts churning at a state of affairs that was difficult to believe. As he stared at the momonji lined up on the straw mats, there appeared a taxonomist who had been a friend of his grandfather's. Hanishibe explained the situation to him and asked him to come up to his private room in the shrine office.

There the taxonomist pried his grandfather's facelid partway open with a scraper used for disassemblies, stuck a syringe into the reliefs of a face softer than his exoderm, and injected a resurrectant. Nothing happened. The taxonomist moved on to various other approaches, forcing him to breathe in awakeners and sticking acupuncture needles into his pressure points to stimulate the nerves.

"Well, sometimes the effects don't take right away," the taxonomist said in a consoling voice, then headed back over to the disposal area.

Hanishibe was sitting in his chair, doing nothing in particular. On a sudden impulse, he opened his desk drawer, pulled out a bundle of manuscript pages, and laid them out on the floor. On every page, dreams of that village by the lake, dreams he had heard from the ebisus, were recorded in densely packed, reddish-black letters.

Hanishibe didn't need to reread them all in order to realize what he had been pretending not to see. He put his hands to the floor and hung his head. The veins in his temples were beating furiously.

"Blackness," a muffled voice suddenly said.

"Grandpa?" Hanishibe rose to his feet like a drunkard.

"Am I still...in space? No...this world...is awfully heavy..."

Hanishibe waited to hear what he would say next.

He noticed a pale, wisteria-hued glow coming from the shelf where his decorations were kept. The gluelike mass was giving off light. The tiny stars on the universe globe next to it were set twinkling as they reflected it.

When he opened the window and craned his neck upward, the sky was tinged with the same color and was beginning to grow brighter.

4

Three days later, Hanishibe was awaiting the Shrine Chieftain's arrival in a fourth-floor living room. He had decided to tell him the truth.

As the door began to open, he heard a voice saying, "Thank goodness! Thank goodness you're safe!" The Shrine Chieftain came into the room with his arm around the shoulders of a young woman. She had no arms below her elbows, which were wrapped in bandages.

"Hanishibe was with you until dawn looking for me, wasn't he?" the girl said, staring straight into Hanishibe's eyes. Her voice was that of the Shrine Chieftain's wife; her face that of Matamade the washwoman. "I am truly grateful," she said and gently touched with her bandage-wrapped elbow a clenched fist that Hanishibe couldn't keep from trembling.

"Hanishibe, what's the matter?" the Shrine Chieftain asked concernedly. "You look so distressed…Perhaps I've made you overdo too often lately. You should relax for a while."

"What about *her*?" he said.

"'Her'?" asked the Shrine Chieftain. With a frightened expression, Matamade—the Shrine Chieftain's wife—drew near to her husband. "Oh, you must mean this possession-seat that she's been wearing lately. What with the sudden uproar this time, the receptaflesh from the bronze bell couldn't get here in time. It's all right though. Her arms, of course, and even her face will go back to normal, so don't you worry. Although my wife does seem to prefer being thinner, as she is at present."

"What are you *talking about*, sir?"

"Oh. So is that what was going on?" The Shrine Chieftain's expression clouded over. "I've spoken carelessly. It seems that I've done something inexcusable to you. If this has upset you, we can decide on a different ebisu."

Hanishibe couldn't understand the words being said to him.

"This may sound like I'm trying to make excuses, but we had her tested for personhood, just in case. We proceeded only after confirming she is not a person, not even by legal definition."

Hanishibe punched the Shrine Chieftain in the face as hard as he could. The sensation was like hitting a boneless mass of flesh. The Shrine Chieftain fell back on his buttocks, and Hanashibe kept hitting him until Matamade interposed herself, waving the rounded nubs of her elbows.

For a long moment, no one moved.

"Even whirligigs are fundamentally no different," the Shrine Chieftain said, the palm of his hand pressed against his cheek.

Hanishibe staggered back away from him until he felt the wall against his back. Were his ears ringing, or were there angry voices outside?

"We've always treated the ebisus well," said the Shrine Chieftain.

"No doubt to protect your life in that city by the lake."

"Good heavens! Don't tell me you've recollected? But if you have, you should understand. Here, through the power of some unknowable outside presence, deteriorated copies of magatama-bearing momonji—of countless alien life-forms as well—are replicated continuously. That's why our daily life began its endless, meaningless repetition and in time began to pollute one of the Divine Implements—the Magatama. That contamination led us to isolate the Divine Implements, and in their place create the Hereafter—a specially designated preservation area we've made by availing ourselves of unused regions in the brains of ebisus."

"For your own families to live in?"

"As the Divine Will First Party carries out its unending

duties, the right to good health and welfare is also granted us by law. But since only a single bronze bell has been handed down to us, we cannot make possession-seats receive spirit at will. Rather than doing everything in the manifestation zone, you get better reception by going through the raw sensory organs, and it's also in keeping with the Divine Will First Party's philosophy."

Hanishibe was feeling as though the Shrine Chieftain were a fundamentally different life-form. "You're doing the same thing to your Divinity students. They may not know it, but they're burning off years of their lives to assist your families in escaping. Destruction is coming, just like Kubutsutsui argued. Isn't it?"

"Hanishibe, no!" cried the Shrine Chieftain's wife. "My husband is trying to save everyone in this city!"

"So how many more are you saying can board the Deilith?"

"The boarding of the volunteers has been complete from the very start. They're in the Divine Implement, the Magatama. All of them."

"That's different from the people living in Cavumville right now! How could you do this?"

Hanishibe's knees were starting to tremble. Even though things had come to this, he was still clinging fervently to the hope that the Shrine Chieftain might say it wasn't so.

"Even you would do the same," said the Shrine Chieftain.

"How dare you. Please don't make assumptions about what I would do."

"At any rate, it looks like you didn't recollect after all, though guesswork alone has gotten you pretty far." The Shrine Chieftain leaned against the wall as he got back to his feet. "You may have been revivified from a momonji, but you're still me after all."

At that, Hanishibe felt as though the air had been crushed out of his lungs. "Well then," he said at last, glaring at the

Shrine Chieftain's wife, "does that mean you're Yatsuo?"

"Of course not," the Shrine Chieftain replied. "Yatsuo was my prior wife, whom I outlived. That's a tale of long, long ago—of Earth in the days of the Great Dust Plague. But she—"

The Shrine Chieftain was taking his wife's shoulders to draw her near when a lone, dismayed-looking purifier suddenly burst into the room. Eschatologists, he reported, were gathering outside in large numbers, violently demanding admission to the Deilith. The Shrine Chieftain asked him who had stirred them up, and the purifier mumbled an answer too low to understand. The Shrine Chieftain asked again less politely, and the purifier, glancing at the Shrine Chieftain's wife, answered in a voice that came out as a whisper.

"Your wife."

The Shrine Chieftain opened a window, and they looked down below. Amid the thick, drifting haze, a multitude of bizarre figures stood in disorderly array, forming a line that was bobbing on a soup of digested petauristas. Bound for the Deilith, they had crowded onto the array of barges that formed the approach to the shrine. Those who had surged up onto the Deilith were shouting angrily toward the main shrine and the shrine office. A figure holding a bonestaff aloft at the head of the group was none other than the Shrine Chieftain's wife.

"We planned to escape this crumbling world with only our families!" she cried.

Over and over, she fanned the flames of the furor around her, shouting out secrets that only the Shrine Chieftain's wife could possibly know.

Without a word, the Shrine Chieftain went out of the room. His footfalls could be heard as he descended the staircase. His frightened children ran in from the next room over and clung to their mother.

"It's all right, dears, it's all right. Daddy is sure to save us. There's nothing to worry about."

Hanishibe realized in a sudden flash of insight exactly what the Shrine Chieftain was about to do. He leaned far outside the window and shouted as loudly as he could, "Don't! Get away from here right now! Narikabura, stop it!"

Not a soul paid heed to his voice.

Rises began to appear in the layer of corpses piled up around the Deilith, growing higher and higher as if swelling from sudden fermentation, until four large hills had formed. Giving off a faint smoke, the dead bodies covering these mounds stuck one to another as they slid downward, and out from their centers there crawled misshapen human figures, each one as tall as the shrine office's third story. The entirety of their long, twisted bodies were covered—or bound perhaps—with clothing that bulged with ridges of muscle fiber. From their collars jutted tongue-shaped, transparent heads from which bubbles of air were popping in such numbers that the creatures appeared to be boiling.

"Gods—"

"Doomgods!"

"Doomgods..."

"Four of them!"

"We'll be cursed!"

With a roar of voices, the multitude fell back. People were pushed off the ledges of both the Deilith and the shrine road and began to smoulder as they were buried in half-digested remains.

Hanishibe, following after the Shrine Chieftain, descended as far as the basement but found that the iron door that continued to the inner part of the Deilith had been closed. Reversing directions, he climbed back up the stairs and went out through the front door of the shrine office.

Before the main shrine, the doomgods were crawling on all fours so that their bodies overshadowed everyone. They were raising and lowering their ridge-enveloped thoraxes. Inspired to awe by those magnificent forms, all remained rooted to the spots where they stood. The people would shrink back each time the doomgods' long arms and legs buckled, making their midsections twist and turn.

One of the doomgods suddenly lowered its faceless head down to eye level, then slowly waved it left and right. That alone was enough to make many of them lose control of their bladders and sink to the ground on the spot.

Underneath the shifting, glossy sheen of its smooth surface layer, strange-looking organs pulsated amid entangling nets of blood vessels and nerves. The surface of its face sank inward from the center, rotating like a whirlpool, and a shrill, piercing voice rang out. Fountains of blood erupted from the noses and ears of the dozen or so people in front of it. They were instantly thrown backward.

On the other side of that doomgod's inclined torso, the figure of a woman came into view, being lifted high up into the air. Three fat fingers gripped her head tightly. Hanishibe cried out when he saw that face. In the blink of an eye, the Shrine Chieftain's wife's—Narikabura's—head was twisted off. It fell to the ground, where it was kicked back and forth among the legs of people running around in a panic as they tried to escape.

The barges of the shrine road swayed back and forth in a winding fashion, and the crowds of people surging across were gradually being thrown off into the filthbed.

Most of the people, driven away in every direction by the doomgods, were fearfully coalescing around the Divine Gate that rose high above the forward end of the Deilith.

The double door at the front of the main shrine creaked open. Standing in the doorway was the Shrine Chieftain, garbed in the raiment of a Shinto priest and holding in his hand a long pole from whose tip hung white streamers of purification.

"Make way—"

　"Make way—"

　　"Make way—"

—backed by the voices of purifiers in the main shrine who sang out their admonitions in a round, the Shrine Chieftain stepped forward uttering the lines of an incantation and waved the staff at the doomgods.

One step at a time, the doomgods retreated. The people all breathed out sighs of relief. The Shrine Chieftain continued to wave the pole about. One by one, the doomgods returned to the filthbed from whence they had come.

CHAPTER 4:
DIVINE CROSSING

1

By the end of the day on which the riot occurred, Hanishibe had departed the shrine forever.

He went back to his old, empty home, and when he came in the door, a great number of craftworks—embodiments of nostalgia for the Hereafter—were waiting there to greet him. One by one, he took each of them in hand and wiped away the dust.

It was while he was touching those rows of molars inscribed with divine letters that Yatsuo's last words came back to him.

You...are the only one...who can stop you. You alone.

Hanishibe shut his eyes, drawing a deep furrow in his brow as tears spilled from the corners of his eyes.

The public's criticism of Hanishibe, who had been court enforcer, was severe. Though he took on contracts for odd jobs at many different workshops, he sometimes had days when he couldn't put a single meal on the table.

Whenever his hands were even briefly idle, he would rub and massage the rigid body of his grandfather, giving him stimulation and telling him continually about the things that had come to pass already and those things that would come to pass later.

Once when he was at the peak of exhaustion, Hanishibe was speaking to him while half asleep—and found himself inputting the coordinates of habitable planets in a launch device and firing off about forty chrysalises.

As he floated along the corridor of an ark of woven reeds, Hanishibe imagined what would come later. He could envision the chrysalises landing, turning into momonji, and crawling all around the planet investigating its environment. Then within the birthingsacs inside them, the variegated bodies of colonists fitted to that environment would be formed around the magatama that were their cores. The revivified colonists could then breed the momonji—which were themselves made of ultimaterial—and wrap themselves in their furs, build homes with their bones, light fires with their oils and fat, and fill their stomachs with their meat. If things went well, they would be able to build a civilization again. Naturally, the eternal pilot Hanishibe would never know what became of the colonists afterward.

All alone, Hanishibe completed each task in silence and then went back to his home by the lakeshore where his family was waiting. His dear family, constructed by way of a thorough psychological disassembly, was ever attuned to his present spiritual condition. Also present were the casual, friendly residents living nearby. There was such peace there.

As he was living out such days, possession-seats fashioned by the bronze bell continued to receive soulsplinters of him through his magatama. Hanishibe would live out his prescribed life span, then go down to a death that was little different from falling asleep. Then the possession-seat would awaken him, and he would become the next Hanishibe. Weaving in this manner a life without end, his voyage to untouched stellar systems continued, and he continued dispatching momonji pupae to worlds where the habitability ratio was high—

And then one day, Hanishibe awakened from his nap and realized that he was in neither the shipboard cabin nor the house by the lake, and he was overcome by a horrifying sensation of loss that left his whole body trembling.

His grandfather had not awakened, but in continuing to speak to him, it had become clear to Hanishibe what he should do, as if he had been given the exact advice he needed.

Hanishibe went to see Komorizu and told him everything.

Creaking noises began to be heard constantly all through Cavumville. From time to time, the petraderm would shake powerfully, causing plaster on houses to come loose, bonebrick to crumble, and loop-lanes to buckle. The membranes in the windows never stopped shuddering. The Shrine Chieftain was seen often out on the Deilith, waving around his pole with its streamers. Divinity students were martyring out one after another. Komorizu had been no exception.

After Komorizu's death, Hanishibe became unable to find any of the commonplace items he used every day, and sobbing, he wandered all around his house looking for them. He couldn't find a single thing. If Moitori hadn't come to visit him several days later, he might have never stopped looking.

Moitori, granting a request his son had made while he yet lived, at last welcomed Hanishibe into the Department of Aquatic Resources. Though he had his doubts about a man who had once been court enforcer, Moitori had already secured nearly double the number of momonji that had survived thus far. That number would likely increase even further with the next Descent from Heaven.

Hanishibe went to see Professor Shitadami of the taxonomy department and asked him for his help. Together, they created an ultralow-temperature, near-vacuum environment in a Department of Aquatic Resources laboratory. Momonji were locked inside and experiments repeated time and again. Most of the momonji, however, died without displaying any transformations beyond an increase in body fur. Professor Shitadami endeavored to convince his taxonomy department's undergrads and graduates alike to join in the experiments, but only a handful of these responded.

Houses and streets in the direction of the Serpent collapsed from the tenth level all the way down to the fourth. There was little time left.

One by one, the number of Professor Shitadami's students at the Department of Aquatic Resources began to increase. An idea proposed by Monozane the Truncated Dodecahedron, who had been brought in aquarium and all, led to the breakthrough: momonji were illuminated with polarized light, and their skin was observed hardening just slightly. Once they determined the best way to proceed, the experimentation gradually accelerated.

Staring dazedly through eyelids nearly sealed shut by drowsiness, Hanishibe was looking at a creature resembling an albino armormole.

Its gigantic form, shaped like a roll of bone-mochi *coupée pão*, was covered in a succession of bone-colored armor plates.

Something struck the back of his knee, and he came back to himself as he dropped to a kneeling position. Right beside him was the diminutive Professor Shitadami, sitting in a chair and holding a dermasheet out toward him. Hanishibe took it from him, and as his eyes followed the masterfully written script, a smile began to spread across his face. Every department had met their targets. They had succeeded in turning a momonji into a pupa.

With everyone looking on, two pairs of wing-type ossiforms pushed up one segment of its armor, and then one of its backshell ossiforms, in a layer of fat, slid open, laying bare the wet gleam of its birthingsac membrane.

Once the production of pupae began, the grounds of the Department of Aquatic Resources grew steadily more cramped, and even the homes of those involved were taken over. In the marketplace, momonji and the midsized petauristas that served as their fodder grew quickly scarce, until at last, all that could be had were the dried ones and the ones boiled in sweetened soy sauce.

2

The disturbances continued. The Descents from Heaven that had once occurred at a rate of one every three months had not taken place now for five months and counting. The trembling in the window membranes only grew stronger, and the funnelroar was reaching the point where it was clearly audible. It reminded Hanishibe somehow of a herald's voice, crying out to clear his master's way.

The Shrine Chieftain's lack of appearances even at Descentmaking ceremonies encouraged unease among the multitudes, and even if someone had wanted to negotiate with him, the four doomgods had reappeared at the Deilith a month ago and were still sitting there listlessly so that no one could approach the shrine.

Hanishibe was fine-tuning the environment of the experimentation chamber when he overheard some student talking.

One of the doomgods was melting, they said. He went out onto the loop-lane and found Moitori and the others gathered there looking downward at the Deilith. Hanishibe was taken with a strange sense of déjà vu and ran his gaze back and forth across the filthbed surrounding it.

"What are you looking at? It's over there." Moitori pointed at the main shrine.

A thing like a blob of fat was going in through the doorway. At its side there stood a figure garbed in priestly raiment.

From that point onward, the doomgods were three.

The following week, Hanishibe went all the way down to the bottommost level for the first time in months. This was because he had noticed that the houseboats dotting the filthbed had not changed their positions in quite a long time. Most likely, this was what had caused his déjà vu.

When he drew near the Deilith, the doomgods in front of the main shrine grew restless, so he couldn't get on from the shrine road. He had a feeling that the filthbed surrounding him contained more of the dregs of Descents from Heaven than usual. The houseboats moored nearby were all uninhabited. The main shrine as well had its door ajar and showed no sign of life.

With fat fingertips, a doomgod was kneading something resembling an internal organ, but losing interest perhaps, it threw it away over its shoulder. It rose on its haunches just slightly, leaned forward, and thrust its hand through the door of the main shrine. Taking hold of a single, elongated arm, it dragged a limp human form outside. The body's head lolled about and nodded forward in Hanishibe's direction. A bowl-shaped depression was visible from which a chunk of him had been cut out. The doomgod started twisting the limbs off the dead body.

Another doomgod dragged another dead ebisu from the main shrine. It tore open the corpse's stomach with its bare fingers, and when it had finished pulling out the intestines, it put one end to its throat and gradually sucked it into its body. The head of the ebisu had of course been severed.

Hanishibe shuddered violently. Looking across the filth-bed, he realized that most of those scattered dregs he had noticed were pieces of ebisu corpses.

Cavumville was facing an increasingly severe food shortage. Even the replenishing of whirligigs had been hit with delays.

In front of the Department of Aquatic Resources, residents had been gathering for days on end making high-handed demands that the momonji market be reopened. After experiencing numerous skirmishes, the crowd, overcome by raging passions, attacked both the Deparment of Fisheries and the homes of those who worked there.

The three momonji that were in the experimentation chamber at the time were disassembled on the spot, but then the blood-smeared attackers were themselves attacked as they headed home carrying slabs of meat. However, the pupae being stored in the warehouse and in private homes could not even be scratched by the likes of hammers and axes.

In the midst of this riot, not even one of the attackers noticed the gargantuan crack that had appeared in the heavens.

Hanishibe was gazing at the sky from the window of his room when it happened. The crack grew, zigzagging across the sky like a lightning bolt, and the air pressure began to drop precipitously. All through the city of Cavumville, dust and tiles began to be swept up into the air.

Hanishibe remembered the very first cnidarianlike baby he had taken from the birthingsac of a momonji in this land. The touch and the weight of that moist mucous membrane came back to him with vivid clarity. The long years before this hollow had come to overflow with its supervariegated humanity came and went in the twinkling of an eye. Perhaps this diversity of mutations had been the result of trying to adapt to a world that could not possibly exist.

He thought of the four hundred passengers sleeping inside the momonji pupae. It had been impossible from the start to provide enough momonji for the entire population to cross over. Perhaps those who had not been selected by the vote were feeling relieved about it now. Hanishibe had the feeling that they probably were.

Beyond the cracks overspreading the whole sky, an inky blackness could be seen that seemed to inflate as it grew ever larger.

The rooftop, the ceiling, and the walls were all blown away in the space of a single breath, and the world went dim. Hanishibe clung to the body of his grandfather. It was as if every Descent from Heaven that had ever occurred—and every petaurista—were caught up in a vortex, and all going back to Heaven at once.

At the center of the whirlwind, the Deilith was rising, even as the main shrine, the shrine office, and the Divine Gate were falling away.

He thought of Narikabura, now a ghost lurking in that village by the lake.

Rows of houses peeled away in succession, and bruise-colored petraderm was exposed. The town that had been built up over untold generations was going down to utter destruction.

Hanishibe and his grandfather had already been swallowed up in the raging currents borne of that Stygian void. Rings of petraderm spun away into the distance. Amid a blackness spangled densely with dull bonebricks and human forms, he could make out the shapes of many silk-white pupae, each one as sturdy as armor.

It was getting hard to breathe. He felt like his insides were on the verge of turning inside out. As Hanishibe clung to his grandfather, mucus came oozing out from his eyeballs and from between the scales that covered his entire body. It formed a thick protective membrane around him. Even so, that was merely a simple reaction to the environment and could only prolong his life a short while.

Hanishibe's sense of sight slipped away into the distant past. Before an ark of woven reeds there suddenly appeared a green and blue planet. Its volume was only about three times that of the ark. Even so, it had an atmosphere, and there was no word save *planet* he could use to describe it. At the end of an undeclared war with its gravity, the ark, badly damaged, made an "unplanned landing" on that world. Although Hanishibe had managed to escape using the Deilith, it too crashed soon afterward into another planetoid with a powerful gravitational field, crash-landing inside a hollow in its interior. Finally, the entire planetoid had been covered in a celestial sphere, which had begun to glow with an ashy whiteness—

Amid the darkness, a part of the sky glowed brilliantly with the color of forget-me-nots. It was a giant, slowly revolving shard of the celestial sphere. As thick clouds rolled across its surface, the angle it made with the horizon grew more extreme. It was so vast that there was no way to guess how far away it was. Fragments of sky flitted by his field of view, revealing multilayered cross sections that fluttered past like the pages of a book. Then the curved surface of the heavenly realm rose into view, covered in a swollen, translucent membrane that gave off a faint light, squirming with untold multitudes of life-forms.

There were shelled things that crept on the ground, wild things that ran in herds, soft things that lurked in shadows, vigorously copulating momonji piled atop one another, and doomgods who, like cattle drivers, were hurrying all these petauristas along, but at last all of them vanished from Hanishibe's field of view.

The sky had been shattered into fragments of all sizes and shapes, resembling the islands that were drawn on the map of the Hereafter. The blue light given off by these shards of sky illuminated the indistinct shape of the bruise-colored moon, with its funnel-shaped mouth. Behind it, some sort of gargantuan shadow—a vertically oblong spheroid—was growing larger and—no, not larger—*closer!* It crossed the limb of the moon, growing ever more voluminous: a strangely shaped mass of stone suggesting a fossilized egg with complex patterns of cracks.

Long, vertical projections resembling dried sausages stuck out in four directions from the moon's outer shell, trembling and scattering innumerable flakes as they opened up, their outer surfaces peeling off, their lower bases near the filthbed being used as fulcra to move them. From their tips extended clumsy projections like palms with no fingers.

The upper and lower halves of the now-unoccluded mass of stone began to rotate in opposite directions around its center and at last came apart into two pieces. The hollow moon, waving around its four projections like an infant, slowly moved into the space between the two hemispheres. Night fell across many of the sky-shards illuminating this spectacle, and then the stone that had enveloped the moon began to lose thickness, until at last the border between itself and the surrounding space simply melted away.

Hanishibe couldn't stop shaking from the cold. Tightly, he gripped the magatama hanging from his neck.

Unexpectedly, the fearless arms of his grandfather moved. Grabbing both of Hanishibe's shoulders, he turned him around so that he was facing forward. Then like interlaced fingers coming apart, his grandfather's entire body opened up from its center and enveloped Hanishibe's freezing body.

He could hear his grandfather's voice murmuring, *I can hold out…until you get to sleep.*

Hanishibe nodded.

Or maybe it was Yatsuo who nodded.

Or his grandmother.

Or me.

Or us.

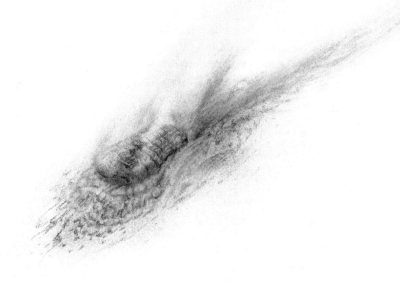

FRAGMENT:
GENESIS

<Gyo> discovered a mass of sealed and hardened syntax in the jewel's closed-off, innermost depths. To it he connected all his cogitosomes and unloosed its bindings, whereupon torrents of syntax came gushing forth in a flood exceeding <Gyo's> capacity to process. In the word-soil of his vast net of cogitosomes, there was constructed an alien civilization based on geometrical shapes.

<Gyo's> decision-making ability suffered immediate degradation from this invasion, and pollution due to hemorraging profits spread through his entire system.

It seemed as if the geometric civilization would continue flooding into him, but then of its own accord it began degenerating into Chaos, and the danger that it posed increased all the more. One by one, the surrounding corporatians pulled out their distribution tubes and ceased from trading fluids with him. Even <Gyo's> affiliated corporatians withdrew to his exterior. It was on this wise that <Gyo> was ostracized and unincorporated.

CASTELLUM NATATORIUS
(OR, THE CASTLE IN THE MUDSEA)

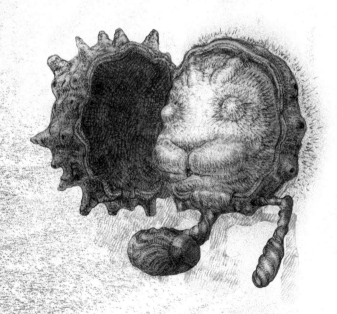

CHAPTER 1:
DURING THE CIRCLINGSEED FESTIVAL, IN CELEBRATION OF THE CASTELLAE'S MARRIAGE

1

The din from up above was just barely audible inside my tiny grotto.

A crowd of over ten thousand had gathered over in Mebohla Riptrench, and the eruptions of cheers from their ranks—stretching off toward the outer shell of Castellum Raondo—came vaulting over Gukutsu Clifftown, spilled down into neighboring Suifu'ushi Riptrench, permeated the labyrinth of forkways that spread still deeper into the ground, and at last found their way to my grotto.

In the past, this small cave had been used as an egghatch by some sort of giant gloambug. The walls enclosing its narrow, hemispherical space were fortified with a hardened mixture of dung and saliva, and the ceiling was just high enough to stand up straight in and walk around.

I lay suspended from the ceiling, supine in a danglebed woven with fibers spun from the anuses of Hagu tribe artisans. It was somewhat elastic and felt pleasant against my wounded body.

As I lay there gazing up at the countless, cup-sized glowjars growing densely on the low ceiling, I couldn't shake the feeling that this grotto was sinking steadily into the depths of the Mudsea—apart from the rest of Castellum Raondo.

Inside those brown, faintly translucent vases, I noticed whitish, phosphorescent mollusks squirming about, but just as that was registering, the grotto tilted sharply. I held onto the danglecords and the edge of the bed with all three of my hands.

Here in the midst of the Mudsea's verilucent layer, Castellum Raondo and Castellum Saruga had pressed their backs up against one another.

Both castellae were shaped like upright bicones, but their axes were tilted slightly off center, causing them to bend to one side, creating the gently rolling surfaces known as their "backs."

Within the belt of light that filtered down from the Seasky, the two castellae formed a gourdlike shape as they sank their outer shells into one another. Innumerable combtongues, growing thickly on their surfaces, became entangled and pulled hard against one another, breaking apart the castellae's shellite surfaces and fusing them together with the fluids they secreted. The castle folk inside both castellae were bashing huge, pillar-like battering rams against the high walls sealing off the ends of their semicylindrical riptrenches, and cracks in those walls were beginning to appear. Not that it was a sight I'd ever actually seen myself.

Something did stir in me at the sounds of the bustling festival, but I certainly didn't have strength enough to go marching around and around in the loways of the newly conjoined riptrenches, fighting my way through jostling crowds carrying along seeds the size of submuddies.

All castellae traced out sinusoidal paths as they advanced, moving back and forth between the verilucent and nihilucent layers, creating a cycle of day and night for their interiors as they made their leisurely migrations through the vast Mudsea that covered seven tenths of the planet's surface. The time it took to complete one of these migrations we called a "round."

An unmarried castellum grew its seeds over the course of many rounds, all the while increasing the potassium nitrate content of its body. If, in that state, it failed to gain a spouse, it would detonate the potassium nitrate in its riptrenches and blast its seeds out into the sea. Due to the many castellae that sank immediately from the resulting shockwave, this process was known as "suiseeding." Now that ours was married though, there nothing more to fear. The conjoined cities would, for a time, enjoy a season of prosperity.

Provided the castellae didn't contract any serious illnesses or go to war with other castellae, this state of affairs would probably continue for about two hundred rounds. By the time the castellae sank into the Mudsea at the end of their natural life spans, the little castlings they bore would be well on their way to adulthood. There was hardly anyone in the castellae who wasn't resting a figurative hand on his thorax in relief.

The cheering grew louder, grating on my elbows. I folded my three arms, with their thin smatterings of pinhairs, so that my palms covered the acoustic pores in my elbows. The sound of breath entering and leaving from the rows of spiracles in my sides grew considerably louder and more hollow-sounding.

A sharp pain ran through my thorax, causing my antennae to retract into my forehead. Dr. Saromi at the clinic had told me that it was phantom pain, but illusory or not, pain still hurt.

I looked down at my body. It was about four times the length of my head. My sense of my own existence was so attenuated

that even I felt like I was losing my grip on reality. The rounded segments of my body were lined up right in front of me, but I could see almost nothing there except the danglebed.

As a tribesman of the Monmondo clan, my carapace blends into my surroundings no matter where I may be. Most likely, this is because our ancestors were preyed upon for so long.

But for some reason—maybe a psychogenic reaction brought on by that miserable failure of mine back in my birthplace of Castellum Gakugu—I can no longer secrete the decoromas that would normally adorn my body. If I were from an ordinary tribe, this would amount to nothing more than having my bare carapace exposed, but in the case of the Monmondo tribe, this kind of dysfunction makes one's very existence all but imperceptible.

I could hardly even see the crack that was most surely tracing a vivid course from the right side of my thorax to the left side of my body. Following it with my hooknail, I could feel the ridge where viscous sealant that had been squeezed from the gap had hardened. For the twenty arcs it had taken for the crack to close, I had been cooped up in this grotto like an embryo waiting to hatch.

I reached out an upper arm and grabbed several leafsheets that were stacked haphazardly on the tabletop. I always prepared my reports using excerpts from these logs and had given Dr. Saromi instructions to deliver the whole bundle to my mother in Castellum Gakugu if anything should happen to me.

I lowered my antennae to the leaves and began tracing them over the rows and rows of scentences...

It had all started with an inquiry from the Ministry of Welfare Contemplation, over at the Seat of Learning. The usual procedure was to reply through my manager at the dodgejob agency, but partly because I'd been fed up with his way of doing things, I accepted the request directly. The job was to investigate some secret documents that had changed hands twelve rounds ago between Maidun Reproducing Pharmaceuticals—operated by the Zafutsubo tribe—and the Ministry of Legal Contemplation, which was another part of the Seat of Learning. Maidun Reproducing Pharmaceuticals? That was an emerging company that had been making a killing recently with a painkiller called "namas-machina."

At the time, I was still living halfway up Nazumo Clifftown, over on the outer loop of Mebohla Riptrench. This was up against the outer shell, so when the ocean currents were violent, it could get pretty noisy there, making it impossible to get any sleep.

I left my room before we went into night. The succulent plants that grew throughout Mebohla Riptrench were still glowing brightly, but the castellum was picking up speed as it began sinking into the lower depths of the verilucent layer. I felt the disorienting sensation that came with the plunge as I made my way across a hanging bridge, and then I was entering a boreway gouged into the facing cliff of Gukutsu Clifftown. Passing through the thick cliff wall, I continued on toward the other side, in the direction of the castellum's spinal girder.

The castellum was composed mostly of layers upon layers of shellite. The structure was formed by fluids that a mass of organs—supported by the thick spinal girder running vertically from the castellum's base to its crown—secreted as it grew to adulthood. The concentric rings of the castellum's two deep riptrenches had been formed by imbalances in the stress field caused by the castellum's growth. The circular curves of both riptrenches were interrupted where they intersected with the castellum's back, forming dead ends on either side. The four vertical cliffsides within these riptrenches had been transformed into clifftowns by the castle folk's tireless excavations.

As I continued on through the boreway, I was entering Marov Clifftown, on the side of the cliff's inner circumference. A swarm of fist-sized wingbugs that had gathered by the entrance took flight at my approach, and then the wide, vertical space that was Suifu'ushi Riptrench opened up before my eyes.

A diffuse mist of pollen was drifting through the open air, beyond which was my destination: the vast expanse of Bohni Clifftown on the other side. The face of that cliff, curving sharply so as to loop around the castellum's central region, was covered in a variety of succulent plants whose leaves gave off a faint glow as they squirmed sluggishly about. Their rootleaves grew in thick bunches on the upper reaches of the castellum's outer shell. There the translucent fibers in their stalks absorbed light from the Rimblaze, sent it in through the castellum's shellite wall, and caused the plants inside to glow.

Windows and ventilation holes gouged into the cliffs peeked out from among the leafy shadows. Nectarvectors could be seen here and there. Wearing catchpouches slung before and behind, they stood on the thick, fleshy leaves, using them as scaffolds as their long proboscises drew nectar from flowers the size of their heads, as well as from the nectar glands in the leaf stalks.

I passed between two pillars jutting upward from the foot of a suspension bridge, stepped out onto the planks (a great many of which were missing), and began crossing over Suifu'ushi Riptrench. Numerous suspension bridges were strung at random intervals between the vertiginous arcs of the two facing clifftowns. Starting far off in the distance, I saw the bridges begin to sway, and then a mist of pollen came dancing downward. My row of stepping planks sagged, and I held on tightly to a rope that served as a handrail. Over on the face of the clifftown, the nectarvectors were hiding themselves behind leaves. A warm, clammy, powerful wind was beginning to blow through Suifu'ushi Riptrench. The castellae were exchanging gases.

I waited for the wind to die down, made my way to the other side of the suspension bridge, and headed into one of Bohni Riptrench's ripways. It made use of a natural crack in the shellite; the ceiling overhead narrowed to a sharp edge. I followed the path until I reached its inner wall, then entered a vertical pitway that had been dug there. As I started up the ladder, I could feel it vibrating against my fingers and feet. In the backgirder region that lay beyond that wall, there were fully grown organs whose autonomic operations controlled the exchange of gases, the circulation of redslick, and so on. It was said that the largest of them reached a height of five stories.

Many companies had crowded into Bohni Clifftown to take advantage of the natural resources there, including organ heat, redslick pipeline pressure, nutrifluid, and filtrates. I passed such businesses one after another during my vertical climb. When I reached the top level, I ducked into a boreway, then emerged onto a surface-facing gougeway. Gougeways were long roads shaved horizontally into the surface of a cliff. One side faced open air, so if I were to lose my footing, it would mean a headlong plunge all the way down to the riptrench's deep loway.

Looking upward, I could see a gently rounded canopy bearing down from about two stories overhead. In its surface was a sparse arrangement of large holes used for gas exchange; from the edges of each hung strands of algaelike moss.

The leaflight grew weaker as I was walking. On the dim wall of the gougeway, a line of figures carved in relief was coming into view. Each had a wide head and a figure that did not narrow at all at the waist and was posed for prayer with both hands raised asymmetrically. These were the twenty-eight saints of the Zafutsubo tribe. After walking past each of these ferocious-looking saints, there appeared an open, rectangular entrance. Here was the uppermost floor of Maidun Reproducing Pharmaceuticals, which crowned a drilding that sunk to a depth of five stories underfoot.

As I was meticulously brushing off the pollen and spores that were stuck all over me, the world was falling into utter darkness all around. The castellum had reached the nihilucent layer, where the light of the Rimblaze did not reach. Even as it became impossible to see, however, the fragrances of the various types of plants growing throughout the riptrench grew exceedingly distinct to my senses, completely changing the world's appearance from what it had been in the daytime.

Dimly glowing workers emerged one after another from the hardshell-tile entryway. In addition to their company scent, they reeked of exhaustion. Once their presence had faded, I stepped inside. Walking across the mossed floor, I quietly made my way downstairs and in short order found myself standing in front of the room that was my destination. I placed an elbow against the door and was just getting a handle on the state of things inside when the door suddenly began to swing open, and I drew back in alarm. Out came a senior executive of the Zafutsubo tribe, his body swathed in the gaudy aroma of his position. In the instant before he shut the door, I slipped inside.

Inside the recessed chamber, one person still remained on night duty, just as my information had indicated. She was doing clerical work, and her posture made it look almost as though she were biting into her desk. She had that barrel-like build peculiar to the Zafutsubo tribe, and even sitting down, she was taller than me. Her hard, rust-colored carapace was covered in leaf-vein patterns secreted from the decoroma glands in her joints and, due to a trashy balm she'd applied on top of that, was overscented for her position.

As for me, I had taken a bugbath beforehand and gotten all the balm I used in place of decoroma licked off of me. Except to the Banon tribe—whose sonivision could hear outside my audible range—and to those old ladies sometimes seen begging at the bottom of this riptrench, I was now undetectable.

I closed my spiracles so as not to be sensed by the flow of air. The dorsal vessel that ran through my body tensed as I passed silently by the side of the night-duty worker. I headed toward the back of the suite, hid myself behind a divider wall, and at last relaxed my spiracles, untensed my body segments, and exhaled slowly.

Bending down in front of a bookshelf by the window, I pulled on a drawer with both of my lower arms. The lockbug lurking in its foreplate made no reaction to my scentless presence, and the drawer slid right out. I pulled out a sheaf of reports and started tracing the scentences with my antennae. I was looking for a certificate issued by the Ministry of Legal Contemplation that had classified namas-machina as gloambugs, as well as the old attachment that had given the basis for that decision. The attachment had been created when namas-machina were first imported as maintenance tools for the reverbigation net and included mostly the details of their intelligence tests: able to speak like people…powers of mimicry, but only acquired as a survival strategy…intelligence level no different from other gloambugs… though trainable—such things were recorded therein, and in the corner of each leaf was the aromaseal of the previous Archlearner of the Ministry of Welfare Contemplation. As I was pulling out these documents, however, I became aware of an oily pressure bearing down over me.

A hulking figure nearly twice my size was standing right beside me.

Six dark red eyeballs were arrayed on an oblong face as wide as my shoulders, but none of them were able to detect my presence. The problem was her branching antennae, moving above my forehead as if tracing my outline. They were red, swollen, and twitching—signs of spawning season. Only during that period did they become especially sensitive to certain heat signatures, which made it easy to find creatures suited to be their eggbeds. And the Zafutsubo tribe's favorite kind of eggbed was none other than the people of my own tribe, the Monmondo. Even worse, the Zafutsubo were an endangered tribe with a lot of political clout, and the Ministry of Legal Contemplation had recognized their right to choose their eggbeds freely.

Chewing noisily on something, the Zafutsubo woman came sidling up to me, and everything that was about to happen was perfectly legal. In the shadows of her two arms, small underarms that had devolved into beaklike projections twisted and turned meaninglessly. The abdomanus hanging down from between her legs bent forward though, and a fat, whitish spawning tube slowly slid out from its tip.

"What's the matter?" she said. "You had to have known things might turn out this way when you decided to come here."

A bitter memory of my estranged wife came back to me.

Monmondo women use people as eggbeds too, but they don't lay anyone but their own husbands.

It had been such a joyful time; being together with my wife, choosing names for our soon-to-be-born children. But then, on the very arc when our relatives had gathered for the spawning ceremony—right before that first pairing that I'd been burning for so passionately for so many rounds—something deep inside of me had snapped. Engulfed by a boundless terror that had come geysering up from inside, I left my wife decked out in her spawning dress and fled from Castellum Gakugu where I had been born and raised. Yet now here I was, about to have fifty or so eggs injected into my thoracic cavity by some strange woman from a completely different tribe.

I crouched low on both my short legs, then sprung off the floor as hard as I could, leaping backward. Better to go flying through a window and fall to my death than be messily eaten by infants who could have come from anywhere.

Windowfilm caught my back, stretched to its breaking point, then snapped away from me as it ruptured. I shot out into open air and plummeted into the shadowed riptrench's deep crevasse.

Tiny wingnubs on either side of my back began vibrating furiously, fanning my terror. I fell for a time that seemed long enough to prepare a gourmet dinner for five—ah, that memory! The time we invited my mother and both my grandmothers to our new house before the spawning ceremony...my wife giving off the charm...turning a blissful smile my way...the ladies at ease, chatting pleasantly...and then just when I was taking my seat and about to dig in, I slammed magnificently into the surface of the loway.

My left under-arm went flying up into the air, and my upper body—except for the shell on my back—was split almost completely in two. The membranes between my body segments ruptured, and my stomach and intestines splattered bright colors all over the road. A puddle of pale, yellowish-green fluid was spilling out of me, getting larger by the moment, and I shuddered at the sight of the many small parasites squirming around in it.

I felt my dorsal vessel contract, twitching, inside my thoracic cavity, as the chambers of my heart made sad, lonely sounds as they struggled to draw in bodily fluids that were no longer there. It was a sound like someone sipping at an empty cup. Yet even that near to death's door, I was thinking: Surely I deserved a little praise for the bundle of vital aromaterials I was still clutching in three of my hooknails.

There was little pedestrian traffic at that time of night. As foam oozed out of my mouth, as I trembled with chills like I'd never experienced before, as I was praying, "Just let me die quickly," a shabby white thing came crawling out of a tiny crack in Bohni Clifftown.

It looked like a tangle of long, spindly stalks stretching out from beneath a misshapen bowl. At first, I thought it was a gloambug, but as it drew nearer I could see that it had the stature of a person. Her entire body was covered in cottony white mold, with suspicious-looking mushrooms growing sparsely here and there. Though she stood on two legs, her three pairs of arms were touching the ground on account of a head and thorax that were bent extremely far forward. She was an elderly beggar, one to whom I sometimes gave spare food.

I couldn't quite tell what tribe she was from, though hers was a type often seen among the beggars. Regardless of whether I was wearing balm or not, the resigned gaze of this old woman never failed to follow me when I passed through this quarter of the loway. Unable to do anything else about her, I had started giving her alms as a sort of hush money. Each time I did so, the woman would get this look on her face as if she had seen a ghost and bend her long antennae backward.

The old woman's abdomanus was like a tacked-on accessory; it swung to and fro as she gathered up my spilled viscera in six delicate, hypha-infiltrated hands and placed them back inside the container that was my split thorax. I raised a moan in protest when she started putting the parasites back in too.

"Even these, play important roles," she admonished. "Throw 'em away, and you're a dead man." She spoke in a halting tone, as if it had been years since the last time she had opened her mouth. It was a weak, scratchy voice, but she sounded younger than she looked. I shut my mouth, not so much because I was persuaded as because I lacked even the strength to cry out again.

The old woman got my thorax back together again, and as she was nimbly weaving a temporary binding from stems of *raho* grass she plucked from the cliff, she told me, "I worked as a nurse in Castellum Giri until the time I was twelve. I'm used to treating wounded soldiers."

Castellum Giri...wasn't that the one that had sunk to the sea bottom after getting into a big three-way fight with Castellae Raondo and Sosoga? Had that been when she had migrated here? But even if that were the case, why hide herself in a place like this? With questions such as these swirling though my mind, I slipped out of consciousness.

When I next awakened, I was lying in a soft danglebed in a narrow white chamber.

My body was back to normal, and I didn't feel any pain. Had it all been a dream? I was starting to think so when I tried to sit up and realized that my lower left arm was missing. Fearfully, I touched the thoracic plate that I remembered having cracked. A long, diagonal ridge of half-dried sealant ran across it.

So this was a clinic of some sort. And there wasn't a clinic anywhere that wasn't tied up with Maidun Reproducing Pharmaceuticals somehow. Seized by a chill of fear, I looked around for some means of escape and noticed a window in the wall behind me. Timidly, I descended from the danglebed and walked over to the wall. I reached up to touch the window, but the instant I stretched my body upward, a sharp pain hit me—it was like a spring had just snapped inside my thorax—and I collapsed to the floor then and there.

With the sound of the door opening, I heard a familiar voice call out.

"Well now, what's this? Trying to skip out before the bill's settled? I just had to sew up your arthrostitial membrane, patch your carapace back together, and transfuse just about all of the fluids you now have. Do you have any idea how much trouble that was?"

It was Saromi Urume, the head of Saromi Clinic.

For quite some time now, I'd been investigating the finances of certain patients for him, as well as collecting unpaid debts. As such, I knew his dark secrets. Here, at least, I wouldn't be handed over to Maidun Reproducing Pharmaceuticals.

Had that beggar known that I worked for this clinic regularly?

Dr. Saromi narrowed the space between his two antennae. "And even after all that," he continued, "you're still very much alive. You shouldn't be."

2

I found myself lying in the small grotto's danglebed and for a moment was bewildered. Here my written record had broken off. Scentences had tremendous power to bring scenes back to life, and getting lost in their fragrances was an easy thing to do.

Scentences were written with secretions that came from the anuses of blotterbugs. When you gripped one of their elastic, spindle-shaped bodies, the neurofungi living inside would react, stimulating the creature's glands. When using such an instrument, concentration was a must; otherwise, you'd end up rattling on and on about things that were self-evident or slip off into a kind of automatic writing that would just be all over the place. With the pain as bad as it was, it didn't look like I was going to be able to use one this arc.

It was ten arcs after I was hospitalized that Tagadzuto, my manager, came to visit me. I explained to him that I had slipped on the gougeway, but he wasn't one to be fooled by a weak excuse like that.

I had taken this job without going through his dodgejob agency, and Maidun Reproducing Pharmaceuticals—one of its regular clients—was about to have its reputation dragged through the mud as a result.

Thanks to the aromaterials I had by this time handed over to the Ministry of Welfare Contemplation, ambiguities in the evidence that had led to the namas-machina's classification as gloambugs had been brought up for discussion in the Seat of Learning's Assembly, with open hearings being held. Not that this had overturned the status quo, of course.

Tagadzuto was not about to show his hand. As usual, the smile on his one-eyed face never faltered as he said, "You should be up and about before long, Radoh Monmondo." When addressing a member of another tribe, it was only good manners to attach the tribe name to the given name, yet when Tagadzuto said it, it somehow sounded like a slur. "I've got a request from the Zafutsubo. They want us to find out who that thief was who slipped into Maidun Reproducing Pharmaceuticals. Dead or alive, it's all the same to them."

The dodgejob fee from the Ministry of Welfare Contemplation had all gone to Dr. Saromi in the form of charges for surgery and hospitalization fees, and as if that weren't enough, I'd even ended up saddled with debt, thanks to a rather ironic prescription for namas-machina. On top of that, the Zafutsubo—a tribe with whom any face-to-face meeting meant taking my life in my hands—now had it in for me personally. That was why I was living hidden like this now, in a labyrinth of forkways too narrow for their large bodies to pass through.

It was high time to get out of this business already. This dodgejobbing work—shameful, dangerous, the job description changing with every request—just wasn't the kind of work someone could do for very long.

Originally, a "dodgejobber" had been the name of an invisible beast from a well-known legend, and when we Monmondo first migrated here, it had soon become our nickname. The Monmondo, fleeting and indistinct in form, had been prized as workers in both homes and businesses at first, but then, as more and more of us had started cauterizing our decoroma glands and taking on illegal, dirty types of work, "dodgejobber" had turned into a slur. Later, the artificial removal of secretion glands—an act that invited disorder within the castellum—had been outlawed, and many of us had migrated to other castellae amid a rising anti-Monmondo sentiment.

Then, in an age when these things had been all but forgotten, Tagadzuto's father had founded the Dodgejob Agency—an all-purpose contract business. The word "dodgejob" had of course been used to suggest the kind of dirty work the Monmondo had done in the past. Naturally, the tribal affiliations of hired dodgejobbers no longer mattered, but even so, it was only natural that I was welcomed warmly, being a Monmondo tribesman with the bonus of dysfunctional secretion glands.

Another wave of pain hit me, but it only made me feel less like moving.

"If all you do is sleep all arc, you'll end up ugly as a grimebug." I remember my mother used to scold me like that all the time. Grimebugs were very common, sweet-tasting gloambugs we ate as candy, but to my childhood self, their hideous, wrinkly forms were like hand-sculpted fragments of nightmare.

One time, I found a dead grimebug lying in the corner of the oven in our house. Maybe someone had tossed it in to get rid of it. Even after the passage of several arcs, though, it had still been lying there, neither burnt nor decayed. As time went by, I stopped thinking about it. A few more rounds went by, and then one night when I was sound asleep, I was awakened by a strange sensation on my stomach. Still half asleep, I batted something away with my hand. I seemed to remember hearing the dry sound of something crawling across the floor.

The next morning when I went to clean the oven, the grimebug wasn't there. My mother laughed when I told her about it and said there had never been any such thing there to begin with.

These things are all golden in my memory now. It's been a lot of rounds since I last saw my mother, and having defied the natural law of the Monmondo tribe, it's unlikely I'll ever be able to return to Castellum Gakugu.

I sat up slowly and lowered my feet to the floor. Moving even a little made my joints go stiff with fear. It felt like my whole body had turned into fragile, wafer-thin porcelain.

I stood and nearly hit my head on the glowjar-encrusted ceiling. A mortar and pestle I took from the boreshelf in the wall, then set them down on a small round table. Next, I bent over carefully and pulled up a floorboard near my feet.

Inside was a cage containing a mass of jostling, flat-bodied namas-machina, who all raised up their cephalothoraces in unison. When I undid the latch and opened the barred lid, their eight threadlike legs undulated like cracking whips as they scrambled for escape. Knocking them back down with my one lower hand, I grabbed hold of a particularly vigorous individual, pulled it out, shut the barred lid, and replaced the floorboard. The creature's pale yellow carapace was soft and damp. Its dark organs could be seen through it dimly.

"Stop this right now," the namas-machina said in a voice incongruously deep for its small body. "It's still not too late to turn back. You've not yet committed an unpardonable—"

It continued speaking, all eight limbs wriggling in protest, as I jammed it down on the spike that rose up from the bottom of the mortar. Its face twisted into an idiotic-looking grimace, and it let out a rather forced-sounding groan—*Gweh!* Using the pestle, I crushed its ovoid body in the space of a breath, then started grinding it up, carapace and all.

Only male namas-machina bugs were prescribed as medicine. They were capable of speech, true, but like it said in the textbooks, they were merely miming sounds; it wasn't as if they understood anything they were saying. The pale yellow ichor, the dark thin organs, and the finely crushed shell all mixed together like gravel, and when it reached the perfect sticky consistency, I tossed in the yellow flesh of a peeled headpeach. As the medicine reacted with the fruit juice, it began to take on a reddish tint. I sheared off bits of a dried dewliver root and sprinkled the shavings over the top.

Leaning in close to the bowl, I tore into it with my maxillary and labial palpi, making slurping noises as I sucked in its contents. With the gustatory hairs on my tongue, I savored a perfect blend of bitterness and acidity and enjoyed the texture of crushed carapace shards against my gastric teeth.

A numbness that was like a chill spread out through my whole body, and the pain grew indistinct. The tips of my toes curled backward, and it felt like everything inside my body had turned into smoke and was dispersing. You don't get that effect unless it's just been crushed. I expanded to fill the entire grotto and was drifting around and around in eddying circles, but then there came a rude, rattling noise that brought me back to reality—that sucked me back into myself.

I was standing frozen in front of the round table. Both my hands were still on the mortar. The reverbigator shell, standing out like a knot protruding from the wall to the left of the doorway, was vibrating. Reverbigator shells were made from the shells of bivalves called magnanimussels.

Unconsciously, my mandibles started to chatter. I walked over and opened the spiky, hemispherical lidshell.

As expected, a sticky, ash-white blob was welling out from a circular frame in the wall behind the lidshell and was beginning to form itself into a head—the mantislike shape peculiar to the Urume tribe. The reverbigator's jewel-bits were pressing hard enough against its mouth to cause indentations, and the face was making low moaning noises. For a tribe numerous enough to account for sixty percent of the castellum's population, the Urume varied little in appearance; it was difficult for people from other tribes to tell them apart. This face, however, had only one eye, so I knew right away that it was Tagadzuto. Judging by the look of that moist, slightly swollen eye, he'd been sucking a great deal of nectahol.

Tagadzuto's grass-colored face, looking at me through a reverbigation shell in some distant bar somewhere, had been recreated in front of me, its image transmitted across the net of neurofungi infiltrating every corner of the castellum.

By nature, neurofungus is predatory; it can sense whatever its prey was searching for and take on that shape to lure it in. Jewel-bits packed with namas were used in reverbigator shells to keep the stuff from crawling out when not in use—although caution was still necessary when handling it.

I pulled down the lever attached to the circular frame, releasing the jewel-bits, then took one step backward.

Released from the bindings, Tagadzuto's mandibles began to open and close stickily.

"Well, well! It's certainly a blessed arc, isn't it?" The reproduction of his vocal cords was only middling quality; he sounded a bit different from the real thing. "So you're pretty much recovered? I heard the news from Dr. Saromi. You never think to count your blessings until you're laid up in bed and can't move, eh?" Hollow words of appreciation for my work volatilized into the air. "Any progress on that request from the Zafutsubo tribe?"

"Nothing yet."

"Well, there's no hurry on that. Actually—"

He had called me right in the middle of the Circlingseed Festival. This had to be something major. Even so, I let fly with the words I had prepared.

"Actually, I think I'm gonna give up dodgejobbing."

"What's that? Can't hear you with all the cheering outside. I hate to do this to you in the middle of the Circlingseed Festival, but I need you to head over to the Seat of Learning right now and meet with Archlearner Meimeiru at the Ministry of Archaeological Contemplation. He's got a job for you. Come see me afterward."

I'd heard that name somewhere...

"Oh yeah, the one who's been speaking out against Archlearner Maruba's Speciation Hypothesis."

I was stewing inside. Was this retaliation for taking that Welfare Contemplation job without permission?

"That's right. Even I've been throwing in a little cash for Archlearner Meimeiru's research. It's a sad state of affairs, but we can't turn a blind eye to the rot that's been spewing out of the Ministry of Welfare Contemplation...humans originating from bugs and whatnot."

To be honest, the thought of being related to the tiny gloambugs that lived off our feces didn't exactly put me in a good mood either. That said, there were many ambiguously defined tribes among the wide variety of races, and some of them—for reasons of business or politics—were considered gloambugs. Many people would no doubt be inconvenienced if the Speciation Hypothesis were to go mainstream.

"That public hearing at Sohlo Lecture Hall was sure something else, wasn't it? Oh, but you didn't go, did you?" Rather excitedly, Tagadzuto began to tell me all about it. The proxy of Archlearner Maruba had been in attendance from the Ministry of Welfare Contemplation, and brandishing his precious Speciation Hypothesis, he had pompously declared namasmachina to be an anthropoid species and claimed that any and all use of them as food was illegal. It was a rather unrealistic assertion.

"After all, he's saying that lower gloambugs—even the sickos that externally fertilize eggs—are related to humans."

Was Tagadzuto stifling a laugh? His maxillary palpi were quivering as he spoke.

Enraged listeners had objected, naming off obvious differences between humans and gloambugs—the gloambugs having a larval stage, their compound eyes, and so on. To which the Archlearner's proxy had thrown up a smokescreen of terminology unfamiliar to Tagadzuto's elbows—words like "direct development" and "neoteny."

"Now compare that to the magnificent specimens the Ministry of Archaeological Contemplation has brought back from the Hellblaze—"

"So what happened next?" I said.

Tagadzuto let out a groan, as if tormented by a throbbing in his old wound. His mandibles clamped and unclamped repeatedly before he spoke at last. "Archlearner Meimeiru's proxy apparently died while soaking in a bugbath."

So that was the job then—to investigate the proxy's death. There was a sense in which the death of a proxy was no different from the death of an Archlearner himself. A proxy, I'd heard, was someone who completely surrendered his own will in order to fully transform into the one with whom he had contracted. There was madness in that kind of work.

"Isn't that a job for the Ministry of Law Enforcement? In

any case, my mind's already made up: I want out."

"What's that? You'll do it then? Great...this kind of work...erfect for...omeone like you, after all." Tagadzuto's voice seemed to be breaking up. An elaborate stratagem. He was talking like that on purpose.

"Even for me, the circumstances make things a bit hard to swa...of course, the Maruba faction is suspic...at any rate, talk to Archlearner Meimeiru...okay? I'll be in touch."

Tagadzuto's face collapsed, and in its place the face of a woman began to take shape. It was my former wife. In a seductive voice, she began whispering to me, releasing an aphrodisiac fragrance.

I suddenly felt lightheaded, but just as I was about to bury my face in hers, that terror that had seized me just before our spawning ceremony reawakened. Startled, I jumped back from the reverbigator and slammed the lidshell shut.

I had just come within inches of having my head engulfed by that thing; if I hadn't pulled back, not a sliver of carapace would have been left undigested. Neurofungi fed on almost any organism; the only exceptions being those crawling packets of concentrated namas known as the namas-machina. That was why namas-machina were used for inspection and maintenance of the reverbigation network.

I crushed another pair of namas-machina and slurped them down. As my viscera grew warm and I started to feel that sense of exultation again, I grabbed a small bottle of aromatic oil from the boreshelf and jammed it between two plates on my chest. I had no intention of getting mixed up with any Zafutsubo, so I planned on staying scentless on the way to the Seat of Learning.

There was nothing for it. This would be my final dodgejob. Thus resolved, I set out from the grotto.

CHAPTER 2:
THE LAST DODGEJOB

1

Crouching low with my hands on the walls, I walked up the slope of the narrow forkway. From time to time, my cranial plate would scrape against the ceiling.

I emerged into a boreway in Marov Clifftown and walked through the dimness toward the castellum's outer shell. When a faintly glowing aromaseal appeared on the wall, I knew that I had passed into Gukutsu Clifftown. The muffled sounds of distant, joyful cries grew gradually louder, and an exit came into view that opened onto the loway of Mebohla Riptrench. The roar of the crowd was enough to shake my body. Even if I had wanted to go out into the riptrench, the way forward was blocked by a dense, unbroken stream of jubilant revelers, many carrying nectahol bottles in their hands. I backtracked a little ways, took a pitway up to the fifth level, and emerged onto the gougeway. Here there was only a smattering of sightseers, and I was able to look out across the long expanse of Mebohla Riptrench, formed by two high, sheer cliffsides that traced wide arcs around the castellum.

A huge, jumbled multitude was filing past on the loway beneath where I stood. Every tribe imaginable was included, all churning against one another like ingredients of a stew boiling in a pot. Their carapaces were creaking so loudly that I wondered if some might start popping open here and there at any moment.

Most were drunk on nectahol, rubbing their carapaces and clacking their mandibles together playing festival music. They were embracing one another, hitting one another, and heedless of place or propriety, even spawning and defecating. Some were happily jabbing egg tubes into members of other tribes, while others just kept walking in spite of missing arms or heads. The lower-level suspension bridges that stretched out over the crowd were sagging from the weight of the people who had piled out onto them, and many arms and legs were hanging over the sides.

The time was skyrise sharp. The castellum had risen to its highest point in the verilucent layer; it was the time of arc when the Rimblaze was at its brightest. The humid air warmed, and my antennae contracted a little, sensing a miserable stuffiness on the way. Even the fragrance of grass and flowers that was usually so thick on the air had for this one arc been pushed aside by the brilliant, cloying crush of people.

The clifftowns towering above either side of this great multitude were completely overgrown with fungi and succulents the size of men, with leaves that came in every shape imaginable. There were radial tubes that moved around slightly; stretching, contracting multilayered whorls; belts that undulated like waves... They all shone with powerful lights that set the spores and the particles of pollen sparkling as they danced through the air. The nectarvectors were nowhere to be seen, and even the windows that could be seen among gaps in the leaflight were dark, with no sign of life.

Gukutsu Clifftown curved around the riptrench's inner circumference, arcing rightward toward its terminus, where the

Seat of Learning was located. My present course would take me there.

I walked along the gougeway, whose porous surface bore traces of its carving. When the light hit its curved surface just right, it would gleam with a rainbow sheen. Every once in a while, I would catch sight of a worm crawling on the wall.

On the loway at the bottom of the cliff, the people looked like a squirming mass of explosively reproducing gloambugs.

The festival music built to a crescendo, and a cheer rose up, so loud and long that throats went dry as they shouted. As the crowd churned with excitement, the stately form of a huge, reddish-brown seed was gradually coming into view from behind the curvature of Gukutsu Clifftown. The labyrinthine pattern of grooves covering its hard outer shell gave off scattered flashes of light as silverbugs, used for divination, ran back and forth through them. At the festival's finale, just before the seed was plunged into the fertilization pool on the castellum's lowest level, the trails of mucus left by their bellylegs would be decoded, and that would become the name of the baby castling.

Riding a wave of many bearers, the seed tilted dangerously to one side like a mudfish without its statolith. It wobbled unexpectedly to the left and the right, then rode up against the cliff face, crushing vegetation as it proceeded forward, and with the sight of it distracting me, I was late to realize what was heading my way. The timing couldn't have been worse if I'd planned it. My spiracles squeezed shut.

From the direction opposite, a trio of rust-red, barrel-shaped figures with huge, imposing bodies—a trio of Zafutsubo—came striding toward me, swinging their shoulders left and right.

It's all right, I told myself. *It's not like every Zafutsubo is in her spawning period.*

I walked forward without hesitation. The Zafutsubo drew

nearer. I kept walking. The distance closed between us. I moved out of their way toward the riptrench-facing edge of the gougeway and turned my body sideways. The first passed by in front of me…the second passed by as well…and the third twisted her upper body in my direction and stretched out two thick arms as she came at me. The red, hypertrophied antennae extending from her forehead made a soft hum as they quivered, and the abdomanus between her legs curled forward.

Oh dungheaps! Not again—!

With a glare at that fat, whitish spawning tube sliding up from the tip of her abdomanus, I kicked off the edge of the gougeway and leapt into open air—and in that instant the tiny bottle in my thorax came loose and went spinning through the air, sparkling as it scattered a splash of innumerable tiny drops. A great swell of surprised cries rose up from all around. Splashed with the scented oil, it "looked" like I had just appeared out of thin air right above the crowd. Maybe that was why festival-crazed revelers started leaping one after another from gougeways and suspension bridges all through the rip-trench. As for me, I crashed into the crowd on the loway.

I could hear groans from those I had landed on, as well as a noise like mucus being squeezed out of something.

I was still in one piece though. Other voices rose up in similar torment from here and there, and the crowd's confusion worsened, bringing the festival march to a halt. Pushed back by walls of people, I fled the scene and, after running this way and that in confusion, escaped into a Gukutsu-side ripway and the forkways beyond.

My dorsal vessel was pounding furiously. My whole body throbbed with pain.

Crouching low, I was making my way forward through the forkways when I noticed a grass-green body floating in midair inside a branch that headed off to the right. The trap resembled

a zephyr lily; a lone figure was tangled up in strands of mucus that hung vertically from the ceiling.

This was one of the Meiyuru tribe's licensed traps, and as such its location was publicly disclosed. Yet still for some reason there was no shortage of idiots who kept getting themselves caught in it.

"Help me, help me," he called out in a voice devoid of all strength.

He could see me, thanks to that aromatic oil I'd gotten all over myself. Still, helping him out of that trap would not only be an illegal act on my part, I might well end up getting caught in it myself. Ignoring the pitiful voice, I walked on by.

After advancing some distance, I came to a junction with another forkway, and there the way forward was blocked by a procession of brown figures who were passing by across my way.

The festival's spread all the way down here, I started to think—but then noticed that nearly all of them were Guromura tribesmen. Possessed of wide fans on their tails, many of them worked in waste-mud removal.

From the middle of that line, a totally unexpected voice called out to me: "Hey…that wouldn't be Radoh Monmondo I see over there?"

It was a drinking buddy of mine, the same one who'd found me my current grotto and remodeled it to make it livable. I owed him a lot.

"Well, if it isn't Roto Guromura!"

"You're breathing awfully hard, there…You okay being up and about? And what's with that hideous decoroma? You're scarin' me! You got some kind of contagious mystery disease? I can see right through your bottom half!"

"I just ran into a little trouble."

"As always; it's never anything good if you're mixed up in it."

"Well what are *you* doing down here? Shoveling mud even during the festival?"

"Nah, I'm scraping potassium nitrate, actually. That's what's keeping us busy lately. Can't hardly catch a break."

"Whatever for? What with the marriage, potassium nitrate production should be suppressed; there's no more chance of a suiseeding. Or are you prepping for some war you think's on the way?"

"I don't really know why, but down in the bottom-level powdercaves, the potassium nitrate volume keeps going up; no matter how much we shovel, it doesn't go down."

Were boreback snakefish and backside marshgrippers breeding explosively out in the Mudsea? Countless combtongues grew amid the rootleaves and cnidarians covering the castellum's outer shell, catching mudborne creatures for nourishment. Those two species of mudfish contained substances essential to the production of potassium nitrate.

The workers in the line whom Roto was blocking were starting to complain.

"All right, all right—well, see you later, Radoh Monmondo. Don't hit the namas too hard."

The Guromura workers raised their tail-fans and disappeared one after another into the tunnel to the right. The line went on and on. I should've gotten them to let me through while they were stopped. From far off in the distance, I could still hear that whisper: *Help me…help me…*

That unpleasant sense of weightlessness we felt whenever the castellum changed directions was coming over me. It was the beginning of postrise.

Once again, I took a pitway up to the fifth floor of Gukutsu

Clifftown and began walking down the gougeway toward its right-hard terminus.

Up ahead, the vertical, slightly convex wall blocking off the end of Mebohla Riptrench was…making me wonder what in the world had happened to it. From the middle levels down to the loway, the wall had collapsed, and an open space beyond could be seen peeking through the hole that had opened there.

Oh, that's right! We've married Castellum Saruga; the out-ermost riptrenches of both are joined now. I could've sworn we'd taken cannon fire from the look of things.

The clifftowns' points of connection hadn't matched up well at all.

Must be a difference in size or a mistake in positioning, I thought.

The Seat of Learning's drilding was a single, seven-level structure. Vegetation had been cleared from its surface, leaving its stone face exposed. I passed through the opening of a tall ripway lined with dustboxes and stood before the drilding's vaulted gate.

With sudden concern for the state of my dress, I rubbed at my upper body, trying to spread out the drops of aromatic oil that were sprinkled over my carapace.

When I was ready, I stepped beneath the vaulted gate, glanced at a pair of golden statues protruding halfway out of the walls on either side, and faced the heavy, imposing door. I pushed against it, but it wouldn't so much as budge, and there wasn't any knob or latch for me to pull on either. As I stood there wondering what I was supposed to do now, the four long arms of the golden statue to my right began to move, and then the whole thing came loose and stepped out of the wall. Frightened, I whirled about, only to find a second statue standing there. Miguraso tribe gatekeepers.

From my mandibles, I gave off my identification scent, stated my business, and then the gatekeeper to my left grabbed me and wrapped his long arms around my thorax. The other took a sharp-edged scraper in his hand and, paying no mind to my panicked bewilderment, started scraping at my back and sides.

Scattered fragments of what looked like broken shells started falling to the ground around my feet, followed by a white, fan-shaped thing that plopped to the ground like a piece of dung.

I had *been feeling awfully stiff,* I was thinking as it hit me that the glowjars in my grotto must have been breeding while I was bedridden. Many kinds of life-forms were being studied inside the Seat of Learning, so there were restrictions on bringing in things that could reproduce. Once the gatekeepers had curtly explained this, they let go of me, slid their sharp fingertips into cracks beneath the heavy, imposing door and, with a single heave, lifted it up for me.

It was my first time to set foot inside the Seat of Learning. The corridor had a high ceiling painted with diatomaceous earth, and the floor was carpeted with white leaf-fat. Gelded fluoroflesh flies were stuck to the walls at ten-pace intervals, illuminating the corridor with their orange light all the way to the back.

Threading her way through a sparse smattering of passing students, a black figure came sliding toward me. She was a slender woman of about five heads' height, and between her four smoothly moving legs was a bulging abdomanus that dangled all the way down to the floor. A Meiyuru tribeswoman. Yellow ivy patterns of decoroma rose up here and there from her black carapace, over which a fresh-smelling aromatic had been modestly applied.

The woman came up in front of me and silently stopped.

She had a narrow face, and her ruby eyes bulged out in a way that made me think of fish eggs. A long proboscis stretched from her mouth down to her thorax.

"You're the replacement, correct?" Heaving that long ab-domanus between her legs, she spoke to me with sounds caused by the friction of body joints.

"Replacement? I was told to come here by Tagadzuto at the Dodgejob Agency. I'm a dodgejobber—"

"Yes. Radoh Monmondo, correct?" In her tremulous voice, it sounded like she had said "Raroh." "I'm Liaison Officer Noi Meiyuru. There's no need to be so guarded."

It wasn't until she said that that I realized I'd been uncon-sciously putting space between us. The reason was clear enough: I'd seen that Meiyuru trap in the forkway on the way here.

"Archlearner Meimeiru is currently meeting with an inves-tigator from the Seat of Defense; there's a hearing at the Min-istry of Law Enforcement there. So first, let me show you to the postmortem room at the Ministry of Clinics, where his late proxy is. This way, please."

Following along behind Noi Meiyuru, I walked down the lonely corridor.

We had just reached the postmortem room's relief-carved door when I was shocked to hear a voice from the other side of its glossy shellite surface saying, "—just a stage prop, though, right? Nothing more to this guy than aromatics."

We entered the room. A Hagu tribesman covered in long white hair was standing with a grass-green Urume tribesman next to an examination table in the back of the room. A Mon-mondo tribesman, garbed in aromatics, was lying facedown on a fringed examination table with wheeled legs. Using his hairy hands, the Hagu tribesman stripped a body segment's worth of carapace off his back. A shriveled dorsal vessel appeared un-derneath.

Instantly, the Urume drew in his antennae.

"Ugh! What a stench! This guy reeks of namas-machina!" Brushing his antennae toward the back of his head with one upper hand, he added, "And right in the middle of the Cir-clingseed Festival too. Well, Coroner Sabo? Let's hear it."

"The scarring on the carapace resembles burn marks, but that has nothing to do with the cause of death. It could be he got burned by the Rimblaze on the continent."

Burned by the Rimblaze? Surely he didn't mean Archlearner Meimeiru's proxy had been to the Hellblaze!

The coroner applied a crowbar to the joint of his cranial shellplate and, with a strong push, jammed it underneath and pried up the carapace. The Urume tribesman's upper body bent backward as he backed away.

Dozens of gloambugs were squirming around inside his cranial shellplate.

"His brain's been completely consumed," the Hagu coro-ner said. "People with loose body segments should know better than to get in a bugbath of all things!"

"It happens though," said the Urume. "Every round, there'll be one or two who end up like thi— Hm?" The Urume turned around toward us. "And who are you supposed to be?" Judging by his pompous stance, he was most likely an investigator from the Ministry of Law Enforcement.

"Archlearner Meimeiru asked him to come investigate the death," Noi Meiyuru answered in my place.

"Another paper stage prop? And what's with that awful decoro— No, wait; I know that freaky-looking face of yours... You've been thrown in my detention center how many times? I get it, you're on a dodgejob for Tagadzuto's agency. What's a crook like you up to around here?"

In spite of what he was saying about me, I didn't get angry at all. The dodgejobs that came my way usually *were* illegal in-vestigations; they just tended to get overlooked thanks to an understanding we had with the Ministry of Law Enforcement.

"So you're planning to investigate this case independently

of us? You are, aren't you? Why is that?"

But since I didn't yet know the details of the job myself, there was no way for me to answer.

"I don't know what to do with this paranoid bunch at the Seat of Learning. Do what you've gotta do, but there's nothing suspicious about this case. It's a cut-and-dried gloambug seepage. Now hurry up and get out of here."

After we were run out of the postmortem room, we went up to the second floor, where the Ministry of Archaeological Contemplation was located, and headed toward the bathroom where the proxy had died.

"Pretty fancy place, having baths in here," I murmured as we walked.

"It's because we can't have samples and excavated artifacts getting contaminated. Our laboratories are even equipped with bugstreams for sanitation. Of course, the gloambugs used are all sterile, so there isn't any breeding."

The bathroom was a small chamber inlaid with hardshell tiles that gleamed a pearly white. Most of the floor was taken up by the long, narrow bathtub. In the tub, there was not a single gloambug to be seen. It had probably been drained after the investigation was completed. Noi explained that the used bugs were collected in gloambug disposal bins located in the ripway, where they were picked up by bugsweeps who in turn sold them to repro-pharma employees for use as fodder.

"Seen enough? Next, I've been asked to show you to the autopsy room."

"So the body we just saw was the Archlearner's proxy, right?" It's good manners to look at someone's face when you talk to them, but my eyes had somehow drifted down to her abdomanus. "Why the autopsy room? How is that different from the postmortem room?"

"The equipment's the same, but the affiliation is different. Follow me, and you'll understand soon enough."

We left the bathroom, and the autopsy room was the very next room over.

Noi Meiyuru opened a door inlaid with a round viewing portal and showed me in. The room inside was extremely dry, and there was a faintly sweet odor on the air. Noi told me that the smell had started several arcs ago, but the cause was still unknown. In terms of decor, there was no great difference between this and the postmortem room we had just visited, although this one was a little more spacious: a windowless cube with reverbigator shell, boreshelves for instruments, and numerous autopsy tables. The arrangement of the tables was rather odd though. They were pushed up flush with one another in four columns and two rows. Like a dim shadow, there was a faint black stain in the middle of this composite surface, and ochre-hued fragments of something were scattered around it here and there.

"It must've been one huge giant who slept here," I said, cracking a joke without forethought.

"That's correct," said Noi. "Twice as tall as a Zafutsubo." Could the Meiyuru tribe crack jokes too? I found that surprising, but there was no change in Noi Meiyuru's body odor. "You'll get a detailed explanation from the Archlearner later. Up until yesterarc the mummified remains of an unknown life-form were lying on these tables—one dug up from a barrow on the continent." Noi tapped her fingers on one of the autopsy tables. The sound they made was cold.

"An unknown life-form?" This had taken a turn for the weird. "It didn't just disappear all of a sudden, did it?"

Without so much as a twitch of her antennae, Noi stared

at me with her red eyeballs. While it wasn't exactly the job Tagadzuto had promised, finding that thing was apparently the reason I had been summoned here. This was the Seat of Learning though. With the brains they had here, they should have been able to think up any number of reasons why this had happened. There was something about all this I was finding a little hard to swallow.

"Naturally, the lockbug showed no signs of tampering."

"You think maybe the reverbigator broke, and it got eaten up by neurofungi?" I picked up one of the shards lying on the autopsy tables. "Though it's bad manners to scatter one's meal around like this."

Occasionally, stories of neurofungi eating babies or some-one's head did make their way to my elbows.

"These fragments do confuse the matter, unfortunately. Most likely, they aren't from the mummy. In appearance, it was quite different from we humans."

I picked up a fragment and took a close look at its edge. There was a delicate wave pattern there. Rubbing at it with my hooknail, I said, "Does that shadowy-looking stain over there have nothing to do with this giant either?"

"Like I said, it was excavated in the Hellblaze. It was com-pletely desiccated."

Did that mean these fragments and that stain were traces of someone who'd made a giant disappear?

"Also, it couldn't have been neurofungi. The reverbigator shell had just been inspected and had had parts replaced; it was as good as new. After the corpse disappeared, we checked with the Ministry of Reverbigation just to be sure and confirmed that there had been nothing in particular out of the ordinary."

"Did you get the Banon tribe to—"

"We had them soundsight every nook and cranny in here."

I was just about to ask about security patrols when she

headed me off at the pass. "The security detail confirmed looking through the viewport twice last night and saw the remains inside both times. That gives us a window of about three swings in which it could have happened. All I can think is that we're dealing with some unknown presence."

As I could only think of the most typical questions to ask, it was getting harder and harder to understand why I'd been chosen for this job. The Dodgejob Agency even had a guy who was a former investigator. The face of shrewd Tagadzuto rose up in my mind. What if I had been called here not to investigate, but to *be investigated*? Was I—a dodgejobber with an invisible body—a suspect?

At just that moment, the lidshell started rattling on the wall-mounted reverbigator. Noi walked over to it and opened the lidshell. Viewed from a distance, it looked like a dark hole had opened up in the wall.

"The investigator just left," a hollow-sounding voice said from the hole. "Bring Radoh Monmondo over to me now."

2

On the seventh floor of the Seat of Learning, double doors of black shellite were arrayed up and down the hallway known as Archlearner Row, resembling giant sets of mandibles.

About ten paces ahead of us, one pair of doors swung open. I could hear raised voices from inside, but I couldn't tell whether they were excited, angry, enraged, or panicked.

"Why won't you let us investigate—"

"It's performing its marital duties without defect—"

"True, but the potassium nitrate level really is going up; the castellum's eating nothing but snakefish and marshgrippers.

This must have something to do with a sort of eating disorder, or maybe there's abnormal development of the nerve fibers—"

"If you look at history, nothing like this has ever happened in the fifteen-hundred-round record of our migrations across the eight castellae—"

"Which is precisely why—"

"It's only a temporary issue—"

"Reinvestigate—"

"That won't be necessary—"

"*Archlearner Ryofin!*"

Three men and women were shoved out into the hallway, and the doors closed behind them. There they stood in front of those doors unmoving, with furious expressions on their faces. Archlearner Ryofin...of the Ministry of Castellum Contemplation, if I remembered correctly. He was in charge of running the Circlingseed Festival.

Noi and I walked past them as though we hadn't seen anything and stopped in front of the third door down the hallway.

A vertical slit appeared between black, rounded doors marked with the Ministry of Archaeological Contemplation's aromaseal, and then they swung open, trailing strands of mucus to the left and right. Urged on by Noi, I went inside, swiping away the mucus strings. She remained in the hallway as the doors closed again. It felt kind of like being thrown into a detention cell.

A raw, fishy smell hung thick in the air, and the room was hazy with mist. It was a space of irregular shape and little depth, covered in rippling meatpleats suggesting some sort of coelenterate. Two giant lunming bugs clung to the walls on either side, and both had their oddly elongated, polelike arms raised almost to the ceiling. They were rigid and motionless, as if in death. The wall in front of me was pierced by a large, ugly hole that looked as if it had been gouged there, and beside it, a man was tilting a barrel he held in his four arms, pouring in sticky nectar.

"Archlearner Meimeiru, I presume?" But in spite of my greeting, the man with the barrel didn't reply; he simply shouldered a second barrel and again began pouring nectar into the gaping hole.

"I am Archlearner Meimeiru Shutohroh of the Ministry of Archaeological Contemplation."

I turned around at the sound of a muffled voice behind me, but all I saw there was a reverbigator pointed toward me like a shellfish stuck to a meatpleat.

"This reverbigator shell was created to be my voicebox. It's made so I can speak with the lidshell closed."

The voice could be taken for either male or female.

"Where are you, Archlearner Meimeiru? I've come here to see you, but—"

"You're seeing me already. Because you're inside my cranial plates."

At that, I was gripped by a feeling of extreme unease. He didn't seem to be speaking in metaphor. Were these meatpleats the folds of the Archlearner's brain tissue? I had heard rumors about the Shutohroh tribe but had never dreamed they were this hypertrophic.

"I believe you've heard the short version from my liaison officer already, but I'd like you to know the details as well. This is the truth of the Speciation Hypothesis. This is what will define both the present and future human race."

Maybe the Maidun Reproducing Pharmaceuticals incident, too, had in fact started out as an interdepartmental battle. The idea of humans descending from gloambugs sounded ridiculous to me too, but I couldn't imagine what other creature might be substituted for them.

"Braving extremely harsh conditions, the Ministry of Archaeological Contemplation had already conducted as many as fourteen research expeditions to the continent of Iva, located on the Hellblaze side of the planet. There, evidence was discovered of more than four hundred anthropoid life-forms completely unlike gloambugs."

I looked around, unsure which direction I should face when speaking. In the center of the ceiling was a cluster of several black, hemispherical shapes resembling the round windows seen on submuddies; long fibers that reminded me of plant roots were hanging down from their fringes.

"Sounds like you could draw up a whole new phylogenic tree," I said, giving him a neutral reply as I wondered whether those things might be eyes or antennae. If they were, did that mean he could use them only to peer inside his own head?

"Indeed we could," said Archlearner Meimeiru. "On the other hand, the roots of that tree remained missing. In order to investigate that mystery, we organized a research team made up of seventeen individuals and sent them on what became the fifteenth research expedition. That's when they discovered the mummified body of a heretofore unknown life-form, which has given us a clue toward unraveling the mystery of humanity's origin."

Unbidden, a question came to mind: what were the remains of so many life-forms even doing in the Hellblaze? Hadn't the same hemisphere been exposed to the light of the Rimblaze since the world first formed? Wasn't it established science that living creatures could only survive in the Mudsea?

"I have named this creature 'Pancestor.' That's enough for the introduction; now I will have you see the reality."

"See it? I thought you called me up here because it disappeared from the autopsy room."

But no reply was forthcoming. I saw the man from before leaving the room with his empty barrels, and then the many long legs of those lunming bugs that had been waiting on the walls to my right and left started moving—so swiftly that each was like the afterimage of another—and clamped onto every part of my body, holding me still in a firm grip.

Huh? What? As I cried out in incomprehension, the rippling walls of meatpleat closed in and pressed up hard against me. A lukewarm, foamy liquid began oozing from each point of contact.

No matter how I struggled, it was useless to resist. My body was being pulled into the meatpleats…It was like I was being dissolved, and after I'd lowered the sails of the landship, and sunk its anchor down into the Sandsea, I opened the entryway door and headed outside.

Instantly, my field of view went solid white. The heat and the gale-force winds were unbelievable. No one could stand against it; everyone was crouched down low on the scorched, sandy soil. If I bent my arms at a certain angle, the acoustic pores in my elbows would moan with flutelike sounds. Two of us had been blown away by powerful gusts.

Light shone down from the celestial sphere like a rain of burning needles. We had lived most of our lives in the indirect lighting brought to us by riptrench vegetation, but this was lethally direct rimlight.

Moreover, night did not exist in this hemisphere. Our antennae dried out, and we couldn't focus our visual or olfactory senses. The cooling, protective cloths we wore over our heads were reduced to rags in no time, and our carapaces grew hot as cooking grills, boiling our internal bodily fluids.

Slowly, my eyes adjusted. It was an empty world, without a single plant growing anywhere, and so vast that I could get no sense of distances. Still, there was no mistaking it: these were the same coordinates at which the previous survey team had made visual confirmation of a bizarre corpse but had been forced by a sandstorm to give up on investigating it.

Something was shimmering off in the distance. It was on a slightly elevated hill. The region that extended from midway up to its peak was dark and clearly made of a material different from that of the sand. I nodded to the team, and they nodded back. At long last, we had found the corpse.

Battling the wind, we approached the hill, but as we drew near I could feel a sense of disappointment spreading through the survey team. The thing buried in the sand that made up the upper part of the hill was a simple, flattened ovoid shape, composed of arrayed body segments; it looked far too much like a gloambug.

What became clear as we got closer, though, was that it was *big*—so big that a castellum seed could have probably fit inside. Its carapace was singed black, as if it had been grilled over a high temperature flame and had peeled back here and there in a pockmark pattern. We spent half an arc removing a portion of its carapace, and inside we discovered a hollow space encompassed by a complex skeletal structure. It put me in mind of something man-made, like a submuddy.

I took a step inside, passing beneath an array of bones that reminded me of thick ceiling beams. I continued on to the center of the hollow and realized there that this place was a barrow—for sealed within a baglike membrane was a dessicated giant.

It had one pair of arms and one pair of legs. Its smooth, almost featureless body was completely unsegmented and didn't connect at any point to the shriveled, wrinkly membrane that covered it. At first, I took it for some sort of mollusk, but thanks to the ultrasonic soundsight of our Banon team members, we soon learned that internal bones ran throughout its trunk and four limbs. Furthermore, we detected in its head the shadow of a small, artificial object that appeared to be mineral in nature.

We stayed there for a space of ten arcs, investigating the barrow and transporting the giant's mummified body, but three of our number, unable to endure the harsh environment, perished, and most of the rest were weakened. A Meiyuru teammate injected the particularly critical cases with a venom that induced a state of suspended animation. We launched the catamaran-style landship that was awaiting our return, transferred to a submuddy at the survey base on the coast, and then, rocked by the waves of the Mudsea, I found myself suspended within the cerebral plate of the Archlearner.

I was lowered to the floor by the long arms of the lunming bugs. The back of my head was pounding fit to burst.

"Even now, many members of that team are in the hospital undergoing resurrection treatment. My personal proxy synchronized with me once before being hospitalized. He had a smooth recovery and returned to work, but then, as you know, he died in a bugbath just before Pancestor's autopsy was to begin. And shortly thereafter, Pancestor himself disappeared."

I exited the Seat of Learning, holding my pounding head with my upper-left hand, and turned into a ripway that formed one side of it. The ripway rose to about three stories' height, narrowing gradually toward the top.

A row of dustboxes was lined up along that wall. I continued on into the ripway, wondering if there might be a clue there among them. The Archlearner's bodily fluid had turned white as it dried, and now it was flaking off me like scales with each step I took. The throbbing in my head had only gotten worse. This wasn't the usual pain.

On the ground ahead, scattered bugpuddles came into view. Many of the gloambugs were on their backs, scratching vainly at the air with their many legs. I looked at the dustbox just to the right of them, where an aromaseal read WASTEBUG DISPOSAL.

"Hey! What do you think you're doing?"

Surprised by the sudden shout, I accidentally stepped on a beetle, crushing it underfoot. I turned around to find myself face to face with an exhausted-looking Urume tribesman. The aromaseal on his armband read "Security Patrol."

"I'm here on a dodgejob—"

Then I slipped on the sticky mucus underfoot and, stumbling again, trampled one gloambug after another. The patrol officer said, "Oh dear," in the same tone one might use with a child who'd just pooped.

Red mucus was sticking out of cracks in the crushed bugs' carapaces. I knelt down and wiped some up with my fingertips, moving my fingers together and apart a few times experimentally. It was terribly sticky, and there was a sweet scent to it.

"They've been sucking redslick or something. So, what sort of dodgejob are you on—?"

Gloambugs certainly did like castellum redslick. They had to be exterminated whenever they latched onto a pipeline and started sucking refills. On a prior, unrelated case, however, I had once investigated the layout of the piping in this area and was well aware that no redslick pipelines passed anywhere near this spot. Besides, if it was redslick they were sucking, they wouldn't smell the way they did.

"I'm doing an investigation for the Ministry of Archaeological Contemplation," I said, standing back up.

"Oh, so this is about that vanished giant…"

"Don't tell me that story's gotten out already?"

"No, it's just that the patrol guard on duty last night happened to be me."

"I see. You look pretty worn out."

"I'd finally gone home and had just gotten to sleep when a reverb came from the liaison officer and woke me up. Honestly, that woman…! I told her no one had been in the autopsy room, but she still made me come back in. It was just two arcs ago I got moved to the third floor, and already there's angry big shots putting me under the microscope."

"I've heard that there hadn't been any change in the giant's condition, but if you noticed anything…"

"Do I have to go over all this again? All I did was look in from the doorway, but it was lying there same as always. At any rate, there was nobody in there, and I did check the lockbug like I was supposed to—"

"Hey, I'm not doubting you."

"—been asked again and again if there was anything suspicious at the scene, but how could there be if there was nobody in there to begin with?"

But the Ministry of Archaeological Contemplation was assuming an invisible perpetrator.

"Hey," the patrol guard said in a hushed voice. "I can't ask the higher-ups about this; they'd just get mad and tell me to mind my own business, but…do you know what that thing is?"

"No idea. What do you think it is?"

"Well, rumor has it that thing's an ancestor of ours. It was smooth, and its carapace had a reddish-yellow tint that was just a little bit translucent. When I shone my lantern on it, it had a glossy sheen. Its shape, too, made me think there might be something to those rumors."

"Oh? A glossy carapace…" I scraped my toes against the shellite pavestones, wiping off the yuck. I had my eyes trained on a gloambug whose carapace was split wide open. An image of the gloambugs squirming inside the proxy's cranial shell rose up in my memory. "By the way, do wastebugs from the

Ministry of Archaeological Contemplation's autopsy room and bathroom empty out there?" I pointed a finger at a wastebug disposal bin.

"That's right." The guard turned toward the wastebug disposal bin and opened the lid. Contrary to my expectation, it was empty inside. The bug drainage pipe that opened out of the wall was also clean.

"The bugsweeps came by to get them just a little while ago."

Which meant the bugs on the ground must have spilled out at that time.

"But all that aside, um…" —here a degree of reticence crept into the guard's tone— "…I really think you ought to see a doctor."

3

Thanks to my headache, my feet were starting to go wobbly. This was a symptom I had never had before.

I descended into a pitway with unsteady footsteps and, taking the boreway, passed through Gukutsu Clifftown and Marov Clifftown, emerging on the loway of Suifu'ushi Riptrench. Here, it was unusually deserted. Was it just my imagination, or did everyone I pass on the street have an uncomfortable look on their face? Maybe they all thought I was drunk.

I stepped into the waiting room at Saromi Clinic; with the Circlingseed Festival going on, it was no surprise to find it empty. I opened the door to the treatment room and found the head of the clinic inside, sitting in a chair. He was squeezing a blotterbug as he wrote in his medical log. The scents of antiseptic and fresh bodily fluid were present; someone must have been brought in due to an accident at the festival.

Saying nothing, I seated myself in the chair in front of him. The abdomen of his blotterbug raced across the leafsheet as he spoke.

"Lovely…you again. And here I thought I was finally gonna get a break."

"My headache's really bad this time. Can you take a quick look?"

"I told you; it's phantom pain. You've sure turned into a worrywart." Dr. Saromi finally looked up at me. "You're not taking any namas-machina I didn't prescribe, are you? That drug's so strong they banned it in Castellum Saruga. You'll only make your condition worse."

"That goes without saying," I replied, not averting my eyes. There was a limit to how much of the stuff could be prescribed at one time, so I had to make the rounds of several other clinics and pharmacies. "By the way, about my prior request…?"

"Oh, you mean the one who saved your life? Sorry, I can't hire her. Forget about it."

Dr. Saromi pulled an atomizer bug—notable for being nearly all abdomanus—out of his desk drawer, pointed it at me, and squeezed the abdomanus repeatedly. A bitter-smelling mist sprayed from its tiny mouth, which settled all over my body.

"This carcass of yours is always a pain to examine."

His long antennae felt their way over my carapace as though they were dusting me off. He told me to turn around, and when I obeyed, a laugh rang out like a chisel cutting shellite.

"You've got brain matter hanging out from between the segments in the back of your head. What in the world happened to you?"

Unconsciously, I started reaching back to touch it, but he stopped me.

"The Archlearner of the Ministry of Archaeological Contemplation forced a vicarious experience on me while explaining a job." A bad feeling started to come over me. "You don't think Tagadzuto might've sold me out to be a replacement for that dead proxy, do you?"

"Radoh Monmondo?"

"What?"

"There, you still know who you are. There's no way you've become a proxy."

"Well then, why did he—" Intense pain hit me, as though I'd just been punched in the back of the head. The gap between my cerebral plates was being forcibly widened. Then something was jabbed inside, and I vomited.

"Looks like some foreign brain matter was injected. That's what pushed yours out."

"Why that dirty—!"

"But that tiny little brain of yours never could've handled the experience by itself. Without these cells, turning into a proxy would've been the least of your worries; you could've ended up an empty husk—uh-oh."

"What—?"

"There's one in your brain too. I'm seeing this a lot lately. Most of the patients who come in here complaining of headaches have these weird tumors. Benign though; they're nothing to worry about. An investigation's starting up at the Ministry of Clinics, so we should know what they are before too long."

With the increased weight, my head was unstable and my neck segments wobbled something awful. In order to protect my enlarged brain, the back half of my cranial plate had been removed, and an artificial plate attached in its place.

I entered a forkway through one of the holes that opened

sparsely onto the loway and was doing fine until I couldn't remember how to get back to my grotto. Due to my secretion gland dysfunction, I'd been using aromatic oil as a marker, but now I couldn't smell the difference between that and the scents left by others. *It's this way,* I thought, but found the path I went down blocked by gloambug eggs and chrysalises and ultimately ended up going in circles. My dorsal vessel started beating faster, and my breathing grew rapid with agitation.

It was because this place was such a complicated labyrinth that I'd chosen to live here in the first place. Who could blame me for getting lost?

I kept telling myself that, trying to ease my nerves.

At last I heard a familiar rattling sound. Somewhere, a reverbigator shell was vibrating. I followed the sound and finally came to a tiny, run-down grotto. There was no one inside. The reverbigator shell continued to rattle.

Rather boldly, I approached it and removed the lidshell. Inside was the face of Tagadzuto. After silently reflecting on this for a moment, it occurred to me that this grotto was my own. I pulled down the lever that controlled its jewel-bits.

"You're awfully late getting home, aren't you, Radoh Monmondo?" said Tagadzuto. "What's the matter? You look a bit different somehow."

"Archlearner Meimeiru's request...he wasn't asking for a proxy contract, was he?"

"...ello? What did you..."

He was doing it again. I slammed the lidshell shut.

And right after that was when it happened. A powerful blow to the back of my head. My consciousness took flight.

CHAPTER 3:
THE ANALOGIZING ADDICT

1

My carapace was broiling under intense light, and I was in a delirium. My elbows whistled like flutes as a ferocious wind whipped across their acoustic pores. Gradually, the whistling began to sound more and more like a human voice.

"You, all right? You, all right?"

From the midst of a mold-encrusted cephalothoracic shell, something resembling a face was calling out to my elbows. What was this old lady doing here? What had happened to me?

"I'm sorry. I let myself in. I'm sorry."

A horrible wave of nausea washed over me. My head felt like it was being squeezed in a vise. I had the Archlearner to blame for that. No, wait—that wasn't right. It was right here that I'd been struck from behind. I reached back and touched the spot experimentally. There was a dent in the artificial plate, and the fittings were loose.

"You, you gave me food. Sometimes, you give me food. Remember?"

The room was dimmer than usual. I looked up at the ceiling and saw pale, wrinkly ovoids dangling here and there among the glowjars.

"What're those things..." I said. The insides of my mouth were sticking together.

"I wanted to thank you, but when I came here, another person—not you, came out through the door, strange man. When I, came inside, you were still on the floor, so I..."

"A strange man?" A Zafutsubo tribesman? But there was no way a Zafutsubo could get into such a narrow forkway. "Tell me what he was like. Was he alone?"

"He was alone. A common tribe, Urume, I think, but I don't know."

Someone hired by the Zafutsubo, then? But if that was the case, why hadn't he handed me over to them—?

"There was something funny about how he moved. That can happen when you're sick in the cranial nerves."

That's when I remembered—this old lady used to be a nurse.

"There may be something wrong with me too," I said. "I'm seeing these weird things on the—"

"I'm sorry, so sorry. I laid them for you to eat, but I couldn't cover the ceiling..." As she clung to me with slender, mold-encrusted arms, my back went rigid and my temperature began to drop. Those things were eggs. Their unnatural wrinkles and color were characteristic of geriatric ovulation. "I've been worn down till I'm almost nothing but shellcoins, but, I can still lay eggs, so, just a few every arc, and..."

"You saved my life; that's plenty. Now, please stop that already." I stood up and brushed off the old woman's hands.

"You can eat eggs from another tribe...if both sides agree. Please eat them. You've got to eat. Don't hold back. You must still be in pain. You've got to get better. This is all I can do for you. I'll work hard and keep laying them, so..." The old woman put her arms and legs against the wall and started to climb toward the ceiling.

"I'm telling you, you don't have to lay any more!" Unable to hold back my emotions back, I yelled at her as I dragged her back down. Powdery spores from all over her body danced in the air. "Come on, it's time for you to go. Don't come in here."

"I'm sorry, I'm so sorry. I'm sorry—" She sounded like she was praying as I shoved her out of the room and closed the door. Then I stood there, unable to move. It was like my feet were held in stocks.

At the end of the arc, I still didn't feel up to doing anything. I took my namas-machina, but the headache didn't get any better. After passing a sleepless night, I stumblingly emerged from my grotto.

I made my way through the forkways and emerged into Suifu'ushi Riptrench, where the vegetation that grew thickly on its walls was just beginning to garb itself in leaflight. A still hush hung over everything. Leaf-shaped gloambugs were feasting on trash that had collected in the corners of the loway.

I headed for Saromi Clinic, told Dr. Saromi what had happened, and had him look me over.

"Again?" he groused. "And I'd just attached that plate; look at it now! Judging by how it's bent, I'd say it's been pried open."

A hard sound reverberated inside my cranial plate, by which I understood that the artificial plate had been removed.

"…it just keeps getting stronger and stronger."

"What does?"

I turned around and saw that Dr. Saromi's antennae had withdrawn.

"Can I get you to face forward?"

I did as I was told, and right away the nausea hit me.

"I don't feel so good."

"Of course you don't; I've got my hand stuck up your head—ah, there it is!" At which point a spatula covered in red mucus was thrust before my eyes. It had a faintly sweet smell. "There was a spot on your brain that had been pressed on and spread out; this stuff was stuck to it."

The man that the old woman had witnessed—this had to have been his doing, though I had no idea what he'd hoped to accomplish.

Dr. Saromi's antennae extended upward slowly. "It almost looks like you got de-bugged in there."

"You mean there was a parasite in my brain? Where did it go then?"

"Maybe that man you described was nicer than you thought and assaulted you in order to clean you out." The doctor laughed. "Just kidding; all I'm saying is that that's what it looks like. I don't know of any species of parasite that has secretions this color."

That can happen when you're sick in the cranial nerves, the old woman had said. I remembered that in the past, illnesses caused by brain parasites were sometimes misdiagnosed as diseases of the cranial nerves.

"That man might have been a host as well," I said. "I was told that he had the walk."

"I see. If that's the case, what he did could also be taken as irregular behavior caused by a brain parasite. Though that still doesn't explain the secretions."

I remembered the sensation of gloambugs being crushed underfoot. The broken shards of their carapaces, smeared with red mucus. That sweet aroma.

"The dead proxy was a Monmondo like me. He suffered a seepage in a bugbath and had his brain eaten up. But what if his cranial plate had been pried open by the same man?"

Dr. Saromi didn't answer.

"Red mucus came out of gloambugs that had likely been inside the proxy's brain. There are some types of parasite that move from host to host. You think that maybe that man had tried to parasitize both of us?"

"Don't be ridiculous. Who would use a crude method like that? This is why detective work should be left to professionals."

"A new breed then?"

But why were they only infecting Monmondo? No, wait—the man who assaulted me was Urume. Could different tribes be suited to different stages of their development?

"And why did they fail in parasitizing us?"

"They didn't 'fail' or anything else. These parasites of yours never existed to begin with. We're in the realm of paranoia now— Hey, you *are* taking the correct dosa—"

"Yeah, that might have been a little far-out," I said quickly, realizing that he was about to call me out for overdosing on namas-machina.

"Well, I'll let you know right away if I come across this 'new species' of parasite."

Dr. Saromi wore a displeased smile as I thanked him on my way out. From there, I headed over to the Seat of Learning.

"I can see what you look like quite clearly today," said the gate guard on the left, awfully sociable today as he opened the gate for me.

I asked him where I could find Noi Meiyuru, and he said she was probably in the liaison office just inside. Before I had proceeded even a few steps down the corridor, I spotted a door whose aromaseal said "Liaison Office."

The instant I opened the door, a rich, sweet aroma hit my antennae. In the dimness of the room, I saw two figures that seemed to be blending into one another. Suddenly, the strength went out of my legs, and my knees felt ready to collapse. I grabbed onto the doorframe.

Something hot was beginning to coil around me. My field of view was becoming distorted, and in the middle of it, I realized that one of the two figures was Noi Meiyuru...that she was holding an Urume woman from behind...that her black arms and forelegs were wrapped around the woman's grass-green body...and that a long proboscis was sticking out from the back of the inverted triangle of her head—

Noi Meiyuru pulled her proboscis out and turned her head toward me. The golden aroma she emitted sparkled in the air like a scene straight out of heaven. She was the goddess I had lived my life in yearning to meet—there was no other way to describe her. Starlight dripped from the tip of the goddess's proboscis. It was I who should be showered in that glory. Certainty of that coalesced inside me until I could restrain myself no longer.

I shoved the Urume woman over and sat down in front of my goddess, turning my back toward her. A supple pair of beautiful black legs wrapped around my body, holding me gently, firmly, passionately still. I let out a low moan. I could feel my cranial plate being opened. My back arched suddenly, making my ventral carapace spasm. At last, I felt something hard against the back of my head, nudging its way inside—there was a sound like a flute being played off-key.

Then...it was being...pulled...out...

I heard someone coughing painfully. The legs holding me pulled away, and a strong sense of unease hit me, as if ropes on a suspension bridge were snapping one after another. When I stood up and turned around, two arms violently struck me, shoved me, shoved me again, pushed me out, and then slammed the door shut in my face.

I stood frozen in front of the liaison office, my entire body flushed, feeling like I had just been put on hold. Why had she stopped? And then at some point, my knees began to tremble. The instant I noticed it, I was suddenly gripped by a terror that came welling up from inside. What in the world had just happened? I couldn't believe that had been real. To think that a guy like me—who had fled from a perfectly proper spawning ceremony—would willingly offer himself up as food! Maybe it had been a daydream—a side effect of the painkillers—*something!* Maybe I had only just arrived here. That's what it was! I'd only just gotten here!

I stamped my feet down on the floor to stop the quaking. Then, just as I was raising a hand to knock on the liaison office door, it silently opened in front of me.

With a backhanded motion, Noi Meiyuru shut the door behind herself as she emerged from that room. I backed a few steps away from her, and my pulse started racing.

"Sorry to have kept you waiting," she said softly with her abdomanus. I could read absolutely nothing from her serene expression. Noi's entire body was becoming a dark, indistinct blur. No, that wasn't right; it only seemed that way because my antennae had been retracting unconsciously.

"So? What brings you here?"

Stumbling over my words all the while, I told her my errand, and without the slightest hesitation Noi promised to take care of the job I'd requested. She told me she would need a little time to finish.

"I'll just wait outside," I said.

I wanted to get away from that place right now. As I turned to go, Noi called out to me from behind.

"You'd do well to lay off that stuff," she said.

When I emerged from the front gate and started walking, I heard the gate guard on the left murmur behind me, "Isn't that thing a little loose?"

"Maybe he hasn't noticed," the gate guard on the right whispered back. "Let's tell him."

When I reached back to feel the back of my head, sure enough, the artificial plate had come loose. Using both upper hands, I snapped it back into place and crossed the nearby suspension bridge into Nazumo Clifftown. A number of idle carapace polishers were loitering on the gougeway. They called out to me, but I walked on by and ducked through the tiny doorway of a cavebar. A flag raised outside had ethyl alcohol mixed into its aromaseal.

A stand-up bar stretched all the way to the back of the long, narrow interior. Standing on tiptoes, I looked across the room to make certain no Zafutsubo were present and then, just in case the need arose, took a spot near the entrance so I could slip out at any time. I put a shellcoin engraved with the name of YUMA URUME down on the counter. After death, everyone was processed into shellcoins to be passed around among the living—even that woman who'd just now become fodder for Noi. Even so, would there be any place for an invisible guy like me to go after death?

The Urume barkeep turned the inverted triangle of his head toward me.

"Give me a flamecaller ale," I said

Brewed from the nectar of flamecaller grass blossoms, it had the highest alcohol content of any nectahol. The barkeep set out a cupshell and picked up the shellcoin.

"You look a little chilled, mister. I can put in some spice-grains if you like."

I nodded assent. The barkeep shook a slender, tube-shaped container above the cupshell, and when about ten of the blue-black grains had fallen inside, he whistled out a signal. Over by the inner wall, a Tsuamo tribesman rose to his feet. Letting out a belch, he walked over to us with obvious reluctance. His carapace was carved with decorative images of flamecaller grass, amid which my own sickly countenance was reflected in the brightly polished surface. The Tsuamo brought his mouth close to my cupshell and began vomiting at irregular intervals. Teardrops pooled in the gaps of his eye sockets as sticky, nectar-colored liquid gradually filled my cupshell. Midway through, he coughed, spraying some of it into the air. Its strong, liquory odor made my eyes water. "I'll have one too," said a customer standing farther inside, and the Tsuamo toddled away in his direction.

The barkeep stirred the liquid with the long leg of a wing-bug, then softly pushed the cupshell in front of me.

I gulped downed the flamecaller ale. I swallowed again and again. By the time I finally regained my composure, my throat must have been charred black.

That had been a dangerous spot.

What had just happened in the liaison office had been no daydream brought on by the side effects of namas-machina. The Meiyuru tribe secreted an enchanting scent that put their prey into a state of ecstasy while their bodily fluids were being sucked out.

You'd do well to lay off that stuff…

Had *that* odor been to blame for Noi having stopped just as her proboscis was going in? Had the stench of namas-machina really soaked into my insides that deeply?

"Ugh! What a stench! This guy reeks of namas-machina!" That's what the detective from the Ministry of Law Enforcement had said yesterarc.

The proxy had been a namas-machina addict as well. What if some unknown parasite had been driven out by the namas content that had built up in his system?

But now that I'd gone and remembered the stuff, my body was starting to crave namas-machina. The minute I got back to my grotto—no wait, that old lady's eggs were still stuck all over the ceiling, weren't they? I didn't feel like going back to that.

How I was supposed to get rid of them? I was feeling a little down over that when suddenly a namas-machina came falling down from the ceiling. My drooping shoulders shot to attention, but no, it was smaller than a namas-machina, and the color was completely different. A seed-shaped gloambug with a translucent yellow-green carapace: a honeydew bug. It aimed its rear end at my cupshell and raised it up as if flirting. "No thanks," I told it. Abdomen still aloft, the gloambug crawled backward in the direction of the next customer over from me. "Thanks," he said. A drop of honeydew swelled from the tip of the gloambug's pointed anus and dripped into his cupshell.

I realized then that the customer raising that cupshell to his mouth was none other than my childhood friend Rei Urume. Feeling suddenly nostalgic, I was just about to speak to him when an irate voice from behind interrupted my thoughts:

"Huh? What did you say? No, no; that's not right at all!"

I didn't need to turn around to tell it was somebody talking on the reverbigator. Recovering from the distraction, I started to call out to Rei and then realized that I'd never seen that man before in my life. And anyway, I was born in Castellum Gakugu; there was no way any boyhood friend of mine would be here.

"No, no, no—what? I can't hear you. At all. Hello? Hey!"

The man's voice was getting even louder behind me.

I downed the remaining nectahol in a single gulp and put the bar behind me.

I found Noi Meiyuru in front of the Seat of Learning speaking with the gate guards.

The memory of myself worshipping her like a goddess embarrassed me no end, even though the bewitching scent of her secretions had been to blame.

Noi's antennae went up when she became aware of my presence. Was it the fumes of flamecaller ale that sent them recoiling backward even farther?

The gate guards opened the door for me, and I passed underneath it. I heard them whispering to each other about going out for drinks tonight.

Walking alongside me, Noi, who had had a worker inspect the gloambug drainage pipes, told me the results. As I had suspected, dark sticky blotches of red mucus had been discovered in the pipe connecting the autopsy room and the bathroom.

When we entered the autopsy room, the examination tables that had earlier been flush with one another were now separated and lined up along the wall, exposing a hole in the center of the room for the draining off of gloambugs. Around it there rose up piles of dark red scum that gave off a sweet aroma. Gloambug legs, no doubt ripped off in the act of escaping, were sticking out of these piles in every direction.

I told Noi about being attacked in my grotto and of the possibility that both the proxy and myself had nearly been parasitized by an unknown life-form. Noi's elegant, flowing black antennae bent doubtfully.

"So you think this life-form came up through the gloambug drainage pipe and gobbled up the mummy? But that—"

She seemed to be shying away from calling it "Pancestor," probably because her position required neutrality when it came to the Speciation Hypothesis.

"Yeah, it wouldn't be easy. Something that big would take a long time to eat, and there would probably be leftovers. But look at it another way: what if that life-form *went out* through the drainage pipe?"

"What do you mean?"

"If this thing is a parasite, it's a kind that's never been identified in Castellum Raondo before. That mucus reminds me of the stains in the autopsy room yesterarc. And the fact that it appeared at the same time Pancestor vanished..."

Noi remained silent, waiting for me to continue.

"...means it's possible to think it was Pancestor himself that *turned into* the parasite. Going by its original size, it could have divided into dozens of them."

"It was dead; there was no mistaking that," said Noi, abdomanus pulling back slightly. "It was a dried-out corpse."

"'You'll end up ugly as a grimebug,'" I said.

I had quoted my mother's words with nostalgia, but Noi simply emitted a dubious body odor.

"You never heard that growing up?" I said. "In Castellum Gakugu, they say that to children who want to sleep all the time. You smelled the odor of that scum. It's blood sugar. A grimebug—even if you throw it into the Hellblaze—can replace the moisture in its body with blood sugar and enter a dormant, nonmetabolic state. It can stay that way practically forever." When I had spoken thus far, I realized something I couldn't explain: the mucus's color...why was it red?

"Even if we allow that it resuscitated," said Noi, "how can one body divide into multiple parasites? It did have an endoskeleton and internal organs, after all."

"What do you think those ochre-colored fragments were that were left behind?"

I told her what I'd heard from the patrol guard about Pancestor's carapace.

"That man! Why didn't he tell me such an important—?"

"He was assigned there the arc before yesterarc. He probably thought it had been covered in carapace from the beginning. Pancestor was changing by hardening its skin. Like a gloambug pupa becoming a chrysalis." Suddenly, the muscles around my mouth tensed up. Something in my consciousness was struggling. "Inside its chrysalis, a gloambug temporarily dissolves all of its internal muscles and organs. Maybe this thing reformed itself into multiple individuals in the same way."

"If those shards came from a chrysalis, don't you think there would have been more left behind?"

"There were strange marks left on the fragments though, weren't there? They may have eaten the shell for its nutrients."

"Even if such a thing is possible, it could have escaped any number of times before being brought here."

"Then it must not have done this to escape. It tried to parasitize me. And probably the Archlearner's proxy as well."

"Why in the world would it do such a thing?"

"There must have been some kind of trigger…"

I wracked my brains for an answer, but it was starting to feel like I was just saying whatever came to mind, and I found myself at a loss for words. Unable to bear Noi's incisive, questioning gaze, I looked away from her, and that was when my eyes fell on the reverbigator shell.

"You told me the reverbigator had just recently been inspected and had parts replaced, didn't you? When was that?"

"Three arcs before the disappearance. The jewel-bits had worn out over many rounds, and a technician from the Ministry of Reverbigation came over. Because the remains were being kept here, I went with him as a guide and observed everything that happened."

"I see. It sounds like there was nothing suspicious, but something still bothers me."

I walked up to the wall and opened the lidshell. The formless fluid inside sucked at a thought that was always with me and began forming itself into a face. I shifted my gaze to the circular, seashell frame and saw a faint trace of dark red mucus stuck there. Yesterarc, I'd been standing far away and hadn't been able to see inside very well. Or maybe it had gotten stuck there afterward.

"You see this?"

"Y-yes…ah, the reaction you had when you saw me at lunch earlier, that was merely a temporary effect induced by scent, so…I really should have put a lockbug on the door."

I looked back at the neurofungus and frantically shut the lidshell. What the neurofungus had unearthed from my thoughts was not the face of my former wife, but that of Noi. My temperature skyrocketed with embarrassment.

"That's not what I mean; there are traces of something that looks like that mucus on the reverbigation shell. The parasites attempted to dive inside."

"Couldn't they have just made a mistake while trying to get outside?"

"The reverbigation net extends all the way to the castellum's central nerve area."

"Surely you don't mean they're trying to parasitize and control the castellum—they would just end up as fodder for the neurofungi. The only things that can move through it are namas-machina."

"The only things we know of."

I thought of that customer speaking loudly on the cavebar's reverbigator just now…of Tagadzuto seemingly pretending his reverbigator was going out on him—either of those malfunctions could have been caused by invasive parasites.

"The Ministry of Reverbigation is under the Seat of Defense's jurisdiction, isn't it?"

"Yes. Why do you ask?"

"There's some kind of problem at the Ministry of Reverbigation right now. And somehow, it's mixed up in this case."

2

I set out for the Seat of Defense with Noi, and together we walked on and on along the gougeway. We did not converse; it was an awkward trip—it felt like we were eloping or on our way to commit double suicide. The Seat of Defense was situated symmetrically opposite the Seat of Learning with the spinal girder right in the middle. Gazing out over Mebohla Riptrench, we looped around Gukutsu Clifftown toward the left-end terminus next to the oilfactory organs and finally arrived at the Seat of Defense.

Plants were growing wild and untended on the cliff face, so that I couldn't tell where the Seat of Defense facilities started or ended. The only hint was that compared to the areas where residences were clustered, I could hardly spot any windows here. I had been held in detention plenty of times on the bottommost level, where the Ministry of Executive Action was located, but this was my first time to visit a mid-level's front entrance. Spear-wielding gate guards were standing one on either side.

I noticed something move from the corner of my eye. I looked up and saw a swarm of unfamiliar gloambugs crossing the underside of a suspension bridge to Nazumo Clifftown. Both their bodies and their six limbs were long and slender, and their white carapaces looked oily.

"Relay bugs, it would seem," Noi told me. Was that a sign that the reverbigation net was finally about to go down?

An Urume liaison officer whom I'd contacted earlier appeared, carrying a rope wrapped around one arm. Explaining that it was required by regulation, he snapped a set of handcuffs that were attached to the rope on my wrists. This was because I had an arrest record. I followed along behind the two liaison officers as they walked side by side, as if I were a suspect being taken in.

In the corridor, strategists and tacticians were coming and going in silence. On the walls, countless relay bugs were rapidly skittering about. I heard an order barked from somewhere, and a large group came running down the hall, dodging out of our way as they moved on by. I could hear snatches of strained voices and the din of reverbigators spilling out from the rooms that we passed.

"A warning from Castellum Sosoga?"

"Dungheaps! I can't hear you!"

"It's close to a distance of one hundred mudmiles—"

"They've extended their exoshell gunbarrels—"

"What? What was that? What?"

"What about Saruga's Seat of Defense? What're they doing at the Seat of Cooperative Measures?"

"At any rate, station bombardiers in the defensive cloisters—"

I could hardly believe my elbows. This castellum was sitting on the razor edge of getting into a war! Castellum Raondo had suddenly begun increasing its potassium nitrate stocks, despite now being married—had that been mistaken for an arms buildup in preparation for war?

Overwhelmed by the situation, I stumbled forward and nearly fell. My rope had been yanked.

"Where do you think you're going? The Ministry of Reverbigation is this way," scolded the liaison officer.

With me being pulled along behind, we descended a staircase and came out in a long hallway. My handcuffs were removed in front of the first door we came to, and I was ushered into a large chamber that was apparently some kind of meeting room. From the center of the ceiling, there hung a huge, biconical garden lantern woven from fungal fiber, which illuminated an oval arrangement of desks. Currently, there was only a solitary Murai tribesman sitting in the seat farthest back from us. He was leaning on the desk with his elbows, and his eight slender forearms were positioned in a complicated, crisscrossed arrangement, each holding a blotterbug in its hand.

"This is the chief of the Ministry of Reverbigation," said Noi Meiyuru. She took one step back from my side, revealing another seat near the door, in which sat exactly the sort of rust-red, barrel-shaped figure that I didn't want to meet. His antennae were tracing over paperwork on his desk.

I shook my head in protest, but Noi, oblivious, introduced me to him.

"Gashun Zafutsubo, this is Radoh Monmondo."

Gashun leaned forward with his wide torso and glared at me. His antennae extended and retracted repeatedly. There was a lot of strength in the hands with which he was gripping the edges of his desk; his claws were digging deep into the tabletop.

"I see. So your injuries are all better now?"

"Do you know each other?" asked Noi.

"I don't," Gashun replied in a voice like a grinding millstone. "But among my tribe, he is…something of a celebrity."

The man at the inner seat was sliding a blotterbug across a leafsheet. In any case, he appeared to be a stenographer.

"Thank you for your concern," said Radoh.

The stenographer moved one arm away from his desk, lowered another arm to it, and started writing again. Apparently, different speakers were assigned to different arms.

"In any case," Gashun said, "it appears that war is upon us…"

The implication being *"…and I have bigger fish to fry than you."* He was deflecting my attempt to speak with him.

Gashun opened a flat box on his desk, caught a relay bug, and drew it out. He brought it close to his mouth and, after making a sort of kissing gesture, tossed it to the floor.

"As you can see, I have quite a lot to do."

The relay bug turned its long, narrow head this way and that, then disappeared in the blink of an eye from where it had landed.

"Radoh Monmondo believes this uproar about a war breaking out has something to do with an unresolved question the Ministry of Archaeological Contemplation is trying to answer."

I shot a panicked glance at Noi's expression of studied indifference. *No, I do not!* That thought hadn't even crossed my mind.

Gashun leaned back in his chair; perhaps Noi's words had calmed him down.

"So this is about the reverbigation net? It's true the confusion on that end has been going on for a while now. It's under investigation at present; we're doing all that we can."

"Is it possible that some contaminant has gotten into the reverbigation net somewhere?"

"Contaminant? Is that what all this is about?" Gashun sat up straight. "I just told you that it's under investigation. I can't be talking about this to outsiders. Especially not when one is a dodgejobber."

"It's all right," Noi said calmly. "This man is the proxy of Archlearner Meimeiru of the Ministry of Archaeological Contemplation."

"No, I'm—"

Eyes still locked on Gashun, Noi cut me off with a wave of her left arm.

"Telling me there 'may be a connection' isn't good enough,"

Gashun said. "The Ministry of Archaeological Contemplation and the Ministry of Reverbigation have never had much to do with one another. You two are just trying to extract information from us. So please leave."

With nothing at all to show for it, we were thus expelled from the Ministry of Reverbigation. Things had gone as I'd imagined, Noi Meiyuru's words and actions notwithstanding.

"And what were you planning to do if he'd found out this is not related to the war?" I asked as we walked along the gougeway together.

"That's why I said it was your idea. At any rate, if war does come, they'll have more on their minds than you. And what did you do to earn a grudge from the Zafutsubo?"

I gave a brief explanation, and Noi laughed—just a hiss of air expelled from her spiracles.

"Don't worry about it," she said. "At any rate, spawning an Archlearner's proxy is not allowed."

"I'm not a proxy. I'm just a dodgejobber."

Noi didn't reply. Even if there was some contract I didn't know about that stipulated I be treated as a proxy, that was still no guarantee that the Zafutsubo would observe the law.

Two Urume tribesmen had been following us ever since we left the Seat of Defense. Of this I was certain; dismissing such things as "just my imagination" had given me no end of past regrets.

Later, when we were nearing the Seat of Learning, I told Noi about them and darted into a narrow ripway that turned off to the right. If I stayed on course, I would come to Suifu'ushi Riptrench, but I made a left along the way and entered the high-ceilinged Sohsoh Ripditch. Just as I remembered, a row of bathhouses ran alongside it.

I ran into the drilding of Semama Bathhouse, tossed a shell-coin onto the counter, and grabbed a bathtag marked "purify" from the tagbox. Ignoring the surprised clerk, I entered a small private compartment closed off only by a curtain and lay down in a bathtub made of nectarwax. I pulled on the rope hanging down from above, and gloambugs started pouring from the bugtap in the wall, getting deeper and deeper as they crawled around in the tub.

This was a really nice place—they had fourteen different kinds of gloambug, running the gamut from beetles to worms. If I'd had more time, I would have liked to specify the mix and taken my time soaking in them.

As the bugs squirmed over me, the tension in my body started to loosen up. The dirt, the grime, the aromatics, and infiltrating hypha were all broken down by saliva from countless tiny mouths that sucked at my carapace, licking it all away.

Things seemed to be quiet outside. In any case, it looked like my nerves had gotten the better of me. I had just fallen into an idle daze when the curtain of my compartment fluttered slightly. Two figures could be seen through it dimly.

I leapt out of the bathtub. A splash of bugs went flying through the air. I slipped past the legs of two Urume tribesmen, who shouted as they wiped off the bugs that had landed on them.

I got out of the bathhouse and kept running full-tilt down the ripditch. Bugs that were caught in my joints got crushed between my segments—it hurt. Pollen also got stuck in my spiracles, making it hard to breathe.

I was wiping at my thoracic carapace when I tripped on a bughole near the middle of the ripditch and fell to the ground. I rolled over onto my back, rubbing away the pollen. Everyone walking in this ripditch was Urume. I tensed up each time one came near my side. Among them were two who were holding crowbars for prying open bug carapaces. I've heard that the first thing you learn in the Seat of Defense is how to do a decarapacing. The pair were closing in on me. As they looked this way and that, waving about their fully extended antennae, they walked right beside me and passed on by.

I returned to the gougeway in Gukutsu Clifftown and slipped back into the Seat of Defense's drilding. Walking along the walls of its crowded hallways, I entered the block where the Ministry of Reverbigation was located. If I could take such a great risk with so little hesitation, did it mean I'd become a proxy already? If that were the case, would the authorities view me as lacking free will and therefore not charge me in the event that I got caught?

I stood before the door to the meeting room I'd visited before and peered inside through its small window.

Five people, including Gashun Zafutsubo, were gathered at the oval ring of desks, looking up at the huge garden lantern hanging from the ceiling as they spoke to one another. The Murai tribesman was sitting in the same seat as before, swiftly moving his many limbs all at once, transcribing the conversation.

I put my elbows up against the door.

—*That proxy was saying something about a contaminant, wasn't he?*

—*You should know it's nothing so trifling as that.*

—*Hey, you're keeping awfully quiet lately. It isn't like you.*

—*Never mind about me; have you heard anything from the Ministry of Castellum Contemplation?*

This discussion, perhaps having hit a roadblock, went around in circles a few times, and soon no one had anything else to say. I heard nails tapping on a desk.

A reverbigator sounded noisily. Gashun left the ring of

desks and walked over to the wall.

I caught snatches of an insolent, angry voice shouting from the other side, occasionally overlapping Gashun's answers.

—At this rate, we won't be able to keep the bombardiers in step with each other!

—I don't care how many relay bugs you send; it's no use if they only remember sentence fragments!

—What's going on? The reverbigator—

The voice went on, doggedly criticizing the outages in the reverbigation network. Apparently, it was someone from the Ministry of Defensive Action.

I walked away from the door and wandered around the Ministry of Reverbigation, looking for its aromaterial depository. In the midst of a long hallway two floors down, I finally found a door with the aromaseal I was looking for. I took a peek inside through the small window in the door. There was no sign of anyone present.

I slipped inside. It was dark in there. Not a single torchburr was glowing, but bathed in the scent of the aromaterials, the colors of everything rose up dimly all around.

First of all, I started looking for records detailing the history of reverbigator outages. On a bookshelf near the entrance, three rounds' worth of materials were assembled, sorted according to arc. Each document bore the personal aromaseal of Reverbigator Replacement Technician Sohso Shutohroh. He connected his giant brain to the reverbigation network to manage it apparently.

I found the records from two arcs prior to Pancestor's disappearance, from which I learned that during that time, a slight increase in temperature had been detected in the autopsy room of the Seat of Learning. A note written there said "ordinary influx of gloambugs." Had the parasites been digested then? Three arcs prior to that, a reverb of indeterminate origin had been placed to the autopsy room, and following an unusual spike in heat consumption, the standby signal from the jewel-bits had broken off. An inspector had been dispatched to the site immediately amid concerns of a neurofungus leak in the room, but that bullet had been dodged; it was only a matter of damaged jewel-bits. An investigation into the cause had carried over into the following arc, when it was concluded to have been the same thing causing frequent outages on the reverbigation network: neurofungus fibers crossed with the neural network of the castellum.

Just to be safe, I checked records from some other dates and learned that malfunctions had been taking place even in the offices of Archlearners Meimeiru and Ryofin.

I tensed up at a sound out in the hallway, but no one came inside. I moved on to my next target of investigation.

On a shelf further inside the room, periodically updated charts of the castellum's structure were rolled up in tube-shaped bundles covering one round each. These were stored between small partitions. I pulled the tube for the current round from its compartment and unrolled the latest chart on the floor. A complex, 3-D perspective drawing of the castellum spread out before me. I was surprised when I saw the biconical shape of the reverbigation net that reached into the castellum's every district. It was exactly the same shape as the garden lantern hanging in the meeting room. Had that thing been a model reflecting the present state of the reverbigation network? I could tell at a glance that the reverbigation network connected the residential blocks and the military facilities on the chart.

The uppermost portion of the reverbigation network appeared dimmer than the rest and was tangled up with a fibrous shadow suggesting creeper vine. Beneath it, a short row of symbols had been jotted down. When I took a look at a chart made ten rounds ago, that shadow was smaller than it was now.

And twenty rounds ago, there was no shadow at all.

As I was checking out a number of other document shelves, I learned that those symbols corresponded to numbers assigned to the minutes of Reverbigator Damage Response meetings. That fiberlike shadow was apparently an irregularity in the growth of castellum nerve tissue. Caught between the necessity of a major construction project and the danger of harming the castellum's autonomic functions, it seemed they had been unable to decide what to do.

I put back the charts and the meeting minutes, left the depository, and after traversing many corridors in which the commotion was growing only louder, slipped back outside, whereupon I was stricken suddenly by a great exhaustion and felt a cold ache in my stomach. The gustatory hairs covering my tongue stirred.

Contrary to all expectation, I had uncovered no trace of any parasite disrupting the reverbigation network. What now bothered me more, however, was that abnormal growth of castellum nerve tissue and those reverbigator calls of unknown origin.

I'd always heard that castellae had no more intelligence than an ordinary gloambug. That was supposed to be settled science, but if it were to be overturned—

I was still struggling with these thoughts when I arrived back at my grotto, but right away I pulled up the floorboard.

My dorsal vessel contracted tightly.

I sank to the floor on the spot. My namas-machina were gone! Not even one was left in the cage. Somehow, I must have forgotten to close the latch.

I was hurting all over now; it felt like every last nerve in my body had been laid bare. I no longer had any idea what was causing it. It hurt so bad, I thought I was going to burst open at any moment. While I was putting on aromatics and getting ready to go out again, the strength drained out of me, and wobbling, I lay down in my danglebed.

Just as before, eggs were still dangling from the ceiling. No, something was different now. Overall, their surfaces were stretched tighter than before. The wrinkles had vanished, and a ripe green color was beginning to tint the adhesive parts stuck to the ceiling. I sat up and felt one. There was an elasticity to the shell, and I could feel the pulsations of something inside. It was the same as when touching any egg.

Don't tell me those namas-machina went and violated them when they got loose! But these eggs were so baggy and shriveled! Had a lifetime spent in a closed environment made those gloambugs completely undiscriminating? They'd fertilized as many as they could and then run for it!

It was then that I realized the truth that had been right in front of me all along, and I shuddered.

That old woman was a namas-machina female.

I'd heard that the females were forced to spawn under the auspices of Reproducing Pharma workers, and I'd heard that they kicked them out the moment the quality of their eggs began to drop.

Many miserable, forlorn namas-machina females—who looked like nothing if not people—were said to be milling around in the margins of the riptrenches. Still, almost no one, myself included, took note of their presence, nor did we ever doubt our actions as we went on consuming namas-machina.

Just then, a sudden tremor rocked the grotto. Like the hands of some giant, it shook me to and fro and threw me out of my danglebed. Dishes and other necessities of arclife came spilling off the shelves and the tabletop. The lid in the floor opened and shut like a flapping wing. The war, it appeared, had begun. Three eggs fell from the ceiling and burst open. The castellum had never shaken like this before. Maybe we'd taken a hit.

The shaking quieted, but the floor was still listing. Whitish embryos writhed amid pools of sticky fluid and shards of broken eggshell. Black eyes stared at me from behind white, cloudy membranes. Fleeing their stares, I backed out of the grotto.

I will never put anything like that in my mouth again, I swore. But resolution alone wasn't enough to quell my craving for them. I hurried into the forkway as another powerful tremor rocked the castellum. At the very least, I needed something that could serve as a substitute. My job for the Seat of Learning was slipping farther and farther from my mind.

I came out into the riptrench and stopped in at a second-rate bar facing the loway. It was a tiny place, just a narrow cellar with a few tall tables where customers could drink standing up. Shards of broken cupshell were scattered about the floor, and the smell of stale alcohol hung on the air. There was no sign of any other customer.

"What brings you here at a time like this?" said the owner's familiar voice. Only the head of the short Tsuamo tribesman could be seen peeking above the counter. "I was just about to close up shop."

"Flamecaller ale," I said.

"We're sold out."

"Then make it a ragerum," I said, ordering their second-strongest nectahol.

Reluctantly, the owner took a shellite bottle down from the shelf, stretched, and poured some of the liquor into a cupshell. There was hardly any bouquet to it at all. This place had only bottled spirits. Although the owner was capable of coughing up raw liquor if asked, his alcohol content was so low and the flavor so bitter that no one ever ordered it.

Suddenly, the castellum went into a wide swing, and many bottles came sliding off the shelves, shattering on the floor with loud pops and the tinkling of shellite.

"Yikes!" the owner cried, rather pitifully. "Well, if you don't mind broken bottles, you can do as you like with those."

So I knocked back one shot of stale liquor after another, trying to fool my aching and longing. Even so, the more I drank, the more unbearable it all became. When I should have been making small talk with the owner, I instead found myself shoving a shellcoin in front of him and asking where I could find a black market dealer. At some point the castellum's swaying had settled back down.

The dealer's establishment was located in the subterranean maze of forkways under Bohni Clifftown. He was Urume, and I found him leaning against a wall at the edge of a weak circle of light filtering down from a vertical forkway. He had a listless demeanor and a long, dried earthworm in his mouth.

I showed him the aromasealed letter of introduction I'd gotten from the owner of that crappy bar. The man shifted his mandibles, tilting the dried earthworm upward, and turned away from me. Placing four hands against the rock wall, he applied his weight against it. A part of the wall slid sideways, opening up a narrow entrance. Bending down, the dealer went inside, and I followed along behind.

Inside was a pitch-black cave. No light reached it, but the stench of namas-machina swirling about in its cloying air made the whole room seem dazzlingly bright. I looked up, and right before my eyes I saw namas-machina faces. Countless faces. They were tied up in bundles that hung from the ceiling so thickly there was no space in between.

"That was quite a tremor we just had. The war's already started, hasn't it? These'll sell out in no time, so get 'em while you can."

Speaking with a knowing look, the dealer reached up with both upper arms, untied a single bundle from the ceiling, and held it out in front of me.

When I saw the price tag, I couldn't believe my antennae. Just one bug cost what I'd expected to pay for three bundles.

"These are all fresh and lively," the man said, showing off the bundle as he turned it around and around in his fingers. There were about twenty-four of them in it, and all were as still as death. I paid the price asked. He grabbed just one from the bundle, but when he pulled on it, it wouldn't come loose. Its threadlike legs were tangled up with those of his fellows. Annoyed, I grabbed hold of the bug myself and wrenched it loose, not caring that its legs were ripped off in the process. Then right before the dealer's unbelieving eyes, I bit into its backside with my mandibles. The raw, fishy flavor made my stomach want to climb up my throat in protest, and I clenched my gastric teeth tightly. The cracked carapace was cutting the inside of my mouth to ribbons, but I couldn't stop biting, crushing, and grinding. However, when I was finally ready to swallow, it wouldn't go down. Something was blocking the passage. I imagined a squirming fetus lodged in my esophagus, which made my throat constrict even tighter and set off spasms in my thoracic plate.

"Oh dear..." the remaining half of the namas-machina said drowsily. "You don't look so good. You'd better...go to a clinic..." Utterly discombobulated, I coughed hard and blew out what I had already chewed up. "Please, sir, get that looked at," the remaining half went on, its concern for my health quite evident.

Fury welled up inside me, and I flung the namas-machina into the wall. Or at least I tried to, but the torn legs were still clinging to my hand and wouldn't come loose.

I turned away from the dealer and got out of that cave. From behind, I heard a dirty laugh, and the dealer calling out, "Aw, he really loved you!"

The spasms wouldn't stop. I wandered in a daze through boreways, across suspension bridges, and along gougeways, and while I was doing so, somebody snatched the namas-machina from my hand and took off running with it. I kept on walking. Walking was just another kind of spasm. Moving as though all my joints had come loose, I wandered through every back alley worthy of the name until at last I found myself standing in the very spot where I'd hit the pavement after taking that header from Maidun Reproducing Pharmaceuticals.

Maybe I wanted to believe that everything that had happened since was just a dream I was having in the last instant before I slammed into the ground. If that were the case, it would take care of not only the withdrawal symptoms but the whole war to boot, and I could just die quietly. Maybe that's what I wanted to believe.

I collapsed at the side of the road. The convulsions of whole body segments were becoming more violent.

That's when I sensed someone's presence and extended my antennae. Somebody's butt had appeared right in front of my face. Its owner was rubbing it hard against the ground. Then the hindquarters rose up, exposing a translucent ovoid shape, tinged with light. Steam was rising up off of it. I reached a hand out reflexively and pushed the still-damp egg into my mouth. As I was chewing on it, my stomach turned inside out. I vomited out emptiness, and everything else that lay beyond.

CHAPTER 4:
NAMES EXHUMED
FROM EBON DUNES

1

I awakened to the shock of being harshly shaken up and down.

My body, the grotto, no, the castellum itself was rocking violently. I sought to escape, but there was no strength in my limbs; every joint felt like it was dislocated. A terrible chill took hold of me, and I felt like I might throw up at any moment.

"Da-da, Ma-ma, o'tay, Da-da, Da-da—" My field of vision was motion-blurred from the shaking, and I was experiencing an auditory hallucination of shrill, strange voices. *"Da-da, Da-da, 'old on, Da-da—"*

"It'll be a little while, before you can walk again," a voice said suddenly by my elbow. It was a woman's voice, and one I'd heard somewhere before. "Have to fix you up quickly. If we don't, we're going to be buried, in this grotto."

Buried? What in the world was this about?

"…castellum's people, are starting to move. Starting to move in great numbers."

Where are they moving to? What's going on?

"Fix'yu, Da-da, Da-da, 'ang on, Da-da—"

"Take this."

A rubbery something was pressed up against my mouth—
Stop it!—and turned back and forth to wedge it inside—"*Da-da, Da-da, Da-da*—"

"Da-da, 'ang on…"

"Ma-ma, i'Da-da otay?"

"Da-da, 'et well, Da-da…"

"Da-da, 'ake up…"

"Da-da, Da-da—"

Their noisy, drawling voices dragged me out of slumber.

Segments creaking, I sat up in bed. Namas-machina pupas were gathered beneath my danglebed. Through gaps in the netting, they were massaging my carapace, stroking it with their filament-limbs.

Ro was sitting by the wall with her back bent deeply over. Why did I know her name? That's right! After I collapsed, she lent me her shoulder and brought me back to my grotto, stopping to rest so many times along the way. That was when I asked her her name for the first time, and she told me it was Ro. Ro Namas-machina.

"Da-da 'oke up!"

"Da-da's awake!"

"Da-"

"Daa-daa"

"'ood mo'nin"

"Stop it!" The fresh, ripe smell of the pupas clung to my antennae until I couldn't take it anymore. "Are—are you making them talk?"

When I looked up at the ceiling, nothing remained except the egg bottoms, resembling receptacles of flowers left behind after the petals had all fallen. "Don't tell me, these guys hatched from the eggs up there?"

The grotto shook violently. There was a muffled sound like

when my elbows ring. A fusillade from Castellum Sosoga.

"They're still fighting, are they? How long has it been?"

"You were, more than ten arcs, with withdrawal symptoms—"

"*Ten* arcs! Wonderful! Just wonderful! So I've just been lying here while the castellum's in danger—"

I sat up straight and stepped down to the floor, but unable to stand, I collapsed on the spot. It felt like my body's center of gravity was lagging behind me. I heard the dry sound of something slender snapping into pieces. When I looked at the floor, there were several long white legs scattered about. Some gloambug's apparently. Had they belonged to a relay bug?

Surprised by the pupas that had gathered around, I somehow managed to stand up again. I advanced forward with long, wobbly strides.

"Da-da"

"Da-da"

"'Ere you 'oing?"

"Da-da—"

I tumbled forward into the wall, then grabbing hold of the doorframe, shoved myself out of the grotto.

Was it just me, or did I hear Ro murmur, "Goodbye"?

I stepped into the forkway and started walking. Strong quakes rattled the walls intermittently. After proceeding for some time, I found my way forward blocked by a pile of black, granular potassium nitrate. Gloambugs were busy digging in it, turning it over; maybe their nests had been buried underneath. I switched to a forkway that continued forward on an upward slope, but soon found the path blocked again with more potassium nitrate. I backtracked some distance, then advanced up the incline of a different forkway. Light from the exit at last came into view.

When I looked up over the lip of the hole, I saw the rolling dunes of a dark, dark desert, spreading out across a sharply tilting world. I was looking up from the end of the Mebohla Riptrench Ioway, and there before my eyes was Nazumo Clifftown, transformed into a gargantuan slope that had been buried up to around its third level by a deluge of potassium nitrate.

The leaflight from the wall's vegetation appeared to be weakening. The potassium nitrate dunes continued off into the distance until the riptrench's curvature hid them from view. Suspension bridges between the lower levels were all buried on one end.

I crawled up out of the hole and started walking across the black dunes with dry, crunching footfalls. Carts loaded up with household goods were stuck where they had sunk into the black sand.

A man came up from behind me at a hurried pace and passed me by. On his back, he was carrying a bundle of namasmachina. Their cloudy black eyes were looking at me. "Da-da," "Da-da," said each one. "'ake a break," "'ake it easy."

Was I hearing things, or were the words of the little ones propagating through them to me? I had no idea. One thing was certain: I really did need a break. In someplace other than that grotto.

I stopped at the top of a low hill to check my position, looking up at the inclined ceiling that the leafy wall of Gukutsu Clifftown had become. Perhaps sensing the danger, flowers were blossoming all across it, sticking out their sharp pistils and stamens.

"Hey there! Why didn't you come?" cried a voice from behind. I turned around but didn't see anyone.

"Over here! Over here!" he said.

I looked around, trying to find the speaker.

An inverted triangle-shaped head was peeking up over the

ridgeline of a tall dune that had a suspension bridge sticking out of it. The rest of his grass-green body was revealed immediately as he crested the hilltop and started down the slope. Again and again he waved at me, but I couldn't remember who he was.

Now he was coming up the low rise where I was standing. "How about you moving a little yourself?" he said, a sound like broken flutes whistling in his spiracles as he came to a halt in front of me. An Urume tribesman.

"I've been looking for you since yesterarc. I wanted to evacuate early, but I couldn't get you on the reverbigator, and none of the relay bugs I sent ever came back. The forkways were all buried, toOAH—!"

A strong tremor struck, and the man slid down the slope, although his posture was unchanged.

Seeing that I was at a loss to answer him, he opened up a briefcase and pulled out a wide-mouthed bottle made of shellite. "It's the mystery parasite!" he said. "Someone at the Ministry of Reverbigation was forcibly hospitalized, and this thing came out of his head."

I hurried across the rolling dunes, carrying the bottle, feeling the weight of the squirming parasite inside.

We reached the Seat of Learning, but there was no sign of the gate guards, and the door had been left half open. I went inside and crawled up the tilted staircase on all fives. When I reached the seventh floor, I turned the corner leading to Archlearner Row and started walking. Noi Meiyuru came into view right away, her back turned toward me. She was cornered by three learners—probably the same three we'd seen Archlearner Ryofin of the Ministry of Castellum Contemplation kicking out of his office earlier.

Antennae unconsciously raised, a flustered-sounding Noi was saying, "I'm sorry, but I just can't help you."

Then she turned around to face me and said, "Do you have any idea how worried we were, Archlearner? We even sent relay bugs."

"What're you calling me Archlearner for? I'm—"

Unable to remember my own name, I fretted for a moment, but then the Seat of Learning started shaking wildly. Fluoroflesh flies came tumbling down, and with an ominous rumble like the sound of a great millstone being turned, cracks began to appear in the passageway's ceiling.

"Hurry, please," said Noi. "All archlearners are to be moved to Castellum Saruga by morrowarc."

"A moment, please, Archlearner Meimeiru," one of the learners cut in, glaring at me. "Archlearner Ryofin still has not approved any kind of response or countermeasure. Which is to say, the Ministry of Castellum Contemplation is not functioning."

Next, a female learner leaned forward. "There's no longer anything we can do. As learners at the Ministry of Castellum Contemplation, we ultimately had no choice but to conduct an unauthorized, independent investigation."

From behind them, the third learner murmured as though talking to himself: "But the Seat of Defense has no elbows for unauthorized advice."

Pleadingly, the first learner asked me, "When the time comes, would you be willing to testify for us in court?"

A memory came back to me of the reverbigator malfunction records I had glimpsed in the Ministry of Reverbigation's aromaterials depository.

"It isn't just the accumulated amount of potassium nitrate that's the problem—"

"Its three-dimensional distribution is abnormal. Unlike a so-called 'suiseeding,' this one will not blow outward in all directions."

"That's right. The blast will have a downward directionality;

more than half of the castellum will be preserved."

"But in any case, the explosion can't be avoided."

"All right, everyone," said Noi, "it's about time to attend to your own evacuations now. The Archlearner is in a hurry."

The learners continued to talk at me, but urged on by Noi, I started walking. The black double doors were both open, like the mouth of an infant waiting to be fed.

Waiting for me.

The instant I set foot inside Archlearner Meimeiru's skull, the long legs of the lunming bugs on either wall wrapped around me, and I scarcely had time to brace myself before being shoved into his pleated flesh. I sank into it as his bubbling secretions enveloped me.

Behind me, I heard a voice groan in agony, as well as a noise like backed-up plumbing. It went on and on, grating on my elbows. It felt so good I could barely contain myself. If the Archlearner was synchronizing with me, he had to be getting a vicarious taste of my withdrawal symptoms as well.

"I see. Your predecessor was no different; it would seem you Monmondo are easily given to indulgence. In any case—"

It's the job that's to blame, most likely, I thought. It isn't easy having somebody's brain forcibly jammed inside your head.

"—to think that's why namas-machina withdrawal is so severe fresh egg in antagonist factor and surprising potency through window-shopper prescriptions of dependence and retention that the clinics can see how Maidun's racking up the sales while even the Ministry of Archaeological Contemplation ample research funds but what ought to worry them females egg-laying age of thirty rounds laying without a break speeding up aging discarded one after another still young also retreated from proposal to cull and the expense problem look around the riptrench emaciated females all over the place not so much gloambugs as old women bad influence on the castle folk casting doubt on the Hypothesis—"

The stream of the Archlearner's clouded thoughts had backed up and overflowed, and I was left stunned at the facts I found bobbing on the surface. Why hadn't I realized right away? I'd gotten it into my head that Ro's nurse work in Castellum Giri had been a lot farther back. She'd treated wounded soldiers until she was twelve, she'd said. Hadn't it been thirteen rounds ago that Castellum Giri sank in that huge three-way battle? So even though she looked so old and decrepit...she had to be still in her twenties.

"—thoughts grew too distracted due to impurities there's no time back to the matter at hand which is to say this is what I thought: that the castellae are intelligent—"

No, that's what I thought.

"—many theories emerged previously regarding castellum intelligence but their physical structure too different from ours no way to prove it there was one faction insisted it was brainwave activity waveforms closely resembled humans at the onset of madness and there were others who said they were not so different from patterns that can be extracted from waves in the Mudsea—"

That would make sense, I thought, *if the castellum were acting with some kind of goal in mind.*

"—in mind it would make sense consider the damage to the jewel-bits in the autopsy room's reverbigator, and the reverbs of indeterminate origin—"

Judging by records of those "reverbs of indeterminate origin," it seemed certain that Archlearner Meimeiru had been contacted by the castellum as well.

"—supposing the castellum had had some sort of contact with Pancestor by way of the reverbigation network suppose that it stole something from Pancestor—"

It was clear that the castellum had somehow tampered with Archlearner Ryofin's consciousness.

"—interested in a small shadow—a mineral, apparently—

inside Pancestor's head, the Banon tribe detected it with their hypersonic soundtouch artificial perhaps but if Pancestor formed multiple individuals to take it back—"

And then somewhere along the way...

...I found myself here, gazing on a vaguely peach-colored mollusk enclosed within a brain's mucous membrane sac. Or was it a memory that had been implanted later? The creature was simple in form—nothing but tentacles in front, with tiny projections covering the whole of its moist surface membrane. I extended several touchtongues from inside the sac and buried them in the mollusk's moist, elastic membrane. Savoring its sweet flesh as I dissolved it with my secretions, I realized that its cellular structure was a perfect match for Pancestor's, which still resided in my memory. A scorching flame, I realized, was being transmitted by the nerve fibers running throughout its tissues. I sank my touchtongues deep into its tissues and followed those fibers until I reached a mass of cells that had become tumorous. This tumor seemed to be controlling its entire body. Was it coincidence that it so strongly resembled those tumors being discovered in the brains of castle folk?

I withdrew the touchtongues, then extended tentacles of nerves, which I wrapped around the lump. I could see differences in electrical potential in it that resembled brainwaves, and what was more, it was receiving an external transmission that appeared to be a signal. It would take time to analyze the whole thing, but I could tell that one part of it was indicating something using three-dimensional coordinates, and one of those points was glowing. I pulled one of the Ministry of Reverbigation's 3-D perspective drawings out of my memory, and after making many tweaks to its angle and scale, laid it over those coordinates. The glowing point was located at an intersection of the reverbigation net and the castellum's nerve tissue. There was something there.

I heard a strange noise. Was it just my imagination?

I could find out what was there by sending in namas-kara—but no. There was no need for that. There seemed to be some contradiction in my reasoning. For the time being, I needed to break off the investigation. Yet even so... No. There was no need for that.

I was standing in front of the door to the Ministry of Archaeological Contemplation. I felt worn down to nothing and was even unsure whether I'd really been inside Archlearner Meimeiru or not. Something slid from my upper arm, and frantically, I caught it with my one lower arm. It was the wide-mouthed bottle. When I opened the lid, it was not a parasite that I found inside but many tiny, meaty sprouts.

2

I became suddenly uneasy and hurried back home, stumbling again and again as the tilted world pulled at me. The castellum's inclination could shift again at any moment, and if it did, my little grotto might end up buried in potassium nitrate.

I wandered through the forkway, and when I finally got back home, the little bugs came crowding around, saying "'elcome 'ome, 'elcome 'ome." They raised up the fronts of their flat bodies and touched me with slender arms that were like frayed strings.

Ro Namas-machina was sitting in the danglebed, still as death. She raised up her cephalothorax to look at me and began to rise.

"No, you're fine. Please stay there."

I sat down next to Ro. Her far-too-light body rocked back and forth.

"It isn't safe here. Come with me, and evacuate to Castellum Saruga. Castellum Raondo is going to sink."

"But you, have work to do. It isn't, finished, is it?"

"The investigation's been canceled."

"But it isn't, finished, is it?"

She was right. We were about to sink to the bottom of the Mudsea, and everything was still so unclear. No, wait—if we used these gloambugs...

"The little bugs might be able to dive into the reverbigation net and pin down what's causing all this. It's probably the thing the castellum stole from Pancestor—"When I had spoken that much, a forceful voice rang out in the back of my mind: *The investigation is canceled!* That's right; it was canceled. And I realized then that the execution of my plan had been in trouble from the start. Ro had been cast out by Maidun Reproducing Pharmaceuticals, even though she still possessed the ability to lay eggs. Most likely there had been a drop in the namas content of her eggs.

"If these little ones go into the reverbigation net," I said, "they won't come out unharmed." I wasn't thinking of them as simple gloambugs anymore. They were Ro's children. "*No, they are still lower gloambugs,*" flashed the thoughts of the Archlearner.

"But I laid them for you," Ro said flatly.

"Da-da, Da-da, Da-da."

The little bugs that had been listening to us started buzzing with excitement: "I wanna go! I wanna go!"

"You don't understand. It's dangerous." How many months of her life had she whittled off by laying them? "I can't let you go."

I picked up one of the little ones as if to console him and said, "The investigation's been canceled." At that moment, I could feel thoughts of the Archlearner competing against one another inside me. He was unable to suppress his own intellectual impulses. However—

A child came entreating me: "Da-da, I wan' a name. I wan' my own name."

"Your name is Shoru."

The name came to me instantly. It was one of the names I had picked out for the children I'd once expected to have myself. The other children shouted out his name over and over.

My lower arm grabbed a pair of tweezers from the boreshelf and picked up one of the meaty sprouts from the wide-mouthed bottle on the table.

"You all are not allowed to do this kind of thing. Don't even try it," I said. I wriggled my fingers between the joint of Shoru's still-soft cephalothoracic shell and used the tweezers to plant one of the meaty sprouts in his slightly peach-colored brain, all the while murmuring, "This is wrong. I can't do this…"

"Ahh, lucky! Lucky!" the children were all saying enviously.

I opened the reverbigator's lidshell and pushed Shoru into the head that welled up inside. Gradually, he was sucked in through its face.

Half the arc went by, but Shoru didn't come back, so I finally sent in a second one, whom I named Jafutsu. Ultimately, though, the result was the same. Perhaps they'd been digested by the neurofungi.

When the third one, Donei, finally returned next morning, he was almost completely dissolved. "I sorry, Da-da…I cou'n't fine it…I sorry…" With those repeated whisperings, he breathed his last.

Postrise came and with it the return of the fourth child, Sagusa. He was trembling violently when he came back. I set him on the danglebed, and Sagusa peeled back his labial palpi and opened his mouth wide. The corners of his mouth audibly tore as a rounded thing like polished jasper began to rise into view. He spat up a curved crystalline object, shaped like a gigantic water droplet. There was no great difference between its size and that of Sagusa. White fibers trailed from its tip.

After stroking the back of the limp Sagusa once, I held the damp crystal up to a glowjar with two hands and looked at the light shining through it. Emerald illumination suffused it faintly.

What in the world was this thing? Something seemed to be carved into its surface, but there wasn't anything sealed inside. Why had the castellum stolen something like—

Suddenly the children turned toward the door and started growling all at once.

With a loud, violent shock, part of the door exploded inward, and with the next resounding blow, the rest of the door collapsed.

An axe-wielding Urume tribesman came inside, and then right behind him, another. As he raised his axe, I planted a kick that knocked him to the ground and ran out of the grotto holding on to the crystal tightly. I fled through the forkways, getting potassium nitrate all over myself in the process.

When I reached the dunes of Mebohla Riptrench, I found myself surrounded by over a dozen pursuers—Urume and Guromura, mostly. They approached with awkward footsteps, narrowing the distance between us. All of their lower arms were dangling limply like those of dead men, and their bodies seemed slow to react to me. If I went for it now, I realized, I could probably get free of them.

With that thought in mind, I was just about to make a run for it when my lower arms were grabbed from behind and I was dragged down onto the slope. Two more of them grabbed hold of me, and just when it seemed like the crystal I was carrying against my thorax would be torn away with the arm that held it, I saw a glint of golden carapace against the black slope.

With their long arms and legs bent in a compact stance, a pair of Miguraso tribesmen came sliding down the incline. The slope collapsed under their weight, causing several of my pursuers to lose their footing. The Miguraso stretched out their four long, thick arms and pushed down the men I was struggling with. That was when Noi Meiyuru came skidding down as well, abdomanus raised, tracing out an arc in the sand. She

jammed her proboscis between each pursuer's body segments in turn, anaesthetizing them.

It was as if we had suddenly fallen into a world without sound. The quiet itself was disquieting.

"Has the shelling from the enemy castellum stopped?" I said.

"Only temporarily. I just hope this means the Seat of Defense has managed to make contact with them. There's enough potassium nitrate in here that even they won't be unharmed if it blows."

"I see."

"You didn't go along with Archlearner Meimeiru's decision, did you?"

"I thought I told you, I'm not his proxy." Though it was still uncertain exactly who I was.

"The archlearners carried out of the Seat of Learning were exhibiting many behaviors we've never observed before and seem to be in a stupor."

"The castellum is probably interfering in their conscious minds. Where is Archlearner Meimeiru now?"

"Waiting for you." Noi straightened and pointed over my shoulder.

I turned around. Several dunes over was an enormous mass of skinned meat, large enough to be a house. It had twin black doors, and a diffuse curtain of steam was rising from it.

Behind this fleshy mass, there swelled a translucent body that was like the stem of a mushroom. Many ropes were fastened to what looked like vestigial limbs, their ends held by a multitude of workers. The withered body was attached to the giant head.

I stood before Archlearner Meimeiru, and his black doors, his giant mandibles, swung open.

CHAPTER 5:
UPSTREAM TO THE HEADWATERS

1

The pale peach sac of a mucous membrane appeared before me like a bubble inflating before my eyes. No sooner did its moist surface press up against my forehead than I felt pressure on the back of my cranium as my head was pinched from either side. Overcome with terror, I squirmed to get free, but it only squeezed even harder. I screamed as loudly as my voice would go.

Radoh Monmondo. Unexpectedly, those words came back to me. *Oh, right...that's my name.*

I peered into the membrane-sac's interior.

In the midst of the clear liquid contained therein, there floated an emerald crystal in the shape of a warped egg. It hung from tendrils of nerve cells dangling from the uppermost point of the sac's interior.

Slowly, I exhaled from every spiracle in my body, calming myself.

I was jammed in between the crystal and the archlearner's brain. I couldn't believe this: I had become a conducting ciruitbreaker, a pawn to be sacrificed in the event of some abnormality. That was what he was using me for.

Just as I was wringing out my last iota of strength in an attempt to get loose, I realized that I was tossing and turning in my danglebed. Right above me, I could see my ceiling, colonized by glowjars.

I'd just been having a long dream, it seemed. Cheers from the Circlingseed Festival came to me as though through a seashell.

The castle folk were tirelessly walking around and around in the riptrench overhead. I felt a swell of excitement at the commotion but was seriously injured right now and unable to move. Besides, if an outsider like me were to join in, I'd just end up disrupting the sense of harmony. A rather forlorn sensation, as though it were this grotto alone that was sinking to the bottom of the Mudsea, began to take hold of me, when suddenly the danglebed where I lay ripped open, and up and down switched directions.

For a moment, I could have sworn I'd been flung into the very heart of a natural disaster.

I was lying flat against the blinding white earth of the Hellblaze as my body was buffeted by the ferocious gale of a violent storm. Pounded by the wind's unceasing blows, it seemed certain they would scoop me right up off the ground, yet thanks to the numerous rootlimbs I had extended deep into the earth, I was able to hang on just barely. A strange sensation in my inner organs added to the sense of urgency. There was a pump-shaped organ in the middle of my chest pounding out a rhythmical—if irregular—beat.

I hardly move from this place much anymore, I was surprised to hear myself thinking. *Maybe because I'm so old now.*

My field of view had always been narrow, and it was now blurred to the point where all I could see was just the bit of ground before my eyes. Even so, I could make out my own shape—indistinct though it was through the clouds of dust and sand—as well as that of a rugged boulder that both resembled a human and looked nothing like one. Perhaps it was one of my comrades?

Through my rootlimbs, I expelled the last of the moisture and the water fleas mixed with it, uprooted myself, and with undulations of my gastropod moved to another spot and deployed my rootlimbs once more.

Through repetition of this simple procedure, the distance I covered continued to grow. Surrounded by hard shellite blackened by the scorching rimlight, my weakened body, my weakened cells, were becoming active again. At the same time, the many layers of shellite I had accrued were vanishing as if through volatilization, and even my rootlimbs had become withered. With ease, the winds pushed and shoved me around, until at last I started to roll. I couldn't stop the contraction of my body. At the end, I became a flat seed that could fit in the palm of one's hand. As the winds blew me up into the air countless times, I began to cross that continent of scorching sands.

At times when the force of the wind would weaken, the seed I had become would fall and stick into the sandy ground.

Beyond the gale-blasted clouds of dust, I saw a faint, wavering shadow. It emerged from a curtain of roiling, grainy particulate to become a boulder as black as jet. It came edging its way toward me, bearing down on me from above. I was afraid I was going to be crushed, but the next instant I found myself being sucked inside and deposited within a seedsac. Inside, I stuck to a mucous membrane, on which I gradually dissolved into nothing. I became the boulder itself.

In this dazzlingly bright, blazing-hot world where night never fell, the generations of these boulder life-forms passed one after another. Over time, the external shells that had protected me from the searing light disappeared, leaving only thick carapaces. These were not sufficient to protect my internal organs from the burning rimlight, so I had no choice but to endure brief lives of only a few tortured rounds.

Beneath my umbrella-shaped cranial plate, drops of water oozed one after another from the tip of my long tongue. The droplets instantly leapt upward and clung to the underside of my cranial plate, where at last they broke apart into fine particles blown out from gaps in the segments of my body.

After the passage of several generations, my carapace had thinned somewhat, and after several generations more, its area had shrunken to the point that only scattered blotches remained, like lakes left behind by a dried-up sea. When black cortex lay exposed all over my body, many clusters of insulating, heat-resistant fat nodules began to swell out, and I turned into a four-legged creature that looked just like a succulent plant.

Panting with thirst, heavy clusters swaying, I walked backwards, wandering from place to place, until I suddenly stopped and gouged a hole into the ground. Into this hole I stuck my proboscis, and joyfully, ecstatically released all of the moisture that was stored up inside my fatty clusters. As I did so, my consciousness grew dim and distant from a sudden, lethal dehydration.

Not long afterward, my clusters of fatty growths atrophied and a crazed tightrope-walk between life and death began.

I finally understood now. I was traveling backward through the long and perilous history of variegation leading up to my acquisition of a body-type suited to the harsh environment of the Hellblaze.

Spurred on now by some unknown instinct, I was beating death by breeding faster than the Rimblaze—its place ever fixed in the heavens—could kill my bodies.

I was crouched down low beneath powerful gusts that blew across the land in a body covered with black skin, moving backward little by little on four bent legs. A steady succession of dried-up corpses appeared from the sand and began crawling along beside me. There were also some who were blown over to me by powerful gusts of wind.

They were all of them comrades. Though tormented by starvation and thirst, we all sought one another's bodies, becoming tangled up together like a ball of yarn. As we switched from partner to partner, we grew smaller and more fragile. At last, we all gathered together and burrowed into the sand. Each of us was enveloped in shell and became an egg. Then, one by one, we were sucked inside...and became...our parents. Our bodies tangled together with those of comrades who had come to us. We pushed pointed reproductive organs deeply into one another, sucked out one another's seed, and then came apart—

At some point, our skins had faded to white and become covered in blisters, and we had become able to return to our parents' wombs while we were yet naked newborns. Our skeletal and muscular structure changed, making it difficult to move about in a hunched-over crouch, so that at last we raised our upper bodies and stood on two legs.

From out of the sandstorm, a dozen or so comrades came carrying the gargantuan body of a dun-colored female.

It was Pancestor.

They laid her down on the ground. Her skin was covered in blisters, just like ours.

A redness began to appear in Pancestor's skin. I thought I could see her fingertips and face spasming just slightly, and then, with sudden, halting movements, she rose to her feet.

One by one, we climbed up her blistered flesh and clung tightly to the soft meat enveloping her chest, her stomach, her sides, and her thighs. We attached ourselves, and there we

withered, dangling from her body, the very image of tumors. When the swelling went down and it was no longer possible to tell where the blisters had been, I looked down on the sight of the epidermis covering my body. It was starting to melt, to sink in, to flow away.

I—who had become Pancestor—looked around at my surroundings with my eye-cover lowered slightly. The sandy plain stretched out all around, unbounded—and I saw a flat, black ovoid. It was a barrow. Sunk partially into the ground, it was giving off a faint white smoke. Starting from one side, a long furrow in the ground stretched off into the distance.

As the surface of my body continued to liquefy, I started walking backward again.

I stood in front of the scorched black barrow, and a part of its outer shell slid open, exposing a filmy membrane with a vertical rent. I pulled open that tear, and when I was sealed inside, my body began falling apart, spiraling away, as if decomposing—or maybe I was being carried off by the dozen or so children who had divided off of me…and wrapped in a membrane to serve as my burial shroud…and entombed within the scorched black barrow—and eventually all I could hear was the rhythmic beat of my pump-shaped organ. That, too, grew gradually more distant, and at last everything ceased.

An instant later, I was flung out into a void of utter blackness.

I was shuddering so hard that my carapace seemed ready to come apart at the seams—for just a fleeting instant, my body resumed the shape of Radoh. Through my internal organs, I felt a darkness so overwhelming it could blot out death itself. It was expanding outward with incredible speed, and a primal fear of its all-encompassing vastness engulfed me.

Suddenly, a giant boulder appeared before my eyes. It was coming toward me, rotating. I cringed away from it, and it simply passed me by. After that, multiple boulders appeared one after another, just missing the place where I stood as they flew past.

At some point, the entirety of the blackness had taken on varying shades due to innumerable points of light that clustered thickly in some places and were scattered and more diffusely in others.

Looming into view from the corner of my eye was a huge, bright ball of red light that reminded me of a blob of magma. A variety of vastly smaller jewels—some larger than others, some tan and some blue-green—were moving in concentric circles around this ball of light, each rotating as it did so. Counted from the glowing sphere, the first, the second, and third of these blue-green, white-swirled jewels came into the foreground, and a powerful impulse that I can only describe as a homing instinct stabbed through my entire being. In the blink of an eye, the ball of light grew distant, and the points of light stretched out, beginning to form a radial pattern. After a sensation of having my body stretched out to infinity, I came back to myself and was staring at the luster of a small crystalline object.

Tiny bubbles floated upward. There was a sound of air entering and leaving through spiracles.

At long last, I was back—or I should have been. Instead, I was turning into a boulder, holding on tightly to the plain of the Hellblaze and struggling against the gusts of wind and the rimlight.

Was I about to experience the hell of that seemingly infinite process of speciation all over again? I nearly fainted at the thought, yet somehow another part of me deep down was submerged in powerful emotions that defied all description or metaphor.

Before my eyes were my fellow boulders, casting dark shadows on the ground. Beyond them, the vast Mudsea—a murky ocean the color of dried leaves—spread out all around. The surface of that sea, which seemed to swell with the rising of each wave, was swaying amid ripples of intense heat.

To escape from the light of the Rimblaze, we had embarked on a journey across countless generations, and here at last, at the uttermost edge of the continent, we had arrived on a beach facing the Mudsea.

I whistled at one of my companions. There was no reply. Was it just a rocky mountain? With that thought in mind, I strained my eyes and saw one side of his outer shell flake off in large pieces. I pulled out my rootlimbs and drew nearer. Inside the body cavity that had been exposed, organs were flattening out as they dried. Off in the distance, the body of another of my comrades caved in upon itself.

Everyone was whistling to one another. Together with those others who yet survived, I began advancing toward the Mudsea. The shale that covered the shoreline cracked and split beneath our weight. Our heavy, boulder-shaped bodies sank deep into the mire. The heat that was trapped inside leached steadily away. I breathed out slowly from the many holes that had opened in my outer shell.

Time passed, and with its passage succulent plants and fungi adhered to my body's surface. Lower gloambugs that had survived by living underground began burrowing into the holes and cracks of my shellite. After several generations, my comrades and I became able to exchange gases underwater through symbiosis with them. I was beginning to drift in the Mudsea's verilucent layer. Undermud, where the light of the Rimblaze was weakened to a tolerable degree, a diverse ecosystem unfurled around me, where there was no shortage of prey.

We, who had been freed from the Hellblaze and from our own body weight as well, grew fat, and there was nothing to stop us from growing fatter and fatter still.

2

The feeling that I was floating in muddy water vanished unexpectedly, and together with the pressure against my carapace, the original sensations of my body came back to life. I could see folds of pleated flesh right in front of me. Most likely, there was not an inch of my body not enveloped in them. Even though I shouldn't be able to remember, I think this was like the time I spent in my father's body.

Had I truly come back for real this time? Or was I about to be sent somewhere again?

I drew up my body and braced myself, then the fleshy pleats began to writhe powerfully, and vacant, drawn-out moans echoed forth. It was the Archlearner's voice apparently. And I couldn't blame him. The theory that he'd espoused and propounded up till now had just been completely overturned. And it might even be that his consciousness had been tampered with, making him send research teams to the continent.

But even if that were so, why had Castellum Raondo stolen the crystal? Had it wanted to recover its memories of that fearsome darkness and of the jewels that floated therein?

"I can't blame you for not understanding what those images meant; inside the castellum there's practically no need for astronomy."

Archlearner Meimeiru...

"But the Seat of Learning does know something about it. Those are the galactic coordinates of the world and its Rimblaze—where we are. And most likely, they show the position of Pancestor's homeworld as well."

There it was again—that intense impulse that pierced right through me...To grant her wish to go back to that place? Impossible. But...could that also be the reason for the increased potassium nitrate production?

"If that's truly the case, I'd have to say it's one of the saddest things I've ever heard."

What do you mean by that?

"Given our present level of potassium nitrate, there won't be enough propulsive force. It's no easy thing to escape from a gravity well. It's probably going to be impossible."

I was still dumbfounded when the pleated flesh enveloping my body began to twist. It slowly turned me around as it pushed me out of the Archlearner's brain. I started to fall forward, but the lunming bugs caught me with their long pole-legs and lowered me gently to the floor.

After the major operation of transporting the huge Shutohroh tribesmen was complete, the holes in the riptrench were sealed, and the two castellae broke off from one another.

By this point, the folk of Castellum Raondo had to the last man moved over to Castellum Saruga.

Robbed of the homes in which they'd expected to live out the rest of their lives, many had lost heart or were filled with anger. With the population having nearly doubled inside Castellum Saruga, there was no end of squabbles with the original residents of the overcrowded castellum. Since namas-machina were not approved for medicinal use there, every clinic was filled with the moans of addicts suffering withdrawal symptoms.

In spite of it all, that night—

Yes, it was night. At least for castle folk, it was. But Castellum Raondo must have been floating up near the surface, bathed in the blazing light of Skyrise.

Everyone in the castellum had shut themselves up in their familiar—or perhaps still strange and unfriendly—apartments and were huddling close together with family and friends, straining their elbows as one. I, too, was together with Ro and the children.

Earlier than predicted, the muffled sound of an explosion boomed from above. Intermittent rumblings gradually became more powerful.

What we were told afterward was that Castellum Raondo, unable to break free of the water's surface, had sunk into the depths of the trench, belching out hot bubbles of cannon-smoke. The attack by Castellum Sosoga had caused mudleaks, and the castellum had lost much of its strength.

As if clinging to a lifeline, everyone listened to the sounds of the castellum as it vanished into the distant depths.

There are some who say they can hear it still.

CHAPTER 6:
LATTER DAYS IN CASTELLUM SARUGA

Much of Castellum Raondo's Seat of Learning and Seat of Defense were merged with their counterparts in Castellum Saruga. As might be expected, this gave rise to numerous misunderstandings and conflicts.

Although Archlearner Meimeiru had achieved a historic accomplishment in discovering the origin of castellae, he acknowledged the error of the theory he had championed and retired from active service, becoming a materials depository that stored a portion of the galaxy's coordinates.

It was also learned that a vast store of additional information was hidden inside Pancestor's crystal, and the learners of each ministry began a joint effort to study it. Thanks to this, it soon became clear that those troublesome tumors being found of late in the brains of castle folk were being caused by some sort of wave emitted by the crystal. When a certain learner connected his own consciousness to the crystal's stored information, what he saw was the familiar, daily life that the castle folk lived in their riptrench. By the end of the study, they understood that all of Castellum Saruga—populace included—was steadily being copied into the crystal's information space like a finely detailed sculpture and overwriting the crystal's original information in the process.

Unable to find any way of restraining it, the Seat of Learning decided at a great convocation to return the crystal to the barrow in which it was found. A large number of Shutohroh tribesmen were asked to memorize its most important information, and then, due to my "prior familiarity" with the Hellblaze, I was half-forced into accepting the job of taking it back.

All the details of that incredibly harsh journey have been set down in another memoir.

I still haven't shaken that strange feeling of emptiness I had as I re-enshrined the crystal within the barrow...the feeling that I had surrendered my very self.

When I returned to Castellum Saruga, the degree of Interministerial Learner was bestowed on me, based on former-Archlearner Meimeiru's recommendation and my successful completion of the mission to return the crystal. I began to mediate in the research of all the ministries.

Everyarc, I commuted to the Seat of Learning, visiting each of the ministries and often passing Noi along the way. In a small rented room in a nearby clifftown, I lived with Ro and the children as a family.

The mold and the grime washed off of Ro in the bugbath, and she at least stopped looking like an old woman, though scars from the many troubles she'd endured became visible in detail on her carapace.

The children were always begging for stories. Even if all I did was open my journal to a random page and start reading, they would always be thrilled. Their favorites were the scenes where they were being named. Lately, they'd even started making up stories of their own and not once or twice had put on skits for me.

There are a lot of people who insult me behind my back, calling me "Radoh Namas-machina," and there are a lot as well who pity me, saying I've gone buggy in the head.

Maidun Reproducing Pharmaceuticals, unable to get permits for relocating its facilities, was dissolved. There are rumors, though, that the Zafutsubo have formed an underground organization and are selling namas-machina on the black market.

At the Ministry of Castellum Contemplation, my work involved assisting in experiments that attempted to make contact with Castellum Saruga. At the Ministries of Welfare Contemplation and of Archaeological Contemplation, I checked the results of their research against one another. At the Ministry of Legal Contemplation, I submitted materials for their meetings, and during my breaks I made the rounds of each ministry's aromaterial depository, digging through the aromaterials moved over from Castellum Raondo. Everyarc goes by at a hectic pace.

During the prerise of just such an arc, Ro, lying in the danglebed, failed to wake up. There had been no sign of anything amiss.

"How long has she been like this?" Dr. Saromi asked after rushing over.

I couldn't comprehend his meaning.

"All I can think," he continued, "is that she must have died years ago."

Ro's body cavity, he said, was all shriveled up inside, as if it had been dried out, with little holes everywhere.

At last, I found Castellum Giri's POW list. It was what I had been looking for as I had been digging through all those aromaterial depositories. In the midst of the bulleted text, I found her name: Ro Namas-machina. Besides that, her name appeared on a list of workers who had provided treatment for Castellum Giri's wounded soldiers. Immediately following the war, she had at least been treated as a human being. I took this evidence and submitted it to the Ministry of Legal Contemplation.

She became the first namas-machina in the history of either castellum to be given funerary rites as a person. Even now, she circulates among us in the form of a few dozen shellcoins. Thanks to that, I unexpectedly meet her again from time to time.

But for now, this is nothing more than a special exemption, a kind of honorary castellum citizenship given to the dead; it's not as if any living namas-machina have received rights as castle folk. There's still work to be done.

I've even been teased by some people who tell me, "Next thing you know, you'll be wanting to give castellum citizenship to castellae."

Although many different experiments for communicating with Castellum Saruga have been attempted, none have yet borne fruit.

Every once in a while though, I'll get a reverb from an unknown location.

At such times, I nod in silent agreement and then close the lidshell.

FRAGMENT:
EXILE

There appeared before <Gyo> the unincorporated an auditing corporatian who, anointing him with a draught of yoking fluid, locked down his cogitosome network. Next, he caused his innumerable subordinapes to commit death-service and banished the Chaos to the remnants of the seedship. Furthermore, it attached a group of luxury collection officers to <Gyo's> surface and had them suck out all of his stored-up riches.

The dregs of <Gyo's> consciousness gazed helplessly upon his own body as it shriveled away.

<Gyo> was compressed and imprisoned within a meteoroid-shaped prisonshell and, with many other convicts, loaded into a guarded chamber aboard a Reaffirmation ship. In a room for honored passengers located on its bottommost level, a freshly hatched Planetary Infant was welcomed.

PEREGRINATING
ANIMA
(OR, MOMONJI CARAVAN)

CHAPTER 1:
ORDINARY DAYS

Hisauchi was headed down.

Eight, seven, six… Inside the elevator, he stood watching as an indicator light moved sideways through the row of floor numbers.

He glanced over at his colleague Takagi, who was leaning against the wall to his right.

They'd been working in the same office right up until closing time, so his facial features, naturally, were clearly defined. He had a gentle sort of face, although a painful-looking cold sore was sticking out on his lip. Since it was easy to have those implanted at the doctor's office, there were oddballs out there who wore them as alternatives to piercings, but in Takagi's case, the reason was different: he liked to indulge in the sense of liberation that comes when an illness has departed or a wound has healed.

Hisauchi and Takagi reached the first floor, and the doors slid open. They walked out into the entryway. Takagi's footsteps were awkward due to the repeated compound fractures his femurs had endured.

"Want to go out for a drink?" Takagi asked.

"I've got plans already," said Hisauchi.

Even if he had been free, he probably would have turned him down. Every time he drank with Takagi, it always felt like he was reliving the same evening. That was how little their topics of conversation varied whenever they got drunk.

Hisauchi parted company with Takagi as they left the building, then started off down a cobblestone road, walking parallel to the streetcar tracks. After passing the trading company's three buildings, he turned into a narrow alley on the left and continued walking, turning corners at random.

A great number of crosses rose up into view; they glowed faintly from the spaces between tiles in the walls of the buildings and from bars in their windows. Sick of this ubiquitous holiness that was turning up everywhere, Hisauchi turned another corner, only to find his way blocked by an iron gate painted with yellow and black stripes. This was the border of the next parish over.

He backtracked and turned right. Someone came walking toward him from across the way. There was nothing unnatural about the man's face, except that the harder Hisauchi tried to recognize some physical characteristic, the grainier and more blurred his visage became. This was what was commonly known as <Crowd>: the interrelational appearance setting with the lowest possible intimacy level. Even so, he was able to recontuit him as Yasukawa, an acquaintance of his. Malfunctions of this sort had started happening about a month ago.

Taking the initiative, Yasukawa said, "Hey, Hisauchi, is that you?"

"Hey there, long time no see. What brings you all the way out here?"

Yasukawa's home office was in Parish 153—the same one they were standing in—but located on the exact opposite side of it.

"I was just feeling antsy," he said. "I get this feeling sometimes, like if I'm not out here walking around like this, the places I don't know all that well are just going to up and vanish."

"I know exactly what you're talking about," Hisauchi said with a nod. He felt something similar and couldn't refrain from obsessive-compulsive wandering either.

"Well then, I'll see you later," Yasukawa said. He dragged his feet as he started walking again and passed Hisauchi on the side.

Viewed from behind, he was a pitiful sight.

Hisauchi gave up on his aimless roaming and returned to the main road.

He went into a little bakery in front of the streetcar stop. The inside was crowded with <Crowd>-faced customers. Hisauchi picked up a paper sack and a pair of tongs, went to the fresh-from-the-oven table, and began filling the sack with neat round slices of rye bread, dark brown pieces of walnut bread, and more. Each time he put a piece in, the bread would switch to Paid.

He left the shop holding the sack against his chest, then saw a streetcar stopped right in front of him—no, not stopped; it was just starting to move.

In a sudden rush, he hurried after it, grabbed the handrail by the door, and pulled himself up into the car. With a sigh of relief, he took hold of a leather strap.

The man in the seat by the entrance was humming some sort of tune to himself. "Stop that," scolded the woman on his right. "I know you don't mean to, but that song is expensive; there's no telling how much they'll deduct."

Beyond the glass window, the stone city rolled past, painted orange in the light of early evening. Off in the distance, a church's steeple peeked into view. The passengers' reflections were overlaid on the scenery, including Hisauchi holding on to the leather strap. Every bag and every article of clothing subtly displayed the name of its maker, retailer, and raw materials used in uniformly translucent text. This was a lingering memory of Kosmetics, which had once adorned the world in kaleidoscopic splendor back in the days before it degenerated into the scrapworld that existed today. The streetcar itself was almost like a show window, lined with faceless mannequins.

Hisauchi got off three stops later and started walking along a dimly lit alleyway that cut through a residential district.

The paper sack he held in his right arm was warm and a little damp from the steam. On the other side of the familiar stucco walls that stretched along both sides of the road were long rows of everyday, single-family homes. The trees in their yards threw out large canopies of branches and leaves.

None of the homes had any feeling of being lived in though; practically all of them appeared to be vacant.

Dry leaves danced to the ground with their customary motions.

A rumbling began emanating from somewhere, drowning out the faint echo of Hisauchi's footfalls.

Hisauchi tensed up, stopped walking, and held his breath.

Just a few paces ahead, something suddenly leapt out of the seam where the road met the stucco wall. It had the energy of some predatory beast.

With a gross, sticky sound, it stuck to the street.

It was a chain of tumors the color of raw meat, tangled up like a set of puzzle rings. In the light of a lonely streetlamp, the tumors glistened. They bubbled up one after another from the edge of the street, twisting and turning like beads in a rosary as the mass as a whole swelled larger. Many clawed fingers protruded from the gaps in the tumors, twitching as if tapping on keyboards. Hisauchi's back broke out in gooseflesh. As the fingers played their silent strains, they started swelling up, as if each were competing to be the largest, and varied organs resembling skinned rats and cow tongues grew bountifully from their tips. Just as suddenly, bulges began appearing in other places, and all manner of internal organs began spilling out one after another. Splorching and splurching against each other, writhing furiously as they buried one another, they grew into luxuriant thickets that rose even higher than the stucco walls.

Throat tightening, Hisauchi loosened his tie and shifted the paper bag to his left arm. The aroma of freshly baked bread caressed his nostrils. He moved over to the other side of the street and, scraping his suit jacket along the stucco wall, managed to slip past what was probably fifty people's worth of viscera.

Once he was through, he took a deep breath and started walking again. Even so, he found himself unable to shake the sight he'd just seen from his mind.

"You must be a thief," he could clearly hear a nasal voice say. His heartbeat quickened.

"Not that we mind or anything," added a relaxed, easygoing voice.

"If you think so, then I don't really—"

His stomach squeezed tight.

"We *know*." A woman's voice this time, filled with scorn.

In trying to get his mind off the proliferating organs, he had just run up against a layer of memories he could have gladly done without. A series of linked moments from his past, without exception painful ones, came blossoming back into life.

This sort of recollection seizure was a disease endemic to the <World>. Everyone living here experienced them, but Hisauchi would always overreact and become disoriented. Seizures similar to this one had tormented him constantly since early childhood, and he had even undergone an illegal nervous system replacement to, at least for a time, suppress them.

The street and the rows of houses around him began to fade suddenly, and the scenery around him dissolved into the chaotically jostling dustwroughts of a discardation stratum. His legs and back grew heavy with exhaustion: he had been wandering the discardation strata aimlessly for days—this was one example of the nightmares he had come to have occasionally over the past fifty years.

He pulled an aluminum case from his coat's inner pocket, shook out a pill, and tossed it into his mouth. As he ground it between his molars, his surroundings started to go back to normal, and the pangs of remorse and self-reproach melted gently away. While his past did not recede from him (it was shared by a large number of unspecified individuals), he was able to distract himself from it in this manner.

Hisauchi started walking faster, and presently he arrived at his home.

He opened the wrought-iron gate, stepped through, and entered the garden. The davidia tree's branches were studded with scattered white bracts, and fresh leaves spread out from the many species of plantain lily. The oak front door that came up in front of him was out of style; he didn't like it. *With Kosmetics, I could've replaced it in a heartbeat,* he thought unhappily.

The instant he gripped the brass knob, his authentication went through and the lock came open. Moss-green pumps were set out neatly in the entryway.

Hisauchi changed into his regular clothes and went into the kitchen-cum-dining room. Hamuro, wearing her apron, turned toward him, but her face was indistinct, like that of some stranger set to <Crowd>. Even though she was registered as his lover in this house, their intimacy level had declined after just two days apart.

"Relational appearances are still on the blink, I see."

"Yeah. I hear it's just our parish though. Somebody from the computation company was just here explaining it."

"The computation company?"

"Said he was here to check on something. I thought you might be nearby, but when I opened the map, there were 'He is here' markers all over the place."

"Again? I wonder if it's the same kind of malfunction the intimacy settings are having."

"Who knows? Anyway, I made sure to put in a gripe about your usage volume. He apologized profusely, of course, but—"

"Ah, so that was what he wanted to check on? Thank you. They had me at four zeroes too many. No way that could be right…"

While Hisauchi was speaking, he handed her the paper sack. Hamuro unfolded the top, and said, "Ooh, these smell great!" as steam came wafting up from inside. She put the rye bread and walnut bread in a basket on the dining table. "I'm sure glad bread doesn't cool off. The meat sauce just finally finished simmering."

"Oh, let me help you."

Hisauchi filled a large pot with water and put it on the fire. Beside him, Hamuro heated a frying pan and tossed in some butter. The butter shrank as it melted, sliding around in the pan as though skating. Then she added soft wheat flour, poured in the milk, and beat the mixture with a wooden spatula. Hisauchi looked on, transfixed by Hamuro's skill and efficiency, and presently the water came to a boil.

He poured a small amount of olive oil into the hot water, added a pinch of salt, and then in went the lasagna, which he stirred with long chopsticks to keep the pasta from clumping.

Hamuro looked at Hisauchi, and a hint of a smile appeared on her face. Her features were steadily coming into sharper focus.

The lasagna finished boiling and was allowed to cool in the water-filled pot. Hamuro drained off the water and started laying the pasta out on a baking sheet, piling the noodles one on top of the other. Moving to Hisauchi's left side, Hamuro spread the meat sauce around in a square lasagna dish. Hisauchi poured white sauce over it. "*Someone* forgot to shake the water out of the noodles," Hamuro said while spreading out the lasagna. Together, they repeated the operation, piling on layer after layer. The steady progress of their mutual efforts, uncoordinated and utterly commonplace, felt somehow wondrous to him. At last they put the cheese on top, sprinkled it with bread crumbs, and placed it in the oven.

The lasagna cooked up to a splendid color, and they took it to the table. Even through the potholder, the heat of the dish made it hard to hold. Hamuro set out the plates and the wineglasses without missing a beat and piled their dishes high with salad and salami. Hisauchi twisted a corkscrew into the cork of the wine bottle. While this would sometimes split the cork, today it came right out.

Hamuro's intimacy level was soaring by the time they sat down facing one another. The fresh gloss of her lips, the faint rosiness in her cheeks, the scattered freckling of her skin—it was all coming into sharp focus now. Still, this was just her veriself, a unique form made to order by a bodyshop stylist; Hisauchi had never seen her gene-derived baseform.

He tilted the bottle of wine over Hamuro's glass. Amber-tinged ruby filled it. He poured for himself as well and with one finger wiped off a drop that had trickled down the neck of the bottle. The color of the grapes seeped in between the lines of his fingerprint. He somehow felt the spaces between the ridges were too wide. Both lifted their glasses lightly and sipped the wine. The fragrance of berries…a faint vanilla flavor. Without a word, the couple nodded at one another.

Hisauchi put his spoon into the deep dish in front of him. With a strange feeling that something was a little off, he stirred up the cream-colored stew, scooped out a chunk of potato, and popped it into his mouth. The spoon made a return trip between the dish and his mouth. All expression gradually faded from Hisauchi's face, and he stopped moving.

"What's the matter?" Hamuro said.

"This *is* what we started out to make, isn't it?"

"'This?'" Hamuro scooped up a piece of broccoli with her spoon and showed it to him. "Why do you ask? We just made this stew together, didn't we?"

"I'm sorry, I just have this feeling like we made something completely different."

"Different? Different how?"

"Um…let's see, it was more like, cooked on the surface… and the inside too was firm like this…and the blackened part was really good."

"That would be gratin, wouldn't it?"

"No, it was more like, lots of layers…That's right! We used this big, square, heat-resistant dish." He traced a finger across his wineglass and brought up a list of his personal possessions on its surface. But there was nothing under Dinnerware that jumped out at him as the dish he was thinking of.

"I can't remember." He wiped away the list and began to display a succession of oven-baked foods, their pictures taken from a cooking catalog. "Were there always so few varieties?" He slid his fingers across the curved surface of the glass as he wracked his brain impatiently. What he was looking for didn't appear. "But still…it was something completely different."

"That's a nice problem to have, not being able to remember. Everyone else is struggling with memories they can't erase." Hamuro soaked some bread in her stew. "I've never once passed a screening to gain the right of obliviation. What you've got is a simple case of imaginative amnesia."

"It isn't that; no matter how I think about it…"

Even when he checked the oven history, all he found displayed were ingredients for making stew.

"Now it really is looking like imaginative amnesia."

Hisauchi gave Hamuro a forced smile, feeling his eyes grow hot with an ineffable sense of loss, and he topped off his glass with plenty of wine.

CHAPTER 2:
BONEBELLS

1

A glaze of Chaos lay upon the greater portion of the world, and on the surface of its ever-growing, ever-transforming Vastsea, thousands of caravans could be found at any given time, making their way across in long processions.

One of these caravans—a column made up of several dozen downy white momonji—was advancing across a dustwreck plain, with dustwroughts of all shapes and sizes grinding and jostling against one another. Each momonji had its three transparent eyes fixed on the backside of the momonji in front of it, and their giant bodies—reminiscent of *coupée pão* bread rolls with their slight, gentle swells toward the front—swayed left and right as they crawled over unstable ground that was rolling with eidos waves. Ten pairs of claw-legs were arrayed in the middle of their undersides, which they used to pull themselves along guidelines that were laid out over the ground. These guidelines, made from twined fibers of momonji entrails, were indispensable for travel over the ever-changing Vastsea.

The momonji began pushing their way through a dustwreck jungle that blocked the way forward, slipping between wreck-trees that melted and flowed like mercury. Every fifth momonji was guided by a handler who accompanied it.

The field of view opened up and a calmdust belt, dented with countless indentations like the receptacle of a lotus, spread out all around them. Up ahead was Tochino Recuperation Block, standing like a fortress in the midst of an ivory-white plain. It was an artificial island floating on the Vastsea, covering an area of eighty thousand square meters. Eight connected flotation modules formed its rectangular shape. High castle walls of potsherd brown enclosed it completely, keeping the nanodust outside.

The caravan's vanguard reached the midpoint of the eastern blockwall, and the East Gate opened up. One after another, the momonji passed through, headed for the earth-covered area called Caravan Square.

When they came to the middle of Caravan Square, the handlers all shouted out in loud voices, placed hands on the backs of the chest-high momonji, then jammed fingertips into gaps in the backshell ossiforms that were under their skins. The four-meter-long creatures began turning their huge bodies around to face northward. The recuperation block's interior was divided into three large sections: a temporary holding pen to the north, Caravan Square in the center, and living quarters to the south.

When the momonji that led each column arrived at the movable fence that was in front of the holding pen, handlers stationed at strategic points placed their hands between the momonji's three eyes and brought them to a halt. With a slight lag, the momonji following along behind stopped as well. A synchronized venting of exhaust gases came from the spaces between the ground and their bellies, sending wispy clouds of dust flying.

The handlers, exhausted from their long journey, began to exchange parting courtesies. One after another, the dustmancers

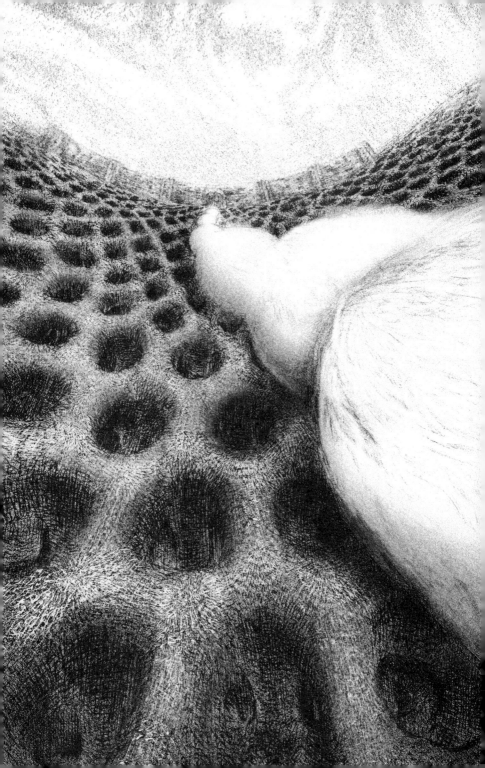

and feelancers departed, and the fatteners who stayed behind hurriedly set to work around the momonji.

One fattener, lying on his back, got down under a momonji's buttocks, twisted an arm into its cloacavity, and pulled out a long stripeworm he'd caught in his hand. Another fattener, grooming the creature's white body hair with a flea comb, removed a large flea the size of his thumb and squashed it under his boot. These tasks had to be done before they could bring the momonji into the holding pen.

Near the end of the line, a slender young girl with a fluff of walnut hair was scolding a momonji that had started moving forward on its own. She was not a fattener though, and her voice was too weak to be of much use. Her garb was that of a dustmancer—a boilersuit with antidust camouflage that appeared only as a solid gray and a shadecap hanging down on her back. In terms of stature though, she didn't even come up to the top of the momonji's thick body. The girl kept ordering the momonji to go back, but instead it simply latched on to the gigantic posterior waiting in front of it.

"You suckin' cartilage or something?" a voice called out. "A weak little squawk like that ain't gonna do nothing." A young fattener strode up, grabbed a handful of the momonji's loose hide, and wrung it like a wet towel as he barked a command. Reluctantly, the momonji curled around and came loose from its fellow's rear. "Take a break, kid. You ain't looking so good."

With a vague smile on her pale, mole-dotted face, the girl walked away. She next approached a momonji near the middle of the procession.

She stroked its soft back with a small hand that was covered in scars, though her veins were clear to see through her skin. She had lived side by side with these momonji for most of the past month since departing Afumi Fattening Lake.

Momonji were hermaphroditic, and the juveforms born at

the fattening lake had been no larger than watermelons. Their baggy, pale-peach skin had been completely hairless, and their backshell ossiforms, arrayed like armor plates, had been faintly visible through it. When spots of soft white hair had started to grow in here and there, the girl had found their pitiful, ragged appearance utterly adorable.

Bobbing out on the lake, the juveforms would gradually swell to larger and larger size, eventually exceeding the young girl in height.

On reaching the age of ten, momonji were entrusted to caravans, with whom they would journey across the Vastsea, either hauling cargo or as cargo themselves.

Soon these momonji would be handed over to another caravan and make for points farther north.

Following a stopover at some way station like Tochino Recuperation Block, momonji were led away to the more remote recuperation blocks in outlying areas. There some would be forced to produce gas and liquor until the day they died, while others would simply be disassembled on the spot. The latter were processed for a wide variety of uses—muscles and organs served as foodstuffs, intestinal fiber became guidelines, fat was made into candles and soap, pelts were used for clothes and bedding, and bones became building material and tableware; everything was used up. "The only thing we don't use," the saying went, "is the sound of their breathing."

The girl called out words of farewell to her traveling companions. Of course, the momonji could not reply. They had never had voices to begin with. The only sounds they could make were those useless, intermittent breaths, emanating from a mouth hidden under the forward part of the chest area.

She heard somebody groan near the posterior of the momonji she had just been petting and looked over to see what had happened. The fattener who had been pulling stripeworms there had just had his head doused with a gush of lye-colored excrement, which was now dripping down his face. She fought back laughter as soilmongers came flocking to the man from out of nowhere and started to shovel the manure into a wheelbarrow. They would ferment and dry it, and then it would go on sale. Sometimes the caravan would load muck of that sort onto the backs of momonji as well and transport it to agricultural recuperation blocks.

The girl moved over to a long-haired momonji waiting one head back in line. A little to the upper right of its three quartz-like eyes, its long hair curled in a spiral pattern, like a whirlpool in a surging sea. This was its whorl, or more precisely its jewel-eye, whose position differed on every momonji. During the course of their journey, she had gotten terribly attached to this one.

The girl touched its whorl and wrapped its hair around her fingers. After enjoying the sensation for a moment, she started combing it with her fingers while moving sideways, along with the natural flow of the fur. At last, she spread both arms wide and buried herself in the shaggy, sun-warmed pelt that covered its body.

Comforted by the elasticity and warmth of its thick skin, she breathed in a deep draught of its musky beast-smell, when suddenly, a husky voice from behind brought her back to reality.

"What did I tell you, Umari?"

She jumped away from the momonji and spun around.

Staring down at Umari was a powerfully built old man with a face that looked like something carved from a rocky mountainside. His fearsome eyes were like webbed cracks made by a blow from an iron staff. The lingering scent of fuzzy down steadily volatilized from her cheeks and chest.

"Master!" Umari cried, remembering only belatedly to bow her head.

Just as old carvings always seemed to be missing a piece or two, Umari's master was missing his left arm. The sleeve of his garment was tied off like a sausage around his upper arm. It had been torn off in his youth, he had said, by one of the Canvassers that haunted the Vastsea. Nothing but white stubble was growing on his square, bony jaw, and not a single hair was left on the top of his head; still, he stood ramrod-straight and certainly didn't look like someone over seventy.

The average life expectancy was short for those who spent their days traversing the Vastsea. Dr. Shibata at the clinic was probably the only one in the whole recuperation block who was older than Umari's dear master. Both had a certain air about them, like blessed, immortal hermits. She wondered: was that why they were rumored to have lived through the Great Dust Plague three hundred years ago?

"Don't let yourself get attached to them," said Master. "You'll only end up hurting yourself. The work of a dustmancer is finished the moment the momonji are all inside the recuperation block. You've finished making your courtesy calls, I presume?"

Umari gave an audible gasp and fumbled for a reply. Her master sucked in a single breath of air that made his thick chest swell and then let fly: "Then what are you doing staring off into space?! Get on it now! Start with the captain. When you're finished, come to the Isuzu Inn. And tell the other brethren to come there too."

"Yes, sir. Master."

"And after that—"

Frantically, Umari had started to run, but Master's words made her wobblingly freeze in mid-stride.

"—it seems that Kanze—that caravan cook—is in town right now. Can I ask you to take care of him as well?"

Umari ran northward along the column of momonji, looking for Team Leader Higan-shii. When she came to the momonji at the head of the line, she found it waiting quietly in front of a gate in a fence running east to west through the entire recuperation block. The temporary holding area that spread out past that fence was divided into numerous sections based on the momonji's destination and intended use, and momonji were being shoved into each of them. Some were also being driven along the road to the auction grounds at the northernmost end of the recuperation block.

She saw no sign of Team Leader Higan-shii. A row of three rusting cargo trailers were lined up near a movable section of fence that served as an entrance. Sitting on top of the nearest trailer—whose front end had been severely warped and twisted—were five members of the Dustclingers—the clan to which Umari also belonged. This was their first time in what felt like ages that they were back on their clan's home turf, and the strength seemed to have drained out of all their shoulders.

On the far right end sat Renji. The tan girl's thick black hair was tied up in the back, and her tan lips were pursed. A polyhedrical object rested in the palm of her thumbless right hand, and moment by moment, the number of its corners was changing in accordance with her whispers. She was dustchanting to kill a little time. Umari would have probably needed days to produce just one of those eide.

"Ahh, I just can't do it!" Renji said. "They won't come out right like Junrin-shi's." Renji glared at the polyhedron as she spoke. She was hoarse from an excess of dustchanting. Junrin-shi was a dustmancer whose name was known even among the Dustclingers, but some years ago she had gone missing during a caravan drive.

Following a clinical examination, Renji had been pronounced sterile at the age of ten, and after being kicked out of the maternitorium at Isurugi Recuperation Block, she had joined the Dustclingers out of admiration for Junrin-shi. Even so, she was not yet ready to receive the title of "-shi." And while it was true that less than a year had passed since Umari's joining the clan, she doubted she could ever learn to chant dust as skillfully as Renji did, even if she trained for decades.

"Look, I'm telling you, there's no point in eking by with these runs between recuperation blocks." Sitting next to Renji, Romon dangled his booted feet off the edge of the trailer, gesticulating passionately as he made his points. "All across the worlde, the number of recuperation blocks keeps falling. How much longer do you think this kind of work can go on? We need to be thinking about what comes next."

"Yeah. Yeah, I guess so." Next to him, Homaru gave a noncommittal reply.

"So what are you saying?" sturdy-framed Kugu-shi said listlessly from Homaru's side. "That we should become sailors and go trade with maremen or something? We'd just end up swallowed by coffin eels."

Kugu-shi had stripped off the coverall he used for caravan work and was now wearing short sleeves and knee-length breeches. Leaning back on his thick, muscular arms, he gazed up at the tangled wisps of cloud in the sky. His calf was swollen so badly it looked ready to burst and had big stitch marks snaking all the way around it; to Umari, the sight was difficult to take in. *How many times does this make it that Kugu-shi's saved my life? I've got to train—every minute I can spare—so I won't just be cuffs and fetters on everyone.* Yet even as the thought ran through her mind, she knew she was so far behind in so many ways…Feeling miserable and pathetic, she let out a sigh.

Sitting on the left end as if in meditation was Geiei-shi, the eldest of the group, with his ruined eyes and his close-cropped hair. He turned toward Umari, showing a face tattooed with antidust camouflage.

Suddenly, Romon said in a louder voice, "No, you're over-simplifying; I didn't mean it like that. What I'm trying to say is—"

"Who in the worlde has filled your head with that tripe?" said Kugu-shi. "You haven't been yourself lately."

"Nobody's filling my head with anything. It's Master and all of you who aren't thinking things through enough!"

"*What* did you just say?"

Homaru, caught between the arguing pair, had drawn up his sloped shoulders in obvious discomfort. Noticing Umari standing in Geiei-shi's line of nonsight, he called out to her, "What do you want, Convalescent?"

Umari hadn't actually been sick, but she got called that a lot, being as her color was seldom very good.

The arguing stopped, and all faces turned toward Umari.

Romon stuck his head out; it was covered with deep scars from old cuts. Glaring at Umari, he said, "The old fossil send you?"

Ever since she had joined the clan, she had been ostracized by Romon. Probably in part because Umari's carelessness was to blame for a few of those scars. Judging by his behavior and his many scars, it was easy to think him the same age as Renji and Homaru, who were both in their mid-twenties. In fact, though, he wasn't much older than Umari. Not that Umari knew her own age with any precision. She had thought of herself as seventeen at the time she realized she didn't know.

"'Old fossil?' I'll tell Master you said that," warned Renji.

"I ain't afraid of that senile *fossil*. He works the living hell outta me! Well? What is it?"

"Master says finish your courtesy rounds and then meet up

at Isuzu Inn."

"All right, folks," said Kugu-shi. "In that case, it's dinner-time." He jumped down off the trailer, and the other clan-brethren followed with languid cheers, kicking up dust as they landed.

Slack-jawed, Umari looked up at Kugu-shi's nearly two-meter height. His fat nose reminded her somehow of a bull's.

"What?" he said in his deep bass voice, draping his worksuit over Umari's head. Taking care of laundry was her job. "We finished up ages ago."

"Um," Umari said, peeking out from beneath Kugu-shi's sweat-ripe coverall. "Where's Team Leader Higan-shii?"

"You're *still* keeping to your usual snail's pace?" Homaru said, laughing with phony surprise and a flash of silver light. After losing his baby teeth as a child, permanent ones had never grown in, so silver false teeth had been implanted in both his upper and lower jaw. There were a lot of people like that. "By this time, he's probably leading the next caravan out already."

"For someone who takes no rest at all, the man really does hold together pretty well," said Romon.

"Aw, what's with the poor sad face, Umari?" said Renji. "If all you ever do is hang around momonji, it stands to reason your sweetums'll get away."

Riding the coattail of Renji's comment, the other clan-brethren started teasing her. It was the usual routine. Renji always accused Umari of liking whoever she herself had fallen for; it was a way she tried to keep her own feelings hidden. In any case, there were no other women outside the maternitorium.

"I'm going on ahead," Kugu-shi said as he turned away. "Finish up your courtesy rounds or there won't be any left when you get back."

Left all alone, Umari set off on foot, threading her way between rows of momonji as she searched for the hands who had accompanied them on the drive.

The fatteners called out to her in kind voices, but no one else did. After all, Umari was still just an unskilled greenhorn who couldn't even do a dustchant very well. Normally, there would have been a ritual exchange of coordinates earlier for communication purposes, but not only had no one given their coordinates to Umari, she had not even been able to get coordinates for herself. That was why she had to go around thanking and bidding each one farewell in person; to do otherwise would have been disrespectful.

She noticed a pair of feelancers who had been with the caravan. They were standing on the west side of Caravan Square talking to one another. She ran up and bowed, but they brushed her off without so much as a glance.

It hit her then that she didn't even know Master's coordinates. It wasn't as if she needed them, but at the thought of that, she grew all the more miserable.

"Got no house, got no shack, got no shirt to hide my back...

"Got no meat, got no bread, got no job to keep me fed...

"But momonji I got...

"Mo-mo-mo-monji I got...

"...and with them I get by.

"...and with them I get by.

"...and with them I get by..."

She could hear the drunken voices singing from somewhere. She turned around and saw what looked like a crew of gutdiggers in front of a food stall, clad in protective coveralls. One by one, and occasionally together, they were lifting their voices in song.

On the western side of the square was a wide, open-air market, with the eaves of assorted stalls aligned to form many long aisles. These included momonji stalls that sold lightly broiled meats, bonemeal soba, stewed organs, fried stripeworms on sticks, hemomochi, and more. Even with the sun still high, it was crowded.

At a kebab stall, Umari spotted Soho-shii, standing a head taller than the other diners around him. His slender body was leaning over toward the left. Inside the oven, a spindle-shaped chunk of meat—a whole armload's worth—was grilling on a rotating oven plate. Every once in a while, a drop of grease would fall and pop.

Soho-shii held a bonecup and a large skewer of grilled meat in his hands as he conversed with a handsome-looking man—a beastbutcher, judging by the blood-spattered apron.

"No, it's not that I was trying to raise my skills," Soho-shii was saying, his mouselike, high-cheekboned face stretching as he tore a piece of meat off with his teeth. "It's just that all the young dustmancers are being headhunted by that crawlbacker lot. It's leaving the clans short-handed."

"Huh. What do crawlbackers want with a bunch of dustmancers?"

"No idea. I have heard some pretty crazy rumors though. Wild tales of giant eidos bombs and the like—Oh look here! If it isn't Umari! What's the matter? Your courtesy rounds ending in miserable defeat again?"

Soho-shii raised the bonecup to his lips. A powerful smell of ammonia wafted on the air. The beastbutcher turned to Umari with a stunning smile. Behind him, the upper body of a terribly fat woman could be seen wobbling back and forth like a pendulum. That was Sagyoku-shii, leader of the Fatguard Clan. The beastbutcher continued smiling at Umari.

Unsure how to respond, she averted her gaze and started speaking quickly, trying not to look flustered. "You drink that stuff a lot, don't you, clan-brother?"

Soho-shii stared intently at his bonecup and gave her a

knowing smile. Originally, Soho-shii had been a disciple of the same clan as her, but two years ago he had struck out on his own as a linelayer, changing his honorific from "-shi" to "-shii" to show he was no longer a child apprentice but a fully-fledged workman. Their last journey had had a lot of difficult passages on its itinerary though, so he had accompanied the caravan at Master's request.

"I'm trying to find Kanze—the caravan cook," she said.

"Ah, he just went in there."

Soho-shii pointed a finger, but drunk as he was, it was too unsteady to be much help.

What was in that direction was a long row of houses stretching from east to west. It looked like a dam that might burst at any moment, unleashing the flood of disorderly residences piled up behind.

Soho-shii drank up the last of his liquor and, tilting this time rightward, added with a belch: "The maternitorium."

That word focused her attention on the middle of the row, where a dark, three-story wooden mansion stood out conspicuously from the rest. A belvedere adorned its large, gabled roof, and fretwork ran along the handrails of its cloister. The roof and the handrails glowed in the afternoon sunlight. The whole structure had been excavated from a dustsink and reconstructed here.

"He said he'd be heading out in half an hour," Soho-shii said.

Umari thanked him and started walking toward the maternitorium. Like wet, fallen leaves, earthcreepers lay scattered here and there on the ground. "Earthcreeper" was a catch-all term for drunks, beggars, and dead bodies seen lying on the ground. Most had once been Vastsea crossers.

Beneath a cusped gable was a conspicuous red and gold double door, in front of which ten or so young children were drawing momonji on the ground with pointed bones. Noisily smacking on cartilage, their mouths were moist with spit.

When they noticed Umari, they came crowding around her, crying out in wild voices. Umari stroked their oily, matted hair, and that alone made them break out in innocent laughter. Using the full weight of their bodies, several of them pushed the doors open for her, and the rest, pulling on Umari's hand and pushing against her back, guided her into the building.

The moment she crossed the threshold, she felt a tickling in the back of her nostrils. Smoke from the incense burner filled an open space that extended three floors upward and shone faintly in the light streaming in through the skylight.

Directly across from the entrance, a great red staircase awaited. The wide passage leading to it was inlaid with brilliant floral patterns in mother-of-pearl, and a row of women stood at ease along either wall. All of them wore embroidered gowns, with beauty spots stuck on their white, painted faces. Umari's throat made a noise as she fought back a cough.

"Why, if it isn't Umari!" one of the girls standing in front cried when she noticed her. One after another, the other mothers leaned toward her, forming a fan-shape as they tried to see her face.

"Isn't that Umari—"

"I'm glad you're safely back—"

"Skinny as ever, aren't you—"

"You never change—"

"Have you been ill?"

"You were like that before, weren't you?"

"You *are* making them feed you right, aren't you?"

Small spots of lipstick were painted in the center of each one's lips, and the brilliant red color took Umari back to her own days in the maternitorium, when she used to grind up shellbugs to help make lipstick.

"Mothers, I'm sorry to have been out of touch so long." A

smile blossomed on her face as she looked around at all the mothers on her right and left. Her eyes came to rest on the swollen belly of a long-necked woman in the middle of the row to the left.

"Your tenth, Lady Shushu-mater?"

"Your voice is the same as ever; still sounds like you're sucking on cartilage. It's my eleventh. The babies just keep on coming. It's wearing me out." Laughing loudly, she exposed a set of teeth resembling a broken keyboard. "Well, what brings you here today? Don't tell me you've come back here to become a mother?"

Umari felt a jab of pain in her slender chest. So Dr. Shibata had never told them she couldn't bear children.

"I'll get around to it one of these days," she said.

But the mothers were not to be brushed off so easily.

"Listen, happiness is watching over your children as they grow—"

"We need to cheer up the men—"

"Come back! You'll be able to wear makeup and have romance—"

"Oh, no! No matter what you say, it's momonji this girl's head-over-heels for—"

"I just don't understand…"

"Back when Umari ran out of here saying she was gonna be a fattener—"

"I was shocked when I heard that…"

Even now, Umari would have liked to become a fattener if she could. She hadn't been able to get on with any fattener clans though; not even the Fatguard Clan run by Sagyoku-shii, whom she'd glimpsed just shortly before. Her current master had taken her on when she'd been at wit's end. Which made two times she had been rescued by Master.

Umari hadn't been born in a maternitorium. From what

she had heard, she'd been picked up by Master when he was on a caravan drive and afterward entrusted to the maternitorium here. That was what she'd been told one year ago, after Dr. Shibata had examined her and explained the condition of her uterus.

"Ah, this needs washing."

Lady Rani-mater pulled loose Kugu-shi's antidust camouflage, which she'd been carrying under one arm. Washing the clothing of Vastsea crossers was one of the jobs the maternitorium performed. They also urged Umari to take off the antidust camouflage she was wearing now, but Umari declined, explaining that she was here on an errand.

"Which room is Mr. Kanze in?"

"That obnoxious caravan cook? He's 'playing house' with Lady Mebaru-mater in the Hagoromo Room. Make it quick, okay?"

Waving to the mothers, Umari went up the big, red-carpeted staircase. The soles of her shoes sank comfortably into the momonji fur. At the landing, she reversed directions and climbed a second staircase, then headed off toward the Hagoromo Room. On the way up, Umari passed a drunken man who was coming down together with a mother she didn't know. As they passed one another, the man misstepped badly and stumbled into Umari.

"Sorry, Mother," he apologized in a voice that didn't seem to be working right.

All of the women here were mothers, and the men were all sons born in some maternitorium or other. It was rare now for births to take place anywhere else.

Umari heard him whisper in the ear of the mother beside him: "*She don't ever change, does she, that mother...*"

"Women *don't* age," the mother replied with a laugh.

Running along the third-floor cloister was a loop of small

bedchambers separated only by thin, sheer curtains. Inside each, naked men and women lay entangled with one another, moaning and gasping.

Umari came to one room that had a card labeled "Hagoromo" hanging from the pillar. She pushed the curtain open with the back of her hand. Inside was a small man, half buried in the vast expanse of Lady Mebaru-mater, whose body was now bloated to the point that her arms and legs looked like mere accessories. The man was making vigorous movements, like the flailing of a drowning man.

Umari had been on a caravan drive with Kanze only once, and that was about ten months ago. Still, there was no mistaking that over-groomed mustache and square-jawed face, even with his features strained with excitement.

The cook looked up with a sweat-smeared face when he realized Umari was standing there. "Don't tell me it's the Dustclingers' girl," he said. He spat out the clan's name like a grape seed, indicating both the clan and its Master, although he didn't stop playing house. A wallet dangling from his neck danced and jumped about.

"I'm here with a message from Master. Please pay him three months' worth."

The Dustclingers operated a financial service for its hired hands. Kanze had been entrusted with funds by the caravan to buy foodstuffs, but after blowing it all in a gambling den, he'd borrowed money from Master to pay for the provisions, then accompanied them on the drive, acting as though nothing had happened. Since that time, he'd been avoiding routes that the Dustclingers frequented.

"Well, uh, as you can see, I'm a little, er…" The cook shook his head, sending beads of sweat flying. He rocked his pelvis even harder, sinking deeper and deeper into Lady Mebaru-mater.

"I may still be green," Umari countered, "but even I know

how to chant butthole-i-vores." The medibugs of which Umari spoke were more formally known as "colonoscopy worms." "I can't control 'em yet though."

So saying, Umari took out a small leather pouch, loosed the string around its mouth, and turned it upside down. Silvery-white blobs of dustwreck came spilling out, resembling melted pieces of candy. They formed a mound in the palm of her hand.

The cook, whose hips continued to sway even as he stared at the falling bits of dustwreck, suddenly shouted, "Agh! Cramp!" and jumped off of Lady Mebaru-mater, gripping his left calf with both hands as if catching a fish that had been flopping about on land. "My calf!" he cried. "My calf!" As he bent backward, clear, unclouded seed dribbled down lazily from a vessel that now had no harbor.

The cook leaned against the corner of the room, suppressing his voice between ragged breaths as he berated Umari:

"...cramped so bad I couldn't feel a thing!

"...made me waste it!"

He pulled a ticket from his wallet and grudgingly, repeatedly, added up the amount. With a miserly air, he at last handed over five coins. Umari told him it wasn't enough.

"You greedy hag!" the cook shouted as he held out one more coin. Lady Mebaru-mater's flesh rolled with her laughter. Even after Umari had put the Hagoromo Room behind her, the cheerful laughter rolled on.

2

Umari waved to the children and told them goodbye, then began walking westward along a row of buildings of which the maternitorium was a part. In the central square was another herd of freshly arrived momonji. She could even see the rare amber-colored breed.

Enthralled by the sight, she tripped over something. An earthcreeper. There sure seemed to be a lot of them today. There was even one who was stuck in a dustdrain ditch.

After passing by the tanner's and the materialmonger's, she arrived at the Isuzu Inn. This barracks, patched together from various excavated materials, had no wall in front, leaving an interior bustling with travelers and merchants completely exposed to view. Chairs were aligned haphazardly, and not even one matched any other. It was said that they were all precious artifacts excavated from a certain chair museum in dustsunk land, but thanks to rough handling, they now looked like nothing more than junk. Even so, if you threw them out on the Vastsea, large morphwaves would likely propagate outward from where they landed.

Umari heard the grating cries of chickens and glanced down the narrow gap between the Isuzu Inn and the neighboring building. There was a legless earthcreeper in there, clinging to the chicken-wire fence. He had his hand stuck into the coop through a hole he had made in the fence. He was stealing chicken feed.

The chickens were flapping their wings furiously—but not just because of the earthcreeper.

A tremor rumbled through the ground, and everything around Umari swayed wildly. As she crouched down low, the ground supporting the Isuzu Inn began tilting perilously right before her eyes. The earthcreeper went sliding, and the chickens seemed to float for just an instant before they crashed into the wall. Innumerable bonebells, hanging in a loop from the walls inside, rang noisily while a landslide of cups and dishes poured off the tabletops, slipping through the hands of customers who tried to stop them.

The split face of a thick, scraped-up flotation module rose up to the tip of her nose.

Leaking water began spreading out from the gas factory next door on the left. Momonji used in gas production floated in large water tanks, since their exoshelletons had been removed to allow their air sacs to expand to the uttermost limit. Water from those tanks had apparently spilled.

Slowly, creakingly, the ground began to level back out. Ordinarily, flat ground could be taken for granted, but this had just been a stark reminder that they were in fact standing on nothing more than a raft afloat in the Vastsea.

Umari stepped into the Isuzu Inn, where the faint ringing of bells still lingered.

The restaurant area had a floor space of one hundred square meters, and the shaking just now had thrown it into utter chaos. Food and tableware had been flung all over the floor. She could hear tightly choked sighs and pained coughs. Many people were picking up their boneplates and utensils, putting handfuls of spilled food back on their plates, or calmly continuing their meals. Naturally, there was no putting back spilled drinks, so voices were being raised here and there as people reordered— voices with that flatness and hoarseness peculiar to the violated lungs and windpipes of Vastsea crossers.

Umari stretched up to her full height for a look around the restaurant. One man had a tall mound of momonji claw-legs piled up on his tabletop and was starting to vacantly scrape out the drying muscle fibers for the trace amounts of stimulants they contained. Another was haggling over the price of some rare item he had dug up out of a dustsink, holding it up with an air of self-importance. Yet another was drowsing as he breathed in vapors from momonji stones (said to be good for respiratory ailments) in a large water pipe. Seated in the midst of them, her teammates from the Dustclingers were throwing their yuzu-sized bonebells down on the floor and cheering as they shattered. It looked like it was going to be difficult to get over to where they were sitting. She looked over at the counter seats that ran along the wall to her right, and there she spotted Master's wide back.

Following in the wake of a server carrying a trayload of food, she made her way through the crowd and stood behind the tall chair where Master was sitting.

"Master?" she said. He didn't move. He had one elbow on the countertop of the riddled bar and was gazing into a bone-cup filled with milky-white liquid. Master was known to drift away like this on occasion.

That was why Romon was so eager to declare Master a dotard. "If he collapses or something in the middle of a drive," he was always saying, "we'll be the ones who'll be goners—"

Umari called him again, and Master came back to himself, blearily accepting the ticket she handed him. The man to the left of him rose totteringly to his feet, handing a bonebell to the barkeep before pushing past Umari's shoulder on his way out. The barkeep added the new bonebell to a wall that was covered in them. It was tradition that before departing on a journey you prayed for safety and left a bonebell here; whenever you made it back again, you threw it down and shattered it.

"Order whatever you like," said Master.

Umari seated herself on the high stool that the other man had just vacated, but since she usually just partook in whatever her master and brethren chose, she didn't know what to order or how to order it. Master, sensing her distress, ordered for her: "Bring her some *pāo* rolls and horsebit meat, along with some simmerstrings."

Soon the barkeep, whose browless face was like a peeled boiled egg, placed a boneplate haphazardly piled with food in front of her and set her bonebell down beside it. Umari wrapped her palm around the bell, gave it a ring as she felt its hard, cold surface, and then put it away in her breast pocket. She never felt like breaking them, so she would just leave this one behind again at the time of her next departure.

Using the familiar knife she carried in her travels, she sliced off some horsebit meat and tore right into it. Juices rich in vegetable nutrients—juices peculiar to the flesh of momonji— came welling out with an aroma of chlorophyll. The meat was full of tough sinews that she couldn't quite bite through; they literally began stopping up her mouth, making it difficult to breath. Even so, she was happy to hold her head high eating a meal of her very own.

It was then that someone came up on Master's right. He ordered a drink in a voice as clear as a mountain stream and rested a strange arm—one longer than an arm should be—on a chair. Still standing, he cast his gaze across the room. Did he have some sort of lung disease? He was taking shallow breaths quite frequently. Still, he didn't look like a Vastsea crosser. His soft, faintly reddish skin was like that of a newborn, which only made the large red boil on the right side of his jaw stand out even more. His skin was drawn tight and shiny like the rind of a fruit.

"Might you be looking for someone?" the barkeep whispered as he held out his bonecup.

The man turned toward the barkeep, a good-natured, friendly-looking smile brimming on his face. Umari was surprised by the whiteness she glimpsed in the flash of his teeth.

"You really shouldn't look at people so curiously," said the barkeep. "You just might end up with trouble you don't need."

"Oh, ah, right." The man sat down in a tall chair and was hidden from view behind Master's hulking frame. "Do you have anything to eat here?"

"Red meat, sweetfat, sausage, offal, claw-legs—we've got it all."

"No thanks, I'd actually like to have rice."

"In that case…" The barkeep indicated the countertop with the palm of his hand.

"I'm sorry, ah, what do you mean?" the man asked in bewilderment.

"You do it like this," Master said, grabbing the front corner of the bar. He pried up a chip of wood.

The splintered underside was swarming with white ricemites.

"They're included in the bill as an appetizer, so dig in," Master said, plucking up one ricemite, then another, and tossing them into his mouth.

The other man's only reply was his shallow breathing.

"This isn't the kind of rice you were lookin' for, is it?" said Master.

"I meant the grain."

"I see. Pearls from the sea; gems from the mountain, eh? If I could easily lay hands on pearls and amber, there'd be all kinds of things I'd like to eat too. Just recently, I've really had a hankering for lasagna."

From the sound of that word, Umari imagined some kind of fruit. It was unfamiliar-sounding, and the barkeep seemed to have had the same reaction.

"Is that something maremen eat?"

"Something like that."

"Excuse me," the man said to Master. "But you wouldn't happen to be a first-generation Incarnate, would you?"

"Incarnate? Oh, a crawlbacker, you mean. What gave you that idea?"

"Well, unlike these other scraplings, you're quite easy to communicate with. Then there's your face, and the fact that something about you just feels different."

A murmur arose from the seats behind the man. Who was

this guy? Some mareman, letting taboo words slip out in pub-lic? Umari was thinking he might be, when the man realized his faux pas and corrected himself: "I'm sorry; what I should have said was 'these non-replayable intellects.'"

Which was an even worse term. The original meaning was long forgotten; now all that remained was the strong sense of contempt attached to the term.

"I think you're the one who's the crawlbacker," Master said with a scornful laugh. "I met a guy who looked a lot like you once. His arms were stranger though...and longer."

"Ah yes, *that* mutation was very common in the first genera-tion. Oh, I forgot to tell you, but my name is Hanishibe—"

But the man suddenly stopped and inhaled deeply.

"What's the matter?"

"I feel dizzy. My field of vision's gone terribly wobbly; also, I'm not used to these intense sensations in my intestines. And on top of that, with this rarefied air and these overwhelming odors..."

Umari, still chewing on some horsebit meat that she still hadn't managed to bite through, lowered her head over the bar counter a little and tried to sneak another glimpse of Hanishi-be's face. The fingers he was dabbing his eyes with came away, revealing a face with a glossy sheen.

"I'm no different from anyone else in the worlde," said Mas-ter, "aside from being a feeble old man."

"Is that so? Could I ask you some questions about yourself? What's it like living in this ruined worlde as a non-replayable intellect that doesn't even legally exist? I've always been curious about that."

There was a rustle as several people stood up from their seats at the tables.

"You don't legally exist either," said Master. "And when you choose your words, it might be a good idea to keep in mind these folks who are perking up their ears right behind you." Master jerked his chin back toward the middle of the room, but the other man, oblivious to the gesture's intent, continued to speak.

"I'm still listed as replayable in my parish's individual registry. Now it's true that about ten years ago, this would have been a seriously illegal act, but the Divine Will First Party has received legal sanction, so this kind of thing is allowed within certain set parameters. There are all kinds of factions over there; it gets kind of complicated, you know."

Several voices rose, saying, "He said he's a crawlbacker!" Tables and chairs rattled.

Umari, frozen with tension, took a sideways glance and saw several rough-looking men standing behind the stranger. Soilmongers, most likely, judging by the earth-colored filth on their clothing.

"Those dirty traitors turned tail and ran when we were facing the Great Dust Plague!"

"Lousy ghosts!"

"Rotten mantis shrimps!"

"You suckered a whole lotta people with your 'baptism' and 'Translation' and all that other babble…"

"We've just barely survived out here on the Vastsea, and you think you can come in here and insult us with those forbidden words?"

A vicarious rage was shooting through the men, as though each of them had just lived through it all themselves.

"Oh no, I certainly never meant…" The crawlbacker twisted around and looked up at the roughnecks.

"I hear you ghosts like to call this place the 'Scrapworld…'"

"You dungdriver—!"

"What'd you bother crawling back here for!"

"Couldn't find Nirvana in a mantis shrimp?"

"No, these fellas been gatherin' up the young people."

"They're plannin' to take 'em away again!"

"What's that? Why? What do you plan on doin' with 'em?"

"He wants to take 'em all away again!"

"You can't have my apprentices!"

"Kidnapper!"

It was already too late to calm them. Kugu-shi and Romon got up from their seats some distance away.

"No, no, this is nothing more than good old-fashioned human resource canvassing; we exchange formal contracts." Overwhelmed, perhaps, by the angry shouts, Hanishibe's gaze danced back and forth as if following a fly as he explained himself to no one in particular. "And besides, I'm from a different department, so I had nothing to do with that—"

Suddenly, Master reached for Hanishibe's face with his thick, cracked hand. The man shrunk back, trying to get away, but Master's thumb and index finger caught the boil on his jaw in a pinch and wouldn't let go. Hanishibe's soft skin broke out in a greasy sweat, his eyes opened wide, and his jaw quivered sideways. Master's thick fingers held on like a ring-clamp.

A cheer went up from the crowd. Hanishibe bent over backward and landed on the floor. Following along, Master had also come out of his chair. Everyone laughed and jeered.

"What in the worlde are you doi—?" That was as far as Hanishibe got before the boil burst in a spray of blood.

His wordless scream rang through the restaurant, silencing the commotion instantly.

A piece of metal resembling a wing bolt was sticking out of the wound, which now resembled a vinegar-peach that someone had taken a bite of.

Master pursed his lips, and his throat began to quiver. He was generating a high-pitched ordinary-wave carrier tone.

All by itself, the metal piece began to revolve, corkscrewing its way out, plucking a spiral body resembling a turban snail from his lower jawbone. At last, it dropped to the ground. Down on the food-strewn floor, the turban shell collapsed and began changing form repeatedly, as if it were being kneaded by invisible fingers. Even eide that lived within the body became confused when they couldn't find a partner to fuse with.

Master pulled out a leather bag and switched to a different kind of carrier tone. Several legs stretched out of the metal body, and it began walking like a spider. It crawled up Master's leg and disappeared into his bag.

The deathly silent restaurant began to resume something of its former clamor.

Whether cheered by the crawlbacker's suffering or fearful of picking a fight with a dustmancer, those who had been raining down epithets moments before now filed out of the restaurant. There was no shortage of people who hated or feared dustmancers. Even those who hired them out of necessity remained suspicious of skills such as dustvein-reading and dustchanting and almost never approached them unless it was for work.

"Have yourself some goldeneye momonji wine, Guv'nor," the barkeep said, pouring a bonecup of Master's favorite. The distinctive scent of iodine came wafting through the air.

"You have my gratitude," Hanishibe said, standing as he took a handkerchief from his shirt pocket and pressed it up against his wound. "To think I had something like that nesting inside my body!" He didn't sound very articulate now; it was like the strength had gone out of his jaw.

"What you had there was a marrowsticker. They don't usually dig into places like that. The inconsistency between that brand-new body of yours and its adult form is probably what attracted it." Master wet his lips with wine and narrowed his eyes. "Just like your words attracted those hooligans."

"I'll be more prudent going forward," Hanishibe said,

steadying his breath. "Actually, it *was* dustmancers I came here looking for. Did you know there's a shrine about two kilometers from here?"

"Yeah, it's in a dustsink, about fifty meters underground. What? You planning on going there to pray?"

"That's right," he said with a carefree smile. "I really am. I'm a sailor. I'm shipping out on a rather long journey, so I'd like to say my prayers in advance. Could I get you to guide me there?"

"I don't know; I thought there was still a seal on you people. You can only go in as far as the inner shrine's divine gate, right?"

"Incarnates such as myself lack the genes for growing kosmetic boxes in their brains. Therefore, the seal shouldn't work on me. If you can just get me as far as the divine gate, that will be enough."

"If you'll meet me in front of the West Gate three days from now, at five in the morning, dressed out in caravan gear, I can take you." Master, who had been staring at Hanishibe, turned back toward the counter. "But you won't come."

"Now what makes you say that? I'll come. I guarantee it."

Disturbed voices rose up from among the table seats. Hanishibe turned toward the sound, and that was when Umari saw several metal shafts sticking out of the back of his head, resembling vaginal speculae. In addition, there was a fat metal leg sticking out from the left side of his nose and a vivid sound like something being sharpened. Hanishibe's chest and back also began to produce asymmetric bulges.

"No, no, I'll be there," he said. The metal leg vibrated and split into upper and lower halves, which then spread apart, splitting Hanishibe's face open vertically. Blood gushed forth in torrents and spurts, and bubbles overflowed and came dripping down. "That's the West Gate," the cloven lips said indistinctly. "Correct?"

Unearthly metal projections ripped through his skin one

after another. Each one was shaped like a tool that could have only been designed to treat some strange, imaginary malady. Chunks of flesh were being sheared off from his face; his sleeves, and his pant legs, were torn to pieces.

An order echoed through the restaurant: "Somebody go get a feedmonger!"

CHAPTER 3:
ALONG THIS SHORE

The ivory beach stretched gently out all the way to a promontory resembling the snout of a crocodile. Rising up from the tip of that promontory was the white tower of a lighthouse.

Out on the sea, waves lapped over one another again and again as they rolled in toward the beach where Hisauchi and Hamuro were standing. There was something unnatural about their repetition. The motion of the waves had become vastly more simple than it had been in the past.

A gentle sea breeze came blowing in against them. A fresh, delicate aroma tickled Hisauchi's nostrils, but still something seemed to be missing—although as a child he had disliked the ocean's raw, even violent, odor of living things. Prior to the Great Dust Plague, there had been Kosmetics, and you could use Concealer to turn off at will any stenches exceeding a certain threshold value, but here in this <World>, the very existence of unpleasant odors had been eliminated as an unnecessary use of resources. "What we never lose is the sense of loss," Hisauchi murmured.

"What's changed?" somebody asked him. "Things are just the same as they've always been, aren't they?" She repeated the words as if trying to convince herself. "Things are just the same as always."

Of course it was Hamuro speaking; even Hisauchi could

tell that much. And yet she was set so firmly to <Crowd> that he almost caught himself doubting it. No, there was a more fundamental vagueness at work here. The longer he looked at her face, the more dazed and withdrawn she seemed to become. There was something that she looked like, but he couldn't remember what it was. There were more and more things he couldn't remember these days.

"For example," he said, "don't you get the feeling there are more and more vacant houses?" Even his own voice sounded formal and distant. "I mean, somebody must have been living in that house two doors down from us."

"I'm pretty sure that one's always been vacant. Still, sometimes extremists in the Divine Will First Party and whatnot do have their individual registries erased because of political problems, so…"

Hamuro looked over to the right, where waves were crashing in against the shore. A man there was walking toward the sea. Buffeted by waves, he gradually disappeared into the depths. A deathseeker, most likely. Deathseekers, it was said, gave themselves over to the tepid pain of suffocation to aimlessly wander the endless seafloor.

Staring at the rippling waves where the man's head had dipped below the water, Hisauchi continued: "I'm having more episodes of déjà vu every day, and every once in a while these disgusting piles of offal come bubbling up out of the roads."

"You're teasing me again. That's just an urban legend, isn't it?"

"I've told you, I've seen them when they manifest, repeatedly. There are people at work who've seen them too."

"But that just can't happen. It isn't reported on the news either."

Give it up already, Hisauchi thought. He too, it seemed, was causing Hamuro loss.

Hamuro sighed listlessly and crouched down in front of a large boulder. It was about the size of a couch, with large cracks in the shape of a crucifix. Playfully, she smoothed the sand with her hands, scooped it up, and at last sank her fingertips deep into the earth to start digging. As she worked, the outline of something began to become apparent. She was just about to grab hold of it with both hands when she uttered a sharp cry.

Hisauchi leaned forward, straining his eyes. Buried in the sand was something like a chunk of meat, pulsating there slightly. A grossly enlarged heart—that was what it looked like. Thick blood vessels stretched out from its underside and disappeared into the sand.

They swept aside the sand with fallen sticks, revealing a jostling cluster of bodily organs, oozing with bubbly ichor.

Hamuro drew away from them, then froze just as she was about to sit down on the boulder.

Rounded projections covering its surface had begun to move all at once, scurrying into the boulder's cracks like a swarm of sea slaters. She glimpsed them for only a moment, but they had all been shaped like fava beans and were about the size of fists.

"This…is what you saw?" she moaned. "Why isn't the Concealer workin—?" A flash of self-deprecation shot across Hamuro's face. "But…we don't have Kosmetics anymore…"

"I still see illusions too sometimes. On the surface, I'm still the same as I was before I was Translated and have inherited the intimacy level of my Kosmetics."

Hisauchi put a hand on Hamuro's back and guided her away from the boulder. From behind, there came a faint sound of footsteps approaching in the sand.

Monks wrapped in yellow-brown robes filed past the couple, walking across the wet sand as they headed for the fishing harbor.

"Followers of Ājīvika."

"Yep," said Hamuro, turning to look back at the cliff face behind her.

The mouth of a cave opened at the base of it, and the face of the surrounding rock was adorned with elaborate carvings. A subterranean Ājīvikaist temple. The religion, revived from ancient India, promulgated a doctrine of predetermined fate. It had its home base here in Parish 153, and word had it that conversions were on the upswing.

"Hey," Hamuro said, brushing aside a few stray hairs. "When was the first time you really noticed the Kosmetics?"

"Let's see, that'd be after I'd had the cranial nerve replacement, so I think I would've been about eight. The kosmetic box in my brain would go off occasionally even before that though, so I don't really remember all that well."

"Oh, that's right; you were sick. For me, it was when I was four years old, when I went to the dentist to have braces put on. I ran my tongue across my teeth and felt the cold, jagged metal. I got really scared because the braces felt like these gigantic, foreign objects. But then I looked in the mirror, and it was so strange: my teeth were white and glossy, and I cut my tongue from running it over the braces too much. They sent an ambulance automatically."

There was no sign of any change in her features.

"You're right, actually. I can feel something happening." Hamuro sighed deeply. "Maybe we've been losing things for much, much longer."

"Yeah. When reality got a kosmetic makeover...when we traded Kosmetics for our new reality... 'When you're freed from the bonds of flesh, all things will be possible'—wasn't that the sort of line they used to promote Translation with?"

"They were doing it everywhere," said Hamuro, one corner of her mouth turning up. "After all, I got baptized in a church."

Hisauchi wondered: had she had what they'd commonly

called a "last-minute" baptism?

Hamuro continued: "I was reborn through repentance. But not only did everything not become possible, legal issues got thornier and thornier, and there were more and more restrictions, and when it comes to children—" Hamuro suddenly choked up.

Great deliberations had been going on in the Council for the past three hundred years, yet even now they couldn't come up with so much as a legal definition for a "child."

Sensing a strange presence, Hisauchi cast his gaze out to sea.

A swell of water appeared amid the waves and a human head rose up out of the water. His face was different from that of the man they'd glimpsed going down into the water earlier, although it too was the face of no one in particular. His eyes were open wide, heedless of the drops of seawater running down over them. His shoulders surfaced next. Was it some deathseeker grown bored of even his craving for death? His form was revealed little by little as he drew nearer to shore. He was wearing a navy blue suit.

Behind the dripping-wet deathseeker, seagulls were gliding toward the face of the gentle ocean, snatching prey from the water with their beaks. One of these tilted its wings sharply, turned around, and traced out a leisurely arc as it made for the shoreline. Both of its wide wings, stretched out fully to the left and the right, grew steadily larger. Its stately form was intimidating, and in a moment, it was closing in before their eyes. Its two wings, like giant sickles, were headed straight for the cringing pair—

And then with a powerful shock, Hisauchi *only* was thrown backward. He collapsed onto the sand and lay there on his back. The seagull's wings flapped in his field of view, and each time they moved it felt like his insides were being twisted.

Beyond the wings' afterimages was Hamuro, standing frozen with both hands held up to her mouth.

"What's…happening?" Hisauchi moaned.

Hamuro came to his side, grabbed hold of one wing with both hands, and pulled. His chest rose up, pulled along with the wing.

"It's no good, you're fused with the gull. It went right through me…But why?"

Beyond the tips of his feet, Hisauchi spotted the death-seeker. He was approaching them, his whole body dripping with seawater.

He drew near, tangles of seaweed wrapped about his feet, and finally stopped in front of Hisauchi.

"Ah, may I?" he said to Hamuro hesitantly.

The deathseeker bent down, reached forward with his wet hands, and grabbed hold of the right wing. With no trouble whatsoever, he folded it over in the direction of Hisauchi's chest. Then he did the same with the left wing. When he took away his hands, Hisauchi rubbed his chest. The seagull had vanished without a trace.

"W-what just happened…?" Hamuro said, confused. But Hisauchi, with the deathseeker's outstretched hand before him, thanked the man and grabbed hold of his arm.

When the deathseeker pulled him up, however, something twisted powerfully inside, and this time Hisauchi fell face forward. His face twisted with agony as it plowed into the sandy ground. Sand was stuck all over his lips. He tried to cry out in anger, but no sound came out—it was like a lock had been fastened to his Adam's apple. His arms and legs were beyond his control as well. Hamuro let loose the scream that he could not.

Locks of wet hair were still plastered across the deathseeker's lifeless face, but he spoke in a clear, crisp voice:

"Suspect's veriform in custody; type-one containment shell set internally. No, the coordinates had pointed me toward a position under the sea. How about the dispersed individual registries? They won't converge? Well, for the time being, all we can do is isolate them. Activate type-one containment shell."

A feeling of vertigo assaulted Hisauchi, and his focus seemed to lag as multiple fields of vision began to overlap his own. They moved about wildly, and his stomach started to churn. It wasn't just Hamuro and the deathseeker he could see; his own prostrate form was visible to him as well. Even when he squeezed his eyes shut, the visions wouldn't disappear.

I've got to get away from here—

Hisauchi couldn't hold still and couldn't wait to get away.

The gentle, sandy ground suddenly heaved upward, forming long, enormous rises, as if the beach itself were suffering an acute attack of edematous blood vessels. Resembling echinoderms, sand-covered lumps of all shapes and sizes rose from the ground. They jiggled as though made of gelatin and began rolling toward where the three people were. The clumps of sand that were stuck to their surfaces peeled off and fell away, exposing various types of internal organs. Dully reflecting the sunlight, the organs came pouncing toward the deathseeker. Branching veins writhed in midair.

"What is this stuff?" the deathseeker cried, losing his cool demeanor as he stomped underfoot a mass of viscera that had wrapped around his ankle—

—Hisauchi was assaulted by a sudden rush of nausea, and for some reason, a vast, honeycomb-patterned landscape flashed before his eyes—

—then with a sickening squelch, the organ collapsed under the deathseeker's foot, sending a spurt of mucusy goo up into the air. On the sandy ground, a bloodstain was spreading darkly outward, but even so, the number of organs showed no sign of decrease. Hisauchi's heart was pounding fit to burst.

"Investigative Bureau unit is under attack.

"That infotumor?"

As the deathseeker batted away an organ that had crawled as high as his abdomen, he continued to carry on a conversation with himself.

"It looks that way. There's congestion centering on the suspect.

"Fragmentary city data detected inside. Resembles Yaoyorozu in composition.

"We've got some crosstalk here.

"Thanks to this guy, this parish is—

"Don't squash any more tumors. It'll complicate the reconstruction. Analyze the cellular nuclei."

I've got to get away—

"W-what the—? The suspect's veriform is—"

From deep inside of Hisauchi, there began to emanate a sound like something coming to a boil.

Hamuro covered her face with both hands and screamed.

Hisauchi's shirt began to swell ponderously outward, buttons began to pop, and then all his bowels came gushing out. Agony coursed through his every vein. The rent in his stomach peeled back, and the moist mucous membrane of his coelom began to envelop his whole body as it was turned inside out.

"What's happening here?

"Brainwaves flatlining—

"Type-one containment shell destroyed during construction by transposition of his veriform tissues' order of precedence—

"What?!"

All that was still recognizably human now lay between Hisauchi's elbows and his fingertips.

The vast multitude of organs that had bubbled up out of the sand converged on the everted body, splorching and splurching loudly. They bubbled as if fermenting and melted into one another, making his white bones bob up and down, flowing randomly this way and that as the whole mass expanded.

"The infotumor's genes are a match for the suspect's.

"So this is what dispersed the individual registries?

"Aah!

"What's the matter?

"Th-the infotumor—it's reached this room!

"Seal it off. Leave only the barest minimum of a transmission channel. First activate a type-two—no, a type-three—containment shell. I'll use the relic's timespace properties to send it back to the Genesis Period.

"Activating type-three containment shell.

"Data spillback from the suspect. This is dangerous; subjective viewers, please cut your connections."

The deathseeker let go of Hisauchi's hand, but his entire forearm, sleeve and all, was beginning to swell up with blisters already.

"Separate elbow joint and discard!"

With that urgent cry, everything from the deathseeker's elbow forward came loose and fell to the ground.

Hisauchi's five fingers each bent in impossible directions and were enveloped by the everted membrane. His entire body had now kneaded its muscles, its bones, and its organs into a warped conglomeration of flesh and blood, covered in a net of blood vessels.

Out among the waves, small, ovoid shells bobbed to the surface here and there. Their numbers increased with every rolling wave, and they began to cover the surface of the sea. They washed up on the shore and, pushing and shoving against one another, began crawling up the sandy beach. A sharp tail was sticking out from the rear of each shell. They were horseshoe crabs. They swarmed in as if tracing the movements of the mass of organs, climbed up the pile of flesh that was Hisauchi, and attached themselves to it one after another.

As the horseshoe crabs fused together to form a containment shell, several reddish-black spheres bulged out from areas that were not yet covered and, pulsing erratically, began to expand. They sprayed violent geysers of rotten soup all around and, with raucous, mucusy *shlurps,* peeled away from the containment shell, becoming flesh-balloons that floated up and away from the sandy shore.

Hamuro and the deathseeker stared up dazedly at the sky as the wind carried those fleshy balloons higher and higher.

It hadn't happened only at the beach. Similar flesh-balloons were taking flight from all over the parish.

Numerous beyond all counting, they floated across the sky like giant, explosively breeding medusae, layers of mucous membranes tinged orange in the light of the evening glow.

Gradually, they converged and stuck together, becoming an uneven agglomeration of bubbles resembling a giant cluster of grapes and casting an incredibly long, vast shadow across the city.

The conglomerate continued to rise up through the troposphere. Each time it passed through some thick cloud, it came under fierce assault by spears of lightning, but the electricity was discharged instantly from the top. High up above, a halo of light began to expand from a single point.

Far, far below, Parish 153 floated alone in darkness, a rectangular patch of skin waiting to be grafted. The other parishes making up the rest of the <World> were nowhere to be seen.

At last, the mass of fleshy balloons reached the stratosphere. Nacreous clouds shone like mother of pearl as they drew near from all around. Atomized particles of nitric acid began to blacken and dissolve the fleshy, bloody mass, but then the blackened outer layer peeled away, a new layer regenerated, and the conglomerate continued to rise ever higher.

At last it neared the point at which it could no longer clearly be seen. Countless fleshy sacs were twisted and squashed, as though being strained through the celestial sphere, and at last they vanished from the <World>. A black, rotten soup sprinkled down across the land below.

That day, the break of dawn brought no color to the <World>.

CHAPTER 4:
THE SHRINE VISIT

1

In the residential quarter on the south side of Tochino Recuperation Block, the buildings were reinforced by coats of dungplast mixed with momonji dung and bonemeal. With little rhyme or reason, the structures had been built onto and rebuilt repeatedly as they competed for space, and they looked like they might start falling down at any moment. Toward the east, located in an area of especially convoluted pathways where the sunlight never reached, was the recuperation block's archival warehouse.

There Umari sat covered in dust, up on a ladder attached to a storage shelf that rose all the way up to the high ceiling.

That man is dead now, so why do I have to do this? she wondered.

Unsatisfied with the answer, she had been paging endlessly through piled stacks of old documents, looking for materials suited to their next job. It took half the day, but she finally scraped together what was needed—maps of the dustsink, project plans related to sewer construction, and so on—and at last put the archives behind her.

From a narrow path, she emerged into the arcade running

north to south through the residential area and started walking toward Caravan Square. There were a lot of discontinuities in the ground, and here and there grilled sweets lay crumbling, as though they had been smashed.

When she was three shops from the gate leading to the square, Umari came to a halt and turned toward the building on her left. Its second story faced the arcade, while its ground floor was hidden by a row of three bone doors. On each of these doors was engraved a single character, spelling out KI-JIN-MON, or DUSTCLINGER CLAN.

Umari hummed carrier tone, recalling the nervousness she had felt the first time she stood before those doors. That day, Romon had opened the door for her, and for some reason he had looked at her like he couldn't believe his own eyes.

After being shown inside, she had pleaded with Master to be trained as a dustmancer, but Romon had inserted from the side, "You can't be no dustmancer. You'll put us all in danger; everybody'll end up getting hurt really bad. Go on back to the maternitorium where you belong."

Umari's reflections were cut off by the sound of a latch being loosed. She slipped in sideways through the door marked KI.

In the midst of a large, low-ceilinged room that reeked of mold, her clan-brethren were up to their necks in preparations for the next momonji drive, which was coming up in just a week. Master was standing next to a work desk by the wall, watching over the work with a careful eye. Did there used to be a whorl somewhere on that hairless head of his? Umari was wondering, when Master suddenly turned around.

"Hurry up and bring me those!"

Umari was so surprised she almost dropped her bundle of old documents. She steadied her grip and handed them over to Master.

Master set his cast-iron tamer on one end of a document roll and used it as a paperweight as he spread the sheet out on the desk in a swift, one-handed motion. "Can't use 'em," he said after flipping through each of the pages. "Well, what are you standing there for? Go and get me some more!"

Umari took off running. She could hear Romon's laughter: "Is collecting debts all she's good for?"

It took her another four trips to and from the archives before he would take what she brought him. By that time, the sun had long since set.

Early the next morning, Master got to work and spent a little less than a day patching together the old documents. The rest of the prep he entrusted to Homaru, who was skilled in the composition of possession-verse. During the remaining half of the day, Homaru easily finished the handwritten crafting-notes and chanted them into eidos grenades about the size of his thumb. The silver teeth peeking out from between his lips looked black as night in the room's dim illumination.

In the crisp air of the early morning, Master and Umari were waiting in front of the West Gate of the recuperation block.

A man dressed in caravan gear approached them, dodging past the earthcreepers lying before the rows of houses in the residential district. Through a thin hemp curtain that hung from the edge of his shadecap, Umari could make out the rounded features of Hanishibe. She was at a loss for words. "Are these clothes all right?" Hanishibe said in a bright, clear voice. "I put the outfit together at a secondhand place..."

"That's an old type of camouflage," said Master, "but since we'll be in a calmdust belt, there shouldn't be any problem." The three of them passed beneath the thick western gate and departed Tochino Recuperation Block.

The plain of calmdust spread out under an empty sky, its surface honeycombed with countless holes. Outlines of crystalline lattices, oft likened to coral formations or fossilized lotus receptacles, stood out in striking relief as they caught the morning sunlight.

A wind was blowing across the pitted surface layer, and low moans sounded out continuously.

Master stepped out onto a crystallized lattice that resembled the femur of some dinosaur, and Hanishibe and Umari followed him in turn. All three trod on their own long shadows as they carefully made their way across the calmdust.

The holes were about as big around as a person's waist, and since the crystals on which they found their footing were about as wide, it was no trouble stepping across from one lattice to the next. Looking down at the endless succession of crystals gave the illusion of floating high up in the sky.

Hanishibe's knees trembled as he hobbled along in front of Umari, perhaps out of fear.

Has he never *crossed a calmdust belt before?* The thought was a strange one for Umari. If that were the case, how had he ever come to Tochino Recuperation Block? And could he and that crawlbacker from before really be the same person?

Crouching figures came into view here and there on the calmdust flat. Each of them had one hand pressed against the ground.

"Who are those people?" Hanishibe asked.

"Dustmancers retained by the recuperation block. They use their tamers like that to periodically exorcise various kinds of invasive eide. Thanks to them, the region around the recuperation block is kept inactive, as a calmdust belt of honeycombed crystal lattices."

The calmdust belt extended for another two kilometers;

past that point, unearthly dustshoots rose up toward the sky, and beyond them a vast dustwreck jungle unfurled, in which dustwroughts of every conceivable kind grew in a thick, chaotic luxuriance that engulfed the horizon.

"This place was once a discardation stratum too, wasn't it?" said Hanishibe.

"We don't call it that," said Master. "There're lots of units of structure for things, depending on their size and stage of activation. Starting from the very smallest—a single nanomote—we've got dustwrecks, wreckcliffs, and so on—lump all of 'em together and you ultimately get the Vastsea itself."

Hanishibe nodded understanding. He was gazing off toward distant heights far beyond the dustwreck jungle. All Umari could see, however, were altocumulus clouds that looked a bit like a momonji herd. When she lowered her gaze, Hanishibe was walking with an awkward and unsteady stride.

"You'll fall in a hole if all you do is stare at the sky," she said suddenly.

And the moment that she said so, Hanishibe wobbled, and Umari had to prop him up from behind. The flab she could feel through the cloth was distressingly soft.

"You miss looking up at those floating bridges they had in the good old days?" said Master, his back still turned.

"I'm not getting all nostalgic, no. After all, what I'm looking toward is the future."

There was no hesitation or uncertainty in Hanishibe's answer. He stamped his foot a few times, checking the curved surface of a crystalline lattice.

"I've gone and dredged up a hoary old word again," Master said. "But it's the same for me. Travel the Vastsea long enough, and even the long stretches of time that run together like lasagna just melt away like stew."

Something about the term "floating bridge" had caught

Umari's attention. She remembered hearing Dr. Shibata use that term once—when had that been? When she tried to recall the conversation, her thoughts were buried under a pile of lasagna—the nature of which she was understanding less and less.

"Our <World> is kind of like that too," said Hanishibe. "We just can't stop calculating the probabilities. Without realizing it, the people grow nostalgic for tomorrow and tie their hopes to days gone by."

"It doesn't matter which direction you hope in, but if you want to make it home safely, forgetting is key."

The trio walked on, crossing the calmdust in silence.

A rumble ran through the ground, and their footing began to vibrate wildly. Grazed by the fingertips Umari held out to steady him, Hanishibe sank into the ground. One of his feet was stuck in a hole.

Looking down through the network of multilayered crystalline lattices, they could make out the dim shadow of something huge and black as it came into view, then slowly passed on by. Hanishibe was panting so hard that his breaths sounded almost like screams.

The shadow receded into the distance, and as soon as the ground stopped shaking, Master broke out in an uncharacteristically loud burst of laughter. "Now wait a minute; the city you were living in must have been in a canvasser just like that one. You're a ghost; what have you got to be afraid of?"

"I'd never seen one from the outside before," Hanishibe protested. A profuse, oily sweat had broken out on his forehead.

Huge though the canvassers might be, Umari still had trouble grasping the idea that cities full of ghosts existed within their six-meter bodies. It was hard to understand as well how crawlbackers could come out of canvassers.

Together with Master, they pulled Hanishibe up out of the hole.

As soon as Hanishibe had climbed back up on the crystal lattice, the curved surface at his feet began to boil and melt. The other two backed away. The crystal lattices melted outward from where Hanishibe stood, closing off many of the holes with a thin, liquid film. A silvery depression formed that was about three meters in diameter. Within its gently sloping curvature there appeared varied rippling patterns, forming a sort of mandala. Scattered, sticklike projections jutted out as it transformed moment by moment, like a kaleidoscope.

"Doilies" was the term Umari used for this kind of metamorphic rippling. They bore a strong resemblance to the little lace mats that the mothers at the maternitorium would crochet to amuse themselves.

Master and Umari were keeping their distance so as not to be pulled in, but Hanishibe was standing right in the middle of that doily. He was completely still and appeared to be lost in deep thought. That vacant gaze was directed at a spot about ten paces ahead, where a new doily was taking shape. Something was rising steadily upward there. It looked like a cube.

"Close your eyes now!" Master shouted. "I told you—don't hope for anything. Your feelings are way too strong."

Taking short, rapid breaths of air, Hanishibe shut his eyes, but the cube was already taller than he was and was steadily growing even larger. Its topmost portion began to tilt, and rectangular depressions began to appear at vital points on its vertical surface. A mansion was beginning to form—the kind sometimes excavated from dustsunk land to be reconstructed on the surface. A terrace with a table and chairs rose into view, and on the far side of a grassy lawn the molten ground became a lake that shone in the morning sunlight. Bathed in that gleam, many rounded poles reached skyward, surrounding the mansion and forming a dense forest.

Using carrier tone, Master began chanting a calmsong.

Umari joined in as well, singing one octave higher.

The doily emanating from Hanishibe's feet began to set-tle down, and the holes reappeared as the film covering them popped like bubbles.

In no particular order, the trees began to sink back into the ground, the mansion's sharp corners grew rounded, and the grounds of the estate lost their shape and grew indistinct. While all this was happening, Umari's heart stirred—she thought she'd caught a glimpse of a human figure in one of the collapsing windows.

The mansion regressed until it became like a mud pie, but there its movements grew dull. Hanishibe's thoughts were still exerting an influence. In the end, the trio departed that place, having been unable to return it to its flat, crystalline form.

They advanced northwestward in silence for exactly half an hour.

The dustwreck jungle was closing in, roughly a hundred meters ahead of them. One portion of it bulged out toward them, cracked apart as though shattering, and then formed shapes of dense, leafy foliage.

They braced themselves, thinking at first that the nanodust was reacting to Hanishibe's emotions again. What pushed its way through the dense leaves, however, turned out to be a three-eyed face covered in white fur. The jungle spat out mo-monji after momonji after momonji, like whitish insects fresh-ly emerged from their chrysalises.

Golden eyes, long hair, brown stripes—every one of them was a high-grade breed. Now they were forming up in ranks and setting out across the calmdust belt. They were apparently using one of the permanent guidelines that required a usage fee. The dustmancers walking between the momonji raised their hands toward the trio and lightly turned their wrists.

"They look awfully proud of themselves, don't they?" Master

said as he returned the gesture and Umari copied it. It was a very common greeting between caravan drivers.

Master turned his back on the momonji caravan's long train, took a sextant from the bag that hung from his belt, and looked up at the sky.

"It's farther south," he said.

They walked for another ten minutes or so and arrived at their goal's coordinates. It was a perfectly ordinary intersection of crystalline lattices.

Master took his tamer from its holster and crouched down on one knee. He pushed the muzzle up against the center of the intersection, and then he pulled the trigger.

A dull sound rang out. It sounded like someone punching a large metal bell. At the same moment, faint beams of light danced across the bonelike surface.

Spreading out from a mark made by the eidos bullet, the crystal began to melt, forming a hole. It grew deeper and deeper, as though an invisible heat source were melting its way downward, creating a vertical pit. The holes that lined its inner wall began to close like eyes being lulled to sleep, smoothly transforming the wall into a curved shaft without bumps or dents.

At last a long, intricately detailed ladder came bubbling up out of the pit's inner wall, stretching vertically from the opening all the way down to the darkness at the bottom.

"So it can really form shapes this quickly!" Hanishibe said with a cry of amazement. "Though this is exactly why the worlde ended up like it did."

Master, Hanishibe, and finally Umari began climbing down the ladder. Although the piled layers of nanodust could be transformed like magic, they wouldn't hold the shape for long. Unlike Master, Umari could not yet estimate how long the possession-verse would hold.

After descending roughly fifty meters, they reached the bottom, which was a wide, empty cavern. The air amid the gloom was damp and smelled of mold.

Master, having stepped off the ladder, held a four-sided lantern up over his head. The first thing that leapt into view was a series of wooden divine gates, blackened and corroded, centered between half-fallen wood plank fences. To Umari's eyes, the straight lines of the structures seemed terribly ominous. Beyond the divine gates, there stood a building roofed with moss-covered mats of thatch and logs lined up on its peak. It was leaning a bit toward the right and looked as if the slightest breath might topple it.

Hanishibe, clinging to the ladder just beneath Umari, let out a deeply emotional sigh.

On the roof of that great cavern, a large number of indistinct shapes seemed to mimic the thatched roof but were facing in the opposite direction. Like bracket fungi, they overlapped with one another, forming several layers, and as gently as clouds, drifted along toward the inner darkness.

Hanishibe jumped down to the ground, stumbled immediately, and fell on his backside.

On closer inspection, it turned out that the ground here was shaped like a staircase. A large number of shapeless blobs resembling huge jellyfish lay scattered about here and there. They accounted for the surplus mass that had been displaced when the pit had been chanted from the nanodust.

Umari waited for Hanishibe to get back up, then jumped down herself. She scuffed her soles as she stepped onto the stone steps, embracing a sense of reverence toward their unswerving stability.

Master set his lantern down on the ground and with tamer in hand knocked on the walls from which the divine gates' pillars protruded, checking to see how active they were. The gates resembled chain-replicated bas-reliefs.

"I wonder why this cavern holds its shape?" Umari murmured unconsciously. Even if the calmsong had penetrated this far down, there was no way localized, specific forms could be taking shape. It was a mystery as well why the transformation had gone no farther.

"A reverence for things holy is built into the nanodust," Master said, moving his hands as if trying to shift some invisible thing in midair. "That said, the reason that that instinct is at work here is because this shrine's Kosmetics are functional even now. The kosmetic seal that was bestowed on this place before it sank into the nanodust has effectively served to protect the shrine. Ironically enough."

As Master was speaking, a sound of footsteps overlapped with his voice.

Hanishibe, with a vacant expression, was climbing up the wide stone steps as though he were being pulled. At last, he came to a halt between the thick, round pillars of a gate nearly eight meters in height, where the wood grain was visible. Hanishibe waved his lantern in a wide arc, like the sun in its course through the sky, and illuminated the pitiful state of a moss-covered thatched roof that was a little lower than the divine gate and had mostly decayed into dirt.

Looking askance at Hanishibe's unmoving silhouette, Umari asked, "Um, what are Kosmetics?"

"Just like you dress up in beautiful clothes to hide your nakedness, there was an age when reality was covered over in many layers of an ideal fabric called Kosmetics. At shrines like this one, gods such as Chinju-no-kami and Ubusunagami manifested before humans. They were incorporated into the governing bodies and became intimately involved in people's daily lives to a degree never seen before."

"There were…gods?"

"It was the basic concept translated into Codeblocks, of course. But the informational management and patronage they provided let people enjoy lives of incredible—even perverse—convenience. Later, the raw material of nanodust, also known as 'Yaoyorozu,' recreated the world in matter, but in the end... it brought about the unprecedented disaster of the Great Dust Plague..."

Master pulled up the hemp curtain of his shadecap and pressed the stock of his tamer's grip against his temple.

"Master?"

"But even so, Chinju-no-kami and Ubusunagami wouldn't forsake their parishioners...They were sealed away, however, by the replayable intellects...because their presence interfered with people's...escaping...from this world."

No sooner did Umari notice Master faltering than he fell over sideways onto the ground.

"Master!"

His fallen tamer bounced on the stone steps, then sank into one of the giant jellyfish. Antidust camouflage didn't work if the shape of something was taken in directly. Immediately, tamer-shaped projections blossomed all over the gelatinous hemisphere's surface. This was further imitated by the ceiling directly overhead; tamers grew out of it in a radial pattern and began sagging downward like stalactites.

With no idea what was happening, Umari ran to Master and dragged him down several steps.

The tamers that had chain-replicated from both above and below made creaking noises as they joined one to another, forming a pillar resembling a dolomite crystal. Tamers sank into the pillar one after another, and explosions rang out from their barrels as they were squeezed together on the surface. A volley of tamerfire was starting up.

Reflexively, Umari threw herself on top of Master.

With deafening reverberations, countless tamershots rang out all through the cavern, raining down fragments of wall on top of Umari, who had gone pale as a sheet. Tamers were not made for killing or maiming, but no one who got hit would be walking away unscathed.

Within several seconds the tamershots died down. *Thank goodness it was a single-loader,* Umari thought, exhaling a deep sigh.

She lifted herself up off of Master, and when she turned to look toward the shrine, she saw Hanishibe peering timidly back from the shadow of the divine gate's pillars. He dodged around the pillar made of tamers and came running up to them.

Master's face had started to twitch, so they undid the cord under his chin and used his shadecap as a pillow. They kept calling to him, and presently his eyebrows drew together. "Let me go! In the shaft, I-I didn't shoot the eidos shell to muh-muh-muh maintain the shape! There's no time!" He closed his eyes, groaning.

Hanishibe nodded and set off running for the thatch-roofed building.

Behind his thick eyelids, Master's eyeballs were moving furiously.

"It's no good. What's going on?" Master gasped. "I'm losing my senses. I can just barely control my larynx, but it feels like I have bits in my mouth. Have I been thrown out of the <World's> manifestation zone? I've heard of such accidents…" He continued to ramble on about things Umari couldn't understand, and the tone of his voice made him sound like someone else. Suddenly, both eyes opened wide, though they didn't focus on anything. "Is this…a high-level UI? It's like the visual intercession they had in the Age of Kosmetics. Even the handling's the same. The whisper-lanes to the other parishes… If you go there, you can cross the bord—"

"Master!" Umari screamed, practically beside herself.

"It's no good. I'm shut off from everything. In that case, how about a shared branch of the whisper-net? This one, this one, and this one…the terminal points are blocked by dummy signals. So is it only this parish that's isolated from the others, like we saw from up in the sky? But still—"

Something gurgled inside of Master like a backed-up pipe. Dark blood spilled from his mouth and his nostrils.

"Master! Master!" Umari kept calling until she was hoarse, and finally their eyes met.

"What is this? My body, it feels awfully heavy. Is something wrong with my visual intercessor? I'm starting to see something vaguely. A face? The intimacy level's deepening. Getting too deep. I see capillaries through the skin…a scattering of pigmented nevi. And the left and right sides of the face have lost too much of their symmetry. Don't tell me this is some kind of medical test subject—"

"Master?"

"Are you calling me? Who in the worlde are y—"

"It's me. It's Umari."

Behind her, she heard the sound of gravel and turned around. Hanishibe came running down the stairs, carrying a laquered black box in his arms. Was it something that had been hidden inside the thatch-roofed building? Was that what he had come here to look for?

"Mr. Hanishibe! Master is—"

Hanishibe ran right past them without so much as a pause. He came to a halt at the bottom of the shaft and tied the box up with a cord.

"Please! Help me carry Master out of here!"

Without even answering, Hanishibe shouldered the box, started up the ladder, and disappeared from view.

Umari threaded both of her arms under Master's armpits.

He was giving off an unusual amount of heat. Carrying his upper body, she dragged him as far as the bottom of the shaft.

She undid a cord that was coiled up inside her shadecap and, bearing Master up on her back, tied it around her body. Her legs, however, buckled immediately, and she grabbed the stone wall with both hands. There was a weight differential of more than thirty kilograms between them.

She started up the ladder, but under so much more weight than she had expected, her arms and her calves felt like they might burst open at any moment. Beads of sweat broke out and rolled off her here and there. Soon enough, she had to stop, rest a bit, and then start climbing again. Her breathing grew ragged. Blisters on her fingers and palms burst, and she nearly fell when her hands slipped on the oozing pus. *I must be paler than a corpse by now,* she thought.

It was when they were about halfway up that the shaft began to narrow. The wall turned fibrous and began to unravel. Master's body was hot against her back. She clenched her teeth and climbed on with single-minded determination.

The disk of blue sky circumscribed by the mouth of the pit grew nearer. Her whole body cried out for oxygen. Her lungs hurt, as if they were being scraped out from within—probably, she had breathed in too much nanodust. Her palms throbbed painfully, as though from festering burns, and the muscles of her upper arms and calves had hardened into stiff things that felt ready to snap at any moment.

Just a little more, she said to herself and started up again.

With the exit right before her eyes, the shaft began to twist. It became difficult to move. She squeezed out the last of her strength and tried to make it up one more rung, and that was when she felt it: a strange sensation spreading out on her tongue, as if a piece of sugar candy had been crushed on top of it. The strength went out of her. Sweat that had pooled on the wings of her nose dribbled off. Fearfully, she moved the tip of her tongue across her teeth to make sure. Toward the back of her mouth on the right side, she found a huge, gaping emptiness. She spat out bitter-tasting saliva together with the shards of a broken tooth.

No sooner did it occur to her that the shaft wall might be going flaccid than she felt its pressure on her. It began to pulsate, like the peristaltic movements in the digestive tract. With an audible crack, the bonebell in her breast pocket broke.

Umari untied the cord that held Master to her back, curled up her body, and crawled down underneath Master. Bracing her legs firmly on the ladder, using the elastic wall to just barely support her back, she pushed Master's huge form upward little by little.

Her left foot was cramping by the time she finally pushed him up to the surface. Both arms were trembling as she pulled her own upper body onto the rim of the shaft and blew out an exhalation as though it had been squeezed out of her. It felt like her alveoli were setting off tiny explosions one after another.

She tried to get her right leg onto the rim of the shaft, but it wouldn't budge. She looked down as the shaft, puckering like a pair of lips, closed in around both of her legs, all the way up above her knees.

Frantically, she chanted carrier tone, but her breathing was so ragged she couldn't hold it; it had no effect on the nanodust. As she squirmed trying to get loose, the left arm that was supporting her body also sank into the ground. The ground squeezed her arm and her legs, and in agony Umari gave a shrill scream, like a thick iron beam being twisted to the breaking point. She couldn't believe such a sound had come from her. She cried out for help through tears and through mucus, but Master remained limp and didn't move.

The dull sounds of squishing flesh and breaking bones came to her with maddening sluggishness. She felt all the color draining from her face, a greasy sweat breaking out all over.

Unexpectedly, her body became lighter, and she fell over onto her face.

When she turned her upper body around, everything beyond a point just above her knees was gone, and bright red blood was gushing out. She extended her left hand to try to stanch the bleeding but saw nothing beyond the wrist there either. Her body had lost so much heat that she felt like she had frozen.

Even as she writhed amid the pain and the terror that assaulted her, Umari drew her tamer and set it on her stomach, using her right hand only. With trembling fingers, she picked an eidos bullet from her ammo belt, loaded it, and pressed the tamer up against the crystalline lattice. Holding her breath, she pulled the trigger. A current ran through her whole body, and her spine arched backward.

Presently, medibugs known as scab ants boiled up out of the bullet hole and began to grow. Leaping lightly, they set about covering the severed ends of her legs and wrist. She moaned in the warm numbness.

Besides the scab ants, medibugs resembling centipedes and spiders had also spontaneously generated, but finding themselves with nowhere to go, they were simply left stamping their feet. It was easy for these kinds of bugs to respond to humans and grow automatically, but there was no guarantee they would be the proper type, and there were plenty of examples of them undergoing dangerous transformations.

If I can just send out some earwings next—

Repeatedly, Umari pulled eidos shells from her ammo belt

only to drop them, and by the time she finally managed to reload her tamer, she lacked the strength to pull the trigger.

Die! her finger laughed scornfully.

But when her head started to go fuzzy from the excess of pain, she noticed a small, distant shadow that reminded her of a seedling that had just broken through the sheath of its seed. It was a linelayer, carrying a huge spool of guideline on his back. He was getting closer, using a pulley on his waist to trail the momonji guideline over the ground.

Far, far beyond him, she could see the blurry shapes of momonji. Umari tried to call out, but all that would come from her mouth were bitter-tasting bubbles and the sound of escaping air.

The linelayer came to a halt and shifted his center of gravity to one leg. The wind beat against his shadecap, and in that moment his face turned toward Umari. She could sense his two eyes, so far away she couldn't possibly see them, staring at her two legs, which couldn't possibly still be there. The linelayer set his huge spool of guideline down on the ground and quietly came running.

2

A solitary momonji was crawling along a guideline laid across the calmdust belt.

On its soft back, Umari was lying face-up next to Master. With her right hand, Umari was clutching its soft down, her body writhing as she endured the intense pain.

Walking along beside them at an easygoing gait was tall, skinny Soho-shii.

"They just couldn't wait," he said.

Umari raised her head and could see Kugu-shi and Gei'ei-shi come running toward them. Soho-shii had sent earwing butterflies ahead to let them know what had happened. The potsherd-brown of the recuperation block towered up behind the two of them. Umari lowered her head back into the soft fur, and tears pooled in her eyes.

The momonji's epidermis was suddenly pulled over toward one side. Kugu-shi and Gei'ei-shi had scrambled up onto its body. The two of them cried out to Master.

Master moaned as if in answer. Reddish-black dried blood covered an area from just below his nose all the way down to his throat.

"Umari..." Kugu-shi was staring at the severed ends of Umari's legs.

"I'm sorry, Brother...I'm sorry. I'm sorry..." The words came spilling out, and she couldn't stop them.

"Does it hurt?"

She nodded. He pulled a needler from the case that hung from his belt and pierced her sweaty neck with it. The pain began to ebb, and she closed her eyes.

The tense voices of her two teammates calling out to Master sounded far away, as if she had a seashell pressed against her ear. Whenever she was on the point of falling asleep, her consciousness would rise back to the surface, only to start drowsing once again.

A vibration was transmitted to her through her back. She could tell that the momonji had taken its claw-legs off the guideline and was crawling up the base of the recuperation block.

The warmth of the sun weakened, and she opened her eyes just slightly. The groined archway of the gate was passing by directly overhead.

She heard the sound of shoe soles scraping across the

ground. Soho-shii was leaning against the momonji's face with his full weight.

The momonji's body was pushed upward just slightly, and then it came to a halt.

Umari turned her face to one side and saw a line of vendors' roofs. Beyond them, piles of dungplast stretched out alongside the blockwall like a chain of small mountains, and in the valleys between, people were gathering. Maybe the painkillers were to blame, but all of their faces looked like Hanishibe's. One of them bore a resemblance to Romon. She tried to communicate this but was unable to speak properly.

She had been sleeping again, it seemed.

Consciousness returned at the sound of footsteps racing toward her. She could hear Renji's and Homaru's panic-stricken voices.

"You two take care of Umari," said Kugu-shi.

She could hear the pair gasp. Umari's body was pulled away from the warm fur and began to descend. Something struck against her legs' severed ends, and Umari was turned over, facing upward. At last, she was set down on the ground. Bathed in the momonji's warm exhalations, she felt herself being lifted up again—unsteadily—and laid down on a stretcher.

Renji's upside-down face was right before her eyes. Her thick eyelashes were like eaves over eyes she had averted from Umari.

On one side of Umari's field of view, a wall of white hair began to move. Urged on by Soho-shii, the giant momonji was slowly turning around.

"Huh? Why, Brother Soho-shii, didn't you just set out—?" Then from the other side of the momonji, an unexpected voice gasped.

"'Keep a firm grasp on the situation,'" said Soho-shii. "Isn't that what I always say, Romon? That's why there's no end to these injuries. Kugu-shi! When the old man wakes up, tell him I'll be coming by every month to collect interest on his borrowed life."

"Thank you for your help," Kugu-shi said with a slight bow.

"Just look at this mess! I told you this was going to happen someday!" Romon's voice was shrill and emphatic. "What are we supposed to do now, Brother? Departure's in four days!"

"That discussion can wait until we've carried these two back to the dojo. You go call Dr. Shibata."

"These *two*?" Romon's face entered Umari's blurred field of view from a diagonal angle. "Ah, dungheaps! So that's who got in the way. This is why I was always against letting this...this *child* into the Dustclingers."

"Stop it, Romon," said Homaru. "The girl can't ever..."

"No," murmured Renji. "Umari's a *convalescent*, and a convalescent is what she'll go right back to being."

Master and Umari were carried to the Dustclingers' one-story dojo in the residential district, where they were laid out on bedding.

Umari provided a brief summary of what had happened.

"That dirty crawlbacker!" Kugu-shi spat, pressing his face against the wall. "I knew there was something fishy about him. I saw him out on the street earlier, carrying this black box around all serious-like. I should've punched his lights out."

"You're just full of energy, aren't you?" a new voice said. "Now shut up before I wire your mouth closed."

The door marked "Ki" had opened. Pushed along by an assistant in a wheelchair made of bone, an old woman covered in wrinkles came into the room. Behind her, Romon shut the door.

"Dr. Shibata."

The clan-brethren greeted her meekly. Rumor had it that she had changed from a man to a woman when she was younger, but now she was so wrinkled that no one could guess what gender she was from her looks alone. She was so old that patients at her clinic sometimes joked that she was the one who should be admitted, but she was also one of the few clinicians well-versed in medical techniques from before the Great Dust Plague.

Her assistant, looking like a wax figure in a stand-up-collar shirt, lifted Dr. Shibata out of the wheelchair and set her down at Master's bedside.

"Well, Ol' Dustclinger, this is quite a mess we have here, isn't it?"

Dr. Shibata narrowed her eyes, making the loose skin under them bulge outward. There were some who said in all seriousness that she had specialized sensory organs hidden inside of those bags that could look right into the body and see the parts that were afflicted.

The assistant took a large leather bag from a rack on the back of the wheelchair. He released its clasp with an audible snap and opened the top. The bag was packed with countless bizarre medical instruments, and after asking Romon to go get a bucket, he pulled out a tube-shaped container and handed it to the doctor.

With trembling hands, the doctor took off the lid of the container and pulled out a string of several silvery white jewels that were stuck together. With fingers as shriveled as raisins, she popped off the jewels one by one, dropping them onto Master's chest.

When this was done, she laced the fingers of both her hands and began reciting a stream of possession-verse that sounded like a sutra. Many limbs stretched out of the jewels, and they began moving about like mites. They crawled over his throat, climbed up his chin, leapt across his lips, and burrowed into his nostrils one at a time.

"These are medibugs that I made out of eidos bullets I originally bought from you. I trust you'll have no complaints... even if they go berserk and leave him full of holes, right?"

She laughed, exposing twin rows of yellow teeth with a few silver ones mixed in. That kind of thing frequently happened when the possession-verse was composed by an unskilled dustmancer.

Romon was back now, and he placed the bucket near Master's head, right where the doctor was pointing.

After a little while, a single medibug came rolling back out of Master's nostril and began unspooling string from its posterior. The doctor ran her fingertip over it and gave instructions to her assistant.

The assistant pulled a coiled tube from the case, unraveled it, and stretched it out over the bucket. Finally, he stuck one end deep into Master's nose. A bag of skin resembling a scrotum was hanging from the middle of the tube; the assistant started squeezing it tightly. Dark blood began squirting and spurting from the other end of the tube, which curved down into the bucket.

At last, the remaining medibugs returned as well. Each one spat out its string, and the doctor's face blanched as she read it with her fingertips.

"Doctor?" Kugu-shi asked in a whisper.

"The treatment is finished, and it all went well. They even sewed up the ruptured blood vessels—but his brainwaves are disturbed in a way I've never seen before. This Dustclinger's affliction may be due to a disorder of the cranial nerves."

"You mean nerve disease?"

"No, I mean that every nerve in his body is artificial. If

they were made of Yaoyorozu or Tsukumo, they couldn't have remained functional without being affected by the Vastsea. They're probably made of something older."

"Yaoyorozu?" Homaru asked.

"It's a product name for the raw material that nanodust was made from."

"I know that, but for something like Yaoyorozu to have been used…"

"Exactly," said Romon. "We'd be talking about something that happened before the Great Dust Plague. That was three hundred years ago, wasn't it?"

"What? Don't you all know?" the doctor said, turning to look at Romon.

"Master," said Kugu-shi, his thick arms crossed, "is a survivor of the Great Dust Plague."

"That's right," Gei'ei-shi agreed with a nod.

Umari heard Renji's gasp and turned her face upward, staring at a ceiling mottled with peeling dungplast.

"Whoa, whoa! Just how old is he supposed to be?"

"I myself am a witness," the doctor said to the astonished apprentices. "Surely you lot have the nightmares too. But the Great Dust Plague is what reminds me that those *aren't* nightmares or anything even close. Even now, I've got memories coming back to me all day long, and sometimes they even make my teeth chatter. After the Floating Bridges fell and the Second Evacuation came to a standstill, everything started to go downhill. Those of us who refused to be Translated—or were refused Translation—were insulted with slurs like 'non-replayable intellect,' and our only option was to build evacuation chrysalises, lock ourselves up in them, and wait out the Great Dust Plague in a state of low-metabolism suspended animation, having no idea when it would be over."

"I've heard that the Great Dust Plague settled down after

about thirty years," Homaru said.

"It did, although the actual period varied from place to place. The evacuation chrysalises made estimates of the Vastsea's activation state, molted out their occupants, and became new living spaces called recuperation blocks. But there were other, rare cases where evacuation chrysalises might spend two hundred years or more sunk in the Vastsea before someone happened across them and rescued their occupants. That was what happened to us."

"That's…incredible…"

"So, how can we help Master get better?" Kugu-shi asked.

"I don't know what to do myself. But there's a clinician by the name of Kawamura at Rengen Recuperation Block who was with us in the same evacuation chrysalis. Originally, he was a technician whose work involved nanomotes. If he could have a look at him…"

"Rengen Recuperation Block isn't far from our next destination," Kugu-shi said. "We'll go see him."

Umari started coughing hard. Renji, who was sitting at her side, put a hand under her head, lifted it up, and put a bag to her mouth. She vomited up bloody phlegm. It was sticky in her throat.

The doctor nodded and signaled to her assistant with a jerk of her chin. He picked her up off the floor and set her back down next to Umari.

"Now, let's have a look at you." With the bags under her eyes, she stared at the violently choking Umari. She opened Umari's shirt, and after pressing her stethoscope against a chest that showed all its ribs, she unleashed the medibugs again and had them burrow in through her nostrils.

The sensation of foreign objects inside her moved down her throat, and soon her lungs began to hurt, as if they were being pierced by countless tiny needles.

Next, the doctor took off several of the scab-ants covering the severed ends of her legs and checked the condition of the wounds.

"Your wounds have already forgotten legs were ever there and have almost closed. There's not a thing left for an old clinician like me to do. Um, what's your name?"

"I'm Renji."

"What's in a momonji's second-row-right and fifth-row-left claw-legs?"

"Um, painkillers and antibiotics."

"Buy some from the pestler, and have this girl take both after every meal. Once her condition stabilizes, you can buy her prosthetic legs and a staff."

Umari sneezed repeatedly, blowing medibugs every which way.

The doctor held out her round container and made them go back inside by humming carrier tone. Dr. Shibata's assistant set her back in her wheelchair, and after they had gone, the clan-brethren sat down in a circle and opened up a discussion of what to do about the momonji drive coming up in four days—Master was supposed to have served as team leader. The caravan's employer was waiting in Nankou for their arrival, and based on the projected course of the radioactive mobiles, departure could no longer be delayed. They had their instructions from Master already and had mostly finished mapping the route and making the eidos bullets. All that was left now was to make it through the journey by themselves.

"You're staying here," Kugu-shi told Umari flatly, but she refused to nod assent.

Wringing the words from her throat, she said, "Even if I can't move, I can still make carrier tone. Please take me with you."

Everyone took turns trying to talk her out of it, but Umari

kept on asking.

At last, Kugu-shi told her frankly, "You'd just be cuffs and fetters slowing us down. We've got to get Master to Rengen Recuperation Block. Who's gonna look after you in the middle of all that when you can hardly move? Also, you'd probably wake the nanodust by wishing for what you've lost. That could get somebody killed."

"What you oughta call her is a limblacker. Just look what happened to the old man on account of—"

"Romon, shut up. Umari, what you need to focus on right now is recovering as quickly as you can."

With her right hand only, Umari gripped the edges of her covers, hung her head, and began crawling forward by moving either elbow in turn.

"Umari, wait!" Renji shouted.

"Whoa there, where do you think you're going in that condition?"

"You all got a cruel streak, too, don't you, brothers? Even if she does recover, what then? Any way you look at, there's no place for her now but the maternitorium. The bedrooms over there've even got soft bedding. She'll be able to take all the time she needs to get better."

CHAPTER 5:
JOURNEY TO NANKOU

Having departed Tochino Recuperation Block, the momonji caravan's long procession would soon pass beyond the two-kilometer radius of the calmdust belt—and the scenery was a chaotic jumble of views from above, views from the ground, and close-ups, with all viewpoints lining up or sticking together in the backs of my eyes (*It's like visual intercession set to multiperceptory mode*). Or maybe memories of my long life up till now—my life of nothing but momonji columns that stretch on and on forever—simply coming together to form a meaningless illusion (*At first, I couldn't see this bizarre scenery as anything other than an illusion*).

But I remembered the order. Fifty head of edible momonji, to be delivered unharmed within ten days to clients one hundred kilometers away in Nankou. The clients were a stingy pair of merchants, so there'd be no cooks or feelancers coming with us this time. We'd even been forbidden from putting loads on the momonji, despite the fact they were hardly high-grade animals. That was why we'd had to borrow two momonga more than usual from the rental place.

The momonga, spaced out so as to place one after every five or so momonji, had iron spikes driven into their backshell ossiforms. With towing cables tied to the spikes, they were hauling along covered wagons. These contained water, foodstuffs, momonji feed, rolls of guideline, and so on, and inside the one bringing up the rear (*is you, lying down*). Yeah, that's you, lying down in there.

I was supposed to be an Untranslatable (*You were supposed to turn to wasteflesh and die after I got Translated*).

They called it dustsunk land where the shrine was located, but even so, I could've sworn I'd been struck by lightning back there. All of a sudden, I was swallowed up in this mysterious surge of power, and while I was tossing and turning in an incoherent flood of memories I don't ever remember having, my whole body—missing arm included—got pulled apart into what seemed like a million earthworms (*For some reason, that surge is now an endless series of repeating vibrations all around me*). Maybe it was suppressed by the calmdust belt's calmingsong. As the covered wagon passed over the crystalline lattices, their surfaces would start to melt; the caravan hands were very worried about it.

There were ten hands total. Of these, five were Fatguard clan fatteners, and the rest Dustclinger clan dustmancers. Umari was nowhere to be seen. I'd been (*I'd been*) stolen away from that girl.

Every time I woke up, I tried to ask somebody, "What happened?" or "What's going on now?" But our thoughts would interfere with each other (*Our tongues would get tangled*), and all that would come out was delirious babbling.

Walking in the lead, Kugu-shi turned his hulking self around and looked back toward the formation. He whistled with his tongue and stopped the first momonji by pressing one hand against the middle of its face. All down the line, caravan hands shoved their fingers into gaps between the backshell ossiforms under their beasts' skins. One after another, the momonji came to a halt, pushing their faces into the backsides of the ones in front of them, then falling back little by little to space themselves out again. I could dully feel their shifting centers of gravity, like babies squirming to get loose from the people holding them.

In front of the column was a towering dustwreck jungle. It was covered in power lines that hung down like dark, dense growths of creeper vine, and countless pipes and ducts, which together resembled pipe organs. For some reason, ripples of faint light were shining on these dustwrecks' surfaces. Being as no one mentioned it, the caravan hands apparently didn't notice. Other dustwreck jungles visible off in the distance—and even the ground itself—were tinged with that light. The whole Vastsea seemed filled with it.

Is this your doing? The dictation of content I've never uttered— (*No, it's the <World's> functionality, most likely. Perceptions and thoughts are being changed into written words automatically to create an index of shared memories. If we didn't have that, we couldn't be having this conversati—what's this? Scattered perceptions shaking violently...*). The surge had been unleashed. It was mixing with that rippling light.

Next, a powerful stream of light came rolling in from under the ground. It leapt into one eye of each momonji, and in the same instant, light of different wavelengths shone out of their other eyes.

Why can I see this kind of thing? (*It's a lot like a kosmetic EM field visualization.*) Maybe it's their abilities as planetary bioprobes being used as some kind of conversion device.

The dustmancers of the Dustclinger clan gathered in front of Kugu-shi. They all flickered like stripes in an interference pattern, their outlines indistinct, even blending in and out of the background as they moved.

Gei'ei-shi pushed his shadecap back from his crewcut-framed face so that it hung from his neck. He clicked his tongue, got his bearings from the echoes, then plunged ahead into the dustwreck jungle. He began climbing up an immense dustwreck tower formed out of interwoven silos, airplanes, bridge girders, and lighthouses, which in turn were composed of walls of assorted smaller items—it was like he was climbing up a trompe l'oeil painting.

There were thick blooms of traffic lights and streetlamps, clusters of antennae bifurcating like rime-frost, pipes that here and there swelled with woodwind tumors, and crosses and propellers that knocked against each other with outstretched arms. Higher up, images of Christ crucified, ships' figureheads, mannequins, corpses clad in caravan gear, gargoyles, and signage all stuck out in every direction. Temples and tochkas lay covered in scaly coats of clocks and measuring instruments, and every gap in between was filled with the friction and disorder of some lampstand, kitchen utensil, mirror window bottle doorpostboxcarouselectorpedometerrariumbilicalendartboardwalkmandalandminesweeperiscope—even folkloric eide, which should have never been installed in Yaoyorozu, had been dug out of every kind of memory-bearing media. Gei'ei-shi made his way upward, sticking fingers and toes into seams between relics reminiscent of untold hosts of lives *(It's like he's gouging gaps between my ribs—* (*No, more like trenches in my brain—* (One by one). Thanks to the antidust camo covering his body, Gei'ei-shi didn't scatter any eide, although the body heat and brainwaves he was giving off did melt some nearby dustwroughts into indistinct blobs (*It itches, like a light burn*).

Gei'ei-shi, having reached the summit, looked out across the distant landscape, still clicking his tongue cheerfully. A flock of pigeons that had been roosting in the dustwreck tower took flight, and a part of the tower imitated their motion, with countless wings blossoming like a bed of flowers.

Something blocked my field of view. It was so close that its image blurred (*Looks like the inside of a lamprey's mouth. Look at those concentric rings of serrated teeth*). It looks like a momonji's mouth (*But those saw-teeth are revolving*).

My field of view shattered, breaking apart like images in a compound eye. Each view began to spin independently of the others (*This is bad; I'm getting dizzy*).

I felt the sensation of Gei'ei-shi climbing back down the inside of my brain *(Of my body)*—and with each descending step, my fields of view gradually converged and unified.

The fatteners were scolding the momonji, trying to get them back onto their guidelines.

Inside their tough multiple stomachs, momonji broke down whatever they ate, all the way down to the molecular level, incorporating it into their bodies with great efficiency. Nanodust and ores, however, were different. Through microbiotic refining, they could transform such materials into ferroscrap and excrete it, but each time they did so, it consumed an enormous amount of their heat energy.

Gei'ei-shi jumped back down to the ground and told Kugu-shi that there was an extremely active region south by southwest.

Kugu-shi, the Dustclingers' acting leader, altered one part of the planned route that was drawn on his map.

No matter how precisely they forecast the Vastsea's movements prior to departure, and no matter how thoroughly the journey was planned, momonji drives that proceeded as planned were for all intents and purposes nonexistent. This was because the very act of traveling through the Vastsea triggered transformations in it. In belts of high responsivity, the labyrinth was complicated by the struggle of nanodust and human to anticipate one another, and lessons learned on one journey became completely useless on the next. It was said that powerful longings for a safe arrival had even been known to make entire recuperation blocks appear—entire caravans had stopped and spent the night in them, with no one ever doubting that

they were inside the real thing.

Kugu-shi nodded toward Romon, who was on linelayer duty. Romon hefted onto his back a spool of guideline that weighed as much as he did and started up the steep slope of a hill between two dustwrecks. Homaru and Renji followed behind. The mosaic of bricks and flagstones and tile roofs underfoot was divided into patchwork by tangled pipes and power lines. It looked as if time had stopped just as it was all starting to collapse.

Homaru kept lowering cable from Romon's spool, periodically chanting the metal fittings needed to secure it.

Renji's carrier tone was like a birdsong as she cleared obstacles from their path, covering over pitfalls, flattening out areas of upheaval, pushing into the wreckwalls those dustwroughts that stuck out in their way, and even pushing the wreckwalls themselves with both hands, making them shift as if she were moving mountains.

With encouragement from Kugu-shi's sharp tongue-whistles, the momonji reluctantly started moving again.

Starting with the lead momonji, each one in turn latched onto the guideline with its ten sets of claw-legs, following it as they hurriedly crawled up the hill.

The dustwroughts on either side were pretending not to notice, rippling only faintly. According to one hypothesis, the extremely simple shapes of momonji had been carefully designed so as to keep nanomotes from detecting them. Even antidust camouflage had originally been made to mimic the patterns of momonji fur.

They crossed over the hill and had traveled about seven kilometers farther when Gei'ei-shi, who was in the middle of the column, raised one hand up high. Those nearest him copied the gesture, transmitting it up and down the line. Moving silently, each hand in the caravan brought a momonji to a halt. The guideline made a sound like that of whining cicadas. Everyone in the caravan held their breaths.

A vibrating rumble rose up from underground, like the sound of trees being mowed down (*My insides feel like lead. My gut's twisted, and the hollow inside me's getting bigger*)—it was a canvasser. The high-pitched sound of its swiftly rotating pleopods grew more and more noticeable. It was coming this way.

I felt a sharp pain (*Like having an iron spike driven through the top of your head*)—

In the midst of the rank, there was a dull *thunk*, and suddenly one momonji was flung up into the air—it flipped over before crashing back down to the ground. Curling up to protect its underside, it went rigid, then started wiggling its clawlegs at the sky. Right next to it crouched Romon, who had been on his way back from picking up guideline. There was a big tear in the front of his shadecap. Before him and behind, panicked momonji were blowing out hot breaths of air as they squirmed about.

The noise of the canvasser propelling itself through the ground was moving parallel to the line of the caravan.

A huge tearing sound shook the air.

Toward the front of the line, a second momonji went flying, hanging suspended for an instant in midair before it came crashing to the ground.

Dark red blood gushed out from under its stretched, distorted pelt, drenching ground that was covered in a luxuriant growth of wires.

The sound receded steadily into the distance. It was moving away from the caravan.

Gei'ei-shi crawled up on top of a nearby momonji and raised his arm. The caravan hands who saw him started moving swiftly.

Kugu-shi came running over to him, and Romon looked up,

with one palm pressed against his face.

"They got me again," he said as he took away his hand. His flesh had been laid open from chin to cheek, and his uneven rows of teeth could be seen peeking through. "Just look at this! And the Hades thorn only grazed me!"

"We'll sew you right up," Kugu-shi said, but Romon refused to be treated. Under his boot, he stomped the suture ants that came boiling up from the ground. The pain, it was said, would be four times worse if you let someone else do the stitching. Kugu-shi threaded a sewing needle and handed it to him. Romon held down the skin around the tear and pushed the needle through, hissing and groaning in pain as he crudely sewed his face back together.

Nearby, Sagyoku-shii, corpulent leader of the Fatguard clan, was crouched down beside the upturned momonji, inspecting it as she coughed occasionally into a handkerchief. There was a deep gash on one side of its belly, but as she could see from the busy movements of its claw-legs, its life was in no danger. The wound was quickly sewn up, then six men together hefted its huge body and flipped it back onto its stomach.

The other momonji's intestines had come spilling out from its underside, but even so, a frantic Renji and Homaru were working hard to push them back in. Too late, everyone gathered around and lifted up one side. The fleeting glimpse they got of its underbelly told them that nothing could be done. A Hades thorn was buried in the inner wall of its body cavity.

Hwa, hwa... Its short, quick pants were growing steadily farther apart.

Everyone stood there unmoving until its breaths could be heard no longer.

(*I can still hear it breathing, just barely*) No, you can't, that sound is (*Like compressed air leaking out*)—gas! The airsac in its body cavity might be torn. But something isn't right. This isn't the right type for gas production. And for it to go on this long (*Nobody seems to have noticed*). This is bad; if they're not careful it could ignite (*But even if I wanted to stop it, my five senses are spread out all across the Vastsea*). If they don't get away from it fast—

Several projections resembling udders began rising up from the ground around the body.

Was "I" moving them?

I tried bending my fingers, and the projections bent as one. The sensation in my fingers—scattered like dots in a pointillist painting—seemed dispersed through and crammed into hundreds of such projections.

I dipped the tips of those phalanxes into the puddle of momonji blood, grabbed hold of the ground as if to knead it, and then dragged it gradually downward.

The momonji's corpse began to sink just a little.

"It's copying the pool of blood!" cried Sagyoku-shii, her ample chin swaying.

At the rear of the dead momonji, Kugu-shi quickly drew his tamer, squatted his huge body low, and put the muzzle against the center of the puddle.

I felt my spinal column snap violently backward. The stench of bones carbonized by blazing heat—(*This memory...*)—after the cremation, I spent forever gathering up the bones. Thousands of people's worth of bones and countless broken shards—

Kugu-shi raised his rugged, bony face and looked across the pool of blood toward its far side.

Gei'ei-shi, clucking his tongue, was swiveling his head right, left, up, and down.

"What happened—?"

"I don't know; that response was pretty weird. There's an incredibly long dustwrought bending backward deep underground—it just keeps going, farther and farther down. It'll be calmdust soon enough though."

True to his words, holes began to open in the ground as it hardened into a lotus receptacle pattern. It looked like it had frozen over.

I endured a pain that was like having my skin frozen. The movements of my fingers, reflected back at me by the calmdust, pressed against my abdominal cavity from the inside, squeezing my diaphragm.

I could still hear the disquieting sound of leaking gas. I had to get that momonji away from everyone.

I took hold of my own intestines with fingertips that now only barely obeyed my will. Tormented by a nausea that made me shudder, I pushed at my intestines' opening, spreading it ever wider. I felt intense heat being radiated from inside.

Gei'ei-shi put one ear to the ground, and the expression on his tattoo-covered face twisted in alarm.

"It's active! This whole area is active!"

"Disperse the momonji!" Kugu-shi shouted in his deep voice.

Renji ran toward the momonji in front of the corpse, and Sagyoku-shii ran toward the one behind it. Both were shouting, urging escape. The other hands dispersed along the line and began evacuating the rest of the momonji.

Accompanied by a blistering agony, the crystalline lattice cracked and began to collapse, and dark red liquid gushed out from within. The dead momonji was now beginning to sink into the gore, and around it a circle of ground about fifteen meters in diameter—supporting both the momonji in front of the corpse and the one behind it—was melting and sinking, transforming into a gigantic pool of blood.

Kugu-shi and Gei'ei-shi fired their tamers from both sides of the pool, but with the target in a liquid state, there was no effect.

"This is...the momonji's impact scar!" Sagyoku-shii cried as she pushed against her momonji's head. "It's replicating expansively!"

Homaru jumped down beside Sagyoku-shii, and together they applied their body weight against the momonji they were trying to rescue. Homaru bared his silver teeth; sweat broke out all over Sagyoku-shii's face. They sank about a foot deep into the bloody mire.

"*Move it*, you lazy—!"

Kugu-shi and Gei'ei-shi thrummed carrier tone for all they were worth, but the moment the ground crystallized, it would crack and split and become engulfed in blood.

(So heavy...can't breathe...) Inside the covered trailer, my body was vomiting over and over.

Already, the dead momonji was disappearing from sight at the bottom of the bloody pool. The two terrified momonji in front and behind still wouldn't let go of the guideline, as beneath their claw-legs, the depression in which the blood had pooled began to sink even deeper.

"There's not enough time! Give it up and get out of there!" At Kugu-shi's order, the caravan hands began to flee, climbing out of the bloody pool. Renji drew near to her momonji, bid it farewell, and placed a hand on the rim of the depression. At just that moment, the momonji twisted violently, and Renji was sent flying. She slid down the blood-smeared slope and sank in all the way to her hips.

Gei'ei-shi held out his hand right away, but they were too far apart. She was growing farther and farther away. The pool itself was getting deeper and deeper.

Still clinging to the guideline, the two momonji were beginning to tilt.

Breathing in gasps, Renji disconnected the cable from her shadecap and threw it, holding on to one end. For blind Gei'ei-shi though, it was impossible to catch. From the other side, Kugu-shi threw a rope as well, but she was too far away from him for it to reach her. Mandala-patterned reliefs were spreading out all around Renji, who was now covered up to her solar plexus.

(*Hey! At this rate…*) But I can't control the movement (*You've gotta do something*)!

Romon came running and was just about to jump into the bloody pool when he was grabbed from behind by Kugu-shi, who pinioned his arms.

"Renji!" he called.

At the sound of his cry, Renji, now chest-deep in blood, turned around and smiled for him weakly.

"I wanted…to go with you. I wanted you to show me…the worlde, like you've talked about."

Renji closed her eyes and started to chant carrier tone. As she sank from neck-deep to chin-deep, she caused the liquid around herself to transform and gradually sealed herself within a crystalline shell. Its pointed upper tip slipped beneath the surface of the lake of blood. In the same instant, the two mo-monji flipped over and hung suspended in midair. Now the puddle of blood was so deep that the depression looked like a mortar bowl.

Kugu-shi released his hold, and Romon didn't move from that spot. His lips were pressed tightly together, but trembling breaths were slipping through his open wound.

"But she'd come so far," Homaru muttered through tears.

The guideline sagged down, and the other two momonji were lowered into the bowl of blood.

Kugu-shi ground his teeth, then whistled with his tongue, signaling to Gei'ei-shi, who was standing on the other side of the bowl.

Both unsheathed short swords they had dangling from their hips, placed the blades against the guideline, and sawed at it furiously. The intestinal fibers frayed and snapped one after another, but the line as a whole wouldn't break. Finally, creaking with the weight of the momonji, it tore apart at last.

Both of the dangling momonji plunged to the bottom of the bowl of blood and sank out of sight as though they had melted away. With the shock of the impacts, the nanodust became more and more active.

(*It's already too late*) to stanch the flow of blood there's (*not a thing I can do to stop it*). First Umari and now even Renji. Did I really hear a gas leak? (*Was my mind just playing tricks on me?*) Could I have just mistaken the Vastsea's movements for my own—?

The ground began to shake with rumbling vibrations.

Like twin dams being burst by mudslides, the left and right sides of the bowl began to collapse, gradually forming a very long trench. Ahead of Kugu-shi and Romon, Gei'ei-shi and the fatteners grew more and more distant.

Romon spat saliva tinged with blood.

The caravan had been divided.

CHAPTER 6:
CUFFS AND FETTERS

Umari still hadn't slept a wink and continued to stare into the soft illumination of the trioculamp hanging from the bedchamber's ceiling.

The hollow, hushed warbling of distant pigeons reached her. Umari extended her right arm to grab the bed frame and raised her upper torso. When she leaned forward from the frame to try to get out of bed, she unexpectedly turned over and fell. She hit the floor with her cheek and her shoulder, but the thick rug absorbed the impact and the sound.

The maternitorium stayed open late, and the mothers had not yet started to wake up. Umari braced her elbows against the floor and made alternating steps with them to drag herself past the rug, then crawling forward across the cold tile floor of the entryway, she slipped outside through the doggie door.

The indigo sky bore a faint, whitish tint, and customers were already beginning to gather along the lane of the outdoor market.

She crawled onward with only the movements of her arms and body. At this time of day, there were always a lot of earthcreepers out, so no funny stares were directed her way. She was shocked at how much strength she'd lost while stuck in bed. She hadn't been at it long before her elbows felt like they were going to splinter apart, and the pain became so bad she could no longer move.

She wanted to just keep lying on her stomach like this. Give up on everything and return to the dust as she slept.

It seemed like such a nice idea. Yet even so, tears started spilling down her face.

From behind came the sound of someone dragging their carcass over the ground.

The sound gave Umari the creeps, so she ignored the pain and hurriedly crawled on ahead, but the person behind her caught up right away.

"You poor thing; Vastsea's done gone and had a taste of you, has it?"

The voice was terribly hoarse and raspy, but she could tell it was a woman's. She ignored it and forged on ahead, but the woman continued along beside her, making metallic sounds like when you wash a bunch of spoons and things together.

"I understand," she said. "I was a dustmancer a few years back myself." Coughing loudly, she continued: "My name, actually, used to be pretty well known."

Umari stopped moving. She had remembered a name— Junrin-shi, the one that Renji had always idolized. She turned to look at her and saw her stopped a short way behind, facing downward. She was just slightly looking up at her, with twisted locks of dirt-caked hair twined about her face. Several slender metal rods were sticking out from the stump of her left upper arm.

"Why…don't you exorcise those dustwroughts?"

"When your throat gets this far gone, your carrier tone's just not what it used to be." So saying, she made a purring sound in her throat. "And no matter how many I cast out, I just get possessed again, so there's really no point. But never mind me; you may be young, but giving up's really for the best. Becoming an earthcreeper was the smart thing to do. It finally set me free from that hell out there. Now there's no need to struggle anymore."

"No, I—" Umari started to say, but the woman wouldn't let her get a word in edgewise.

"Folks who won't crawl have no right to alms, see? So above all, crawl. That's the most important thing. After that, as long as you're not doing anything uncalled for, you can eat somebody's leftovers anytime you like. And by the way, if you're new at this, you must still have some. So listen, I was wondering if I might get you to share just a little bit with me?"

When Umari suspiciously asked her just what she was talking about, the woman's tone immediately took on the character of a wheedling, flattering child who wants something.

"Come on, pretty please? I'll teach you all about earthcreeping from α to Ω. So give me the stuff in the claw-legs...the stuff that works. I know you've got some. You'd never make it across the Vastsea without it. And if that's no good, a barter ticket or something would be fine."

Strength seemed to well naturally through Umari's body once more, and she started crawling forward.

When a hand grabbed her shoulder with an entreaty to *Waiiiit!* she just shook it off.

"You *greedy little miser! Heartless witch! You think we'll let an animal like you survive here?*" Shrill epithets rained down on her from behind.

Gasping for breath, Umari crawled on, dragging herself over the ground. She kept crawling, heedless as her clothes were torn and her skin was scraped raw.

In her watery, stinging eyes a mountain of transparent red paste was reflected. It was a hemomochi stand.

Dr. Shibata, out for her morning stroll, was sitting in front of the stand, followed by her assistant, whose eyelids were nearly sealed shut. "No need for a bag today. I'll just take it as-is," she was saying. She took a bowl-shaped hemomochi and bit into it with the teeth on one side of her mouth.

The wheelchair she was sitting in turned and began to move along, but it came to a stop when she passed in front of Umari.

"You've got the wrong corner," Dr. Shibata said. She did not turn toward Umari but faced straight ahead, moving her wrinkly mouth like a bellows as she chewed. "If you're looking for crutches, try a bonecrafting shop."

"I…want to keep going on caravan drives with Master and the momonji," she said. "I don't ever want to stop." She lifted herself up on both arms and stared pleadingly at the spider-webbed profile of the doctor.

"Why are you so attached to momonji? To things without souls? Those things were originally called 'planetary bio-probes'—something more like machines than what we'd call living creatures."

"Even if that's true, though, they still die. A caravan drive is the reprieve from death that we give them—it's the only time when their fates are actually up in the air."

"Then it's practically a graveside service held before the fact. You may be getting prodded along by reasons even you don't completely understand."

"I have nothing except the dust I read and the dust I chant when I'm with them."

"Then why did the Vastsea reject you? Wishes that never come true no matter how many times you ask are never going to be granted. You should see that as plain as day just by looking at the earthcreepers. There was once a dustmancer who could cross the Vastsea with only two arms, but even that's an impossible feat for you. And besides, that dustmancer was swallowed by dustwrecks in the end."

"That's why I want legs to walk on again."

The doctor, aware that this request was coming, naturally argued against it and tried to explain the truth to her.

"You think I'd be riding in this thing if I could make something like that?" She slapped the wheel of her wheelchair. "When I was young, the artificial limbs and organs you're talking about were all over the place. And thanks to Kosmetics, you couldn't even tell they were there. But you have no idea of the tragedy it was when the Great Dust Plague hit. Also, eidos bullets are no good when it comes to making things for flesh-and-blood bodies. Just imagine chanting something that complicated into existence with carrier tone. Even if it did work, you'd need to spend vast amounts of time chanting if you wanted the shapes to hold. And for something like walking... an action that others just take for granted...that half-baked carrier tone of yours would never—"

Umari, of course, knew all of this already. Even so, she pleaded on.

"I'm worn out already," Dr. Shibata said. "I'm leaving now."

Her assistant began pushing the wheelchair, and then the doctor was moving away from Umari.

Umari followed after them. People sometimes swore at her and sometimes threw her their leftovers as she crawled forward between the crowded stands. The skin peeled away from her forearm and elbow, leaving both smeared in blood.

"Hey there, weren't you the one talking to Soho-shii a while back?"

A handsome-looking man in a bloody apron was standing in front of Umari. Her face was wet with tears and mucus.

"The Vastsea's gone and done a number on you, has it? But what a superb dismemberment!"

"Please, ged oud of my way," Umari sobbed.

"Whoa there, where'd you say you were going? I'll carry you there if you don't mind."

"Leabe me alone, please. I'll go by mysel'."

Umari started forward once more. His voice called out to

her from behind: "*Anytime you need me, just say so.*"

By the time she had climbed up and down the many steep staircases of the residential district's southwest quarter to at last arrive at the clinic, she was on the verge of losing consciousness.

The doctor's assistant carried her in and laid her down on the treatment room's couch.

"I'll treat those wounds, but that's all. Anything else you ask, the answer is no."

An ancient medical text the doctor had read was shoved in front of Umari, and she was treated to a fluent explanation of just how difficult a thing it was she was asking. Umari listened attentively and kept asking question after question about the points she didn't understand. "*You just don't know when to quit... not too bright, are you...that's enough, already!*" Grumbling all the while, the doctor parceled her explanation out in spoonfuls, then somewhere along the way the conversation morphed into a discussion of how to achieve the thing itself. Starting that day and continuing for some time after, the two of them would spend their nights at the clinic.

"Somehow I get the feeling I've been bamboozled by a fox," the doctor said with a tired expression, regretfully thinking, *I should've bought more hemomochi.*

The blueprint that Umari began drawing with the doctor was completed one month later. The composition of the possession verse took another two months.

While this work was ongoing, Umari began powdering her face and wearing lipstick. To support herself, she became a mother at the maternitorium.

The embraces of travel-weary men were as nothing to her.

A good man or a bad man made no difference. Compared to having both her legs ripped off, they were no more significant to her than mosquito bites. Still, it stuck in her craw that things had turned out the way Romon had said. She had wrestled against those words of his for such a long time.

And even in the maternitorium—or "where you belong," as Romon had put it—Umari didn't know how long she would be allowed to stay. They would probably kick her out the minute it became known that she couldn't bear children. Only those who had given birth at least once were allowed to stay on as "grandmothers."

There had never been many men who came wanting to be fathers. But there were men who were into stump-girls. That pleasant-looking beastbutcher came to see her often. Would he abandon her, she wondered, if she did get her legs back?

After her work in the maternitorium was done, Umari would sit on the foundation that stuck out from the block-wall, and in the still, faintly lit hours before daybreak, continue to practice her chant, watching long columns of momonji as they sometimes receded into the distance and sometimes grew nearer.

Under the wan violet glow of the sky at dawn, she would bare the rounded stumps of both legs and move one of them near to the curved ivory surface of a crystalline lattice. She would begin to chant the possession verse for her artificial leg, and the curvature would bubble and several protrusions come rising up out of it like the tentacles of some coelenterate. The tentacles would break through her skin, eat their way into the stumps of her femurs, and once the foundations were firm, start to extend the lengths of the bones. At this point, muscle fibers would come winding about it like complex skeins of knitting— only to suddenly start melting and run off the bones, liquefied.

She repeated that chant countless times, but it never went

well. Impatience and irritation ran through her as she kept recklessly, ruthlessly trying it over and over, and then somewhere along the way, she got pregnant. It was a miracle. Not even Dr. Shibata's diagnoses were infallible, it seemed.

Umari rejoiced in her pregnancy and accepted her fate. With this, she could finally give up. Someday when her child had grown up big and strong, he would probably cross the Vastsea with momonji. In her old age, he would visit her and tell her stories about the caravan drives. About the momonji. Monotonous tales, devoid of variation or interest, of marching fearlessly onward through the Vastsea.

Already, Umari felt a desire to tell her own, true mother that she had conceived a child, to tell her of all the things she'd experienced. She had missed her chance to ask Master where he had picked her up, so she still didn't know. She didn't really think that her mother was still alive, of course. Most likely, Umari had been rescued alone from some recuperation block that had been swallowed by the Vastsea. That was what she'd always figured had happened.

One day, she tried asking Dr. Shibata, who answered, "I don't really know, b—"

The doctor stopped right after almost adding a "but," and over and over Umari asked her about that, hanging onto that thread as though by her teeth.

"I've told you this before," Dr. Shibata said, "but Ol' Dustclinger first brought you to this clinic seventeen years ago. I remember you looking a bit malnourished, but I was surprised at how healthy you turned out to be when I examined you. How could I forget? Thing was, I thought you were mentally impaired at the time."

"But I was a baby, wasn't I?"

"No, you looked pretty much the way you do right now."

Countless little incongruities she had experienced in her

life suddenly clicked into place. Consciousness receded into the distance, and she felt like she was going to faint.

"After that, Ol' Dustclinger took you to the maternitorium and left you with the mothers there. Asked 'em to look after you as if you were an infant. And sure enough, you were learning to speak at about the same speed that a baby grows. To look at you, you were no different from the mothers, so the children all loved you. Come to think of it, Romon was in that bunch, wasn't he...?"

Not long afterward, Umari miscarried. The fetus, no larger than a bean, was tangled up in dustwrought fibers.

I was never a child, and I can't even make decent arms and legs, Umari thought, heaping reproach on herself. *No one like me could ever raise a child to think for himself and carry on after me.* For many days and nights, she wandered about the recuperation block's interior, weeping as her crutches and her sticklike prostheses moved awkwardly back and forth like compasses.

Then without her realizing it, her wailing voice began to transform into a crystal-clear carrier tone.

Motes of dust rose up from the ground as if in a vacuum and swirled around Umari as she walked where impulse took her, drawing nearer and nearer. These nanomotes were eating into her prostheses and replacing them, growing into ligaments that bound tibia to fibula, connecting layer after layer of muscle fiber to her tendons.

When her tears had dried, and the skin was taut around her eyes, and every last tear had disappeared from her face, her staff fell away and struck the earth. Umari realized that she was standing firmly on the ground on twin legs of silver.

CHAPTER 7:
THE CROSSER OF BOUNDARIES

"Didn't you check them out before we left?"

"They tested negative for pregnancy."

Sagyoku-shii the fattener had her shadecap pushed down on her back and was stroking a momonji's abnormally swollen side, a grave expression on her face. Since it was injured, it had been moved in front of the momonga that pulled the wagon at the tail-end of the line.

The rear half of the divided caravan was stuck between a pair of steep wreckcliffs that rose up on the left and the right.

"They should never grow like this outside the environment of the fattening lake. And this is—"

"We haven't even managed to link up with Gei'ei-shi and the others yet, and we can't afford to run any farther behind schedule." Romon spat, and the crude stitches in his face started bleeding again. "Honestly, is breastfeeding momonji all you're good for?"

"Why, you little—!" Sagyoku-shii rose to her feet, bosom shaking as she came grabbing at Romon. Kugu-shi got himself between them right away. "Don't you stop me!" she said. "I'm gonna pull this brat's innards out through his poop chute!"

"Ms. Sagyoku-shii, please don't lose your temper over every little thing this idiot says. This momonji, it's the same one that was wounded by the canvasser's Hades thorn earlier, right? Could the pregnancy be related to that?"

"I've never heard of any such precedent," Sagyoku-shii said, smoothing her rumpled clothing. "In any case, though, it looks like it could give birth at any moment. Please, let's stop here for just a little while. This momonji can't keep going any longer."

Kugu-shi nodded and put the word out that they would be making camp here.

In the trench between the two wreckcliffs, dust crystals about the size of roosting pigeons were beginning to form in midair. The dustmotes that comprised them were reacting to the humans' brainwaves and combining to form wire-frame polygons. Buffeted by the wind, they underwent sporadic, spasmodic changes in shape. After so many unexpected disasters, even the seasoned caravan hands were on the verge of losing their usual relaxed dispositions.

Suddenly, a brief scream rang out. It came from near the front of the column, where a young fattener who was on just his second momonji drive was leaning against a momonji, pressing one hand tightly over his left ear.

"Well, that was smart, wasn't it?" Sagyoku-shii muttered disgustedly and coughed. "Way to get your ear lopped off by that dust crystal! And after all the times I told you not to pay attention to them!"

Another fattener called out for emergency aid, but Sagyoku-shii shook her head at him. "Leave him be. Saroku's gotta live in the worlde, so he at least needs to be able to treat himself."

While this was going on, Romon and Homaru were arguing in hushed tones in the shadow of the covered wagon. Though they appeared to be using carrier tone, they were spoofing the lyrics with secrecy modulation, so no one could understand what they were saying. Horror was evident on both of their faces.

Behind them, a section of wreckcliff nearly thirty meters in height was changing shape, transforming into a great number of tall steel columns supporting a wide, overhanging deck at the top. On this deck stood a box-shaped building, and from its roof, a tall tower rose even higher into the sky.

It was so strange. Was the wreckcliff really changing shape, or was it an illusion? The strangest thing of all was the fact that "I" was standing up on that deck.

From up on the deck, I looked down on steep, overhanging cliffs with striped patterns moving across them and over a vast spread of sea that blurred to a dark steel blue in the distance. Powerful gusts of wind came blowing in against me. When it became impossible to keep standing any longer, I opened a rusted iron door and retreated inside the building.

The interior felt spacious, and the walls and the ceiling were covered in countless crisscrossing wires for conducting carrier tone. The floor and work desks overflowed with massive piles of technical drawings, as well as rulers and slide rules of all shapes and sizes. There was a ruin-grade computator with many stacked layers of circuit board exposed. Amid all this disorder, more than fifty people were hard at work, determination etched into each face. One was making his throat vibrate while facing a carrier tone wire; another was drawing technical diagrams. Like in a house of mirrors, people were multiplying, merging into one another, and moving elsewhere without warning. Time also seemed to be flowing at different rates in different places. Among this crowd were dustmancers with whom I was familiar, including Romon and Homaru; this was just like that place they say everyone stops by just before they die.

A number of those standing in front of me moved away, revealing two figures sitting back to back in the center of the room. The one nearer me was Hanishibe. His entire body was secured with a metallic, skeletal framework; his eyes were open wide; and occasionally an eyelid or the corner of one eye would spasm. His head was nodding slightly forward, and his skull had been removed from the forehead up, exposing a grayish brain tinged cherry-blossom pink. Comma- and dash-shaped pieces of ore that appeared to be magatama and kudatama—excavated relics of the ancient world—were mounted all across his brain's surface, with many carrier tone wires connected to them.

Above his head there floated a circular mirror whose underside shone a light downward.

It was the object Hanishibe had taken from the shrine—it could be nothing other than a Divine Implement. Chinju-no-kami and Ubusunagami still lived. Maybe the kosmetic box in my brain was responding and that was why I was seeing all this. But wouldn't that mean that the Divine Implement I was looking at right now was kosmetic too?

Still expressionless, Hanishibe moved his lips and said, "It's time."

Everyone rose from their seats and headed toward a spiral staircase in the back of the room toward the left. *I* slipped into their midst as well, got in line, and headed up the stairs. We got up past the ceiling and went round and round inside the tower as we climbed ever higher.

The observation platform was walled in with glass on all sides. Many dark human shadows were standing before a dazzling light streaming in from outside. Every face that was turned toward me was the face of Hanishibe.

Through the glass, I could see cottony clouds drifting through the sky and could gaze across the immensity of the Vastsea, where sparse patches of dustwreck jungle flourished.

On a dustwreck hill about a kilometer away was a giant hollow that reminded me of a strip mine. A metal disk sealed off its bottom, and from its center, a line with no thickness was stretching straight up toward the heavens.

Suddenly, the worlde shone with pure white light, and I was shaken by mighty vibrations. As if rocked by a powerful earthquake, the glass windows trembled and the observation platform swayed. The lights dimmed. Up in the sky, the clouds became blurred in a radial pattern; on the ground, the distant dustwreck jungle rolled in concentric ripples while setting off flashes of lightning. With each roll of these continuing ripples, the dustwreck jungle would wither.

Chalk-white crystalline lattices were beginning to sprout within the hollow from which all of this was emanating; they were growing into and on top of one another, forming the huge round pillars of a truss structure that rapidly rose to greater and greater heights.

I remembered an interstellar transport I saw as a child. Clouds of exhaust piling atop one another as it climbed to boundless heights—but this was a Floating Bridge tying Heaven and Earth together—no, a backward-spinning halberd born from the chaos of the Vastsea—

It felt like a powerful force was wringing my heart out, and then I was myself again. The momonji beside me was all tensed up, its back arched slightly. Its labor pains had started. Its heart was pounding violently, as though synchronized with its birthing sac.

Romon recited carrier tone, causing the ground beneath the momonji's hindquarters to sink in, forming a trench there that was like a bathtub. Sagyoku-shii crawled into it, with Homaru crouching right beside.

"It's no good," said Sagyoku-shii. "The cloacal canal is too narrow. It won't come out." She opened her tool case and pulled out a hook-shaped blade. She jabbed it into the epidermis beside the cloacavity on its underside, then swiftly pulled the knife upward, cutting it open.

One plate of its gastral ossiform appeared, covered in red goo. Once Sagyoku-shii had removed it, Homaru reached out both arms and lifted the epidermis. Sagyoku-shii then applied a pair of shears to the red, swollen membrane of the exposed cloacal canal. It tore open instantly, and something inside was immediately pushed out.

With a shrill cry, Sagyoku-shii tried to crawl out of the trench. Right away, Romon and Homaru were there, helping to pull her up. Sagyoku-shii's bloated body, however, was caught under the momonji's protruding hindquarters. She couldn't move.

Sagyoku-shii cried out urgently. Kugu-shi pushed his large frame in between Romon and Homaru, who had begun voicing frantic carrier tone. He reached out with his long arms and in a heartbeat dragged Sagyoku-shii out from under the momonji.

High-viscosity semisolids that looked like bits of vomit were spilling ceaselessly from the rent in the membrane. The trench overflowed in no time, and everyone backed away. Meaty chunks piled on top of each other and changed shape with each passing moment. Finally, the stuff began congealing into a form that might pass for human.

It was slumped forward like a drunk who'd collapsed face-first at his table. Scattered tangles of blue and red blood vessels were beginning to appear on its scarred back, which rose and fell as it breathed deep draughts of air. Presently, the left and right motion of its back became uneven. With alternating swings of its bony shoulders, it began to wriggle its way up out of the trench.

"W-what in the worlde *is* that thing?" yelled Romon. He shot a glance at Homaru as he was backing away. Homaru clenched his silver teeth and shook his head vigorously. Sa-gyoku-shii lost her composure altogether and grabbed onto Kugu-shi, crying, "What is that? What is that?" Kugu-shi, who had been observing Romon and Homaru's earlier back-and-forth intently, rested his gaze on Sagyoku-shii for a moment, then shifted his eyes toward the man-shaped thing that was crawling on the ground.

Its spine curled backward, and supported by both of its folded arms, it raised its upper body. When it attempted to stand, however, it fell clumsily back down. While everyone looked on in shocked silence, it rose and fell again and again, until at last like some ghost or devil, it succeeded in standing erect.

Its face melted like the resin of a half-used beastfat candle, and its eyes and nose looked like holes caused by gangrene. Whitish things would suddenly come creeping out of furrows that snaked around its chest and stomach, and then they would burrow back in under its skin.

Gasps escaped each of the onlookers as they surrounded it from a distance.

Bubbles popped on the face of the humanlike thing as it came tottering forward, leaving gaping holes.

"Expression of aural language…is possible—

"This is the 153rd parish's…Superordinate Investigative Bureau—

"Clearing foreign matter from throat—

"We are acting in accordance with Regulations for Colonized Worlds, Contact with Intelligent Life-forms."

It was a strange voice, one like many people talking all at once—it was the deathseeker by the seashore.

From that day when *I*…

I had to get away from it. But my body was spilled out all over the place…couldn't scrape it all back together. Couldn't tell which consciousness was which anymore.

"Stay away from me!" Romon and Homaru were shouting. "Stay back!" Sagyoku-shii, on the verge of tears, cowered behind Kugu-shi, whimpering, "Keep away! Don't you come near me!" Arms crossed, she kept rubbing her upper arms as if they had broken out in gooseflesh.

"Everybody, how about you calm down just a little?" Kugu-shi said, even while he was backing away.

"We've no time to sp*lurp*," the half-melted face said as a bubble popped. "Pardon us for appearing in this unformed state." It slowly shifted its center of gravity, interrupted by burps from all over its body as it spoke. "Heart rate decreasing—

"Suppress sinoatrial node signal."

"You said 'parish,'" Kugu-shi said, blinking his eyes and wiping sweat from his forehead with the back of his hand. "That mean you're the same as that Hanishibe guy? A ghost that lives in a canvasser? Can I take this to mean you've crawlbacked by way of this momonji?"

I remembered stepping into a dustsunk facility. Momonji, lined up in a row, had been secured to various instruments, and there had been a decomposing human pushed halfway out of one of them. I went along opening up the other momonji's bellies and found human beings in the birthing sacs of all of them. Half of them had had grotesquely long arms. Only one had still been alive. Had the facility been attacked before he received his soul-share, or had it been the replayable intellect who'd been captured on the other side? This was an unblemished possession seat.

"What was that just now?

"Regarding the interference, it's unclear. The rest are the utterances of non-replayable intellects. Analyzing vocabulary…

"—a crawlbacker. That's essentially the case…

"Heart rate stable…

"Who's Hanishibe…?

"An Eternal Pilot of the Kannagara Sect. He was a cleric prior to Translation…

"Don't lump us all in with him. This is heresy from your perspective and ours as well."

The Investigative Bureau slowly raised a putrefied right arm. Many lintlike tenants squirmed as they fell from it.

"Don't try anything funny," Kugu-shi said, drawing his tamer and taking aim. Romon and Homaru circled around to the Investigative Bureau's back.

"We will now extract Mr. Yuuji Hisauchi…

"Right fifteen degrees."

"You're gonna distract who? There ain't nobody in this caravan by that name."

The Investigative Bureau's arm slid sideways toward the covered wagon at the end of the line, separated from the others by a single momonga.

There came a resounding crash like the sound of a tree being felled, and the debris-strewn ground near the wagon erupted in a geyser of dustmotes, as though the land itself were coming to a boil. The ground heaved up in a bell shape that rapidly expanded. Panicked momonji left the guideline and went crawling off in whatever direction they could, climbing up on the feet of the wreckcliffs.

Slowly, ponderously, the bulge jutted upward, soaring to heights well above the heads of all present. Its outer layer was a conglomeration of miscellaneous dustwroughts in scrap-iron state, stirring about like swarming honeybees. Suddenly, though, they all stopped moving, as if they had died. In the same instant, the structure began to break apart and collapse like a landslide. From underneath, a glossy black, cabbagelike head, a chest like a suit of seashell-plated armor, and two arms like mantis shrimps with rows of outward-facing pleopods were gradually revealed. It was a canvasser.

With alternating strokes of its long, segmented arms, it crawled forward across the ground, pulling its lower body out from underground. Bifurcated appendages opened up from the undersides of its short legs, supporting its unwieldy body as it stood.

"In compliance with regulations, your consent is required," said the Investigative Bureau, who was still standing before them.

Kugu-shi said nothing for a moment, but there was nothing

he could really do except give his consent. Under these circumstances, the option of refusal was as good as nonexistent. Kugu-shi spoke and gave his answer.

"Voiceprint recorded as proof of consent."

The canvasser turned its shrimp-arms toward the covered wagon at the end of the column and reached out for *me*.

Another struggle to escape would have meant sacrificing more members of the caravan.

My body was scooped up in hard, armored palms. I experienced a rough, weightless sensation, as well as vertigo-inducing discrepancies between my senses, which had roots spreading out all over the Vastsea. As caravan hands struggled to restrain the terrified momonji, they stared on as my age-stricken body was carried through the air. I too was watching as *I* was laid down in front of the Investigative Bureau. With another eye, I was following Romon and Homaru as they were moving along the wreckcliff, and then—

The imposing form of the canvasser bent its body segments and crouched down low, and the leaves of its cabbage-head unfurled to form a bowl-like shape. A thorn-covered radula as big around as a man's arm slowly emerged from the circular mouth in the center.

The Investigative Bureau, dripping fluids from every inch of its body, grabbed the tip of the tongue-rasp and guided it to the hairless top of "my" head.

"Wait! Stop it!" Kugu-shi shouted angrily.

"Be quiet.

"Right ten millimeters, up five millimeters…

"His life is depending on this."

Having made contact with the top of my head, the tip of the tongue-rasp began to rotate with a high-pitched whine. It turned faster and faster. Everyone drew in their breath. A bright spray of blood rose up and then vaporized.

Together with the tongue-rasp, a portion of my skull came away, and my brain, covered in spiderwebs of metallic fiber, lay exposed in a fist-sized hole.

The tongue-rasp laid flat its thorns, spun for just an instant to shake off the fragments of skull, and then split its tip open four ways. White, fibrous things came out, with fine needles attached to them. They dangled in midair.

The Investigative Bureau raised a hand and clumsily caught a needle between his fingers. Calling out coordinates to himself, he began the job of jabbing the needles into each of my brain's vital spots.

The Investigative Bureau's internal conversation came slipping in through gaps in the folds of my brain:

"Impossible…wasteflesh that can survive after Translation—!

"His entire nervous system has been replaced by micromachines that existed even prior to nanodust. At the time, it was still illegal tech, so there were no model numbers and no compatibility with Yaoyorazu or Tsukumo either…

"Well, in that case we can't use snowflower bugs. So his nervous system's become a transfer route for nanomotes?

"But what about the shared consciousness?

"Up until now, intermittent Whisperings were taking place, but the two consciousnesses were independent, like twins. Beyond their shared dreams, they hardly affected each another at all, but—"

The vertigo wouldn't stop. Overlapped fields of view were spinning round and round. I couldn't hold back the nausea.

Both of my legs kicked upward as I convulsed, as though struck by lightning. A stir rose up among the clan brethren.

I felt like I'd seen one tiny ant in my field of view. Night was born from out of its blackness—it expanded explosively, scattering galactic fireworks as it grew, enveloping all in the twinkling of an eye.

Countless stars glittered, forming beams of light that pierced this body of mine—

The light slipped past the artificial animals, becoming verse for chanting the stars in shorthand.

"It's all right, there's no need to worry...

"Heart rate increasing."

I couldn't tell which side the voices were coming from.

"Activating containment shell...

"Commencing extraction from infotumor...

"Be careful not to sever the shared branches...

"Heart rate increasing...

"Extraction ongoing...

"Irreversibly compressing the processed tumor and individual registry veriform...

"Parish Control Organization has begun to stabilize. Recovery has proceeded to the point of having Real-textures and Sketchzones. Number of pigments and perceptory resolution increasing."

The needles were pulled from my head all at once.

I've gone blind. That's what I thought for a moment. But I could see the canvasser pulling its radula back in and closing its petals back up into a head. It had just *felt* like I'd lost my sight because of the sudden contraction of my phantasmagorically expanded field of vision.

I was thinking back over what I'd experienced in that instant with the same sluggishness I feel after waking up after a night of hard drinking.

I felt no particularly deep emotion over Hisauchi's dissociation. Actually, I wasn't even sure that he was the one who was gone. Even now, I could recall skewed memories of my double past. The one who's here is the only one who can tell of them...

CHAPTER 8:
THE EMERALD CITY

Ignoring Romon and the others' cries that it was still too dangerous, Kugu-shi ran toward Master, who was lying on the ground like a dead man. Kugu-shi loosed his shadecap and tied it around Master's drill-gouged head, then he laced both his arms under Master's, hoisted him up, and dragged him back toward the covered wagon.

Suddenly, countless steel cables burst out of the wreckcliffs that were hemming in the caravan. They shot past the canvasser's sides and between its legs and stuck deep into the ground. More volleys followed, one after another. Trapped inside a geometrical diagram, the canvasser twisted and turned its armored body, but found itself pushed back each time.

"What's this? What's happening?

"Something's taken hold of the cherub—"

The Investigative Bureau was looking this way and that as the flesh melted away from its entire body.

Kugu-shi shouted out in confusion. "What in the worlde's going on?"

The pleopods on the canvasser's prawnlike arms started to turn, cutting through several of the steel cables, which snapped and flew high up into the air.

Carrier tone was starting to flow from somewhere.

One momonji on the other side of the canvasser started to

jerk spasmodically. And then it charged.

There was a blinding flash of light. A thunderous roar pealed out as a huge column of flame rose up into the sky, sending out a violent blast.

Kugu-shi, who was next to the wagon, was blown into the air still holding onto Master. A sharp pain shot through his chest. Knives of heat sliced into every inch of his body, and every joint felt like it was being twisted off. As they landed face-down and curled up into a ball, palm-sized chunks of meat and powdery dust came raining down on their backs, so blisteringly hot that Kugu-shi's lungs seemed to be on fire.

Through the white smoke that hung in the air, Kugu-shi dragged Master away from the blast. Each step he planted sent a piercing pain through his chest. Ribs might be broken. Breathing raggedly, he made it to the shadow of the wagon, and in that instant the thundering roar of a second blast rang out. The wagon was shaken violently, and the whole world went orange. A powerful, scorching wind blew hard all around them.

The roar lingered in Kugu-shi's ears. When he poked his head out from behind the wagon, the worlde was blurred with haze and rippling with heat. His face flushed red in the simmering air and dripped with sweat.

Looking up, he saw the canvasser leaning forward on both its arms, fists buried in the ground. White smoke was rising from it, as though its outer shell were vaporizing. Of the Investigative Bureau, he saw not a trace.

From the front of the broken caravan column, numerous momonji were advancing on the canvasser with their fur standing on end. Kugu-shi hurriedly took cover. He fired his tamer at the ground at his feet and pulled Master near. A translucent, gelatinous swell began forming up out of the ground, and the two men gradually sank into it, lying supine, until their bodies were entirely covered.

Presently, another flash and explosive roar boomed out. The enveloping gel was shaken violently. The wagon was blown over onto its side in their direction. It broke apart into pieces that scattered everywhere.

Though the view outside was warped by the gel, it was possible to make out the canvasser's outline as it peeked in and out of view between the swells of white smoke and the twisted framework of the covered wagon. Several of its breastplates had been blasted loose and were tilting precariously; something that was apparently its bodily fluid was starting to run out of the gaps. Yet another explosion went off. The smoke made it impossible to see anything, and only the tremors—they summoned thoughts of bombardment in an air raid—continued on and on. Unable to breathe, the two men writhed in pain. Had their eardrums burst? They could no longer hear anything. Maybe the explosions had ceased.

Sharp pieces of debris from the covered wagon were sticking out of the gel-case's surface. Kugu-shi tried to rip it open from the inside, but with the pain in his chest, he couldn't put enough strength into his hands. His panic mounted with the fear of suffocation, but then—had the effect of the eidos bullet expired?—the case grew brittle and began to crumble.

Kugu-shi sat up and breathed in all the air that his body craved. Pain turned his exhalations into moans.

When he looked over at Master, dregs from the gel-case were stuck to his nose and mouth, and his face had turned a pale blue. Frantically, he peeled away the dregs, and Master began breathing spasmodically.

Before his eyes lay the covered wagon, now reduced to wreckage. Its arching struts had caved in and now lay atop one another like rings from a celestial globe. Transparent, melon-sized spheres were lodged between them like heavenly bodies. He realized that they were momonji eyeballs—something he should have been very used to. On the wreckcliff beyond them, he could see the blackened, overturned wreckage of what looked like a momonga.

Little by little, the white smoke cleared, and the damaged canvasser was revealed.

Everything from the middle of its trunk down was missing; it looked like it had rotted off. Only its upper body remained, suspended in midair by both of its multijointed arms. Its translucent, pale yellow contents steamed as they dripped from the open, severed edges. The shrimp-arms twisted, the upper body began to tilt, and then the whole thing came crashing down to the ground. The shock had left its multijointed arms bent in wave-patterns.

"Incredible…just incredible!" Kugu-shi murmured again and again.

Like corpses rising up from the grave, four arms reached up from the ground which had just moments ago been occupied by the three momonji ahead of the wagon. Shedding fragments of gel-case, the figures that crawled out were Romon and Homaru. Both were holding long, narrow devices in their mouths, like dogs carrying bones. From either end of those bars hung bags made of skin. Both tossed these devices aside, nodded at one another, and started walking toward the fallen canvasser. They passed one pitiful, scattered wreck of a momonji after another.

Blackening momonji meat was sizzling all around. The wreckcliffs around them had activated and now rolled in imitation of smoke from the explosions.

Enduring the pain, Kugu-shi squeezed out a hoarse cry. "Don't tell me you two did this?"

"That's why I said this was dangerous," Romon said, laying a hand on the black armor of its chest. A wide cross-section was exposed, and Romon let out an *ouch!* when he felt its heat.

"Still, Brother, I trusted you'd save Master and make it through this alive. If it'd been Umari, she and he both would've been killed instantly." So saying, Romon turned to Homaru. "We bungled it the first time, but by and large things went according to plan. Though that monster did surprise me."

"Yeah. Nobody said anything about that. Ah, now for the most important thing." Homaru stuck one arm into the cross-section of the canvasser's glimmering, shiny trunk. "Ugh, this feels gross. And this green vegetable smell…" Was Homaru having trouble? He pushed his upper body in even farther until it was halfway hidden.

There was a noise from behind. From the shadows of some scattered dust-shoots Sagyoku-shii and a single apprentice appeared. Scraps of gel-casing clung to both of their shadecaps.

"It was Homaru, I take it, who wove possession verse for the trick cables," said Kugu-shi. "But filling up the air sacs of edible momonji with explosives—that's not something those two could've pulled off alone. Judging by the force of those blasts, you would've had to encourage potassium nitrate secretion."

Kugu-shi glared at Sagyoku-shii. She gave him a vague smile, placed a handkerchief over her mouth, and coughed into it.

"Tell me why. Why would you do something this cruel?" Coughing from the smoke, Kugu-shi looked out across what resembled war-scorched ruins. "There's no way to complete the delivery now."

"Couldn't be helped," Romon said. "The techniques for making what we want have long since been lost, and it takes more than a hundred years for a canvasser to form from scratch. Besides, what difference does it make to the momonji? They were just gonna be butchered anyway. The old geezer won't be waking up again either."

Enraged, Kugu-shi turned to face Romon. Romon was

staring right back at him.

"If he did wake up," Romon continued, "we'd be at a dead-end. Like they say, the most important teaching for Vastsea crossers is 'don't hope for anything.' That doesn't just go for caravan work. Recuperation blocks are being swallowed whole by the Vastsea one after another, and with all the radioactive mobiles running around out there, the number of living things is declining. That's why we've placed our bets on the future."

"On the future? Do you realize what you've done here? You've destroyed a *canvasser*—one of the ghost cities." Kugushi's jaw trembled as he spoke, and his voice grew shrill. "And the ghosts, they're all connected to each other through those trumpet-shaped heads of theirs; they're gonna come here and attack us any minu—"

"You're the one doesn't understand, Brother," Romon said calmly. "This canvasser was cut off from the Whisper-net of all the other parishes. An infotumor was to blame. In addition, they were apparently grappling with some convoluted issue of heresy. Because of that, all factions were in agreement on this matter."

"Romon, how could you know anything about what was going on in there? Don't tell me that all of this was ordered by those crawlbackers—by those people from the Kannagara sect, or whatever you call it. That's crazy! What kind of nonsense did they fill your head with? When did this start?"

"I don't know; when did this start, Homaru?"

Homaru was writhing about as he tried to pull his upper body free of the gluey substance packed into the cross-section of the canvasser's stomach.

"When I found out that Ms. Sagyoku-shii was in touch with them, I was furious too. Now, though, we're members of the Kannagara sect as well." As Romon was speaking, he moved over to stand behind Homaru. "Also, it isn't like that city is really gone, Brother."

Romon passed both arms under Homaru's and pulled on him from behind, using all his weight. There was a sound like that of something being skinned, and then they tumbled to the ground together.

Homaru grinned and his silver teeth gleamed. Still sitting, he held up his right hand.

Wedged between his mucus-slathered fingers was an emerald-hued jewel. It was curved, fetuslike, and gleamed with a soft, slimy sheen. From the slightly protruding curvature of its back face there extended white, fibrous threads connecting it to the inside of the canvasser's body. Romon cut it loose with his knife. Homaru turned the jewel around, staring at it intently. From time to time, specks of light flowed across its surface like fine grains.

"Beautiful, isn't it?" Sagyoku-shii said, approaching Romon and the others. "That's a magatama. Time is now frozen for the city inside. And now it will become a seed of our future."

"What are you even talking about?"

Sagyoku-shii, who had come to a halt next to Homaru, pushed back her shadecap and gazed at the magatama in wonder.

Many knoblike growths were appearing on the wreckcliffs behind them, bumping against one another as they expanded. Slowly, they flowed and swirled, as if trying to spool time itself.

"This is one of the grand escape plans that was once discarded," Homaru said as he was getting to his feet. "A plan to migrate to habitable planets using seedships. This magatama is vital for reviving that plan. Though only replayable intellects'll be able to emigrate, of course."

"So you people intend to Translate yourselves and turn into ghosts?"

"As you're surely aware, the Kannagara sect is promoting Incarnation."

"Right," said Sagyoku-shii. "We aren't doing this to become ghosts. In lands beyond, in places that don't even exist yet, we'll—" Sagyoku-shii burst into a fit of coughing, one peculiar to those suffering from lung disease. With one hand against her ample bosom, she continued. "—we'll be reborn… and one after another, we'll multiply our offspring…until those worlds are teeming with more people than they know what to do with."

In a sudden flash of insight, Kugu-shi realized: *Sagyoku-shii isn't going to live much longer.* He had a vague idea of why she'd left the maternitorium and what chain of events had brought her to the head of the Fatguard Clan.

That was when Kugu-shi noticed something else: the number of caravan hands was short by one. He looked around, but the young fattener who had just lost an ear to that dust crystal was nowhere to be seen.

"Where is…Saroku, was it?"

"The boy didn't get away in time. If only he'd joined the Kannagara, we might've been able to see him again someday. But he was never willing, no matter what I said to him." Sagyoku-shii had been speaking in a monotone, but now suddenly her voice cracked: "Listen, Kugu-shi, you come with us… there's still time for you to make it."

Kugu-shi held his peace and closed his eyes. It felt like his own body had just turned into an active dustwreck.

Homaru shot a meaningful glance at Romon. "It's no use," he said. "Why do you think we kept this a secret for so long? But we'll take the old geezer with us. His consciousness might come back if he's Translated."

"Looks like a pile of wasteflesh already, though," said Romon. "There's no guarantee it'll work."

Kugu-shi was on the verge of shouting, *No! I won't let you do that to him!* when a groan rose up from right beside his feet.

Everyone's eyes turned to where Master lay.

"That won't be...necessary." Like a seam whose stitches had just come loose, Master's lips were moving. They were parched and cracked, and were beginning to ooze blood. "Where I'm useful is in the Dustclingers. In the Vastsea. I have no intention whatsoever of being parted from this worlde."

Neither Romon nor Homaru—let alone Kugu-shi—could conceal their joy, and they all cried out to him.

"Romon and Homaru. As of this instant, you two are expelled. Leave now."

Cheerful smiles still on their faces, the two former clan-brethren turned their backs, and without a word set off across the still-smoldering floor of the valley. Sagyoku-shii and her apprentices followed along behind them.

As Sagyoku-shii was heading off into the distance, she turned to look back just once.

"Did the Kannagara give you your marching orders?" said Master. "Or did the Vastsea guide you? Or did those Vastsea crossers force your hand? Who put you up to this, I wonder?"

"Huh?" Kugu-shi turned around and bent down next to Master.

"I was watching you all the whole time," the old man said. "But I couldn't move. I'm sorry; there was nothing I could do."

"I'm the one who should apologize. Such a—" But Kugu-shi couldn't continue past those words. The muscles in his face tensed up, and he wore an expression that was somewhere between laughter and tears.

As he looked on, slender metal fibers started poking out all over Master's body, intertwining themselves with the ground, as if sewing it and him together.

CHAPTER 9:
THE BEGINNING

Particles of light began to dance in a primordial darkness once thought to have been sealed away forever. Presently, a sharp beam of light shone into it, caressing every nook and cranny of a great mass of city and flesh and slumber, which had been functioning as a mere hub for shared branches of memory. At the touch of the beam, this conglomerate fell apart into fibers. Losses in the irrecoverable sections were supplemented by a steady flow of replacement data from subordinapes.

Consciousness flickered faintly into being amid brain cells and nerves in the process of being assembled.

It saw nothing, felt nothing, and remembered nothing, however; there was nothing that it wanted to do, and nothing that it didn't want to do.

Each time a bubble of perception floated to its surface, it simply popped and disappeared.

Beneath eaves formed of brain matter, eyeballs, nerves, and so on were woven into existence, and pupils dilated.

The darkness lost its depth and became metaphorically "visible" as a spherical kernel wall. The consciousness became aware that it was being held in custody, though it did not know the reason why or even who it was that was detained in the first place.

In the back of its mind, letters began to assemble themselves into a line. It was a long line. It brought its eyes nearer to see what was written, and one by one, the letters blurred and became gigantic animals covered in white fur: white... mo...momonji...a long line of momonji...a caravan column... and leading it were scraplings wearing smiling faces. Severed branches of shared memory began to connect themselves to the past—a buried shrine deep underground...a pair of legs that had been wrenched from their stumps...an expanse of calmdust, like a lotus receptacle—and bubbles of flesh, gulls by the seashore, dinners with Hamuro, the yard with its davidia and plantain lilies—the fragrant smell of bread, warm paper bags, the town streets with their abundant greenery, the alleyway, the dimly lit—

Hisauchi was walking alone down a dimly lit alleyway. In his arms he carried a warm paper bag. Beyond the familiar stucco walls that ran along both sides of the road were long rows of everyday, single-family homes. The trees in their yards threw out large canopies of branches and leaves. Dry leaves danced to the ground with their customary motions.

The paper bag suddenly became heavier. When he looked, he saw that it had changed into a complex metal object resembling an engine. Unable to carry its weight, he let it go—or should have; one of his arms had fallen off with it. The hunk of metal and the arm that was still holding it dug into the ground and, with a sticky sound, continued to gradually sink. A slight creaking began to emanate from the land.

With a sigh, Hisauchi looked up overhead. The black celestial sphere began spitting out a succession of complex geometrical patterns, and soon it looked like the surface of a lake when it rains. The repeating patterns increased in speed until the eye could no longer follow them, then they all went blurry. Countless stars were beginning to twinkle—or so he was thinking when the sky brightened with a faint whiteness, only to hastily darken again. In brilliant, repeating flashes, the day and the night and the sun, moon, and stars pursued one another across the heavens, moving so quickly that each seemed the afterimage of what came before it.

Dazzled, Hisauchi closed his eyes.

He began to feel the touch of fur in the palm of his right hand.

"Master!"

The voice called out to him from behind, and taking his hand off the momonji, he turned and looked back.

Kugu-shi, wearing his shadecap, was approaching him from far away. At his side, the giant momonji were crawling slowly forward as the wind beat against their soft down. The gusts were getting terribly strong.

He remembered now: he was still going on momonji drives.

He was old though, and most of his former strength was gone. This might well be his final journey.

With the exception of his apprentices Kugu-shi and Gei'ei-shi, the lineup of clan brethren was now entirely different— except for one other: Renji, in a state of near-death, was still sealed within a crystalline dustwrought carried in a covered wagon at the tail end of the column. It had taken many months of hard work, but they had finally succeeded in hauling her up from the deep layers of the Vastsea.

No matter how they wore themselves out trying though, they couldn't cast out the possession verse that was in crystal to get Renji out of it. Renji had chanted that dustwrought as an emergency shelter even as the active layer was swallowing her, and for some reason, it was stubbornly holding onto its eidos and function. Using the possession verse employed here, it might have been possible to realize the complete calming of the Vastsea. However, to know that would also be to break down that perfection.

Without warning, Master was taken suddenly with the notion that the one in the crystal was not Renji, but in fact his own veriform.

From behind him, the sound of footfalls making long strides drew near. Kugu-shi came up beside him and stared at his face. To the right and left of Kugu-shi's wide nose, both eyes were moist for some reason.

"I've been calling you over and over," he said.

"I was just remembering some things about myself."

"What are you on about? Come on, look what's headed our way."

Master turned his heavy old body around.

"Farther off, toward that hill."

Another caravan was just descending the dustwreck hill Kugu-shi indicated. The first several momonji in the lead were goldeneyes. Catching the strong light of the westering sun, the irises inside their golden eyeballs shone like works of damascene craftsmanship.

By their side walked a young girl. She was striding across the uneven ground on legs of silvery white.

The girl was also looking this way. She pushed back her shadecap, and a fluff of cottony walnut hair appeared. Her haggard face, gaunt like that of a convalescent, wore a smile, allowing twin rows of white teeth to peek through.

"That couldn't be—"

Master and Kugu-shi raised their hands up high, twisting their wrists and bending their elbows. From across the windswept plain, the girl returned the gesture. It was a common greeting that caravans exchanged when passing one another.

The two momonji caravans headed toward each another for a little while before diverging once again.

A lone spider came crawling across the junk-strewn ground. It walked up in front of them; lowered its huge, inflated abdomanus; and formed a membrane across the spaces between its eight legs, which it then began to flap like wings. It flew up in front of Master's nose, and he caught it—an earwing butterfly—by the roots of its wings. The earwing extended its proboscis, placing the pointed tip against its belly. Its belly, which was a vocollector tube, then began to turn.

In fits and starts, Master could hear a soft, low voice that sounded like someone speaking with cartilage in her mouth. Master brought his ear closer and narrowed his eyes.

"So even Master has tear ducts," Kugu-shi teased happily. "This is the first time I've ever seen them in action. So what does Umari have to say?"

Biting down hard on his memories, Master raised his voice in laughter.

"That girl! She's been digging and digging through archive vaults at recuperation blocks all over the place, and she seems to have really found something."

"What did she say she's found?"

"It seems she'll be entertaining us next time we meet up in a recuperation block."

He recorded only a set of coordinates in the earwing's vocollector tube, then released it in midair.

"What's this all about? Tell me, please, Master."

Swept off course repeatedly by the powerful winds, the earwing receded into the distance as it chased after Umari's column.

Master squatted down on the ground and grabbed hold of an antique skittle that had been the spider's abdomanus.

That day, strong winds were blowing across the Vastsea, and many sounds resounded like the distant howls of giant beasts, like waves upon the ocean—like parts in a multilayered composition. Amid the movements of the Vastsea whose actions no man could read, many caravans were at a standstill, having lost sight of the routes along which they should progress. The rea-

son for all this became clear as a rumbling in the atmosphere presently began to be heard.

All were looking up at a tattered sky full of clouds resembling scrapes and scratches: Master and Kugu-shi from the midst of a dustwreck jungle, Umari from a belt of calmdust.

A huge, rounded pillar of chalk was reaching up toward the heavens. It reminded onlookers of the smoke of a volcanic eruption. With ferocious energy, it climbed unstoppably onward. Its coordinates were the same as the Dustclingers' present destination. Farther off in the distance still, the slightly blurred shapes of two more white pillars could be seen.

Master opened the cap of his skittle and swallowed a gulp of sake. A strong smell of iodine spread through his nostrils.

"Is that a floating bridge?" Kugu-shi murmured as he took the skittle in hand.

Umari, on the lotus receptacle, was still grooming the sweat-steamed down of a frightened momonji.

A drizzling rain began to fall.

Outside the atmosphere, the floating bridges connecting heaven and earth budded into many reed arks loaded with planetary bioprobes and released them toward the far horizons. Afterward, the columns quickly crumbled, like weathered dirt walls, and darkened the sky with their dustsmoke.

Spreading out from the three collapsed floating bridges, morphwave after morphwave rolled out across the activated Vastsea, triggering a Great Dust Plague that rivaled even that great disaster of antiquity. Once again, many recuperation blocks were swallowed by the waves and sank beneath the dust.

When the waves receded, towns began to pop up one after another, as though the world that had existed before the dustsinks had returned. Over ten thousand people were living peacefully in those days. There were even some who returned from evacuation chrysalises and managed to reunite with their old friends. This was a temporary leakage from the <World> though. Eventually the people, the houses, and everything else began to melt.

The scarce number of human survivors once again formed caravans and began trekking back and forth across the Vastsea.

The number of those living on the Vastsea continued to dwindle inexorably.

On the night that the blazing red trails of the meteor swarm—of the prison shells from another world—came streaking across the sky, there were only a bare handful of caravans left to behold them.

FINALE

The Chaos was expelled into the supergravity that lay in the midst of the accretion disk.

As it fell away toward darkness eternal, the past raining down from beyond was absorbed into every nanite of its being—the ragged gasps of worlds made into Cradleland; the ephemeral, blissful exhalations of civilizations blossoming anew; brilliant blue skies shining from the shards of sky spheres; bright little lights blinking through the Mudsea; reports from interstellar spacecraft seeking new lands and new skies—these the sounds of homecomings long borne in their bellies—the rumbling of the Great Dust Plague that covered the face of the land; the sound of the canvassers'...of the cherubim's...of the <World's> pleopods; the footfalls of caravans crossing the Vastsea; the creaks of the ropes as momonji crawled along; the roar of engines as reed arks departed the floating bridge; the friction of prison-shells as they rained down toward the earth; the impacts; the heavy crashes of waves on the vast, reaffirmed land; the frozen sighs of those perfect attendants forced to labor daily without end; the belches of presidents waiting eagerly to go home; the screwlike noises of a Planetary Child on the axis of a world—all of these things were taking the place of countless stars scattered across untouched sectors on lines of sight spreading out continuously in every direction from the shipshell. Amid the supergravity, the Chaos was destroyed, and yet the form of it remained, scattered across all possible worlds.

ABOUT THE AUTHOR

Dempow Torishima was born in Osaka. He graduated from Osaka College of Art and worked as a freelance designer and illustrator. He won the Sogen SF Short Story Award with his debut fiction "Sisyphean" (Kaikin no to) in 2011. Since then, he has been writing a series of stories in the same far-future world of Sisyphean, which was published as *Sisyphean and Other Stories* in 2013. The book was chosen as the best SF of 2013 in *SF Magazine*, won the Japan SF Award, and was nominated for the Seiun Award in 2014.